Praise for *The Matc*

"Insightful, charming, and packed wit
The Matchmaker's Gift is a tribute to th
chance on true love."

—*Shelf Awareness*

"Loigman's latest is a gem. A scrappy Jewish teenager newly arrived in
1920s New York struggles to follow her calling as a matchmaker—
seventy years later, her cynical divorce-attorney granddaughter real-
izes she has very inconveniently inherited the family gift for matching
soulmates. Both funny and moving, *The Matchmaker's Gift* made me
smile from start to finish."

—Kate Quinn, *New York Times* bestselling
author of *The Rose Code*

"In the inviting *The Matchmaker's Gift*, Loigman takes the readers by the
hand and leads them into the world of *shadchanim*, or matchmakers,
of both a historic and modern variety. This charming story about a
realm that is at once familiar and magical invites contemplation of the
many ways in which the past reverberates into the present."

—Marie Benedict, *New York Times* bestselling
author of *The Mystery of Mrs. Christie*

"Loigman brilliantly illuminates the struggle of two women, generations
apart, torn between society's traditions and expectations and their
own personal fulfillment. The novel bubbles with romance and love
matches, yet the joys of early infatuation are deftly layered over an
exquisite exploration of grief. Glorious and powerful."

—Fiona Davis, *New York Times* bestselling author of
The Magnolia Palace

"Loigman's thorough exploration of turn-of-the-century Jewish immigrant culture and her smooth transitions into the 1990s give the
reader a full and satisfying picture of Manhattan across the twentieth

century. The details are painstaking but never tedious, and the relationships are exciting, sincere, and beautiful." —*Booklist*

"Charming . . . Loigman moves smoothly between the tales of her two spunky heroines and imparts historical details with a light touch. Readers are in for a treat." —*Publishers Weekly*

"Loigman has a gift herself: the ability to evoke places and scenes with the subtlest of details. She takes us all over town in time and space: a crowded French bakery on the Upper East Side and narrow streets lined with sweltering tenements, the audience gathering at dusk for the Shakespeare Festival in Central Park, and a Tribeca party sparkling with celebrities and high fashion."

—BookTrib.com

"The plot employs some magical realism [and] simmers with vibrant detail. . . . Loigman's research exudes authenticity, invoking the sights and smells of a bygone Lower East Side. The historical chapters are compelling; the more contemporary ones are equally so. A fascinating narrative." —Jewish Book Council

"As we follow these parallel storylines, Sara and Abby follow their destinies with an abundance of character and charm. Plus, the dual timelines are rife with fun historical details." —*BuzzFeed*

"Combining authentic historical fiction with mystery and a touch of romance, Loigman artfully reminds us that the past is never far, the present is a gift, and the future is ours for the making. *The Matchmaker's Gift* is timely and timeless, and readers should make time for this original and touching story about the things that matter most."

—Pam Jenoff, *New York Times* bestselling author of
The Woman with the Blue Star

"Written in luminous and lyrical prose, *The Matchmaker's Gift* is a powerful and profoundly emotional novel that charts two generations of women seeking to find their place and forge their independence in an ever-changing world. Exquisitely rendered and masterfully plotted . . . Loigman delves into the mysteries of what makes the heart soar and the soul find its perfect match. As magical and timeless as love itself, this is a book to be shared between generations."

—Alyson Richman, bestselling author of *The Lost Wife*

"Loigman once again taps into her exquisite ability to create rich characters that take us into the past while at the same time telling a universal story about destiny, family, and being authentic. I got lost equally in the stories of both Sara and Abby and was charmed by their connection to each other as well as to their craft. With her trademark ability to spin a tale and the heart with which she does it, Loigman has provided her readers with a story they won't soon forget."

—Susie Orman Schnall, author of *We Came Here to Shine*

"*The Matchmaker's Gift* has all the right ingredients for an enthralling read—history, humor, romance, mystery, and a dash of magic. Loigman's latest book brims with optimism, a cast of colorful characters, and two smart heroines who dare to forge their own brave paths in life. I was completely charmed by this clever dual-timeline novel."

—Elise Hooper, author of *The Other Alcott*

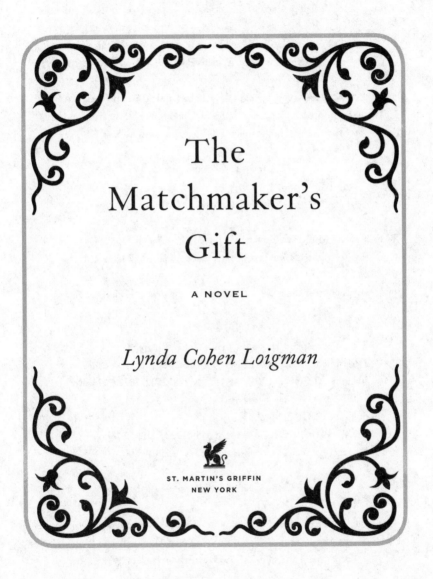

The Matchmaker's Gift

A NOVEL

Lynda Cohen Loigman

ST. MARTIN'S GRIFFIN
NEW YORK

Published in the United States by St. Martin's Griffin,
an imprint of St. Martin's Publishing Group

THE MATCHMAKER'S GIFT. Copyright © 2022 by Lynda Cohen Loigman. All rights reserved. Printed in the United States of America. For information, address St. Martin's Publishing Group, 120 Broadway, New York, NY 10271.

www.stmartins.com

Designed by Michelle McMillian

Map by Royce M. Becker. Originally printed in *The Button Thief of East 14th Street* by Fay Webern. Used here by permission of Sagging Meniscus Press.

The Library of Congress has cataloged the hardcover edition as follows:

Names: Loigman, Lynda Cohen, author.
Title: The matchmaker's gift / Lynda Cohen Loigman.
Description: First Edition. | New York : St. Martin's Press, 2022.
Identifiers: LCCN 2022013545 | ISBN 9781250278098 (hardcover) |
    ISBN 9781250278081 (ebook)
Subjects: LCGFT: Novels.
Classification: LCC PS3612.O423 M38 2022 | DDC 813/.6—dc23
LC record available at https://lccn.loc.gov/2022013545

ISBN 978-1-250-81949-9 (trade paperback)

Our books may be purchased in bulk for promotional, educational, or business use. Please contact your local bookseller or the Macmillan Corporate and Premium Sales Department at 1-800-221-7945, extension 5442, or by email at MacmillanSpecialMarkets@macmillan.com.

First St. Martin's Griffin Edition: 2023

10 9 8 7 6 5 4 3 2 1

For Ellie and Adelle

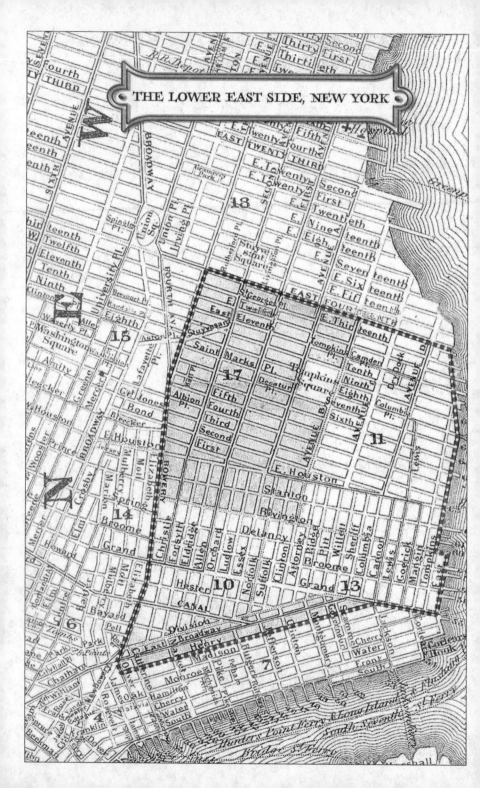

THE LOWER EAST SIDE, NEW YORK

I have always been a woman who arranges things
Like luncheon parties, poker games, and love

ONE

SARA

1910

A Matchmaker for This Strange, New World

Sara was ten years old when she made her first match.

She had traveled for a week from Kalarash to Libava with her parents, her sister, Hindel, and three unruly brothers to board the giant steamship headed for New York. As the coast faded to a blurry mist, eighteen-year-old Hindel wailed like a colicky infant. She wept for the village she would never see again and for the handsome young man she had left behind. Their mother, who had no patience for tears, pointed to the water that surrounded them on all sides. "The ocean is full enough," she said. "If you don't stop crying, you'll drown the fish."

They had come up to the deck from their third-class cabin—a cramped cell reeking of vomit and salt. Sara thought the sea air might raise Hindel's spirits, but the cyan sky offered no reprieve. After soaking through their mother's handkerchiefs, Hindel began using the folds of her skirt. Her eyelids were pink, swollen, and raw, but even in grief, her beauty was apparent. Hindel's skin was as soft as the foam on the waves. The braids down her back were like honeyed silk.

Their mother whispered in Sara's ear. "Find your father and bring me his handkerchief. Quickly, before your sister ruins her clothes."

Sara was more than happy to oblige, to be free, for a moment, from the wailing. Her father's face was nowhere to be seen, but she did not shrink from the crowd. She pushed her way past a group of young men—at least half a dozen bent over a wooden crate, throwing down cards, tossing coins, and laughing. The tallest one winked as Sara went by, but it was the shorter man behind him who caught her attention.

The man stood apart from the rest of the group, staring in silence at the motion of the sea. His reddish beard was neatly trimmed; his woolen suit was worn but clean. Sara watched as he plucked a pair of wire-rimmed spectacles from his face, pulled a handkerchief from his pocket, and set to work polishing the round lenses.

He was gentle with his task, careful and slow, holding the spectacles as if he thought he might hurt them, as if they were the wings of an injured bird instead of two discs made of clear, hard glass.

In an instant, Sara was beside him, pointing to the handkerchief, asking for help. "Please," she said sweetly, "may I borrow it for my sister? She is there, by the railing—the girl with the braids."

The man placed the spectacles back on his nose and squinted. "By the railing, you say? I can't see that far. My eyes are not as sharp as they should be. Still, I'm more than happy to help." Something inside Sara's chest stirred. She knew that when most men saw her sister, they noticed only her flawless skin and the curves beneath her dress. Back in their tiny village, every man over the age of fifteen had leapt to Hindel's aid at every opportunity. They carried her water buckets from the river; they picked up the stray apples that fell from her cart. Sara had seen their wolfish smiles, their hungry stares, their too-close hands. But this short and weak-eyed stranger acted out of courtesy alone.

As she led the man toward the railing, the sun emerged from a passing cloud overhead. Sara blinked once and then again. Was it her imagination, or had a single strand of golden light formed a line from her older sister to the myopic man beside her? "My name is Aaron," the stranger said, as he struggled to keep up.

Three months later in New York, Hindel married Aaron in a one-room synagogue on Rivington Street. At the small reception, held on the roof of the building, electric lights were strung on tall wooden poles, and platters of cake were set out for the guests. Sara's mother told anyone who would listen that her youngest daughter had been the one to introduce the young lovers. "Can you believe it?" she said to the guests. "I sent her for a handkerchief, and she came back with a groom." A few of the guests shook their heads in disbelief, but most of them smiled or offered their congratulations. *Such a good girl you have*, they said. *Such a blessing to her family.*

When all the cake had been eaten and all the schnapps had been drunk, the rabbi—a stout man in a wide fur hat—took Sara's hand gently and murmured a blessing. "Tell me," Rabbi Sheinkopf said, "about the ship. Dozens of men carry handkerchiefs. Why pick Aaron? Why ask *him* to help you?"

A long moment passed before Sara answered. She chose her words like fruits at the market, weighing each one before she spoke. "He was different from the other men. The others gambled on games of cards, but he stood apart. He was polishing his spectacles."

"Ah," the rabbi said. "So, he was the most prudent and scholarly of the men?"

Sara shook her head. "Not really. He wasn't prudent, only poor. And the spectacles didn't make him look scholarly. He was cleaning the dust off of them and squinting. When I first pointed Hindel out to him, his eyes were so bad that he couldn't even see her. . . ."

"So, you chose someone who could see beyond your sister's physical appearance?"

Sara hesitated. "Partly," she admitted. Sara understood that though the rabbi searched for answers, he did not know enough to ask the proper question. She knew that the most important part of her encounter was not what had led her to approach Aaron in the first place, but what she had seen afterward. She did not want to lie to the rabbi, but she was not sure how to explain the phenomenon to him. Eventually, she raised herself onto her toes and whispered the story into his ear.

When she described the filament of light she had seen, the rabbi did not seem surprised. Instead, his eyes sparkled with possibility. "You have a calling," he said to Sara. "You are young yet, but it will wait."

"I don't understand," she said. "What do you mean?"

"The light you saw between your sister and her husband was not a trick of the sun. You have been blessed with eyes that can see the light of soulmates reaching for each other."

Whether it was the rabbi's words, the sip of brandy her father had given her, or the flicker of the strange electric bulbs, Sara's head began to throb. The rabbi's voice was like late spring rain—soft, but steady and persistent. The words he spoke next fixed themselves in her mind and clung to her for the rest of her life.

"You are a matchmaker, Sara Glikman. A *shadchanteh* for this strange, new world."

TWO

ABBY

1994

The night that her grandmother Sara died, Abby dreamed of her in sharp and glowing detail. In Abby's dream, Sara was the same as in real life—a five-foot-tall, plumpish woman wearing comfortable shoes, black slacks, and a cardigan sweater. The skin on her face was wrinkled but soft, her curls freshly dyed Nice'n Easy "Champagne Blonde." When Abby woke in the morning, her grandmother's voice was in her head. *Would it kill you to dream of me in better clothes? Maybe make me taller or a little thinner, at least?*

Grandma Sara had passed peacefully in her sleep, with a smile on her face, a stack of newspapers on her nightstand, and an empty cake plate on the floor by her bed. On the last day of her life, she had walked for three miles around her Upper West Side neighborhood. When she spoke to Abby on the phone that evening, she mentioned an upcoming coffee date with her neighbor. "Mrs. Levitz is coming tomorrow at ten. I promised her I'd make the cinnamon babka, but I don't like to rush around in the morning, so I made two of them this afternoon. I put one in the freezer for you. I'll give it to you when you come on Sunday."

Abby forgot about the babka until the next morning, when her mother called her at work with the news. Sara hadn't answered Mrs. Levitz's knocks, so the neighbor asked the building's doorman for the key. Sara's entryway had been dark and still. There was no coffee brewing, no activity, no noise. An ambulance was summoned, but it was already too late.

Abby shut her office door and let the tears run down her cheeks. It was impossible to believe that her grandmother was gone. Fourteen years ago, Grandma Sara abandoned her retirement in Florida to help Abby's mother raise her two daughters. In the winters, when New York turned snowy and gray, Abby would ask her grandmother if she ever missed the beach. But even on the coldest, most bitter days, Grandma Sara would smile and shake her head. "You and your sister are my sunshine," she would say. "At my age, who wants to bother squeezing into a swimsuit?"

Abby stared at the lone photograph on her desk—a portrait with her sister and her grandmother, taken at Sara's ninetieth birthday celebration. In the photo, all three women held up glasses of champagne. Abby wore her dark curls long and loose, while Hannah's lighter waves were pinned up with flowers. Grandma Sara was in the middle, flanked by her two granddaughters, beaming at the camera.

Pressing the frame to her heart, Abby tried to conjure her grandmother's voice—the vaguely old-world accent that clung to her vowels, the long-forgotten tunes she used to hum under her breath. Abby let her mind drift to the last time they were together, two days ago for their weekly Sunday lunch. The Nichols divorce had been all over the news, and, of course, her grandmother had brought it up. Sara was fascinated by her granddaughter's legal career, interrogating her regularly about the details of her work.

"I read an article today, about the actress and the millionaire. Your firm represents the actress, yes?" Grandma Sara's eyes had sparkled like a mischievous child's.

"Grandma, you know I can't talk about my cases. They're confidential, remember?"

Sara held up her hand. "You don't have to say a word. I have two good eyes and two good ears. I watch the news. I read the papers. I already know everything I need to know. It's not over for those two, not by a long shot."

Abby groaned and covered her face with her hands. "You just said you've read the articles! How can you possibly think it isn't over?"

"I don't believe everything I read. You assume everything they print is true?"

"Grandma, I told you. I can't discuss it. All I know is that I'm working twelve-hour days for people who don't want to be in the same room with each other."

Sara stood from the sofa and refilled Abby's coffee cup before settling back against the chenille cushions. "Sweetheart, you have to stop working so hard. All this tumult will come to nothing. Those two are staying together. End of story."

"Michelle Nichols was in our office three times last week!"

Sara shrugged and sipped her coffee. "I see what I see, and I know what I know. There won't be any divorce. Go ahead, tell your boss."

"Should I tell her that's my grandmother's professional opinion?" Abby had heard a few stories of her grandmother's matchmaking days, back when she was a young woman on the Lower East Side and later, as a young mother after the war. Sara had been out of the business for over forty years, but she still liked to lecture on matters of the heart. It could be a sore point between the two of them, especially when Sara tried to give her single granddaughter advice. In fact, it was the only thing they ever argued about.

"Joke if you want, but yes, that's my opinion. I'm old, but my instincts are still good."

When Abby didn't answer, her grandmother continued. "For instance, I know when my granddaughter isn't happy."

"Grandma, stop. I'm perfectly happy. I already told you, everything is fine. I like my apartment, I have nice friends, and I'm really lucky to have such a good job."

"Lucky is when you win the lottery. Not when you work eighty hours a week."

Abby sighed. "Not my hours again, *please*—"

"You can't do a job like that forever. Every day, another kick in the *kishkes* . . ."

"No one is kicking my *kishkes*, Grandma. Yes, I work very hard. Yes, it's not always the most . . . *uplifting* work. But it's important to me."

"Who's saying your work isn't important? I'm all for divorce—it's a necessary thing. Not just for people like your parents—for other people, too. People even *less* lucky . . ." She paused for a moment. "Of course, none of *my* matches ever needed a divorce."

"That doesn't mean all of them were happy. Times have changed."

Her grandmother took Abby's hand in her own, squeezed it gently, and pressed it to her cheek. "Listen to me, sweetheart. Some things never change. Don't you remember the stories I used to tell you? I should have made you listen better." Sara leaned closer to Abby and sighed. "One day, my brilliant skeptic, I'll be gone, and all of my stories will belong to you. When the time comes, try to remember what I taught you. Who knows? Maybe you'll make a few love matches of your own."

Love. "Grandma, you know how I feel about this. After everything my mom went through, I just don't believe in marriage."

"I know, I know. But listen to me, sweetheart. What happened between your parents wasn't love. That was a match that never should have been made."

❧

Abby's mother and father broke the news of their divorce to their daughters over hot fudge sundaes on Central Park South. Tucked inside a corner of the Hotel St. Moritz, Rumpelmayer's was well-known for its ice-cream confections, elaborate pastries, and fanciful décor. Abby's little sister was delighted with all of it—the teddy bears on the tables, the pale pink walls. The visit to the restaurant was their father's idea, but Abby was not fooled by his subterfuge. She was twelve years old, and she paid attention. She had seen her mother's tear-streaked cheeks. She had heard the late-night arguments coming from her parents' bedroom. Worst of all, she had smelled the unfamiliar perfume—a dense combination of musk and burnt rose petals—that clung to the lapels of her father's trench coat. None of the scents that swirled around the café—cocoa and butter, vanilla and cinnamon—could erase the one that lingered in Abby's mind.

Abby had no power to refuse the family outing, but her father could not force her to enjoy herself. She watched, unsmiling, as the sundae he ordered for her softened and melted to soup in its dish. The unyielding leather of her shoes pinched at her toes and the backs of her heels. The barrettes holding back her dark, rowdy curls bit into her scalp like miniature teeth. Why had they gotten dressed up for *this*? Why were they pretending that they had something to celebrate? Everything about the day was wrong.

Abby was certain her mother felt the same way. Petite and pale, Beverly was nursing a cup of black coffee—a suitable drink for a somber occasion. Abby's father had ordered an oversized ice-cream soda, slathered with whipped cream and topped with a cherry. There was something obscene about the way he devoured it. Normally, her father skipped dessert, but today, he insisted, was a "special occasion."

"Girls," their mother began, ignoring his slurping. "Your father and I have something we want to talk to you about."

"Hold on, Bev." He sucked the last of the soda through the pink-and-white-striped straw and pulled two velvet boxes from the pocket of his jacket. "I have a few presents for them first." Hannah squealed when she saw the silver heart-shaped locket, but Abby frowned and left her box on the table.

"Phil," their mother said through gritted teeth. "We talked about this. We agreed that gifts were not appropriate today."

He smirked and lifted his hands to his shoulders, palms facing outward, as if he were being arrested. "You caught me," he said. "Guess I broke the rules."

"Don't make me the bad guy," Abby's mother whispered. "*You're* the one who wanted this."

Abby searched her father's face for answers. She knew many people considered him to be handsome—that all the pieces (his height, his chiseled jaw, his dark hair) added up to an attractive forty-two-year-old man. But lately, she'd noticed the hidden, ugly parts: the eyebrows raised in mockery, the sneering lips. He had begun to look like a different sort of person.

Hannah was still too young to notice, but Abby had been paying enough attention for both of them. She had seen the recent changes in her father's behavior, the sudden way his moods shifted, like a boat thrown off course. She had kept track of the nights he'd come home late from work, until there'd been so many that the counting turned pointless.

"You want a divorce, don't you?" Abby asked. When her father didn't answer, she repeated the question.

"Shh," he snapped. "Lower your voice." He pushed the velvet box farther in her direction. "Don't you want to open the present I bought you?" His smile was flashy and rehearsed, making him look more like a television anchorman than her father.

"Fine," he admitted when she didn't answer. "Yes, I've asked your mother for a divorce." Abby reached for her sister's hand and squeezed it under the table while he continued. "Sometimes married people don't stay married, but that doesn't mean that anyone is to blame. I'll always be your father. We'll always be a family."

"Are you going to move out?"

"I'm going to get my own apartment," he said. "The two of you will live with your mom during the week, and you'll come stay with me every other weekend."

Abby decided not to protest—at least for now. Hannah's face had crumpled, her blue eyes had grown teary, and Abby didn't want to make her more upset. Hannah hated to be the center of attention. She would never want a room full of strangers to see her cry. Abby knew that was the reason for this outing. Her father was too much of a coward to deliver bad news to his daughters in private.

Outside the restaurant, Hannah whimpered. "My tummy hurts," she said, before heaving the contents of her stomach onto the pocked cement sidewalk. Passersby walked around them to avoid the mess. Their mother took a clean tissue from her purse, wiped Hannah's mouth, and pulled her close. "It's okay, sweetheart," she whispered. "Let's get you home." Their father hailed a taxi, but once his wife and daughters were inside, he told them he would walk back to their apartment. "I need some fresh air," he said with a shrug.

Abby thought all of them could use some fresh air. But the girls and their mother were trapped in the back of the foul-smelling cab, while her father wandered free beneath the cool city skies. The walk should have taken him an hour, at most, but he didn't come home until the whole day had passed. When he came into Abby's room to say good night, she pretended to be asleep. He bent over to kiss her forehead, reeking of vodka, cigarettes, and that strange perfume she couldn't forget.

The months that followed were filled with unpleasant surprises: the process server lurking outside their apartment building; Thanksgiving dinner without their father, who canceled mysteriously at the last minute; a Sunday breakfast with him at their favorite diner, interrupted by the musky smell that hit Abby's nostrils like a punch in the stomach. "Girls," her father said, holding the tall, blond woman's hand, "this is Tanja."

A week before their Christmas break, their mother sat them across from her, eyes red from lack of sleep. Beverly chewed at her lower lip. "We're going to have to make some changes," she said.

"What kind of changes?" Hannah asked, in a voice so shaky that it made Abby's heart ache. Wasn't it enough that their father had left? How many more changes would there be?

Beverly sank deep into her cowl-neck sweater, retreating from the unpleasant truth. "It will take time to figure everything out, but I'm going to have to go back to work. I'm meeting with my old boss at the travel agency tomorrow."

Abby had always enjoyed listening to her mother reminisce about her career: the vacations she had booked for her clients, the family trips, the exotic honeymoons. *One day,* her mother used to say, *we'll take you girls on an adventure. We'll fly first-class and stay at a five-star hotel. They'll serve us champagne and put mints on our pillows and the beds will be so soft that we'll never want to leave.* Abby knew that before she was born, her mother had enjoyed working in travel. When she'd spoken about her days at the agency, her cheeks had been flushed and her voice had risen with excitement. But Beverly didn't seem excited now—only paler than usual, listless, and tired. The only good news was that their grandmother would be arriving soon. Grandma Sara had moved to Florida before Abby was born, but she was coming to New York to stay for a while.

The next day, when their father picked them up for the weekend, Abby and Hannah were less talkative than usual. They hadn't seen him for two full weeks, and though he'd promised to telephone every night, his calls had tapered off to every third day.

"You two don't seem very happy to see me," he sulked. As he led them down the hallway toward the elevator bank, Abby realized that he looked different. He wore a tan corduroy sports jacket, a soft plaid scarf, and shoes she'd never seen before. His hair, which he usually had trimmed every three weeks, had grown shaggier in the front and around his ears. "Your hair is long," Abby said, tilting her head and staring up at him.

"Yeah, well, that's the way men wear their hair these days."

"I've never seen you wear a scarf before."

"Since when do you care so much about my appearance?" he snapped, jamming his thumb against the elevator button. "Tanja helped me pick out some new clothes, okay?"

"Sure," Abby answered. "Your shoes are nice." She didn't want to be critical, but then she thought about Tuesday afternoon, when Hannah's ballet slippers wouldn't fit, and their mother looked as if she might burst into tears. She hadn't said why, but Abby knew: their mother had been worried about the cost of replacing them.

Once they were outside, Abby's father changed the subject. "I have a surprise for you," he said. He led them past the boxy brick building where he'd been renting an apartment and strode confidently in the direction of Central Park West. Next, he sailed them through the elegant marble lobby of an imposing prewar building. Behind a mahogany-paneled desk, a uniformed doorman tipped his hat in their direction. "Good evening, Mr. Silverman," the doorman said, and Abby wondered how the man knew her father's name.

On the eighth floor, Abby's father opened the door to 8D and flicked on the lights. Though most of the windows faced the side street, one overlooked the avenue and Central Park. Abby and Hannah pressed their foreheads against the glass and stared at the treetops a hundred feet below. "Oh," Hannah whispered. "It's beautiful." Abby pulled herself away from the window to investigate the rest of the room. An enormous white carpet covered the glossy wooden floor, and a dozen gold-framed mirrors filled the walls. Identical couches in smooth, cognac leather faced each other in the center of the space, divided by a coffee table made entirely of glass.

Their father interrupted. "Want to see the rest?" He led them both down the carpeted hall, past the marble bathroom and the master bedroom suite. At the end of the corridor was a smaller bedroom for the girls, decorated from floor to ceiling in a jumble of competing florals—bedspreads and curtains in mauve and peach, a seafoam-green carpet, a Lucite chair. "Isn't it terrific?" her father insisted. "Tanja helped me put it all together."

Abby wanted to say that the room gave her a headache. She wanted to say it was all too much—the floral bedspreads, her father's hair. But he was beaming, and her sister was giggling, so Abby decided to stay quiet.

On Sunday morning, over bagels and cream cheese in his kitchen, their father told the girls about his new promotion. He was making more money—a lot more, he said, which was how he had purchased his new apartment.

Abby exhaled in obvious relief. "Now Mommy won't have to worry so much."

Her father stopped chewing. "My new job has nothing to do with your mother."

Abby wasn't sure why he sounded so angry. Her mother needed money, and he had plenty to spare.

"I don't understand," Abby said. "You said that we were still a family."

"It's my responsibility to take care of you and Hannah and to pay for your *necessities*. Any money your mother receives will be calculated by the judge, based on my salary from when the two of us were married. I got my new job after that. Understand?"

But Abby did not. It seemed unfair that her father should wake up to a Central Park view while her mother lay awake at night, worrying about ballet shoes. Suddenly, Abby didn't want to sit at that table, in that sparkling white kitchen that felt nothing like home.

The table wobbled when she pushed back her chair, and her father's cup of coffee toppled to the floor. He jumped from his seat to reach for a towel—anything to stop the steaming liquid from staining the brand-new, pristine tile. Her father saw only the mess *she* had created;

he would never acknowledge the one he'd made himself. Abby felt her face go red with rage.

"If the divorce isn't official yet, aren't you *still* married?"

"That's not how it works," her father insisted. He said it dismissively, as if it didn't involve her, as if the choices he'd made had no impact on her life. He said it as if she didn't deserve an explanation, as if she was too young and too stupid to understand.

"How does it work then? I want to know." She crossed her arms in front of her chest.

He stood from the floor and frowned at the spots where his coffee had seeped into the narrow lines of grout. His voice, when he spoke, was jagged and hard. The words he spoke next fixed themselves in her mind and clung to her for the rest of her life.

"Damn it, Abby, get off my case! You want answers? Be a divorce lawyer, for God's sake!"

⁓☜

Abby was still crying when her firm's senior partner opened the door to her office without knocking.

"Abby, what's wrong? My God, what happened?" Diane Berenson swept into the room and raised a perfectly penciled eyebrow. When Abby didn't answer right away, Diane smoothed the skirt of her elegant knit suit and sat down in the chair across from the desk.

Abby wished she didn't have to say the words out loud. How could death take someone who was so *alive*? Even at ninety-four years of age, Sara still lived on her own. She still did her own shopping, ran errands, cooked meals. "My mom just phoned. My grandmother . . . passed away last night."

"Oh, Abby. I'm so sorry." Diane clasped her hands together in her lap. "Tell me, what can I do to help?"

Abby had heard that tone before—it was the voice Diane used with her most distraught clients. Divorce was a passionate business, after all, and Diane was a master at triaging emotion. She made sure that tissue boxes were placed on every desk, every table, and every credenza in the law offices of Berenson & Gold. When her clients wept and shouted and cursed, Diane waited patiently until they wore themselves out. *Tell me, what can I do to help,* she said then.

The question snapped Abby out of her torpor. She didn't want to be managed like one of Diane's hysterical clients. "Thank you, but I'll be okay. Really."

"When is the funeral?"

"It's not settled yet, but probably the day after tomorrow."

"Thursday then? You should get out of here; go, be with your family. I'm sure your mother will want your help; there's always so much to do at a time like this."

"I'll leave soon, but I want to finish up the Nichols interrogatories before I go."

Diane pursed her lips together and frowned. "That's why I came to see you, actually. I just got off the phone with Michelle Nichols and her manager. You can stop working on those interrogatories."

"What do you mean?"

"Turns out she and her husband aren't splitting up. Her publicist was leaking false stories to the press—marital troubles, an affair with her costar—all to manufacture interest in the next movie. The publicist made her meet with us, and when the paparazzi didn't catch her, he made two more appointments, just to make sure that they'd get photographs of her coming in and out of our building. That bastard convinced her to fake the whole thing."

Abby's pulse began to race. Was it possible her grandmother had been right? *It's not over for those two, not by a long shot.* "You've got to be kidding. That's . . . incredible. Are you sure?"

"Positive. *People* magazine will run a cover story next week about the reconciliation with her husband. Michelle said she was sorry for wasting our time."

"What did you say?"

Diane's face was a mask of mock naïveté. "You know how forgiving I can be, Abby. I accepted her apology as graciously as possible."

For the first time that morning, Abby let herself smile. "Let me guess," she said. "Once Michelle was off the call, you told her manager you expect him to pay our bill in full."

"Close, but not quite. I told that Hollywood son of a bitch that Berenson and Gold will be charging him *double*. I told him that if he doesn't pay us immediately, I'm putting in a call to *People* magazine myself."

Abby coughed. "Sounds reasonable to me."

"I'm always reasonable. But I will not tolerate being used." Diane rose from her chair, buttoned her jacket, and tucked a stray hair behind her ear. "Enough of all that. The important thing now is that you have some unexpected free time—time you should be spending with your family."

"Thank you, Diane," Abby said. She hesitated, debating whether she should share the conversation she'd had with her grandmother. "You know," she began, "the last time I saw my grandmother, she told me she'd been following the Nichols divorce in the news. . . ."

"Good for her for keeping up at her age! Of course, half the country has been following this mess."

"They really have, haven't they? But my grandmother took a special interest. She was kind of an—*expert* on marriage. She used to be a matchmaker, actually, decades ago."

"A matchmaker. Really? Like in *Fiddler on the Roof*?"

Abby thought it best not to reveal how much her grandmother loathed the comparison, how she cringed every time the word *yenta* was used. "Not exactly. Anyway, she brought up the divorce because she was convinced that Michelle would stay with her husband. I told her she was wrong, but she insisted."

As soon as the words were out of Abby's mouth, she wished that she had kept the story to herself. She'd made her grandmother sound like some sort of kooky fortune-teller. Her boss's smile was polite but pitying. "I think it's lovely that you put so much faith in your grandmother's . . . instincts. And that she took such an interest in your work. I'm sure she was incredibly proud of you."

Perfect. Now Diane thinks I'm nuts. "Yes, well, I appreciate that. Of course, I know what she said was only a coincidence."

"Of course."

Later, on the way to her mother's apartment, Abby recalled her grandmother's words. *I see what I see, and I know what I know.* Abby wished she could see what her grandmother saw, wished she could know what her grandmother knew—about life, about people, even about love. If only she had thought to ask the right questions; if only she had thought to write down the answers. In the wake of her grandmother's death, all Abby could see were lost opportunities. She felt poorer, duller, emptier than before. All she had now were faded recollections and a few ancient stories she could barely remember.

Those would have to be enough.

The morning of the funeral was chilly but clear, the sky a brilliant but insensitive blue. The cemetery in Queens went on for miles, with rows of headstones as far as Abby could see. The last time she'd been there, it was to accompany her grandmother on a visit to the grave of her grandfather, Gabe. Abby's grandfather had died in 1954, at the age of sixty, from congestive heart failure. Abby had never met him, but she had heard the stories. She knew how he relished a good cigar, that his nickname for his wife was "the beauty queen." Her grandmother took Abby to the cemetery once a year to savor old memories and place pebbles on Gabe's headstone. In the Jewish tradition, flowers were reserved for joyful occasions—never funerals. It was customary, when visiting the grave of a loved one, to leave small stones behind.

During those visits, Grandma Sara spoke to her husband as if he could hear her, as if he were alive. *Here's Abby, Gabe. Isn't she something? Look at how grown up your oldest granddaughter is!* She liked to catch him up on all the important gossip—the births and the deaths, their old friends' children and grandchildren. *Can you believe Morris Shapiro's grandson is a surgeon? The kid who couldn't eat an ice-cream cone without dropping it on the sidewalk is cutting into strangers' brains!*

Abby's job was to pack drinks and snacks, along with the foldable beach chairs her grandmother kept in her closet specifically for these odd excursions. There was no way to rush the graveside visits. Over the years, Abby learned not to try. Sara alternated between chatting with Gabe, conversing with Abby, and noshing on the snacks. She did not stop until she ran out of news and the last of the nuts and dried fruit were gone. Only then would she stand from her chair, blow kisses to her husband, and say goodbye. *See you soon, my sweet, sweet man.*

And now, at last, they were together again—Sara and Gabe, inseparable forever. Abby hated to think of them both in the ground, hated to say her final goodbye. She managed to keep herself from weeping until it was her turn to heap a shovelful of dirt onto her grandmother's plain, pine coffin. No matter how many times she'd been told that this was the custom, it still felt heartless and unnecessary.

Afterward, when the mourners began to disperse, a woman Abby did not recognize tapped her lightly on the arm. She was about ten years older—thirty-five or so—tall and attractive, despite the fact that she looked as if she'd gotten dressed in the dark. The jacket she wore did not go with her blouse, and she was wearing sneakers with her skirt. "Excuse me," she said, "I wanted to tell you how sorry I am for your loss. Your grandmother was a very special person."

Abby tried her best to smile. The woman's face was not familiar, but Grandma Sara was always meeting new people, always striking up conversations with strangers. "Thank you so much for coming. How did you know my grandmother?"

"I was her ophthalmologist, actually. My staff adored her. Everyone did. She was always so cheerful and so appreciative. Every time I gave her an eye exam, the way she thanked me—you would have thought I'd just given her a winning lottery ticket!"

"That sounds like my grandmother. She worshipped all of her doctors."

"I'm sure people have told you, but you look like her. You have her eyes."

Abby nodded politely, but she had already stopped listening. Her head ached from going for two days without sleep. Her throat was sore from speaking with dozens of people. She wondered how much longer she was required to keep smiling, required to keep listening to other people's memories of the woman she knew better than any of them. Worse than that, she wondered how many times she would have to answer questions about how her father was doing. Abruptly, she interrupted the ophthalmologist, "I'm so sorry, but I need to find my sister. We have to get back to set up for the *shiva*."

The doctor hesitated, as if she had something more to say. She opened her mouth and closed it again. Finally, she pulled a card out of her purse and pressed it into Abby's hand. "I won't keep you, but please, take my card. If you ever need an eye exam, I hope you'll come see me. I just wanted to tell you how much your grandmother meant to me. She truly was . . . one of a kind." The stranger blinked back a few stray tears before following the rest of the mourners to their cars.

A week later, everyone at Berenson & Gold had forgotten about Abby's grandmother's funeral. Richard Gold—the law firm's other senior partner—hadn't even acknowledged it. Of course, Abby could easily count on one hand the number of times Richard had spoken to her. He and Diane never shared clients—in fact, they rarely even shared associates. In general, they behaved more like competitors than partners—like two separate fiefdoms in shared office space. Each had a team of three associates, and Abby had been hired by Diane alone. None of the other lawyers were particularly friendly, but Abby told herself she wasn't there to make friends. One or two associates said they were sorry for her loss, but there were no cards or hugs or sincere condolences.

As for Diane, all she remembered was that Abby had taken a few days off, which meant that she was expected to make up the lost hours. Abby had already been assigned three new cases—two divorces and a prenuptial agreement. But as diligent as Abby tried to be with her work, her eyes kept drifting back to the photograph on her desk.

Two weeks after the funeral, Abby's uncle Ed phoned her at work. He was a few years older than Abby's mother, stocky and bearded, with a gravelly voice. Abby and her sister used to tell him that he looked like the Brawny Paper Towel man. "Thanks for the compliment, kids," he'd say. "But there aren't any lumberjacks in New York City."

Abby hadn't seen Uncle Ed since the funeral. She was happy to hear his voice, but he'd never called her at work before. "Is everything all right? You and Aunt Judy okay?"

"Sure, kiddo, we're both fine. Listen, Judy and I are down in Florida, cleaning out your grandmother's old condo. There were a couple of book boxes in her closet marked with your name, so I'm sending them up north today. I wanted to tell you so you could keep an eye out."

"She didn't leave me those creepy porcelain figurines, did she? The ones in the dining room?"

"Nope. The figurines are still on the shelves. To tell you the truth, we didn't go through the boxes. They're already taped up, and we have too much else to do. I'm going to drop them off at the post office later. They should get to you in a few days."

"Do you need my address?"

"Nah, your mom already gave it to me. I've gotta run, kiddo. Take care of yourself."

The next Saturday morning, Abby's doorman buzzed to say two

boxes had arrived. Once she got them into her apartment, she ran a kitchen knife through the layer of duct tape that held the first of them together. Abby assumed they contained a few cookbooks, or possibly her grandmother's candlesticks. Nothing of any real value, she was certain.

She swore she could smell the faintest hint of her grandmother's chicken soup wafting up from the cardboard flaps. But when she pulled them back, the smells were different—dust and paper, a whisper of whiskey. Six leather-bound journals, in various sizes, were stacked on top of each other. The second box contained more of the same—though the books were newer, and some were binders. Abby's hands shook as she traced her fingers over the covers.

She decided to begin with the pile of older books first and, of those, the most ancient-looking volume. She blinked at the date printed on the inside cover. 1910. The year her grandmother had come to the United States.

Abby scanned the Yiddish words that filled the first faded pages. Although she knew very little of the language, she was able to recognize a handful of words and names: *Hindel Glikman, 18,* kallah. *Aaron Ambromovich, 22,* chossen. Hindel, of course, was her grandmother's sister, eighteen years old, listed as "bride." Aaron Ambromovich was Hindel's husband, the man she had met on the deck of the ship to New York. *Chossen,* Abby knew, was the Yiddish word for "groom." Although there were other notes written beneath the names, Abby could not make sense of any of them. According to the stories Abby had heard, the couple married in 1910, a few months after they arrived in America.

The next several pages were filled with sketches—a drawing of a dog, the Williamsburg Bridge. In 1910, Abby's grandmother would have been just ten years old.

Somewhere toward the end of the volume, the doodles and drawings came to an end. English letters replaced the Hebrew, and the year—

1913—was scrawled in black ink. Abby knew that her grandmother—unlike many of the poorest children at the time—had attended public school. It was there that she learned to read and write in English.

Abby's heart leapt when she saw the writing. What a gift it would be to have her grandmother's diaries, to learn about Sara's early life in her own words!

But the notes were not exactly what Abby had hoped for. Instead of a diary, the book read more like a catalogue. The first entry began with a pair of names. *Miryam Nachman, age 20, bride. Jacob Tunchel, age 21, groom.* A diverse collection of information followed: Miryam was the youngest of three children. Her father's occupation was listed as "scribe," a craftsman who used traditional Hebrew calligraphy for religious items like *mezuzah* scrolls and marriage contracts. According to the records, she was "artistic." She liked to read; she was "stylish." She worked trimming hats for a milliner.

Jacob Tunchel lived on Stanton Street. His mother had passed away on May 30, 1912. According to Sara's notes, he was studying optometry and worked alongside his father in the eyeglass business. Apparently, he had an "entertaining sense of humor." At the bottom of the entry, a few cryptic words were scrawled in messy, tiny script: *The heart is big enough to hold both grief and love.*

As she flipped through the remainder of the notebook, Abby found half a dozen similar entries—couples with old-world names and details, their backgrounds, their jobs, their family histories. Other notebooks were filled with descriptions of eligible men or marriageable women instead of couples. Photographs and cards and newspaper clippings were tucked into the crevices between the pages.

Abby sank down to the cheap parquet floor of her apartment and wrapped her thin arms around her knees. She felt a great weariness creeping in, as if she'd begun a long race and only now discovered that someone had moved the finish line. She had found some peace with her grandmother's death, but now these books raised a thousand new questions. What did her grandmother want Abby to glean from them? How could she make sense of all the pages left behind? Only the strength of Abby's curiosity kept her from giving in to fresh heartache.

She stood up from the floor and surveyed the heap of leather volumes. Somewhere in this stack of washed-out scribbles were the tales Abby's grandmother wanted to tell. Sara had trusted Abby to find them— trusted she would pore through the mountain of papers in order to piece the stories together. Somewhere in this remarkable collection were the lessons Sara wanted Abby to learn.

One day, my brilliant skeptic, I'll be gone, and all of my stories will belong to you. When the time comes, try to remember what I taught you. Who knows? Maybe you'll make a few love matches of your own.

THREE

SARA

1913

Will You Sue a Child for a Piece of Chicken?

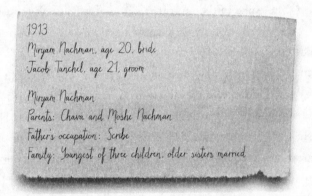

1913
Miryam Nachman, age 20, bride
Jacob Tunchel, age 21, groom

Miryam Nachman
Parents: Chava and Moshe Nachman
Father's occupation: Scribe
Family: Youngest of three children, older sisters married

Despite the rabbi's astonishing declaration, Sara did not think again about making matches until three years had passed. In that time, she'd come to recognize the contradictory nature of her new home: New York was a place of limitless opportunity and shocking scarcity all at once.

The eight of them (including Hindel and her husband) lived together on Cannon Street in a three-room apartment with a hallway toilet shared by too many occupants. The center room was distinguished from the other two by the presence of a heavy iron stove and a trough-like sink attached to one wall. "It's not so terrible," their mother insisted, but her eyes told an altogether different story. They lingered on the flakes of peeling paint, the dusty floors, the water-stained ceiling.

For the first three months, before Hindel married, Sara slept in the kitchen beside her sister. They scrubbed the wooden dining table every evening, covered it with a blanket, and curled on top of it like cats. Their parents took the smallest, windowless room—the only one with a proper bed—and the three boys shared two cots in the living room. Once Hindel and Aaron were wed, however, Sara was forced to share a cot with her youngest brother, George. Night after night, she lay awake in the dark, listening to the ghastly, perpetual concerto of her brothers' snores, her sister's sighs, and the shouting that wafted in from the street. She woke in the mornings stiff and exhausted, took a few bites of bread, and walked with George to the public school on East Fourth Street.

No matter how little she'd eaten or how tired she was, Sara felt a surge of energy when she entered the classroom. Civics and history, arithmetic and reading—there was not a single subject that did not interest her. In Kalarash, only the boys attended school, but in America, half of her classmates were girls. They were not particularly kind to Sara, with her hand-me-down dresses and messy braids, but that did not bother her in the slightest. Living in such cramped quarters with her family meant she longed more for privacy than friends. Loneliness was an unimaginable luxury.

Because of her enthusiasm for school, Sara learned to speak English faster than her siblings. Soon enough, she was borrowing books from her teacher and visiting the Tompkins Square library branch once a week. At night, while her brothers groaned in their sleep, she sat by the window and read her books by the streetlamp's muted glow. The stories snuffed out the racket down the hall. They quieted the stomping from the neighbors above. They charmed and distracted her just enough so that she was able to let go of the clamor in her head.

The downside, of course, was that she slept even less, and all the

squinting in the lamplight weakened her eyes. When her teacher noticed her struggling to see the blackboard, she moved Sara to the front
row and sent home a note.

Sara's mother's hands trembled as she unfolded the paper. Of course,
she could not read the English words. "What does it say?" she asked
her daughter. "What is wrong?"

"There's nothing wrong. Mrs. Stewart says I'm an excellent student.
She wrote the note to you and Papa because she thinks I may need
eyeglasses. She noticed that it's sometimes hard for me to see."

With eight mouths to feed and rent to pay, there was no money in
the Glikman home to spare. Sara's mother refolded the teacher's note,
slipped it into her apron pocket, and frowned. "Don't worry, Mama,"
Sara said. "Mrs. Shapiro owes me some money for helping with her
baby. There are a few men selling eyeglasses on Orchard Street. I'll ask
Aaron if he knows who has the best prices."

The next day, the air of the outdoor market was ripe with the scent
of vinegar and salt. Barrels of pickled mushrooms and radishes, cucumbers, and cabbage blocked the street. Pushcarts were piled high with
carrots, ripe red apples, and sweet golden onions. Children gathered in
clusters around peanut carts while their mothers haggled over the price
of fresh eggs. Tempted as she was to buy a cup of borscht, Sara ignored
the rumblings of her stomach. Before she bought anything to eat, she
needed to know how much the spectacles would cost.

At last, Sara spotted the man she was seeking. Baruch Tunchel sold
wire-rimmed spectacles from a pushcart on the corner of Orchard
Street and Rivington. A black felt fedora sat high on his head, and a silvery beard cascaded from his chin. Somewhere in the middle, between
the hat and the beard, was a noncommittal mouth, a forgettable nose,
and eager eyes watching for customers from behind a thick pair of
spectacles. Tunchel's cart was wedged between a hawkish tinsmith and
a one-eyed woman selling bananas. Sara tried not to stare at the fraying patch that covered the socket where the woman's eye should have

been. "It's not easy to sell spectacles beside a blind woman," Tunchel murmured. "Tell me, young lady, how can I help you?"

"My teacher wrote my mother a note about my eyesight. It's difficult for me to see the blackboard at school."

"You're lucky to have such a kindly teacher. She recommended me to you then, did she?"

"No—my brother-in-law, Aaron, gave me your name. I don't have a lot of money to spend." She glanced at the piles of wire rims and lenses. "Which of these is the cheapest?"

Tunchel snorted. "Before you ask the price, you need the proper prescription. You say you have trouble seeing at a distance? What about up close? How is it when you read?"

"Reading is easy enough," she said. "Though sometimes my eyes get tired at night."

Tunchel made Sara take ten steps back. He held up a chart marked with large and small letters and asked her to read them, line by line. Then he gave her a pair of lenses to try and asked her to read the letters again.

They repeated this exercise several times, with half a dozen pairs of lenses, until Sara could read even the smallest letters with ease. "That's the pair!" Tunchel shouted. "Keep them on for a bit. Have a good look around."

She had been so focused on the chart that she hadn't once turned her head to see elsewhere. When she did, she could scarcely believe her own eyes. She could discern every spot on the blind woman's bananas and every outline of the bricks on the buildings behind her. The sky was not simply a great swath of blue—it was thin lines of clouds and wispy patches of gray. Suddenly, Sara was achingly aware of the edges of every cup and kettle stacked on top of the tinsmith's cart. New York was not as shadowy as she had supposed.

"Looks as if you have another happy customer, Papa." A young man, perhaps twenty, approached the cart. Like the father, the son wore a black felt hat, though his face was clean-shaven, and his eyes were blue.

"I'm not a customer yet," Sara said. "We haven't decided on the price."

Mr. Tunchel cleared his throat. "The thieves at Sears and Roebuck would charge you three dollars and fifty cents for those. But I will let you have them for a dollar less."

Two and a half dollars! Sara never imagined they could be so expensive. The money she had earned from running errands and minding babies did not even begin to come close. She removed the spectacles and laid them down on the cart. Without them, the world grew dull again. "I'm sorry to have wasted your time," she said, "but I can't afford such a sum." Sara wished that she had never come to the market, that she had never glimpsed the city through Mr. Tunchel's lenses.

Luckily, the son chose to intercede. "Come now, Papa. Can't you give the girl a better price?"

"A better price? Better for who? This is why I cannot sleep at night, Jacob! How can I have you take over the business when you want to give everything away for free? How will you provide for your wife and your children?"

"I don't have a wife or any children yet, Papa."

"Thank God! If you did, they would starve!"

"Papa, calm down." Jacob turned to Sara. "How much do you want to pay?"

At this, Mr. Tunchel balled his hands into fists. "Do you hear that?" he shouted to the banana seller. "What kind of salesman asks the customers what they *want* the price to be?"

"I only have sixty cents," Sara confessed. "But I can earn the rest of the money. My neighbor needs help watching her baby, and I could bring you ten cents every week."

"There now," Jacob said. "That sounds fair." But before he could hand the eyeglasses to Sara, his father leapt forward and snatched them away. "Jacob, we don't even know the girl's name!"

Jacob handed Sara a pencil and paper and asked her to write down her name and address. She added her brother-in-law's name for good measure. "See, Papa?" he said. "The girl is respectable. Sara will pay us what she can for today, and she will pay us the rest in weekly installments until we have the full amount."

"The *full* amount was three dollars and fifty cents," Tunchel muttered. He ran his fingers through his silver beard; his shoulders shook with a heavy sigh.

Jacob put his arm around his father's shoulder. "Mama would have wanted you to extend this kindness." To Sara, he said, "Why don't you give me fifty cents for today? You can come back next week, when you have more."

Sara nodded to both the father and the son, but she was so moved that she did not trust herself to speak.

She was back the next week, and every week after that, dropping off two nickels, ten pennies, a dime. She learned that Jacob was twenty-one years old, and that he attended Columbia University's School of Optometry, the country's first university program in the field. "After I graduate," Jacob told Sara, "I'm going to open a store—a proper shop with displays of all kinds of glasses and a separate room for eye examinations."

Jacob's mother had died ten months earlier. Since her passing, Jacob's father had been pushing him to meet with a *shadchan*. "He thinks we need a woman in the house, that I should find a bride and settle down. But I don't like the idea of paying a matchmaker to tell me who I should marry."

Sara knew there were hundreds of *shadchanim* working on the Lower East Side. She'd seen their signs in the tenement windows and their advertisements in the local papers. She'd read the Gimpel Beynish cartoons—humorous tales of an unlucky matchmaker—printed in the Yiddish dailies. Like Gimpel, most of the matchmakers Sara knew were older men in tall black hats and satin coats, strict in their religious observances. Not long ago, a *shadchan* from Lewis Street had knocked on their door to talk to her parents about her oldest brother, Joe. Though her father had sent Sara from the room, she had pressed her ear against the door to listen—not because she was curious about her brother's prospects, but because she wanted to understand the *shadchan*'s methods. What kind of questions did he ask? How did he pair one person with another? She wondered whether her sister's match had been a fluke. Did she really have a gift, as the rabbi believed, or had it been a singular stroke of luck? She thought about telling the story to Jacob, but she was afraid he might think she was foolish.

A few weeks later, on the way to see Mr. Tunchel, Sara spotted one of her sister's friends. Like most of the shoppers milling about, Miryam Nachman wore a dark wool coat, black wool stockings, and sturdy boots. Sara might not have noticed her at all, except for the strangeness of her hat. An enormous green feather—like nothing in nature—exploded upward from the center of the brim. A plait of velvet ribbon secured the feather in place, along with a cluster of artificial violets. Although the hat itself was lovely, it was sorely out of place among the peddlers on Orchard Street. When Sara caught up to her, Miryam explained that she had taken a job trimming hats for a milliner. With palpable joy, she described the shop, smiling as she recalled the mountains of ribbons, the exotic feathers, and the piles of silk flowers, dyed in every possible shade.

"Maybe one day you'll make a hat for me," Sara said.

"Of course I will! A hat to match your new eyeglasses."

"I'm on my way to see the man who sold them to me now," Sara said. "He's letting me pay for them a little bit at a time." She pointed north to the corner where Mr. Tunchel's pushcart was located.

"I'm headed in that direction, too. My mother needs candles for *Shabbos*."

At the corner, the girls said their goodbyes, and Miryam walked east to make her purchase. Sara saw Jacob approach from the west, oblivious to Miryam, whose back was already turned. Neither Jacob nor Miryam took notice of the other; only Sara intuited the connection. The faintest bow of light curved over all of Orchard Street, from the spot where Jacob stood to the candlemaker's cart. Sara removed her spectacles and rubbed her eyes. When she put them on again, the thread of light was gone.

That evening, Sara asked her sister about Miryam. "She's the youngest of three girls," Hindel said. "The older two married wealthy brothers and moved to Brooklyn. Poor Miryam was left behind, but she never complains."

"She seems to like her work at the hat shop."

"It's a perfect job for someone so creative."

"She isn't engaged?"

Hindel laughed. "Why do you ask? Have you found another Aaron for my friend?"

There was too much mockery in Hindel's voice for Sara to tell her the truth of what she'd seen. "What if I have? What would be the harm?"

Hindel put down her sewing needle and patted the peak of her swollen stomach. She would give birth soon, at the end of May. "Your meeting with Aaron on the ship was chance. But to pursue matchmaking here, deliberately? The neighborhood *shadchanim* would be furious."

"Furious that I would interfere in their business or furious because I'm a girl?"

Hindel's answer was swift and certain. "Both." One by one, she counted off the reasons, tapping the tips of her fingers for emphasis. "You are a girl. You are too young. A *shadchan* must be married. If you succeed, they will complain that you have stolen their fee."

Sara hadn't thought about that. "How can I steal what they haven't yet earned?"

Hindel shrugged. "That is how they think. Every person of marriageable age is of potential benefit to them. Miryam may wear out-landish hats, but she is still modest. She is sweet and pretty and in good health. Her father is a well-respected scribe and artist. He will pay a fair dowry, and he can afford the *shadchan*'s fee."

"Our papa did not pay a dowry."

"Luckily, he did not have to. But a dowry is still customary for many families, and the *shadchanim* take a percentage as their payment."

After Hindel finished her explanation, she switched topics to preparations for the new baby. Their mother would knit the hats and blankets; Hindel would sew the shirts and diapers. Sara tried to pay attention, but despite her efforts, her mind wandered elsewhere. All she could think of was the line of light over Orchard Street—the singular strand that filled her with purpose.

Arranging a meeting between Jacob and Miryam proved to be more difficult than Sara expected. "I already told you I'm not interested," Jacob said. "My father and I are still in mourning."

Sara knew that Jacob had been devoted to his mother, but she also understood that this was an excuse. Jacob was not a particularly religious man. Even if he were, there was nothing to prohibit him from meeting Miryam before the anniversary of his mother's death.

Sara passed a dime to Jacob. So far, she had paid ninety cents toward her spectacles. "I'm not asking you to marry her," she said. "I'm only asking that you meet her."

"Between the business and my schoolwork, there is no room for anything else. I'm sorry, Sara, but now is not the right time."

She could not say what came over her then, or what caused her to speak with such newfound authority. "There is never a right time for love. If you wait for the perfect moment, you may lose your chance."

The optometrist tilted his head and stared. "Since when did you become such a philosopher?"

"I'm not a philosopher. I'm just speaking the truth. I want you to meet Miryam, and I don't think you should wait."

"I want to wait until my mother's *yahrzeit*. I want to take a full year to grieve."

Sara considered how best to answer—she did not want to offend her new friend or insult his mother's memory, so she chose to explain in a different way. "Have I told you that my sister is expecting?" she asked. "She's growing bigger every day. Every time I look at her, I'm amazed." Sara lowered her voice to the faintest whisper. "The heart of a mourner is like a woman's womb, Jacob—it can expand to hold whatever is asked of it. The heart is big enough to hold both grief and love."

A week later, when Sara returned from school, Miryam was sitting in the kitchen with Hindel. This time, Miryam wore a hat of dove gray, trimmed with a navy satin bow. Her lips were curved in a hopeful smile; her laughter was warm and expectant.

"Miryam says Jacob Tunchel and his father paid a call on her family yesterday."

Miryam reached for Sara's hand. "You should have heard him play the piano. My parents said that Jacob's mother, may she rest in peace, raised her son well. And, of course, my father is thrilled about Jacob's studies."

Sara pushed her chair closer to the hatmaker. "What did *you* think? Will you see him again?" She knew the answer before she asked the question. It was painted in the glow of Miryam's cheeks, written in her smile, echoed in her eyes. Her happiness filled the cramped, dim kitchen with a light and easy joy.

Jacob refused to accept Sara's next installment. Even the senior Mr. Tunchel told her to put her coins away. Instead of dismissing her as he usually did, the old man insisted on polishing her spectacles. He checked every miniature screw on the frames and buffed the lenses until they sparkled. When he positioned them back on her freckled nose, he did so with all the care and deference of a man placing a crown on the head of a queen.

In August, when Jacob and Miryam were married, Miryam chose Sara for a special honor. Tradition dictated that the bride remove all her jewelry prior to the ceremony so that she might stand before the groom beneath the wedding canopy unadorned. It was considered good luck to wear the bride's jewels, a *segula,* some said—a benevolent charm—one to make the wearer more likely to marry soon and well.

Sara felt silly wearing Miryam's bracelets; she couldn't wait to remove the bride's pearls and earrings. She hated that some of the guests at the wedding stared and pointed their fingers at her. *Perhaps the little one will be next.* Others cared less about the *segula* and were more interested in the story of how the bride and groom met.

Unfortunately, gossip about the match spread, so that a few days after Miryam's wedding, the *shadchan* from Lewis Street came a second time. He arrived unexpectedly after dinner and was invited in for tea. This time, her father sent everyone from the room, including her oldest brother, Joe. Sara took her place again by the door in order to hear the conversation. She left it open the slightest bit so that she could see the men as they talked.

Her father cleared his throat and began. "I'm afraid my son has not changed his mind."

"I did not come about your son. I came here to discuss your daughter." The *shadchan* frowned and pulled at his beard.

"Your timing is terrible," her father joked. "My oldest, Hindel, is already married, and her sister, Sara, is much too young."

"I'm not interested in finding anyone a husband. I'm here because there has been talk that your younger daughter is arranging matches. Several of my colleagues have heard the rumors, and they demand that she stop at once."

Sara was unprepared for her father's reaction, for the laughter that erupted from his lips. "Sara? My Sara? A *shadchanteh*? The girl is only thirteen years old!"

"Even so, it has come to our attention that she is interfering with our business."

"*Interfering?*" Her father was suddenly on his feet, waving his arms in frustration. "How dare you come into my home and disparage a young girl for doing a good deed?"

"Are you saying the girl received no payment? That the families provided no compensation?"

"What kind of a *meshuggeneh* are you? Are we back in the old country, where the innocent are accused? Where women and children are murdered in the dark?" Sara's father struggled to breathe. His round face was red with a savage rage. "We are in America!" he shouted.

Following her father's outburst, the matchmaker lowered his voice, but Sara could see that he was not satisfied. "I want to know more about the details of the match."

Sara's father wiped the sweat from his neck and sank back down into his chair. "Sara!" he shouted. "Come, child. Come!"

She waited a moment before walking through the door so that her father would not suspect that she had been listening. "Yes, Father?" she said, in her most obedient voice.

"This man, do you know who he is?"

"He is the matchmaker, Papa. From Lewis Street."

"Yes, and he seems to think you are meddling in his trade. He wants to know about Miryam's wedding to Jacob."

Sara told the story of her teacher's note, Mr. Tunchel's pushcart, and Miryam's hats. She explained the sadness she felt for Jacob and her own chance meeting with Miryam on Orchard Street. She did not tell the men about the light she had seen. "I mentioned Miryam to Jacob, but I did not know that he would court her."

"And you received no payment of any kind? No commission from either family?"

"I got a discount on my spectacles," she admitted. "And they served us capon at the wedding banquet."

Sara's father glared at the matchmaker. "So?" he said. "What will you do? Will you sue a child for a piece of chicken? Will you break her spectacles in two and take half of them for your own?"

The matchmaker stood from his chair to leave. He did not look at Sara again but addressed his final words to her father. "The matter is settled for today," he said. "But my colleagues and I will not forget. If we hear of any further matches arranged by your daughter, you will hear from us again."

When the matchmaker was gone, Sara brought her father a glass of water. "Papa, remember what the doctor said. You must make a better effort not to get so excited. The *shadchan* is a rude and stupid man. You cannot let such a person upset you."

Sara's father took a sip from the glass and motioned for his daughter to sit beside him. "He is rude and unpleasant, but he is not stupid." He reached into the pocket of his jacket and pulled out a familiar golden bracelet—one of the bracelets Sara had worn during Miryam's wedding ceremony.

"I don't understand," Sara said. "Why do you have Miryam's bracelet?"

"The day after the wedding, her father paid a visit to thank me for your part in his daughter's match. He understands that you are no *shadchan*, but he wanted to show his appreciation. He tried to give me money, but I refused. The next day, he returned with this. His wife insisted that I keep it and accept it as the brokerage fee. When I refused again, he became distraught. It would bring terrible luck, the poor man said, if he did not provide some kind of payment. He told me he could not go home to his wife if I did not accept the gift."

"But Papa, it looks like solid gold. It must be very valuable. If the matchmaker finds out, he'll come again."

Sara's father nodded sadly. When he spoke, his voice was soft and tired. "Miryam's father knows all of this. He has given his blessing for me to sell the bracelet. If I feel well enough, I will do it next week, in a different neighborhood, perhaps. Still, it may be best to save it, in case we are ever in worse need."

"I'm sorry to cause so much trouble," Sara said, but her father waved her apology away.

"You cannot help the gift you have been given." When she did not answer, he continued. "Come now, child. I know the story. I know what you told Rabbi Sheinkopf at Hindel's wedding. To tell you the truth, I am only surprised that the itch to make another match did not strike sooner."

"Does Mama know?"

Sara's father shook his head. "Not yet. The *shadchanim* believe they are the only ones who can do such important work. The possibility that a young, untrained girl could match two souls according to God's will is the gravest insult to their profession. You must wait until after you are wed before you meddle in any more matches. A *shadchanteh*—a female matchmaker—is rare enough, but an unmarried one would never be tolerated by the people of this community. If you were to engage in such behavior, your reputation would be ruined." Behind her father's fragile smile was more than a trace of fear.

Sara was troubled by her father's words. What if she could not help herself? And what if she *never* became a bride? But she did not want to cause her father additional worry, so she swore to him that she would try.

Later that night, as she read by the window, even the stories in her book could not calm her. She worried that the *shadchanim* would find out about the bracelet. She worried that her father's health was poor. She worried that she had sworn a false vow, that she had made a promise she could not keep.

FOUR

ABBY

1994

The blind date was her cousin Jason's idea. Actually, it may have been his mother's idea first—Abby's aunt Judy was always asking about her niece's love life, and lately, there hadn't been much to tell. At any rate, Jason had cornered Abby during the last night of their grandmother's *shiva*. "There's a guy in my poker game— Will Brenner. Nice, smart, around our age. He's a lawyer, too. Okay if I give him your phone number?" The endorsement had been vague and somewhat lackluster, but Abby hadn't been listening all that carefully. She'd been too distracted and far too sad. At some point, she must have mumbled her consent, because a few weeks later, Will left a message on her machine.

> Hi, Abby. This is William Brenner. Hopefully, Jason told
> you I'd be calling. Anyway, he gave me your number,
> so . . . if you have time, I'd love it if you'd call me back.

Abby hadn't been on a date in months, and she wasn't excited about starting now—not so soon after her grandmother's funeral. She was still breaking into tears at odd moments. She wasn't sleeping. She needed a haircut.

She was about to erase the message when she remembered the line from her grandmother's notebook. *The heart is big enough to hold both grief and love.* Abby had never been a superstitious person. She didn't believe in fate or signs. But as she stared at the photo of Sara on her desk, she wondered whether she should give in, just this once. Will sounded nice enough on the phone. She knew that if her grandmother was sitting with her, she would have told Abby to call Will back. Abby imagined how their conversation might go.

It's too soon, Grandma. I should wait a few months.
A few months from now, I'll still be dead.
I'm afraid I won't have anything to say to him.
If all else fails, just talk about me.

Ten minutes before Abby was set to leave work to meet Will at the bar he'd chosen, Diane tapped on her office door. As usual, Diane was styled to perfection—her fitted knit skirt was just short enough to show off legs that any other fifty-five-year-old would kill for. Her makeup was youthful and artfully applied, and her thick brown hair was layered in all the right places. Abby made another mental note to make an appointment for a haircut. Diane's eyes lingered on Abby's paper-free desk and freshly glossed lips. "Leaving early?" she asked. Abby wanted to say that seven o'clock wasn't early, but instead, she nodded and tried not to look guilty.

"I'll let you go then. But first, a quick word about the meeting tomorrow. Victor Étoile will be here at ten. As you know, he's an incredibly talented clothing designer. He's charming, but he's also *extremely* demanding. Nothing gets by him. He should have been a lawyer."

"Is there anything specific you need me to do at the meeting?"

"Nothing I can think of. The most important thing is not to alienate the other side. Victor's fiancée, Nicole, wants us to talk through the agreement together. Be as welcoming as possible to her. She's about your age."

"And how old is Victor again?" Abby asked.

"Forty-five, but don't mention the age difference. When I'm in the middle of prenup negotiations, I never bring up age differences, ex-spouses, or children. Of course, Nicole already knows about Victor's first marriage and his two girls. But I always try to keep the romantic illusion alive. If there's anything unpleasant that needs to be said, let me be the one to say it. You're there to be the good cop, okay? Obviously, Nicole isn't our client, but he's about to marry her, so we need to keep both of them happy."

"I understand."

Diane nodded. "Good," she said. "See you tomorrow."

Will picked the bar of a trendy new restaurant on Twentieth Street, in the Flatiron district. The entrance was marked with a handsome brown awning set inside an ornate marble archway. To the left, a darkened space smelled of wine and mahogany. Painted panels of technicolor fruits and vegetables hung above a lengthy wooden bar. Abby waited for her eyes to adjust before scanning the room for her date. That was probably him—the young man checking his watch, dark hair and glasses, sitting beside an empty seat. The man she thought was Will wore a conservative navy suit, a red-striped tie, and an earnest expression. He was nowhere near as stylish as the bar he had picked. He waved when he spotted her and stood from his chair.

"Abby?" he asked. "Hey, I'm Will."

"It's so nice to meet you," Abby said. She put her bag on the floor and settled into the seat next to him while Will waved over the bartender and asked what she wanted.

After a few sips of wine, she felt more relaxed. She needn't have worried about the conversation. There was plenty to talk about with Will. Aside from Jason, they had a few acquaintances in common. Will had clerked for the Second Circuit with one of Abby's friends, and his college roommate had been in the class behind hers at Columbia. They were both first-born children, both confessed "rule followers." He was a fifth-year corporate associate at one of the city's top firms, and she was almost done with her first year at Berenson & Gold.

"So," Will said, leaning a little bit closer. "A divorce lawyer, huh? Should I be worried?"

Abby downed the rest of her glass. *Here we go again,* she thought. She'd given the speech at least a dozen times—the one she so often felt compelled to make. "Look," she began, "I had offers from all the best firms, just like you. Davis Polk, Simpson, Cravath, Wachtell—"

Will interrupted to apologize. "Oh God, I'm so sorry. I didn't mean to insult you. I wasn't implying that you couldn't get another job."

"People always think divorce lawyers aren't smart or ambitious, but the truth is, most of the assumptions are wrong. Take Diane Berenson. Did you know she and Janet Reno were in the same class at Harvard Law School?"

"Huh. I didn't know that."

"Well, there you go. Let me ask you this, what was the first year at your firm like? What did you work on?"

"I spent nine months in a freezing-cold conference room doing document production for an anti-trust case."

"Did you ever meet a client?"

"I never left the room. It was me and three other first years. We were miserable."

"I sit in on client meetings with Diane every day—even the high-profile, high-net-worth ones. If Diane isn't available, they call me directly.

They want to talk through visitation schedules and parenting issues. They have to find new places to live, they get closed out of bank accounts. Of course, some of them are only out for revenge. Some of them just want a person to yell at. But at least I feel like I'm doing something meaningful. I feel like the work I do is real."

The bartender interrupted to ask if they wanted another round. "Is that okay?" Will asked, and Abby agreed. "It sounds like you're getting amazing experience. But what made you choose divorce law in the first place?"

She took a deep breath. "Exactly what you'd expect, I guess. My parents had a bad divorce. Correction—my *mother* had a bad divorce. My father waltzed off with all the money and none of the responsibilities. His lawyer was incredibly confrontational—aggressive, stingy, and borderline abusive. My mother just wanted it to be over—she was too tired and heartbroken to put up a fight. She hired a lawyer, but not a very good one. I was twelve and my sister was nine."

"That sounds awful."

"It was a long time ago. So, what about you? Did you always want to be a lawyer?"

"Ever since I saw Paul Newman in *The Verdict*. Honestly, that was what did it for me. Of course, what I'm doing now is nothing like that, especially since I'm in the corporate department. It was naïve, I know, to think that practicing law would be the same way they show it in the movies."

Abby smiled. "You're not the first and you *definitely* won't be the last. In five years, every college kid who watched *The Firm* is going to want to be a tax lawyer like Tom Cruise."

Will threw his head back and laughed. "Wait until they find out what it's really like."

"Here's to the tax lawyers," Abby said, clinking her glass of wine against his.

Abby woke the next morning with a pounding headache—the side effect of two glasses of wine on an empty stomach. It was an inauspicious start to a frustrating morning, in which she managed not only to put a run in her last pair of stockings but also to misplace the key to her apartment. She arrived at the office fifteen minutes later than usual, and although it wasn't yet eight thirty, a message from Diane was already waiting, scrawled on a Post-it, stuck to Abby's desk: *Come see me.*

Abby pulled her damp hair into a ponytail and rushed down the hall to Diane's office. Diane kept her waiting awkwardly in the doorway before finally acknowledging her and waving her inside.

"I have something for you," Diane announced. She gestured to the flat, square box on her desk—heavy navy cardboard etched with silver foil stars, the word ÉTOILE engraved across the top. "It's a scarf from Victor's summer collection," Diane said. "Like I told you, he notices *everything.*" She gestured to her own pink-and-white bouclé suit, with two separate rows of silver buttons. "This is from his collection as well." She tilted her head and examined Abby's outfit—a nondescript, pale gray suit and a white cotton blouse with a Peter Pan collar. "I don't think the scarf will go with that shirt—what if you tie it around your ponytail instead? Don't worry, he'll see it. That man doesn't miss a thing."

The only scarves Abby owned were the ones her mother knit for her—thick, cozy wraps made of brightly colored yarn. The scarf in the box was something else entirely—a finely stitched wisp of sky-blue silk, adorned with silver and pearly white swirls. "It's beautiful," Abby said, tying it to her hair. "I'll return it at the end of the day."

"No need," Diane said. "Keep it in the office for Victor's next visit. We'll be seeing a lot of him before we wrap this thing up."

"How much of him could we possibly see?" Abby asked. "I thought the wedding was the first week in September."

"It is," Diane answered. "That means he has two months to torture us. I certainly hope you're up to it."

◦─◉⟩

Victor's fiancée was twenty-five years old, but she was dressed more like a teenage girl, in loose, ripped jeans and combat boots. She had the unmistakable build of a fashion model—impossibly tall and inconceivably thin, with a heart-shaped face and doe-like eyes. Both her lawyer and her mother had accompanied her to the meeting, but it was clear that Nicole Blanchard was the one in charge. Abby could not reconcile Nicole's mother—the round, bland face and the frumpy attire—with the stunning and spirited sylphlike creature to whom she had apparently given birth.

Victor arrived separately, ten minutes later, carrying chocolate croissants from a French bakery that Abby had never heard of before. He was ruggedly handsome, tan and fit, a cross between Michael Douglas and Harrison Ford. His jacket was tailored to fit his burly frame, and his suede loafers (no socks) looked so soft that it took all of Abby's willpower not to lean down and touch them. Victor kissed his future mother-in-law on both cheeks and drew his fiancée into an airtight embrace. Finally, he crossed the room toward Diane, reached for her hand, and kissed it.

Before Victor would allow them to begin, he insisted that everyone try a croissant. The six of them gathered around the ten-foot-long table anchored in the center of the conference room. While Diane's secretary brought everyone coffee, Victor passed out the pastries himself. "These are Nicky's favorite," he said, his slight French accent noticeable mostly in the cadence of his speech and the clouding of his *r*'s. "The best chocolate croissants in the city." Abby caught Diane checking her watch, but her boss did not interrupt.

As the six of them sipped coffee and picked at the croissants, Abby learned that Nicole grew up on a farm in Wisconsin, and that she'd been "discovered" by a scout during a Christmas shopping trip to Grand Chute. At the age of seventeen, Nicole moved to New York, where she eventually signed with the Ford Models agency. The first time she met Victor, she was twenty-one years old, walking the runway at one of his shows.

"Who could look at that face and not fall in love?" he said. And while Abby understood that he might be playing the part of the fashion designer besotted with his muse, she noticed something that caught her by surprise—when Victor looked at Nicole, his eyes lit up. As unlikely as it seemed, Abby got the overwhelming sense that he truly cared for her. Victor Étoile, Abby decided, was a decidedly multifaceted man. He ran an international, multimillion-dollar empire. Reports from various sources (including Diane) painted him as a hard-hitting businessman. Yet, here he sat, with crumbs of chocolate on his shirt, staring at Nicole like a schoolboy with a crush.

When they were through with the niceties, Diane began. "I am thrilled that we could begin today in such a cordial manner. Our goal, of course, is to draft an agreement that will protect *everyone's* best interests. We want to make this process as painless as we can. Soon enough, you'll be walking down the aisle, and this prenuptial agreement will be in a drawer somewhere, forgotten."

"I'm curious, Diane," Nicole interrupted. "Why go to so much time and trouble to negotiate an agreement you're so certain we'll forget?"

If Diane was put off or surprised by the remark, she made certain not to show it. She flashed Nicole her widest smile. "It would be irresponsible for two public figures such as yourselves to marry each other without certain protections, both financial and otherwise. In addition, Victor is bound by earlier agreements, which he is legally obligated to uphold. Without a prenuptial agreement, there is no guarantee he will be able to fulfill those previous commitments."

Nicole crossed her legs and leaned back in her chair. Her posture was relaxed, but her tone was all business. "Are you referring to the children? The child support and inheritance arrangements Victor made with Patrice when they divorced?"

Diane didn't skip a beat. "Among other things, yes," she replied.

"Good," Nicole said. "May I say something before we go any further? I'd like very much for all of us to be completely transparent in these meetings. I know I'm young, but I am not ignorant. There is a large age difference between Victor and me. He is an enormously successful business owner. He has two children from his previous marriage, and they will always be a priority. You don't need to come up with euphemisms for these subjects. After all," Nicole continued, "they are the reason we need a prenuptial agreement. I understand all that, and I understand, too, that this will not be a romantic process."

Abby wondered what Diane's strategy would be, now that Nicole had disproven all her expectations. But Diane's expression betrayed no trace of concern. Was it possible, Abby wondered, that the terms of this agreement could be negotiated more easily than her boss had thought?

As they moved on to a discussion of financial information, Nicole possessed an unnervingly intricate knowledge of the structure of Victor's company and his real estate holdings. Every time she spoke, Victor nodded in agreement—it was clear how proud he was of his fiancée's business acumen. After about an hour, Nicole's lawyer pulled a document from his briefcase and slid it across the table to Diane. "These are some thoughts Nicole and I had regarding what she'd like to see in the final agreement." As soon as the paper was in Diane's hands, Nicole looked at her watch and announced that, unfortunately, she had somewhere else she needed to be.

Insecurity crept into Victor's features. "Are you certain?" he asked. "I thought we were taking your mother to see the wedding venue. She's never been to the Puck Building before." Nicole leaned forward and whispered something into his ear. Whatever she said, it seemed to do the trick—a moment later, Victor's smile returned. "Of course, my love," he murmured to her.

Nicole apologized for ending the meeting abruptly. She slung a giant handbag over her shoulder and rearranged the stack of silver bracelets on her wrist. Abby searched her ensemble—from her leather jacket to her jeans—for anything from Victor's collections, but nothing Nicole wore bore any trace of the famous Étoile silver star logo. Victor excused himself to walk Nicole and her entourage to the elevator, leaving Diane and Abby alone in the conference room.

Abby turned her attention to Diane, who was flipping through the document Nicole's lawyer had drafted. With each page she turned, Diane's frown grew deeper. When she came to the end, she slammed her open palm onto the conference table's glossy surface.

"Uh oh," Abby said. "How bad is it?"

"Let me put it this way," Diane answered. "That woman isn't marrying him for the croissants."

Abby spent the rest of the day on another case, researching child custody issues. She left the office late and took a bus headed up Broadway, but she wasn't able to shake Victor Étoile from her mind. As the bus inched forward into traffic, she considered the assumptions she had made before the meeting. She had presumed that the designer would be the more assertive of the two, and that the model—a woman decades younger without a college degree—would surely be the one making all the concessions.

It was clear to Abby now just how mistaken she had been. Nicole was far more sophisticated than Abby thought, and Victor seemed more smitten than Diane wanted to admit. Of the two, it was Nicole who was the most informed, Nicole who radiated awareness and strength. And even though it was Victor—not Nicole—who was her client, Abby couldn't help smiling as she thought about the way the young woman had commanded the conference room.

At the next stop, several passengers got off the bus and Abby grabbed a seat. She pulled the Style Section of last Sunday's newspaper from her tote bag and did an obligatory search through the wedding announcements. According to Diane, they were mandatory reading, but Abby hadn't had enough time to keep up. The truth was, she despised the overly romanticized stories and put off looking through them as long as she could. Her grandmother, on the other hand, had always read them faithfully, with great delight, every weekend.

"Why do you keep reading those things?" Abby would ask Sara. "It's not like you know the people getting married."

"So what?" Grandma Sara used to say. "I don't have to know them to be happy for them. Sometimes, I like to be reminded that people can find love all on their own."

After reading through the week-old announcements, Abby took the current day's paper from her bag. Diane had taught her early on about the way that news could predict their future clients. How many times had a divorce followed a bankruptcy? How many times had a big promotion led to an engagement ring? Business, politics, real estate, art—all of it was driven by the passions of important people, which meant all of it was worthwhile news to Abby and her boss.

She flipped the pages and sucked in a breath when her eyes landed on a piece about Prince Charles. A documentary had aired on the BBC the day before, in which the prince finally admitted to having an affair. He and Diana had been living apart for years, but despite their separation and the prince's admission, the article provided no new information regarding the possibility of divorce. Abby was sure every divorce lawyer in America was devouring the story, eager for clues.

The royal wedding had taken place when Abby was still a girl—a short eight months after Sara moved to New York. Hours before the sunrise on that day in July, Abby's grandmother woke her granddaughters to watch the spectacle on television. Abby wanted to go back to sleep, but Hannah had begged her to get up. Hannah wore a plastic tiara from the drugstore and had made paper crowns for her grandmother and older sister. Together, the three of them watched Diana's carriage make its way through the city of London. They listened to reporters recite a litany of statistics: two million spectators lining the streets, Diana's dress embroidered with ten thousand pearls, thirty-five hundred lucky people filling the pews of St. Paul's. Hannah was shocked by the number of guests, but Sara was far less impressed.

"It's a lot of people," Sara admitted. "You know, I was at a wedding once with over two thousand."

"Two thousand people! Was the groom's mother a queen?" Hannah asked.

"No, but the father of the bride was a big shot. They called him the Pickle King of New York."

Their grandmother went on to describe the affair—the carriages in the streets, the gaping crowds. "Everyone wanted to see the bride then, too. Not everyone was lucky enough to get a seat in the synagogue."

"I thought your family was poor," Abby said. "How did you get invited to a wedding like that?"

Sara smiled playfully and winked at the girls. "Who do you think made the match?" she said.

As the bus came to the stop closest to her apartment, Abby folded her newspaper and gathered up her things. She tried to remember what else her grandmother had said about the wedding of the Pickle King's daughter, but the only other detail she recalled from that morning was the way her grandmother frowned when Charles and Diana said their vows.

"Such a shame," Sara muttered under her breath.

"What's a shame, Grandma?" Abby asked.

"That they should go to so much trouble and so much expense, all for a couple that isn't in love. Look at them. Those two will never make each other happy."

The severity of the words caught Abby off guard, but it was Hannah who was most affected by them. "Grandma!" she shouted. "That's a terrible thing to say! The wedding isn't even over, and you're ruining it! He's a prince and she's a princess! They have to live happily ever after!"

When Sara didn't answer, Hannah began to cry. Hot, angry tears streaked down her cheeks. She pounded the sofa cushions with her fists. "You're ruining it, Grandma! You're ruining the wedding! Take back what you said. Take it back *right now!*"

The shouting woke Abby's mother, who came running into the living room. She had told them the night before not to wake her. She wasn't about to lose sleep over someone else's marriage.

"Seriously, Ma? You wake her up at four thirty in the morning and then traumatize her? After everything she's already been through this year?"

Sara apologized after that, though Abby sensed how conflicted she was. Her grandmother drew Hannah up onto her lap, rubbed her back, and stroked her hair. "Shhh, *mameleh*," Sara said. "I'm sorry. I take it back, sweetheart. I take it back."

But even as Sara repeated the words, Abby knew her grandmother did not believe them. Sara had sensed something in the couple—something missing, something off. From that day on, Sara was convinced the royal marriage would not last.

At home in her apartment, Abby's answering machine was waiting for her. The first message was from Will, and the second from her mother.

Hey Abby, it's Will. So . . . is it too soon for me to call? Anyway, I had a really nice time yesterday, and I was calling to see if you're free on Saturday. I know it's the Fourth of July weekend and everything. You're probably going away. But on the off chance you're going to be around, I was thinking maybe we could do something. So . . . I guess that's it. Hope to hear from you soon.

Hi honey, it's me. I hope you're okay. I know Uncle Ed sent those boxes up from Florida, but I found another box for you in Grandma's apartment. She wrote your name on it, but there isn't much inside—only two old notebooks. It was in the coat closet behind her suit-case. I don't think they're important, so you can get them anytime. Remember, I leave tomorrow from JFK. I'm supposed to land in San Francisco at three, and your sister is picking me up at the airport. I'm going to miss you, sweetheart. Love you. I'll call you when I land.

Abby listened to both messages again. The Fourth fell on a Monday this year, making the weekend an almost perfect escape. Her mother was flying to San Francisco to see Hannah before traveling for work for the rest of the month. Most of Abby's friends would be away—off to the beach or to the Berkshires. She'd been invited by a few of them, but she hadn't felt up to a big party weekend.

There was even an offer from her father for brunch at his new girl-friend's house in Westchester, but Abby could tell it was half-hearted, at best. After Tanja, Abby could never be bothered to pretend to be interested in her father's lady friends. She knew the invitation was an apology of sorts—Abby was still miffed at him for not showing up at Sara's funeral—but she also knew it would be better for all of them if she did not accept. Abby had learned years ago that the less she ex-pected of her father, the easier the disappointment was to bear.

Abby wondered whether she should admit to Will that she had no plans or whether she should put him off until the following week. It wasn't in her nature to lie, and besides, she thought, Will was sweet. Last night, when they were done with drinks, he insisted on dropping her off at her building. He made the taxi driver keep the meter running while he walked her to her door—an act of chivalry practically unheard of for a first date in New York. As soon as she opened the door to her apartment, Abby's first impulse was to call her grandmother. When she remembered that she could not, the realization left her feeling hollowed out. Her grandmother, she knew, would have told her to go on the second date this weekend.

With Sara on her mind, Abby fell onto her couch and stared at the pile of notebooks on her coffee table. She hadn't had much time to look through them yet, and she wasn't sure how to best approach the task. The more she thought about it, the more she realized that she had no idea what the task even was. Was she supposed to read the notebooks in chronological order? Look for hidden messages? A list of reasons that might convince her to believe in love? As she contemplated returning the books to their boxes, she pictured her grandmother's disappointed expression. *Aren't you even the least bit curious? Do you know so much? Are you such a big shot now that you can't spare the time?*

She sat up from the couch. *The big shot.* The match her grandmother had made for the Pickle King's daughter. Abby wondered whether Sara had included it in her notes, and, if so, what she had written about it. After flipping through the entire first notebook, Abby finally found what she was looking for in the middle of the second volume. The top of the page was dated 1916. Her grandmother had been sixteen years old.

> *Ida Raskin, 19, bride. Parents: Moishe and Bella Raskin. Father's occupation: Owner and Proprietor, Raskin's Pickles of Rivington Street. Owner of four buildings on Allen, Rivington, and Orchard Streets, Owner of Raskin's Farm on Long Island (approximately 1,400 acres).*

Ida was described as "extroverted." She attended Barnard College, where she served as the business manager of the *Barnard Bulletin.* Abby was surprised that a young Jewish woman from the Lower East

Side had been accepted to Barnard in 1916. Ida Raskin must have been incredibly smart—not only smart, but ambitious, too.

Beneath the paragraphs devoted to Ida were those describing her future husband.

Herman Lipovsky, 26, groom. Occupation: Dentist. Education: New York University College of Dentistry and Columbia University. Parents: Israel and Myrna Lipovsky.

Herman, apparently, was "serious" and "reserved." He was the second of the four Lipovsky children and practiced dentistry with his older brother, Isidore.

Pressed between the handwritten pages of the notebook was a faded scrap of yellowed newsprint. When Abby unfolded it, she was surprised to see an article clipped from *The New York Times*. "Pickle King Wedding Splendor Amazes East Side: Rivington Street in Awe as Miss Ida Weds Dr. Lipovsky." One of her grandmother's matches was in *The New York Times*! Abby wondered why Sara hadn't mentioned it before. She scanned the article quickly for her grandmother's name, but when she didn't see it, she went back and read the piece more carefully.

Two blocks of Rivington Street were full of people yesterday, trying to catch a glimpse of the bride, Miss Ida Raskin, as she left her family home for the wedding ceremony. Miss Raskin is the daughter of Moishe Raskin, known throughout the city as "The Pickle King of New York." Fifty carriages and a dozen taxicabs hired by Mr. Raskin transported the most important guests from his home to the family's synagogue, only two blocks away.

Described by friends as "the catch of all the east side," Miss Raskin is the Business Manager of the Barnard College

Barnard Bulletin. Her Pickle King father is known by his colleagues as "a humble man of hard-earned success," determined to make his nineteen-year-old daughter the happiest bride in New York.

That this match was not a typical east side "brokered marriage," in which a professional matchmaker, or *schatchen*, was hired, was pointed out by the bride's father, who said that the couple first met in synagogue on the Day of Atonement, last fall.

Dr. Herman Lipovsky, the groom, is a dentist, in practice with Dr. Isidore Lipovsky, his brother, who gifted the bride and groom a piano. Among additional gifts was a house from the bride's father and a complete set of furnishings from the parents of the groom.

On Sunday evening, five hundred less fortunate members of the community were invited as guests of the bride's family to the vestry room of the synagogue to participate in the "*schnorrer's* tithe," in which the bride passed out five hundred separate half-dollars and helped to serve a lavish supper.

On Thursday, the synagogue was decorated with lilies and roses and a brilliant velvet canopy, called the *chuppah*. Under this entered from one side the bridegroom, and from the other, the blushing bride and her family. The marriage service was recited in Hebrew and concluded with the groom smashing a glass beneath his feet to serve as a symbol of sorrow amid celebration and a reminder of the fall of Jerusalem.

After the wedding ceremony, two thousand guests attended the banquet at Palm Garden, 150 East Fifty-Eighth Street. Among the invited guests were friends, relatives, east side neighbors, the bride's classmates from Barnard, and the groom's classmates from Columbia and the New York University College of Dentistry.

A circle was drawn in smudged black ink around the entire third paragraph of the story. What had possessed the reporter to include such an awkward disavowal of the matchmaking process?

The rest of the notes were filled with details about Ida's older brothers and Herman's relatives. When Abby reached the bottom of the page, the final line made her laugh out loud. In the seventy-eight years since the article was printed, her grandmother's beliefs had not changed.

Don't believe everything you read.

FIVE

SARA

1916

Sweet and Bitter and Gone Too Soon

Ever since Sara made the promise to her father, she'd been careful to avoid arranging matches. Or, rather, to be more accurate, she'd been careful to avoid the *appearance* of making them. With Jacob and Miryam, her influence had been obvious. Everyone knew the part she had played. But in order to avoid the *shadchanim*'s wrath, Sara knew she would have to be more cunning. She would have to be sure that if she paired two people, no one could trace it back to her. She would coordinate from the shadows. She would be invisible, Cupid's ghost.

The first time Sara made a match this way, it was for her favorite teacher, Miss Perelman. At the advanced age of twenty-seven years old, Sophie Perelman was already considered an *alteh moid*—an old maid. Sara spotted her one day, after school, staring at a young mother with a baby in her arms. The teacher's willow-thin frame seemed frailer than usual. The pile of curls on her head flopped to one side, and a thick cloud of longing blanketed her features. Sara walked home with a renewed sense of purpose: she would help Miss Perelman find her *bashert*—the soulmate who was meant to be hers.

As Sara pondered a selection of suitable men, she recalled a friend of Jacob's she had met a few times—the son of a grocer living on Grand Street. After a day of snooping at his father's store, Sara learned that Jacob's friend was married. His younger brother, however, was free from any romantic entanglements.

Sara visited the grocery every day for two weeks, learning more about the young man each afternoon. He kept a book on the counter to read at odd moments. He put out bowls of milk for the neighborhood cats. He told Sara that peaches were his favorite fruit, and he showed her how to test them gently for ripeness. His given name was Shmuel, but his friends called him Sam.

At night, after reading her library books, Sara stared out the window of her family's apartment and imagined the faces of Miss Perelman and Sam. She imagined the faces of other people as well—her neighbor's nephew from Brooklyn who visited every *Shabbos*, the cobbler's assistant who'd fixed a hole in her shoe, the daughter of the midwife who helped to deliver Miryam's baby, the waitress at the coffee parlor on Second Avenue. The faces hung suspended in Sara's mind like stars dangling in a nighttime sky. When Sara shut her eyes, she tried to connect them into tiny constellations—two points of light apiece. The star-faces dimmed and brightened in turn, but when she hit upon a pair that shimmered in her mind's eye, she knew that she had found a match.

It took months of imagining before she figured out the manner in which the combinations revealed themselves. When at last she understood, she was certain that Miss Perelman should be paired with Sam. But how could she manage an introduction without letting either of them know?

She began by bringing Miss Perelman a peach. It was one Sam had helped her to pick—sweet and fragrant, deliciously soft. Sara did not mention Sam at all—only the peaches and the apples he sold.

"It's from the grocer on Grand Street," Sara offered, when Miss Perelman expressed her appreciation.

"I don't think I've been to that market before."

"It isn't far, and it's worth the walk. My mother says the produce is the freshest and the prices are better than all the other grocers."

"Thank you, Sara. Perhaps I'll go. I've been looking for strawberries everywhere and I can't find any at the usual markets."

"The grocer's wife said she'll have strawberries in a few days. She said they would be the first of the season."

"That settles it then," the teacher said.

The next day, Sara politely suggested that Sam trade his soiled apron for a clean one.

Sam looked surprised. "What's wrong with my apron? What do you think aprons are for, anyway? You get them dirty, so your clothes stay clean."

"I know," Sara said. "But yours is *filthy*." Sam looked down at the messy spots of tomato, the splashes of beet juice, and the smudges of dirt. He rubbed his finger over a dried yellow circle of something Sara couldn't identify. "Is that egg?" she asked, but Sam merely shrugged.

A few days later, Miss Perelman told Sara that she'd gone to Grand Street to pick up some strawberries. Sara tried her best not to show her excitement. "How were they?" she asked.

Miss Perelman's cheeks turned glossy pink. Her eyes, dull as soap the day before, flashed with a new, white-hot resolve. "They were the sweetest strawberries I've ever tasted."

The moment the bell rang, Sara ran to Grand Street, where Sam was working in front of the store. Not only was his apron clean and pressed, but his wayward curls were neatly combed. He was stacking pints of strawberries on a long wooden table, displaying them as artfully as if they were flowers.

Sara gestured to the table, to his apron, and his hair. "What's all of this?" she asked, feigning surprise.

"I had a special customer yesterday," Sam confessed. "I am hoping she returns this afternoon."

Sara went on making matches in secret this way, pairing people together like a rogue puppeteer. One year passed, and then another. Slowly, the neighborhood *shadchanim* noticed something curious: engagements and weddings were on the rise, but fewer families seemed to require their services. Suspicious, they listened on the streets and in the synagogues for Sara's name. When they did not hear it, they began to wonder whether a different matchmaker was interfering.

The Lewis Street *shadchan* came to her house again, but this time, Sara's father was not strong enough to see him. Sara's mother asked her to send the man away.

Sara stood in front of the open doorway. "My father is sleeping," she explained. "He isn't well."

"I am sorry to hear," said the marriage broker. "His health should only improve in the future." He shifted back and forth on his feet, clearly uncomfortable in her presence. The *shadchan* was a deeply religious man, and the rules of modesty did not permit him to be alone with her, not even for a brief conversation. At sixteen, she was technically of marriageable age, and in the *shadchan*'s eyes, she was a woman.

He took a few steps backward so that he stood firmly in the hallway. "My colleagues and I have been perplexed," he admitted. "Will you allow me to ask you a question?"

Sara straightened her shoulders and looked the man in the eye. Almost three years had passed since the last time they spoke, and he was more beleaguered than she remembered. His tall silk hat had lost its shine. "Go ahead," Sara said.

"Everywhere we look, our people stand beneath the *chuppah*, yet my brethren and I see our business decline. Do you have any idea why this might be?"

Sara shrugged. "Perhaps, in this country, with all of its freedoms and choices, a *shadchan* is less necessary than in the old world."

The matchmaker wrung his hands and sighed. He tipped his tall hat and made a small bow before shuffling down the hall toward the stairs. "I hope and pray that you are wrong," he said. "My best to your father. *Zie gezunt!*"

Despite the marriage broker's blessing, her father's health continued to decline. Since coming to New York, Sara's father had worked as a presser for a suit maker on the corner of Pelham Street. Sara's oldest brother, Joe, worked alongside him, and her younger brothers helped out after school. Even with all of them holding down jobs, there was barely enough money to cover household expenses. The money Aaron brought home from teaching young boys Hebrew helped a little, but he was still saving to buy tickets to bring his siblings to New York.

When their father became too sick to work, Hindel took a job sewing pockets into women's coats. But soon her stomach swelled with her second child, and the boss of the shop asked her to leave. Sara offered to quit school to take Hindel's place, but her father and mother would not hear of it. "Enough with such nonsense!" her mother cried. "You will be the first in the family to finish school in this country. If you quit now, why did we come?"

Her father called Sara to his bedside. His beard, once so full, had grown sparse and white. His breathing was labored; his face was flushed. "A mind like yours is a gift," he said. "No matter what happens, you must try to get as much education as you can. Will you promise me?"

"Yes, Papa. I promise."

The months that followed brought conflicting emotions. While

Hindel expanded, her father shrank. In the crowded apartment, there was no escape—growth and decay were pressed together like teeth.

Hindel's daughter arrived on an August afternoon, in the middle of a week-long heat wave. Aaron ran down to the pushcart on the corner and bought everyone paper cups of lemon ice to celebrate. Sara spooned the shavings into her father's mouth while he lay propped up against a pillow in bed. The baby was named for their father's mother, Fannie, but they called her Florence, a "good American name."

On the seventh morning after Florence was born, Sara's father couldn't be roused. Her mother's shouts woke everyone but the baby, who slept peacefully through the doctor's visit. "I am sorry to tell you," the doctor said, "but you should prepare yourselves."

In the evening, when Sara's father took his last breath, Florence opened her eyes and began to wail. The noise filled the apartment and flooded the hall. The cries were so mournful, so loud and long, that even the ice man on the corner was concerned. When he learned the sad news from one of the neighbors, he murmured a prayer under his breath. "What is life but a cup of lemon ice?" he said. "Sweet and bitter and gone too soon."

After the funeral came the bills.

There was a bill for the coffin—plain pine box that it was—and a bill for the carriages that took the family to the cemetery. Neighbors and friends brought food for the *shiva,* but there were bills for the liquor and the rented chairs. No sooner had Sara's father been buried than the doctor sent bills for a year's worth of visits. Bills arrived next from the local pharmacy for all the medicines the doctor had prescribed.

When Sara's family first arrived in New York, her father joined a *landsmanshaft*—a mutual-aid society made up of other immigrants who hailed from the same region in Russia. In exchange for paying monthly dues, every member was given a burial plot. The *landsmanshaft* was supposed to help its members in case of job loss or extended illness, but the truth was that Sara's father's society was one of the smallest and poorest in the city. He had indeed been assigned a plot beside his *landsleit*, but that was the extent of the available benefits.

In addition to the funeral-related bills were, of course, all the others: bills from the landlord, the butcher, and the fishmonger. A bill from the midwife who had delivered Hindel's baby. Every day brought fresh invoices, which Sara collected in a tidy stack tied with cotton string. The sight of the stack kept Sara awake at night, thinking of her father and the promises she'd made.

Ever since her father had died, Sara no longer slept in the front room with her brothers. Instead, she was given her father's place in the tiny room beside her mother. Her sleep had been poor on the cot next to George, but in the room with her mother, it was even worse. For the first time in years, she had a proper bed, but the softness beneath her brought no comfort. The room was too crowded with her mother's sorrow and the memories of her father for her to breathe. No matter how many times Sara laundered the linens, the scent of her father's tobacco lingered.

When she did fall asleep, on her father's pillow, visions of him filled her dreams. Her father had loved her as no one else had. He had praised and encouraged her despite her unusual gift; he had taken her side against the *shadchan*. Who would she be without his support? Who would she be without his protection? She had promised him she would not make matches again until she was safely married. She had promised him that she would not quit school. But how was she to reconcile all she had sworn with the ever-growing pile of bills?

School was closed for the rest of the summer, so the next morning, Sara paid Rabbi Sheinkopf a visit. Although her mother understood some of Sara's role in matching Jacob and Miryam Tunchel, only the rabbi knew the full extent of the secret she carried within her. The rabbi had presided over her father's funeral and visited her home each day throughout the *shiva*, but Sara had been too heartsick to say much to him then.

When Sara had first met Rabbi Sheinkopf, he had been the leader of a small congregation in a one-room synagogue on Rivington Street— one of hundreds of tiny *shuls* dotted throughout the Lower East Side. But in the past few years, his congregation had multiplied to include several community leaders and wealthy businessmen. They had all contributed toward the building of a new synagogue, fashioned from a made-over church. The new *shul* boasted a wood-paneled sanctuary and a women's balcony that wrapped halfway around the room. From the middle of the grand, two-story ceiling hung a polished brass chandelier. An elevated center platform was surrounded by a carved wooden railing. As Sara entered the dimly lit space, she saw a group of white-bearded men who had gathered to pray.

Rabbi Sheinkopf was not surprised to see her. Sara supposed this was why she liked him—nothing she said or did seemed to shock him. He excused himself from the other men and led her to a corner, out of earshot. "How is your mother?" the rabbi asked. "Please give her my warmest regards."

"I will, Rabbi. Thank you. She is busy with Hindel's little ones. They keep her from thinking too much about my father."

The rabbi nodded. "A growing family is a blessing," he said.

"It is," Sara agreed. "But it means we have more mouths to feed. And we have too many bills we cannot pay."

"Let me ask the others. Perhaps the congregation can help."

"That is very kind, Rabbi, but I'm afraid we need more help than you can offer."

The rabbi strummed his fingers against his beard. "You have been considering . . . other possibilities then?"

She had not thought he would guess her plan so quickly. "I have," she said. "But my solution is not an easy one. I promised my father I would wait until I was married before I began making matches in earnest. He was afraid of what the *shadchanim* might do if I went against their wishes."

"And have you kept the promise you have made?"

Sara lowered her eyes. "Not entirely."

Again, he did not seem surprised. "And yet, I've heard nothing of your intervention."

"I've been making matches in secret. Not even the brides and grooms themselves know the part I've played in bringing them to the altar. But now the situation has changed. My father is gone, and our debts are too great. I swore to my father that I would finish school, but if we can't pay our bills, I will have to quit. I want to honor my promises, Rabbi, but I can't see any honor in letting my family starve. As far as I can tell, I have two choices—leave school to find full-time work or risk incurring the *shadchanim*'s wrath."

She could see the rabbi weighing the choices, trying to decide the best advice to give. "Please, Rabbi," she said, "what should I do?"

He clapped his mottled hands together. When she looked into his eyes, she saw the same glimmer she'd seen on the night of Hindel's wedding. "Perhaps there is another way. There is someone I want you to meet," he said.

Sara followed the rabbi two blocks west on Rivington Street to a familiar green-and-white-striped awning. Like everyone else in the neighborhood, she had passed Raskin's Pickles hundreds of times. Tall wooden barrels of pickled cucumbers and tomatoes stood on the sidewalk in front of the windows. Sour, sweet, spicy, and dill were among the dozens of choices offered. Behind the cucumbers were smaller barrels of onions, beets, carrots, and cabbage. Inside, the shelves were stocked with glass jars of pickled button mushrooms, black and green olives, and row after row of pickled herring. Rabbi Sheinkopf stopped under the awning and breathed in the briny air.

A short, stocky man wearing a three-piece suit bounded gracefully out of the store. He was in his fifties, bald and bearded, with a robust smile and a hearty laugh. "Good morning, Rabbi! What a pleasure!" He turned to a young man standing by the barrels. "Sollie, get the rabbi here a nice big quart of fresh half-sours!"

"Thank you, Moishe! But I did not come for pickles today."

"You need some herring, maybe? Best in the city!"

Rabbi Sheinkopf gestured toward Sara. "Moishe, this is Sara Glikman." He cleared his throat and lowered his voice. "I believe Sara can be of help with your daughter's situation."

Moishe Raskin blinked his eyes and stared. Sara was already sixteen years old, but her schoolgirl braids made her look younger. "I'm sorry, Rabbi, but I don't understand. I need a *matchmaker*, not a child."

The rabbi scanned the sidewalk for anyone who might be listening. "Let us speak away from your other customers," he suggested. Moishe led them through the store and up a flight of creaky back stairs. To the left was a storage space filled with sacks of salt, sugar, and caraway seeds. To the right, a small room with a long wooden desk, piled high with papers and ledger books. The three of them crowded around the desk and Moishe waited for the rabbi to begin.

"No one must know what we discuss here today. Moishe, do I have your word?"

The pickle man widened his eyes and nodded. "Of course you do, Rabbi. Of course."

Rabbi Sheinkopf told the story of Hindel's wedding, of what Sara had seen, and her extraordinary gift. He described Sara's encounters with the Lewis Street *shadchan,* and the pressure from the neighborhood *shadchanim.*

Moishe scowled when the men were mentioned. "It was one of *them*—Shternberg from Orchard Street—who made such a mess for my poor Ida. I have no loyalty to any of them."

Up to that moment, Sara had been silent, but now, curiosity forced her to speak. "Is Ida your daughter? What happened to her?"

To Sara's shock, Moishe Raskin began to cry. Tears trickled down his ruddy cheeks, landing in the tangles of his beard. He pulled a handkerchief from his pocket and blew his nose with a shameless blast. "No matter how successful my business grows," he sniffled, "Ida is my greatest treasure." He blew his nose a second time. "You tell her, Rabbi. Tell her the story. I don't trust myself to speak."

"Ida is Moishe's only daughter and his youngest child. His middle son, Max, runs the farm on Long Island; and Herschel, his eldest, helps him here. Ida attends Barnard College, on the west side of the city."

"I know of it," Sara said, impressed. "Ida must be an excellent student."

"Hoho!" Moishe Raskin interjected, a sliver of a smile hovering over his lips. "You can say that again."

"Ida is bright and curious, very hardworking," the rabbi agreed. "A year ago, Mr. Shternberg came to Moishe to discuss a young man of similar aptitude, then a student at Yale University. The young people met and were fond of each other. A wedding date was set for the end of May, but less than a month before the ceremony, Max saw Ida's fiancé on Long Island, dancing with another woman."

Moishe interrupted again. "Not only dancing! Kissing! Fondling!"

"Ida must have been devastated," Sara said, at which point Moishe Raskin wiped away a tear. "You, at least, have a heart," he said. "Shternberg, that bastard, saw no problem. *He'll stop such behavior when they're married,* he said. *Remember, Moishe, they're not married yet.* You know what I said? *A chazer bleibt a chazer.* A pig stays a pig, is what I told him. Nobody changes overnight, and who wants to trust an animal like that? Shternberg said he would have a talk with the family, but I told him not to waste his time. *No one treats my Ida that way,* I said."

"And what did Ida think of it?"

"Hoho!" Moishe said, slapping his fist on the desk. "Young lady, my daughter is nobody's fool. As soon as her brother told her what he saw, she called off the wedding herself." The pickle man's eyes welled up again. "The problem is that the pig broke her heart."

"And you haven't met with Shternberg since?"

"Shternberg, Grossman, they're all the same! The men they bring to us now—*dreck*! Ida won't even consider them. The *shadchanim* tell me Ida is *difficult*. They don't see my daughter for the jewel she is."

Sara thought perhaps that she and Ida Raskin had more in common than anyone knew. "Mr. Raskin," she said. "I would be honored to help your daughter."

"But she says now she will not trust any *shadchan*. She says she'll only marry if she finds a love match."

Sara placed her hand over her heart. "That is the only kind of match I make."

SIX

ABBY

1994

Abby was still thinking about the Pickle King article when she got out of bed the next morning. She considered bringing it in to show Diane—her boss might get a kick out of it, especially given the vigilance with which she read the *New York Times* wedding announcements—but by the time Abby's half-hour bus ride was over, she had decided against it. Diane wouldn't want to hear any more about Grandma Sara—the woman who had somehow intuited Michelle Nichols's lie. Better to leave that small humiliation buried in the back of her boss's mind, especially on the day of their meeting with Diane's longstanding client, Evelyn Morgan.

As everyone in New York City knew, it was Evelyn Morgan's second divorce, back in 1979—and the voluminous press surrounding it—that had catapulted Diane from a well-respected divorce attorney to a bona fide legal star. Diane had gotten Evelyn such a favorable settlement that, of course, she'd been rehired for divorce number three. Now, with divorce number four on the horizon, Evelyn had enlisted Diane's services again. Only a meeting with a client like Evelyn could have kept Diane in the city on the Friday afternoon of the Fourth of July holiday weekend. Abby had no plans—other than a possible dinner with Will—but she knew that were it not for Evelyn's request, Diane would have left the city that morning to head to her beach house in the Hamptons.

After a quick cup of coffee, Abby pulled Evelyn's files, which turned out to be more informative than she anticipated. Evelyn was the only daughter of Abraham Morgenstern, owner of Morgenstern's Resort in the Catskills. Born in 1931, she had two older brothers, both of whom had been partners in the family business. At age twenty-two she married Ronald Berkowitz, in a wedding so lavish and over-the-top that every subsequent Morgenstern's brochure featured photographs of the twenty-foot Viennese table. Ronnie was given a position in the company, while Evelyn was expected to stay home and make babies. As it turned out, Evelyn had more business savvy than all the men in her family combined. In the mid-1960s, as the golden age of the Catskills faded, she begged them to sell off the resort. But none of them, especially not her philandering husband, would deign to listen to her advice.

In 1965, Evelyn and Ronnie divorced. As part of the settlement, she traded her shares in her family's hotel for an apartment on Fifth Avenue and East Seventy-First Street. Five years later, when the resort folded, Evelyn's father admitted his daughter had been right. He helped her secure backing to build the Morgan, a luxury "boutique" hotel in midtown, and from there, she swiftly built an empire. Soon enough, she had hotels in London, Paris, and LA, and married the famed British hotelier, Ethan Woodmont.

Evelyn and Ethan lasted seven years together. Given all their overlapping business interests (jointly owned hotels and plans to build more), the marriage took more than three years to unravel. It was, by all accounts, the most contentious and most complex divorce of the decade, covered in every possible publication, from *Vanity Fair* to the *New York Law Journal*.

The next time Evelyn called Diane, it was to negotiate an iron-clad prenuptial agreement for her third marriage to Senator Jack Willoughby. The third divorce—thanks to Diane's foresight—was relatively painless and efficient. It came as no surprise, therefore, when Evelyn hired Diane again to write the prenup for marriage number four.

From everything Abby could discern, Evelyn's fourth husband was an entirely different sort of man from the previous three. Ronnie, Ethan, and Jack were all comfortable in the public eye. They were tall, they were handsome, they enjoyed attention. The fourth, Michael Gilbert, was a professor of creative writing who had published two little-known volumes of poetry. He had no previous marriages, he was not much to look at, and, other than English majors, almost no one had heard of him. Abby remembered studying one of his early poems for a survey class she'd taken her freshman year of college.

According to the notes Abby found in the file, Michael had not asked for a single change to the terms of the prenup Diane had drafted two years earlier. He had signed the document immediately, over the objections of his attorney. Abby wondered what had attracted a glamorous woman like Evelyn to the balding, obscure poet. The story was that they had met a few years earlier when the Academy of American Poets held their annual dinner at one of Evelyn's hotels. Evelyn had been passing by the ballroom as Michael was speaking at the podium. After hearing him recite one of his poems, she had asked to meet him.

Evelyn arrived at exactly two o'clock, walking slowly into the conference room in layers of grays and creams—a bias-cut silk skirt and two overlapping silk tank tops, all topped with a deconstructed linen jacket. Evelyn was only eight years Diane's senior, but on the surface, the two women could not appear more different. Diane's taste ran to close-fitting knits, structured suits, and the boldest jewelry. Abby had expected Evelyn Morgan to dress similarly. But though Evelyn's clothes were surely equally expensive, she favored a more minimalist, loose-fitting look. Her shoulder-length hair was simply styled, her makeup neutral and lightly applied.

Diane stood to greet her client. "Evelyn! You look wonderful! It's so nice to see you!"

Evelyn's voice was soft and strained. "You too, my dear. Of course, I wish I didn't require your services, but it's good to see you just the same."

"I have to say, I was surprised to hear from you. You seemed so happy with Michael, and he was so . . . accommodating."

"Yes, he was. He still is. He really is the sweetest of *all* my husbands."

The words popped out of Abby's mouth before she stopped to think about them. "Why are you divorcing him?"

Evelyn turned to Abby and stared. She squinted her eyes as if Abby were far away. "I'm sorry," she said smoothly. "Who are you?"

Diane gave Abby an icy glare before turning back to her client. "Evelyn, this is Abby Silverman. Abby is my new associate. She's been with us for just over a year now. I asked her to sit in today and take notes. Abby, let's not bombard Evelyn with questions."

"It's fine," Evelyn said. "Poor Michael keeps asking me the very same thing. He can't reconcile himself to the fact that it simply has to end."

With that, Evelyn Morgan began to cry. The tears came slowly at first, but soon, her whole body shook with the force of her sobs. Diane nudged a box of tissues across the table in her direction and waited patiently for the tears to subside. The outburst, as Abby knew all too well, was Diane's cue for the words that always came next.

"Tell me, Evelyn, what can I do to help?"

Though Abby had heard Diane pose the very same question at least a dozen times before, this was the first time she noticed the lack of empathy behind the words. Evelyn Morgan was in real pain. She wasn't pitching a fit about a vacation home she wanted or screaming about child support she didn't want to pay. She wasn't out of control and she didn't need handling; she was a woman heartbroken over the end of a marriage to a man she clearly still cared for.

Abby wanted to hug Evelyn, or to reach across the table and squeeze the older woman's hand. Of course, she couldn't do either of those things—not with a client she had only just met and certainly not with her boss staring at her like that. So instead, Abby kept herself glued to her chair and wondered why it was that a sixty-three-year-old woman on her fourth marriage was sobbing like a teenager in love.

Abby poured Evelyn a glass of water, which gave her something to do with her hands. After a few sips, Evelyn grew calmer.

Diane cleared her throat and leaned forward in her chair. "Now that we're all settled, why don't we discuss how we will proceed. Given the prenuptial agreement Michael signed, this should be extremely straight-forward. Michael is entitled to the house in Lenox and five hundred thousand dollars for each year of your marriage. The Lenox property is worth one and a half million dollars, plus the extra million makes two and a half. There are obviously no children, and Michael has no stake in your business, so, as far as I can see, everything should go smoothly."

Evelyn shook her head. "He won't agree to it," she said.

"He doesn't have a choice. The prenup is binding—"

"I don't mean the prenup. I mean the divorce. Michael won't sign the papers. He doesn't want to leave."

"If he won't leave the apartment, we can file for a—"

Evelyn Morgan held up her hand. "Diane. Please. You're not hear-ing me. Michael isn't trying to make things difficult. He simply doesn't understand why I want the divorce, and I'm afraid that I can't give him any real answers. My reasons are personal, and they are not up for dis-cussion."

Diane nodded. "Of course. I respect that completely."

"There is one more thing," Evelyn continued. "I want to give Michael more than we agreed on. I'm going to increase the payout from one million to five."

Diane's features rearranged themselves into an expression Abby did not recognize—confusion, certainly, but most of all, surprise. Diane prided herself on her vast experience, on the fact that she had "seen it all." No matter how many affairs her clients alleged, no matter how many lies their spouses told, or how much revenge money they spent, Diane assured her clientele that she would never judge, and that she could never, ever, be shocked. But this request from Evelyn Morgan? This was something Diane had not heard before.

There was silence for a moment while Diane struggled to recover. "Do you mind if I ask why? If you're worried about Michael releasing unflattering information to the press . . ."

Evelyn held up her hand a second time. Abby could see that she was a breath away from bursting into tears again. "No. Absolutely not. He would never *think* of such a thing. I'm giving Michael five million dollars and that is the end of the discussion. I do not want to hear him maligned. If we're going to move forward together, Diane, I must have your promise on that. I don't want one bad word said about Michael. I just want this divorce to be done."

Diane tried her best to smooth things over. "Of course, Evelyn. I apologize. But you must understand that it's *my job* to protect you. Believe me, I don't enjoy thinking the worst of people. I get paid to think the way I do, not because I'm trying to be negative, but because I must anticipate every possible unfortunate outcome. Sadly, I've watched too many clients put their faith in the wrong person, only to have that trust betrayed."

"Michael did *not* betray me!" Evelyn stood and then froze in place. She closed her eyes and let out a heavy rush of air. For several long moments, she stood that way, breathing in and out, eyes closed, fists curled.

Abby could see that if Diane pushed any further, Evelyn would leave the conference room. Diane was used to aggressive lawyering, but right now, Evelyn needed something else. A line from the one Michael Gilbert poem Abby knew suddenly lit up in her brain.

"The flower forgives the sun its thirst, the fruit forgives the drought."

Evelyn opened her eyes and stared at Abby. "That's from Michael's first book."

Abby nodded. "I read it in college. I always thought it was a beautiful image. I've been racking my brain, but I can't remember the next line."

A trace of a smile formed on Evelyn's lips. "The moon forgives his banishment when morning snuffs him out." Slowly, she eased herself back into her chair. Abby refilled her glass of water and spoke with Evelyn for a bit about the other poets she had studied. Diane didn't interrupt.

Before Evelyn left, she donned a pair of enormous dark sunglasses. "I want no ugliness with this divorce," she reminded them. "I want it handled as sensitively as possible." She shook Abby's hand a beat too long. "Thank you for reminding me of that poem. I can only hope Michael will be as forgiving with me."

After the meeting, Diane was unsettled. She motioned for Abby to come to her office, where she paced back and forth in front of the window. "I've *never* seen Evelyn like that before. With her other divorces, she was an absolute machine. Assertive, controlled. But today? She didn't even look like herself. Those clothes, that makeup, crying over a poem? It's like she's turned into a completely different person! Whatever she did to that husband of hers, she certainly feels guilty enough about it."

"Why do you think she did something to him?"

Diane shrugged. "Experience mostly. People don't change. Evelyn cheated on her other husbands. Of course, to be fair, all of them cheated on her first."

"I didn't get that sense from the meeting, but you'd know better. I only just met her."

"She liked you though. That was obvious." Diane stopped pacing and tapped her fingers on her desk. She stared at Abby as if she'd never seen her before. "Why don't *you* try taking the lead on this? It really couldn't be more straightforward. I'll talk to Evelyn, but I think she'll agree. For some reason, she wants a gentle approach this time, and she seemed to respond to your . . . sensitivity."

"Thank you, Diane." Abby was grinning in spite of herself.

"It isn't a compliment," Diane snapped. "Maybe that romantic crap worked today, but that's the *last* time I want you quoting poetry to my clients. People come to us for legal advice, Abby. I'm not paying you to run a goddamned book club."

By four o'clock, the office was empty; everyone except for Abby had left early for the holiday. With no one to overhear or interrupt, she decided it would be a good time to call Will back. Like her, he was still in his office.

"Are we the only two losers still working?" she asked. "Sorry—I didn't mean to call you a loser." Abby tried to backtrack, but Will didn't seem to be offended.

"Don't worry," he assured her. "I'm a complete loser, actually. Some say it's part of my charm."

Abby laughed. "Good to know."

"I'm glad you called," he continued. "I was worried I might have scared you off. Jason told me I got in touch too soon. He said I should have waited three days before asking you out again."

"You should never listen to Jason," Abby said.

"I don't know about that. He said you were great. Brilliant and beautiful and—"

"There is *no* way my cousin used those words to describe me."

"Okay, fine. I'm embellishing. But he definitely said that you were smart. What did he tell you about me?"

"Well, I first heard your name at my grandmother's *shiva,* so, to tell you the truth, I wasn't all that focused. He said you played poker together, and that you were a lawyer."

"Your grandmother's *shiva?*" Will sounded upset. "Abby, I had no idea. Jason never said a word about—God, I'm such a jerk. I'm so sorry."

"Please don't apologize. How could you have known? Anyway. I'm pretty sure Jason said you were nice."

"Nice?"

"What's wrong with nice?"

"Nothing, I guess, but calling right after your grandmother's funeral makes me seem anything but. Honestly, I can't believe you agreed to meet me."

Abby wondered how much she should tell him. "I decided that my grandmother would have wanted me to." As soon as she mentioned Grandma Sara, Abby felt something loosen in the center of her chest. It felt good to remember her grandmother out loud. "She didn't think grief should get in the way of things. At least, that's what she wrote in one of her journals. Something like that, anyway."

"Her journals?"

"Yeah. She left me a box of them—not journals exactly, more like notebooks. Or files. I don't know what to call them. It's kind of difficult to explain."

"The two of you must have been really close."

"We were. She retired to Florida, but she came back to New York to help my mother after my parents' divorce. She lived with us for the first year, but after that she stayed—got her own apartment a block from ours so my sister and I could walk over after school. She kept the condo in Florida for a few weeks in the winter. I'd go with her sometimes, on school vacations."

"She sounds like a special person. You must miss her."

"More than I ever thought possible. It's like . . ." Abby felt a catch in her throat, as if she'd choked down an aspirin without any water. She coughed a few times, and then grew silent.

"Abby? Are you okay?"

Her voice returned, smaller than before. "Yup. Sorry about that."

"You don't need to be sorry. Thank you for telling me about her. Do you . . . want to maybe talk some more, over dinner? If Saturday doesn't work, Sunday's good, too. Our office is closed on Monday for the Fourth. I'll probably go in, but not until late."

Abby laughed. "I'm planning to work on Monday, too."

"I guess we really *are* the biggest losers in New York."

"You said it this time, not me," Abby said.

After she and Will made plans, Abby packed her bag and left the office. Normally, she liked having the place to herself—she did her best work when it was quiet—but she was dying to take off her suit and her stockings, and she desperately needed something to eat.

July in the city was never pretty—the air was too sticky, and the streets smelled like garbage. That evening, however, the air was cool and pine-scented, as if a breeze had blown in from somewhere else. Abby put away her MetroCard, ditched the bus, and began walking up Sixth Avenue from Fifty-Second Street. Just before entering the park, she stopped to buy a soft pretzel from one of the carts that was plastered with photographs of hot dogs and Coke bottles. She carried the warm twist of dough in her hand and wound her way northwest in search of a bench.

Abby had been thirteen when her father announced that he and Tanja were getting married. Continuing his habit of breaking awkward personal news in highly public eateries, he told Abby and Hannah over brunch at Isabella's. They were sitting outside, behind the forest-green barriers that shielded diners from the bustling Columbus Avenue traffic, when he pulled two velvet boxes from his pocket.

When she saw the boxes, Abby knew. Hannah was as clueless as ever, of course—her face full of wide-eyed girlish enthusiasm as she pried open the lid of their father's offering. He'd upgraded this time, from silver lockets to slim gold rings encrusted with tiny sapphire chips. Hannah gasped and shoved the ring on her finger before jumping out of her seat and hugging him. "I love it, Daddy! Thank you! Thank you!"

He turned to Abby, who hadn't moved. "Don't you want to open yours?"

At the table closest to them, a waitress set down two steaming plates of eggs Benedict. Abby stared at the runny mounds of hollandaise sauce and felt a wave of nausea stir her stomach. "You're marrying her, aren't you? You and Tanja are getting married."

Her father brushed a few nonexistent crumbs from his lap before flashing his anchorman smile at his daughters. "Remind me never to throw you a surprise party, Abby. But yes, Tanja and I are getting married. She'll be your stepmother. Isn't that wonderful?"

Abby could feel Hannah holding her breath. If Abby pretended the news was good, she knew her little sister would follow her lead. Abby didn't want Hannah to be upset, but she couldn't control the burst of anger that burned its way through her lungs and up to her brain. She bit her lip until she tasted blood, then scooped up the black box with her fingers.

When she did not answer, her father pressed on. "Aren't you happy for me?" he asked.

Without speaking a word, Abby rose from her chair and hurled the velvet cube into the middle of the street. The last thing she saw before she pushed past the tables was a steady stream of wheels running over the jewelry box. She ran to the corner and down Columbus, then west toward Broadway, to her grandmother's new apartment. Only when she was safe in her grandmother's arms did Abby finally allow herself to cry.

She hadn't cried when her parents announced their divorce, or when her father's daily phone calls slowed to once a week. She hadn't cried when she'd had a bad case of strep throat and her father's secretary wouldn't interrupt his meeting—not even when she had carefully explained that her mother was out of town. Of course, Grandma Sara had been there to take care of her, but Abby had wanted to hear her father's voice. She hadn't cried when he didn't call the next day, or the day after that, to see how she was feeling. She hadn't even cried at the restaurant when he'd said he was going to marry Tanja. Abby hadn't cried for such a long time that she wasn't even sure she remembered how.

But cry she did. The tears fell fast on her grandmother's shoulder as Abby shivered through her sobs. She cried for the carefree childhood she'd lost. She cried for the heartache she knew lay ahead. She cried for her mother and for her sister, for the family of four that they would never be again.

By the time she was finished, her eyes were burning, her lips were swollen, and her nose was red. But her fingers were no longer curled into fists and her sneakers no longer felt like lead. Her grandmother sensed the shift in her bearing. "When you have a good cry, the heart gets lighter, no?"

Abby nodded, and her stomach growled. "You're hungry," Grandma Sara said. "Let's go for a walk and get you something to eat."

Together, they walked east on Sixty-Seventh Street into the warm spring afternoon. Grandma Sara hummed softly under her breath, one of the wordless tunes Abby recognized so well. Just outside the entrance to Central Park, they stopped at a group of street cart vendors. "Ice cream?" Grandma Sara asked, but Abby frowned and shook her head. Ever since the sundaes at Rumpelmayer's, Abby had lost her taste for the stuff.

Instead of ice cream, her grandmother bought them pretzels—giant, soft ones, sprinkled with salt. Grandma Sara squeezed some mustard onto hers, while Abby preferred to eat hers bare. They found a bench inside the park and sat side by side, with their shoulders touching.

"Grandma," Abby said, "why is my dad such a jerk?"

"There are worse fathers, sweetheart. Believe me. Some of what I've seen . . . well, I'll tell you one day when you're older. For now, let's just say, he does what he can. It's not what you want, but it's all he can do."

Abby kicked the toe of her sneaker in the dirt. "I know. But why did he marry my mom in the first place? If he didn't love her, why did he do it?"

Her grandmother didn't answer right away. She swallowed the last bit of her pretzel and wiped the corner of her mouth with her napkin. "He thought he loved her," Grandma Sara said. "The same way she thought she loved him. What can I tell you? They weren't a good match."

"Did you know that when the two of them got married?"

Her grandmother wrinkled up her nose. "What did I know?" Abby waited for her grandmother to answer, sensing, somehow, that she should not interrupt. On the path in front of them, a young man walked his dog. A couple pushed a baby carriage; a group of teenagers raced past. A lonesome pigeon pecked the dirt, hoping to find a few crumbs for his lunch. Meanwhile, Abby sat in silence, wondering what her grandmother would say next.

"I've told you before that I used to make matches," she began. "Even at your age, I couldn't stop myself. I would *see* something in two people when they were together, and then . . . well. I could never explain it, not to my father, not to my sister. They understood what I could do, but never *how* I could do it. I was never able to find the right words."

"Did you see something in my mother and my father?"

Abby's grandmother shook her head. "When I looked at my daughter, it was like static on a television set. There was no picture, nothing clear, nothing to help me understand."

"What about when Uncle Eddie married Aunt Judy?"

"It was the same with my son. There was nothing I could see. I told myself it was for the best—I would have driven myself crazy. A mother should help her children, but she shouldn't tell them who to love."

"That makes sense," Abby agreed. "I've never even had a boyfriend, and I hate it when my mom asks me about it. Love is way more complicated now than when you were young."

Grandma Sara's laugh was so loud and unexpected that it startled the pigeon pecking nearby. She reached for her granddaughter's hand and squeezed. "Love hasn't changed, *mameleh*. It was just as complicated back then. If it had been so easy, no one would have needed me."

Abby was skeptical, but she did not argue. A question popped into her head. "What about my dad and Tanja?" she asked. "Do you think they're a match? Will their marriage last?"

Grandma Sara raised her eyebrows. She tried to stop herself from reacting, but this time her guffaw was contagious. Soon, both of them were doubled over on the bench, rolling back and forth with raucous laughter. It took a few minutes for the fit to subside, at which point Abby's grandmother finally answered the question.

"No, my darling. Not a chance."

Dinner with Will was relaxed and easy—comfortable in a way Abby wasn't expecting. This time, he kissed her in the cab; his lips were warm and surprisingly soft, and he tasted like the wine they had shared. When he dropped her off, there was a moment when she could have invited him up to her apartment. But he didn't ask and Abby didn't offer. She didn't want to complicate things—not yet.

He called the next day, just as he'd promised, and invited her to come to his office Monday night. "There's a great view of the East River from our conference room. It's on the forty-first floor. A few of us are going to hang out and watch the fireworks."

"You mean, all the other losers who work on national holidays?"

"Exactly. It's your ideal crowd. Want to come?"

"How can I refuse an offer like that?"

Will was waiting for her outside his office building when the taxi dropped her off. She hadn't known whether she was supposed to bring anything, so at the last minute she'd grabbed a bottle of wine and a plastic container filled with dried apricots and pistachios. It wasn't until she was already in the cab that she realized she'd brought the same snack she used to bring for her visits to the cemetery with her grandmother. *Goddamn it, Abby,* she thought to herself.

It turned out she didn't need to bring anything. The conference table was already covered with pizza boxes, beer, and a few bottles of wine. Despite smelling like a fraternity house, the room itself was designed to impress, with lush silk carpets, steel-framed paintings, and an eastern-facing wall made entirely of fifteen-foot floor-to-ceiling windows. A dozen twentysomething junior associates were present, dressed in standard "weekend-at-the-office" attire: jeans and T-shirts, sneakers, glasses. Abby had put in a little more effort—she'd worn her good jeans and put in her contact lenses.

Will introduced her to a few of his colleagues, grabbed two beers, and led Abby over to a quiet spot by one of the windows. Outside, the sun slipped out of sight; the sky darkened from pale blue to navy to pitch. Someone dimmed the room's overhead lights, and everyone turned their eyes to the river.

Boom! Ba Boom! As the first set of fireworks lit up the sky, oohs and aahs filled the conference room. *Ba Boom Ba Boom!* A kaleidoscope of reds, violets, and blues hung in the air beyond the glass, almost close enough to touch. From the corner of her eye, Abby caught Will staring, a look of admiration etched on his face.

"Thank you for inviting me here," she told him. "The view is absolutely beautiful."

"Like you," he said, leaning forward to kiss her lips. Will had made sure they were far enough away from the others so that the moment felt almost entirely private. But still, Abby was caught off guard. Behind the glass, the skyline erupted again, spraying flashes of color in all directions. It was an intimate moment, and it should have been romantic, what with *literal* fireworks going off around them. But as much as Abby wanted to give in to the excitement, she could not summon the same sparks for Will that crackled outside his office window.

When the fireworks display was over, Abby made her excuses. "I have a lot of work to go over before tomorrow," she said.

Will did his best not to appear disappointed and insisted on walking her to the elevator. They shared a hug and quick kiss goodbye before she traveled down from the forty-first floor to the building's marble lobby. Somewhere in the middle of the rapid descent, Abby felt her stomach flip. Alone in the narrow, paneled box, she could not silence her inner voice—a voice that spoke with her grandmother's lilt and every bit of Sara's trademark nerve. It was as if her grandmother were beside her, whispering into Abby's ear.

He's a nice boy, mameleh, *but nice isn't everything. My urologist was a nice man, too, but I never wanted to marry him.*

When Abby got back to her apartment, she poured herself some wine, plopped down on her sofa, and pulled Victor Étoile's file from her bag. She and Diane had a call with him in the morning, and Abby wanted to be prepared.

Diane had warned her that Nicole's demands were "ambitious," but Abby preferred the more straightforward term—greedy. The model wanted one million dollars plus a 2 percent stake in Victor's company for every year that the two of them remained married. That meant that if the marriage lasted five years, Nicole would get five million dollars plus 10 percent of Étoile. Although the business interest was capped at 10 percent, Nicole was to receive substantial bonuses on the couple's ten-, fifteen-, and twenty-year anniversaries.

There were other demands, including trusts for future children and "reasonable" arrangements regarding the division of Victor's time between the offspring of his first marriage and his second. Any real estate the couple purchased after their marriage would be Nicole's alone in the event of a split.

Abby knew that Diane would never allow Victor to accept such one-sided terms. He had spent the past twenty years building Étoile—last year it did over four hundred million dollars in sales. A man so fiercely obsessed with his company and his brand would never agree to grant his second wife such a huge stake in his business on such an accelerated basis.

But the next morning when Abby joined Diane on the conference call with Victor, the designer did not sound half as resistant as Abby expected. In fact, he seemed more worried about upsetting Nicole than he was about her lawyer's list. He urged Diane to "compromise" and to come up with "creative solutions."

"My priority," Victor said, "is to make sure that Nicole is happy."

Diane grimaced and mouthed a string of inaudible curse words into the air.

"I understand that, Victor," she said carefully. "But *my* priority is to make sure that *you* are happy. And I don't mean *now*. I mean five years from now when, on the off chance that you are not still blissfully wed, Nicole will own ten percent of your company. *Ten percent,* Victor, of the company you spent your *entire* life building. What if you'd given ten percent to your ex-wife?"

"Nicole is nothing like Patrice."

"Patrice was nothing like Patrice, until you divorced her."

From the telephone's speaker, Abby and Diane could hear Victor's heavy, frustrated sigh. "What do you want me to do, Diane?"

"You don't have to do anything. This is what you hired me for. Abby and I are going to draft an agreement, and we're going to present it to Nicole's lawyer. I will go over the terms with you first, but I don't want you sharing the document with Nicole. Let her lawyer review it with her. It will be easier for you both that way."

"Nicole wants this to be a collaborative process. She doesn't want our lawyers to create more conflict."

"I respect Nicole's concern, but please ask her to relay it to her attorney. His term sheet was the most aggressive I've ever seen. Allow me to give you an example—for the sake of comparison. Liz Taylor's latest prenup says that if she and her husband stay married for five years, he gets one million dollars from her. That's it. A million. Not a penny more. Nicole asked for one million for *every* year. *Plus,* ten percent of your company. *Plus,* whatever multimillion-dollar apartment you buy. There's no way I'm letting her lawyer trap you into all that."

"I don't like that phrase—*trap me.* I don't like what it implies about Nicole's character."

Abby watched as Diane grimaced again, closed her eyes, and rubbed her temples. When she spoke, the edge in her voice was gone.

"Victor, I assure you I'm not implying anything. Nicole seems like a lovely person, and I'm sure the two of you will be very happy together. But I am your lawyer, and because of that, I can't let you sign off on what she's proposing."

When Victor responded, it was as if he hadn't heard a single word Diane had said. "I would like you to join us for dinner," he announced.

Abby sensed that the statement was less of an invitation and more, much more, of an ultimatum.

"Excuse me?"

"Dinner, Diane. I would like you to come to dinner. No legal talk, only good food and good wine. I want you to spend some time with Nicole. I am certain that once you know her better, you will change your mind about her. I'll have my assistant call to set up a date. And please bring your associate as well."

"Victor, I really don't—"

"Diane," Victor said, his voice unwavering. "I cannot stress enough how important this is to me. Nicole is going to be my partner."

Diane paused a moment before she answered. "Okay, Victor. Of course. Yes. Abby and I would be delighted to come. Just let us know when and where." She opened her mouth to say something more, but Victor had already hung up the phone.

Diane stabbed her legal pad with her pen. "Is it just me, or have all of our clients gone off the deep end?"

Abby wasn't sure how to respond. She tried to think of a joke to diffuse the tension, but she couldn't manage to come up with anything. "Was that true about Liz Taylor's prenup, by the way?"

"Of course it's true," Diane snapped. "Just don't ask me how I know. In the meantime, I'm giving you a new assignment. Remember when I told you to be nice to Nicole?"

"Yes, of course."

"I want you to try to bond with her at dinner. You're both young women, you're both ambitious. Try to figure out what she really wants. Is she truly interested in having a role in the company? Is there anything else that will satisfy her? If you can get a sense of where she'll compromise, it will really help us nail this down."

"I'll try," Abby said. "But I'm not sure it's worth it."

Diane narrowed her eyes and frowned. "What do you mean it isn't worth it?"

Abby shrugged. "I know Victor is infatuated with Nicole, but maybe it's better if they don't get married. I'm not convinced that they're the right match. I just don't see the two of them together."

Diane's expression turned from mild annoyance to unadulterated fury.

"We are *attorneys*, Abby," Diane hissed, glaring at her from across her desk. "I don't pay you eighty thousand dollars a year to go around playing Cupid for my clients. I don't pay you to ruminate about whether they should get married or whether you think their divorces are a good idea."

"I'm sorry," Abby said. "I wasn't trying—"

"I'm not finished. Maybe your grandmother managed to convince you that she had some special intuition for this stuff. Maybe you think your great 'sensitivity' makes you uniquely qualified to judge. But I didn't hire you to quote poetry to my clients, and I sure as *hell* didn't hire you to sabotage my client's wedding. If Victor Étoile thinks he's in love and wants to marry a model half his age, your job is to make sure that wedding happens without letting him lose the shirt off his back."

Abby swallowed loudly and nodded in agreement.

"And if Evelyn Morgan wants to divorce her husband—no matter how sweet and adoring he may be—your job is to make absolutely certain that she never has to look at his face again."

Abby nodded a second time.

"Do. Your. Job," Diane said. "Now, do we understand each other?"

"Yes. Of course. Absolutely." Abby's cheeks were flushed with embarrassment—blotchy and hot and pink with shame. A stream of sweat poured down her back, and she wished, more than anything, that she had someplace to hide. Diane's reaction was inordinately harsh, but Abby knew that her boss was not wrong. It was time for Abby to stop analyzing, to stop looking for cryptic clues and signs. It was time for her to stop worrying about whether Diane's clients were "in love." Hadn't she already learned from her parents how much damage love could do? Hadn't she specifically chosen her career as an antidote to love's toxicity?

Slowly, Abby gathered her notes and made her way out of Diane's office. She thought about her grandmother and their last few conversations—the way Grandma Sara had taken such a strong interest in her work, the way she encouraged Abby to believe in "soulmates," and "forever."

I'm sorry Grandma, Abby thought. *But I have to put all of that out of my mind.*

SEVEN

SARA

1916

The World Becomes a Brighter Place

With three more weeks until both the public high school and Barnard's fall semester began, Moishe Raskin invited Sara to join Ida behind the counter helping customers at Raskin's Pickles. Not only was it the perfect way for her to get to know Ida, but the salary Raskin paid was double what she earned tending babies for her neighbors.

Ida had been raised to work in retail. She was meticulous in making change; she was outgoing and charming with every customer. After spending only one day in the store with her, Sara understood why Moishe Raskin was so proud of his daughter. From the bristly truck drivers delivering barrels of vegetables from the farm to the local housewives buying herring for their families, Ida made everyone feel at ease. She wasn't a beauty, but she carried herself well, with perfect posture and easy grace. She did not flaunt her prestigious education, but there was no way to spend more than a minute in her presence and not be impressed by her intelligence.

In between teaching Sara how to manage the customers, Ida imparted her knowledge of pickling—from cucumber farming to fermentation to ratios of sugar, garlic, and salt. It was not a glamorous business, she explained, but a necessary one. In the dead of the winter, when vegetables were scarce, a crispy pickle could do wonders—not only for health, but for boosting morale. "Nothing cleanses the palate and the mind better than a bite of a Raskin's half-sour," Ida said. After trying one herself, Sara could not argue.

The two young women fell into an easy friendship, one that seemed to make Moishe Raskin happy. Sara did not mention her matchmaking skills, but she was honest about the other aspects of her life. She told Ida about the first time she had worn spectacles—how the textures of the sky and the street and the city had suddenly come into perfect focus. "What a magical feeling that must have been," Ida said. "It almost makes me wish I were nearsighted, so I could experience it for myself."

"Mr. Tunchel—he's the man who sold me the glasses—said the closest thing to it was falling in love. *The world becomes a brighter place,* he told me. *You notice what you never noticed before, and you can't imagine life without it.*"

Ida's eyes grew cloudy. "Well, that's two magical feelings I haven't experienced then."

"You've never been in love?" Sara asked.

"I thought I had, for a moment. But I was wrong. It certainly didn't feel the way you're describing. What about you?"

"Me? Of course not!"

"Why are you so shocked? You're sixteen, aren't you? You're pretty and smart. I'd give anything to have a figure like yours." Ida looked down at the flat front of her apron and frowned. "My mother is always telling me I'm too thin. Maybe that's why the *shadchanim* suggest such awful men, and so few of them."

"It isn't the number of men that matters," Sara said. "You only need to meet the right one."

Sara's wages, plus the pickles Ida sent home with her each day, helped to ease her family's burden until September began. After that, it was back to school for both girls. "I'll see you in a few weeks, on Rosh Hashanah," Ida promised.

In the days and nights leading up to the holiday, Sara tried to conjure a match for Ida. She thought of the eligible men she knew and pictured them standing beside her new friend. But no matter how many men she envisioned, none of them was right for Raskin's daughter. No one shone brightly enough in her mind.

The day before Rosh Hashanah, Hindel's children were feverish. They sniffled and fussed all that night with their colds, and in the morning, poor Hindel looked ready to collapse. Sara stayed home from the synagogue to care for them, while her sister slept until the afternoon. Later, after a meal of soup, challah, and honey, Sara walked to Delancey Street with her brothers to follow the crowds making their way toward the bridge.

From every corner of the Lower East Side, Jews emerged from their apartments and their *shuls* carrying prayer books under their arms. Men and boys wearing dark coats and hats, women draped in shawls, and young girls in white dresses promenaded together toward the tall steel towers to pray on top of the Williamsburg Bridge.

High above the city's wide East River, in groups of all sizes, they stood against the railing. The men shook the four corners of their prayer shawls, and the women shook the folds of their skirts and coats. As the crumbs from their festive meals fell off their garments and into the water, the sins of the wearers were cast away.

For a mile across the chasm, the prayers were chanted.

WHO IS A GOD LIKE YOU, FORGIVING INIQUITY AND
PARDONING THE TRANSGRESSION OF THE REMNANT OF YOUR

PEOPLE? YOU DO NOT MAINTAIN ANGER FOREVER, BUT YOU
DELIGHT IN LOVING-KINDNESS. YOU WILL AGAIN HAVE
COMPASSION UPON US, SUBDUING OUR SINS, CASTING ALL
OUR SINS INTO THE DEPTHS OF THE SEA.

Ever since her first Rosh Hashanah in America, Sara looked forward to this *tashlich* service on the bridge. From the walkway she could see the other bridges to the south and the great expanse of city and water to the north. There, amid the jumble of cables and girders, she felt an overwhelming sense of replenishment and peace. Wrinkled old men mumbling ancient Hebrew words stood suspended in the sky on a mountain of steel. The scene filled her heart with both comfort and wonder—it was a stunning mosaic of the old world and the new.

The path ahead was full of faces Sara recognized. She waved to her father's pinochle partner before stopping to wish Jacob and Miryam Tunchel a good year. Sara's brothers introduced her to some of their friends, including the two Lipovsky brothers, dentists who practiced farther uptown. Along the bridge, she spotted her teacher, and later, her neighbors from across the hall.

"*A gut yohr,* Sara! Come, say hello!" Mr. Raskin called to her from a few feet away, where he'd gathered with Ida, his sons, and their wives.

"*A gut yohr,*" Sara said. "Happy New Year to you all."

It had only been a few weeks since she'd last seen Ida, but it felt as if it had been months. They had so much to catch up on, so much to discuss, that they could have stood talking together for hours. Eventually, the sun began to set, Ida's family went home, and Sara's brothers disbanded. Sara and Ida linked arms to walk back, making their way westward through the thinning crowd. The dentist brothers Sara had been introduced to earlier stood in conversation with the rest of their family. The men recognized Sara as she passed and nodded their heads to her in greeting.

It was then that she saw it, out of the corner of her eye—the narrow thread of light, linking Ida to the younger dentist. If Sara focused too closely on it, the thread of light disappeared. It was visible only when her eyes were turned elsewhere.

Sara felt her spirits lift and her mood buoy. Her feet, like the rest of her, felt almost weightless, and soon, she was practically skipping on the walkway.

"Slow down!" Ida said. "What's the rush?"

Sara's smile gave way to a burst of laughter. "I'm so sorry! I forgot where I was for a moment. I was busy imagining all the good things the new year might bring for both of us."

The end of the bridge was not far away, so they walked to the railing for one last look over the water. The sky had turned a brilliant, lavender blue, and the gray of the city shone silver in the light.

"Will I see you next week for Yom Kippur?" Ida asked.

"Of course," Sara said. "I'll look for you at the synagogue."

"My father wants me to stay at home until then, but I told him I need to get back to my classes. Maybe in the *shtetl* people slow down between the holidays, but here, in this city, it isn't possible."

Sara thought about all the work ahead of her—the information to be gathered, the introductions to be made. "You're right," she said to Ida. "Now is not the time for rest."

When Rosh Hashanah ended, Sara asked her brother Joe how he had come to know the two dentists. "They're cousins of my friend. You remember Morris? I met them both at his wedding. The older one, Izzy, is friendly enough—he was married himself a few years ago. Herman is the younger one. More serious, quiet." Joe raised an eyebrow at his sister. "Why do you want to know?" he asked.

She grabbed her cheek with both hands and winced. "I have a terrible toothache," she mumbled.

"Why don't you see Dr. Rosenthal?"

"The last time Mama saw Dr. Rosenthal, she couldn't open her mouth for a week! The man is almost eighty years old. I'd prefer to see someone who learned to practice dentistry sometime in the last fifty years."

"That's a good point," Joe agreed. "I'll ask Morris for the address."

After school the next day, Sara walked up Second Avenue and turned left onto East Seventh Street. The Lipovsky brothers' office was on the first level of a three-story house with a polished wooden door. Sara entered the waiting room just as the younger Dr. Lipovsky was finishing up with a patient. The air smelled faintly of antiseptic.

"Remember," Dr. Lipovsky entreated, "no more of that saltwater taffy." Despite the admonishment, the doctor's tone was kind. With great care, he guided his elderly patient by the arm to the exit.

When he was gone, Sara introduced herself. "We met the other day on the bridge," she said. "My brother Joe introduced us."

The young dentist nodded and held out his hand. Beneath his stiff white doctor's coat, he wore a neat white shirt. His manner was as straightforward as his attire. "Nice to see you again. Is there something I can help you with?"

For a moment, Sara forgot her excuse, but then she reached for her cheek and rubbed her jaw. "I have a toothache," she explained. "I was hoping you might take a look."

"Of course," Herman said. "I'm happy to. My brother's wife, Rebecca, usually greets our new patients, but she's not feeling well today. They live upstairs, on the two upper floors." Herman walked to an unoccupied desk in the corner and took a blank card from inside the top drawer. "Would you please fill this out before we begin? Name, age, and address. Oh, and the reason for your visit."

Dr. Lipovsky's touch was gentle. Despite a thorough examination, he could find nothing wrong. "I'm happy to report that I see no cavities and no decay of any kind. You've developed a sensitivity, but it should go away in a week or so." He crossed the room to a wall of shelves, selected a small glass vial, and handed it to her. "This is clove oil," he said. "Rub it on the tooth, and it should help reduce the pain."

Dr. Lipovsky refused to charge her for the visit.

"But you can't go around seeing patients for free! I have to pay you something," Sara insisted.

"All I ask is that you tell your friends about our practice. We are trying to build our reputation, and the best way to do that is through personal recommendations."

"I'll tell everyone I know," she promised. "In fact, I have some friends I'd like you to meet."

On the morning of Yom Kippur, in front of the synagogue, Sara introduced Moishe, his wife, and Ida to the younger Dr. Lipovsky. Every seat in the synagogue was filled as Rabbi Sheinkopf led the service. From their perch high up in the women's balcony, Sara caught her friend staring down at the dentist. Not long after, Herman looked up to scan the upper tier for a glimpse of Ida's face.

After the services, Moishe Raskin pulled Sara aside. "Who is this dentist who keeps staring at my daughter? Is he the man for my Ida?"

When Sara confirmed Moishe's suspicion, the pickle man clutched his beard and moaned. "Why introduce them on Yom Kippur? And here? By the synagogue? It's too solemn! Too serious! I would have invited him to my home, fed him a meal, given him some brandy . . ."

Calmly, Sara disagreed. "Your daughter and the dentist are both serious people."

Raskin wrung his hands in frustration. "What man thinks of love when he's fainting from hunger? What woman thinks of romance when her throat is parched from thirst?"

"Please, Mr. Raskin. None of that matters. I'm telling you, Ida and Herman were meant for each other."

"But how can you be sure?"

Sara gave him her most encouraging smile. "I see what I see, and I know what I know."

Ida and Herman were betrothed in December, but Ida insisted on a long engagement. The wedding date was set for early June, a few days after her graduation from Barnard. Not long after Dr. Lipovsky's proposal, Moishe Raskin paid a visit to Sara's home. He arrived with a basket of delicacies from his store—jars of beets and herring and three different kinds of cucumbers. When Sara's mother wasn't looking, he handed Sara an envelope. Inside was a letter of gratitude.

> *Dear Sara, Rabbi Sheinkopf has informed me of your family's financial concerns, I have taken it upon myself to pay your landlord the rent money that is past due. In addition, I have settled the debt with your father's doctor and the pharmacy. Your credit at the butcher has been restored.*

For Sara, the letter was a miracle. She had never discussed an amount with Mr. Raskin, but she trusted him to help her and her family. For the first time in a year, Sara slept undisturbed.

Her peace of mind did not last long—the *shadchanim* began their assault the next day.

The Lewis Street *shadchan* came in the morning. In the afternoon, Shternberg and Grossman arrived. Representatives from Goerick Street and East Broadway knocked on her door well into the evening. All of them had heard about Ida's engagement. All of them knew about Moishe Raskin's visit.

Sara had expected them to seek her out eventually, but she had not anticipated that they would come so quickly. Her brother-in-law asked them nicely to leave. Her brothers were not nearly as polite. The next day, there was a line of them outside her building—angry men wearing dark coats and black silk hats. They came from Hester Street and Canal, from Hamilton and Cherry and up on East Houston. In twos and threes they banged on the door, demanding that Sara come outside to face them. Sara's mother cried; the neighbors complained. Only Rabbi Sheinkopf was able to stop it.

Like a bearded pied piper, the rabbi led them away from the Glikman apartment to the synagogue. "Come with me, gentlemen! Come with me. You are disturbing the neighbors, your future customers! Let us discuss the matter in private." Anxious for answers, all of them followed. By the time they were seated, there were more than three dozen.

The first of them to speak was Shternberg from Orchard Street, who'd made the earlier matches for Moishe Raskin's two sons. Apparently, the fees for those matches had set something of a record on the Lower East Side. It was said that Moishe Raskin was as superstitious as he was successful. In his mind, a generous fee for the *shadchan* was the best way to ensure a happy marriage. Ever since the second Raskin son had been married, the neighborhood matchmakers had been vying for the opportunity to match the daughter. When Shternberg botched the first engagement, they had circled Ida like hungry sharks.

Shternberg's face swelled purple with rage. "Who does Sara Glikman think she is? Meddling in our business this way? Her father, may he rest in peace, gave us his word. And now that he's gone, she has broken it!"

Grossman stood next and shouted over Shternberg. "We overlooked the gossip when the girl was thirteen, but now she is almost a fully grown woman! We must put a stop to her behavior!"

The Lewis Street *shadchan* tugged at his beard. "We demand to know the terms of her agreement with Moishe Raskin! We demand to see the contract she signed!"

Rabbi Sheinkopf did his best to calm the men down, but their voices only grew louder and more desperate.

"There is no contract." From the women's balcony, high above their heads, came a composed and confident voice. From under their hats, the men raised their eyes in unison to the upper tier and gasped. Sara stood twelve feet above them, grateful that they could not see her knees shaking. Despite the distance, she could hear their murmurs.

"She followed us here!"

"What disrespect!"

"See how she spies on us like a thief!"

Sara took a single step back from the railing, but she did not cry or look away. "I am not a thief," she said. "And I am not spying on any of you. In fact, judging from your accusations, it is all of you who have been spying on me. I came here today because you wanted to talk to me."

For a moment, there was absolute quiet. But then the men began shouting again.

"An unmarried woman cannot make matches!"

"In mocking our calling, you mock God!"

Rabbi Sheinkopf clapped his hands for silence. "Stop! All of you! Stop at once! You're talking to a sixteen-year-old girl!"

"If she is old enough to defile our customs, she is old enough to answer for her misconduct!"

Though the air in the synagogue was cold, Sara could feel the sweat pouring down her back. She was grateful that the men could not hear her heart pounding. There were so many of them, and they were so angry.

"I have no contract with Mr. Raskin," she said. "I became friendly with Ida when I worked at his store. Both Mr. Raskin and Ida have been very kind to me, as has Dr. Lipovsky, my dentist. As Rabbi Sheinkopf knows, after my father passed away, our family was thrown into terrible debt. Dr. Lipovsky is a good-hearted man and agreed to examine my tooth for free. All he asked was that I make introductions in order to spread word of his dental practice. That was my aim on Yom Kippur morning when I introduced him to the Raskin family."

"Then how do you explain Raskin's visit to your home so soon after his daughter's engagement?"

Rabbi Sheinkopf interrupted. "*I* informed Raskin of the family's troubles. The man is a pillar of our community, and I trusted him to act charitably on the Glikmans' behalf. As I'm sure you know from your incessant snooping, Raskin brought the family a basket of food. Are you such a pack of animals that you would deny them that charity?"

Most of the men were shamed into silence, though there were still a few murmurs and grumblings from the crowd. "Enough!" Rabbi Sheinkopf told the men. "Sara has explained herself and so have I. There is no reason for you to harass her further. Now I am going to escort her home."

Once the *shadchanim* were behind them, Sara's eyes welled up with tears.

"I didn't think that those men could scare me, but when I saw them from the balcony, all glaring up at me . . . I confess that I was very afraid."

Rabbi Sheinkopf patted her arm. "You have nothing to fear," he said. "They are more afraid of you than you are of them."

"But why?"

The rabbi sighed. "Life in this country is not what they expected. They are trying to hold on to their traditions, but it is more difficult than they ever imagined. The whole world is changing, and they cannot keep up. Their vocation, their livelihood, their very way of life—bit by bit, it disappears. To be a *shadchan* was a sacred calling; to make marriages was to do the work of God. But now, the *shadchanim* are the subject of derision. The newspapers mock them; they are ridiculed and disparaged. They are painted as mercenaries, as offensive and un-American. They are afraid of you because you are everything they are not. You are young and female and you have a gift. You do not negotiate price or terms. You suggest matches because you are compelled to do so, not because anyone has hired you. You make an introduction and let the rest play out, without force, interference, or manipulation. Young people today want to marry for love, and that is what your gift helps them to find."

"Still, I should not have lied to those men," Sara said. "I'm afraid I forced you to lie as well."

"Neither of us said anything that was untrue."

"Perhaps, but there is more to the story. My helping Ida did not come about by chance. And there is no question that I benefited from her engagement."

"Moishe Raskin is a particularly kindhearted man—that is why I introduced you to him in the first place. Even if you had told him you would accept nothing for your help, he would have found a way to repay the good deed you have done. The man has free will. He will do as he likes. And if he chooses to be generous with you and your family, there is nothing either one of us can do to stop him."

"But what will happen in June when Ida marries? She's already told me her father wants the wedding to be the biggest event the neighborhood has ever seen. Reporters are already calling on her. There will be stories printed in every newspaper in the city. Even if the *shadchanim* let this go for now, in June they will be reminded all over again."

"Moishe is a very influential man. He has friends everywhere in the city, including at the newspapers. Perhaps there is a way to put the *shadchanim* off. I will speak with Moishe tomorrow. Between the two of us, we will come up with something."

EIGHT

ABBY

1994

Dinner with Victor and Nicole took place two days later at Victor's apartment on Madison Avenue. Twelve years ago, he had bought a decaying Neo-Renaissance mansion on the corner of Madison and Seventy-Fourth Street. For two years, he'd renovated the façade and the interior—power washing the stone colonnettes, fixing the broken entablatures, refinishing the slate roof, and fitting the interior with new hand-carved moldings. Once restored to its former glory, the Étoile New York flagship store was set up inside, with the top floor reserved for Victor's personal residence.

"Ralph Lauren got the idea for *his* store from me," Victor said, over apéritifs in his mahogany-paneled living room. A butler (Abby was not sure what else to call him) brought them glasses of dry champagne. It was already well past eight o'clock, but Nicole had yet to make an appearance.

She arrived a little after eight thirty, wearing ripped jeans and carrying a leather messenger bag. Her long blond hair was twisted into a bun. "I'm so sorry," she said, dropping her bag on the carpet and kissing Victor on both cheeks. "My professor kept us late."

"Nicole is taking summer classes at NYU," he explained.

"What are you studying?" Abby asked.

"Business, mostly. I'm hoping to enroll full time next year, but for now I'm just trying to fit everything in." She declined the glass the butler offered. "No champagne for me tonight. I have an exam tomorrow."

Abby felt a surge of sympathy. She knew what it was like to stay up late, cramming and pulling all-nighters for days. "I think it's amazing that you found time for school on top of your work schedule."

Nicole flashed Abby a grateful smile. "It's a little hectic right now," she admitted, "but I wouldn't trade my classes for anything. I can't tell you how refreshing it is to have professors who encourage discussion. When you're modeling, no one wants you to speak. They only want you to wear the clothes and smile."

"Except for me," Victor interjected.

Nicole's face softened, and she patted his shoulder. "Except for Victor," she agreed. "He's the only designer who ever listened. The only one who ever took the time to answer when I asked about the pieces."

"It was impossible not to fall in love with her face," Victor said. "But it was her mind that forced me to pay attention. No other model ever asked about my color palette, about the length of a coat, or the way a seam was finished. Whenever I dressed her for a show, she took every outfit apart in her head, analyzing every detail. *Why put this skirt with this sweater? Why this waist with that sleeve?* The first time I kissed her, it was only because I couldn't think of how to answer her question. I was trying to buy myself a little time."

Abby laughed. It was nice to see the couple this way—at ease with each other, relaxed, content. Perhaps she'd been wrong about Nicole's feelings. *Stop it, Abby,* she told herself. *You're here to help Diane with negotiations. It's not up to you to decide whether Victor and Nicole are right for each other.*

Dinner was served in a small dining room that looked out over Madison Avenue. Abby had a view of a sleek row of stores—clothing, leather goods, and a jewelry boutique—all locked tight and lit up for the evening. While she stared through the glass at the jewelry store, Abby realized that she'd never seen Nicole's engagement ring. Nicole's wrists were covered in silver bangles, but her long, slim fingers were bare.

"Have you picked out an engagement ring?" Abby asked.

Nicole shook her head. "They're not really my thing. I have a few friends who've gotten engaged recently, and I hate the way some of them flash their rings around—like they're trying to make their single friends feel bad."

"Speaking as one of those single women," Abby said, "I know exactly what you mean."

Nicole glanced over at Diane. "What about you, Diane? Have you ever been married?"

Diane stiffened visibly at the question. It was a subject Abby had never dared to bring up with her boss. "No," Diane said. "I never felt the need. Maybe I've seen too many things go wrong."

Before the conversation could veer into awkward territory, Victor interrupted. "Who is ready for dessert?" he asked.

But Nicole was already folding her napkin and pushing her chair back from the table. "I'm so sorry, but I really must excuse myself. If I don't start studying, I'm going to be in real trouble."

"Don't apologize," Diane said. "Abby and I have early meetings, so we should be heading home as well."

"Of course," Victor said, with an easy grace. "I'm pleased that you were able to join us for dinner." He pulled two envelopes from the breast pocket of his blazer. "Next week, I'm hosting a private showing of a very special new collection. Some of the press will be there, of course, but other than that, it will be quite intimate. I hope you'll both be able to come."

Diane pretended to be pleased, but Abby knew the look on her face. There was no way she wanted to give up another evening just to placate Victor Étoile. "I'll have my assistant check the date," she said, in a tone that was pleasant but promised nothing.

Half an hour later, in the hallway outside her apartment, Abby could hear her telephone ringing. It stopped before she got inside, but by the time she'd kicked off her shoes, it was ringing again.

"Did you read that invitation yet? I'm going to *kill* Victor! I'm going to murder him!"

"Diane?" Abby said. "Hold on. Let me look." She pulled the envelope from her bag, tore it open, and read the card out loud. "Join Victor Étoile as he introduces the NICOLE BY ÉTOILE fall collection . . . a fresh, young take on classic Étoile pieces." Abby sat down on the edge of her sofa. "What does this mean?" she asked.

"It means he's creating a subsidiary for her. Or he's hired her as a designer. Or . . . I don't know! Does she have a contract? Has he given her an interest in his company? I have no idea what it means, but at the very least, he should have *told* me about it!"

"I'm sorry, Diane. Is there anything I can—"

"I need to see all the paperwork on this. How am I supposed to negotiate for a man who keeps major decisions like this from me?"

Abby had never been to Diane's apartment, but she could picture her boss pacing back and forth, the same way she did every day in the office. A full minute passed before Diane spoke again. "I'm going over to see Victor first thing in the morning. You're taking the meeting with Evelyn tomorrow, right?"

"Of course," Abby said. "I've got it covered."

"You'd better," Diane threatened before she hung up.

The next morning, Abby went to Evelyn's office in the Morgan Hotel on East Fifty-Seventh Street. She was there to get Evelyn's signature on the summons that would set her divorce proceeding in motion. Evelyn was waiting in the cozy room, all plush carpeting and soft furniture. Instead of sitting behind a desk, she sat placidly on a gray chenille sofa, sipping a cup of herbal tea.

Evelyn took both of Abby's hands in her own. "Thank you for coming to see me, Abby. Would you like some tea? A cup of coffee?"

"Thank you, but no," Abby said. "I only wanted to come by for your signature and to answer any questions you may have."

"Of course." Evelyn swallowed nervously. "I'd like to ask a favor of you. This may sound strange, but would you mind reading the pages to me out loud?"

"You'd like me to read the summons to you?"

"I would, yes. I'm just not . . . up to reading it."

"It's no problem at all. It won't take long." Abby removed the document from her bag and set it on the coffee table. She stole a quick glance at Evelyn's face—the sallow skin, the circles under her eyes, the swollen eyelids, puffy from crying. Perhaps Evelyn was too upset to read the document. Perhaps she was just too damn exhausted. Either way, Abby wanted to help. If it made her client feel better to be read to, she would do as she was asked.

"Supreme Court of the State of New York, County of New York. Evelyn Morgan, plaintiff, against Michael Gilbert, defendant. Action for a divorce. To the above-named defendant: You are hereby summoned to serve a notice of appearance on the plaintiff within twenty days after the service of this summons, exclusive of the day of service (or within thirty days after the service is complete if this summons is not personally delivered to you within the State of New York); and in case of your failure to appear, judgment will be taken against you by default for the relief demanded in the notice set forth below."

"Actually," Evelyn interrupted. "You don't need to read any more . . .

let me get this over with." Evelyn tugged at her linen scarf and twisted the fabric around her fingers. Softly, she muttered under her breath, "Why can't Michael agree to the divorce and make all of this easier on *both* of us?"

Abby wished she had answers for her client, but the best she could do was to try to be encouraging. "Hopefully, once he sees the summons, he'll recognize how serious you are about moving forward." She kept her voice low. "Do you know if he's retained any counsel? I could speak with his lawyer if you think that might help."

Evelyn shook her head. Her shoulders were shaking. "He hasn't hired anyone yet. I suppose I'll just have to be patient."

"Would you like to sign now?" Abby asked.

Evelyn stared at the papers on the table. Her tired eyes filled up with tears. "Abby, I'm afraid I can't . . . I can't see where to . . . would you guide me to the signature line?"

Was Evelyn really so distraught that she couldn't see a few feet in front of her? Gently, Abby pressed her pen into Evelyn's fingers and led them to the proper place. "Here you go," Abby said, as Evelyn wrote her name. "There, that's perfect."

Abby tucked the signed paper into her bag and promised Evelyn she would be in touch soon. As she tugged at the handle of the door to leave, she felt someone push from the opposite side. She stepped back just in time to avoid the man making his way into Evelyn's office. "Excuse me," he said. "I didn't realize Evelyn was with someone."

Abby recognized Michael Gilbert from the author photo on the back of the volume of poetry she'd bought at her corner bookstore that weekend. He was four or five inches taller than she was, with a sparse head of hair that had grayed near his temples. His eyeglasses were thick, his shirt was rumpled, and he shook her hand with ink-stained fingers. "So sorry," he said, pumping her hand. "Michael Gilbert, Evelyn's husband."

Abby heard Evelyn's voice from over her shoulder. "Michael, I told you not to come."

"And I told you, you can't get rid of me that easily. Evelyn, please. Come back home. You can't live at the hotel. *Please.*" Michael's voice was raspy and raw. He didn't care what Abby heard, or what she thought of what he was saying. In a few quick strides, he was beside his wife, reaching for her and pulling her into his arms. Evelyn's body stiffened for a moment before relaxing into his.

"I'll give you some privacy," Abby mumbled. "Thank you, Ms. Morgan." Abby reached for the office door again, her mind buzzing with surprise and confusion. Before exiting, she turned to look at the couple once more. Evelyn's head was on Michael's chest and his arms were wrapped protectively around her. From the window behind them, the late morning sun illuminated them both with a rosy glow. They looked, Abby thought, like a Byzantine painting, encircled in a halo of gold. Abby forced herself to look away and to head in the direction of the hotel lobby. When she got outside, she stopped for a bit to catch her breath on the sidewalk.

She had witnessed an intimate, private moment, something not meant for her eyes: Michael and Evelyn, clinging to each other like two desperate lovers from a Hollywood movie. You didn't have to be Abby's grandmother to understand how deeply the two of them were connected.

Abby wished she hadn't seen it. But even more, she wished that Evelyn hadn't signed the document to begin the divorce. Grandma Sara's voice was loud in her head. *I see what I see, and I know what I know.*

Abby had seen two people deeply in love. And she knew now, no matter what she'd been told, that Evelyn Morgan should not end her marriage.

Back at the office, Diane was seething. "Victor is going to give me a heart attack," she complained. "I scheduled a meeting with his corporate lawyer for tomorrow. How did it go with Evelyn?"

Abby knew better than to mention what she had seen between the hotel maven and her poet husband. Diane had made it perfectly clear that Abby's job was to facilitate their *divorce*. If Abby even hinted at a reconciliation, she wasn't sure how much longer she would have her job.

"Evelyn was having problems with her vision," Abby said. "She wanted me to read the summons to her."

Diane put down her pen and frowned. "Maybe that's why she seemed so off the other day. During her last divorce, she had terrible migraines."

"Hopefully, she's gone to see a doctor."

"I'm sure she has. Evelyn takes excellent care of herself. She goes to a spa for three weeks every January—someplace in Switzerland where they charge God knows what. I've asked her to give me the name a dozen times, but she refuses to tell me what it's called. All I know is that every February, she comes back looking ten years younger than when she left."

Abby tried to chuckle along with Diane, but, in truth, she was worried about Evelyn's health. She knew it wasn't her place to interfere, but as the day went on, she couldn't shake the feeling that she should try to do something to help.

When she got home that evening, she searched through her closet until she unearthed the purse she'd used for her grandmother's funeral. There, in the bottom of the black leather bag, she found what she was looking for—the card from the doctor who'd treated her grandmother. Abby studied the small, printed rectangle: DR. JESSICA COOPER, OPHTHALMOLOGY. Maybe Dr. Cooper would have some ideas about what could be wrong with Evelyn's eyesight. Abby left her number with the answering service and asked for the doctor to return her call.

Later, Abby sank onto her couch with a plate of leftover Chinese food and one of her grandmother's journals. She was curious to see whether Sara had written anything else about the Pickle King's daughter. But she could find no more references to Ida in the book and no more clippings about her tucked between the pages.

At around 9:15, her telephone rang, and Abby let the machine pick it up. "Hey there, it's Will. It's Friday night, so you're probably out . . ."As Will's friendly chatter filled the room, Abby swallowed her sesame chicken and groaned. Will was *nice*. He seemed to really like her. As Abby's mother would say, she could do a lot worse. But when Abby thought about seeing him again, she knew he wasn't someone she *needed* to be with. She struggled to envision a moment with Will where she would ever want to hold him the way she had seen Evelyn clinging to Michael Gilbert.

Abby had heard the stories of her grandmother's first suitor, the man Sara's family had expected her to marry. From what Abby had been told, he had been "nice," too. Good-looking, smart, from a respectable family. But no matter how easy it would have been to marry him, Sara had always told Abby that it hadn't felt right. "Nathan was a good man," Grandma Sara used to say, "but he wasn't my *bashert*, he wasn't my soulmate."

Every time Abby suffered through a breakup in high school or college, her grandmother brought up Nathan's name. "So?" she would say, tilting her head. "What can I tell you? He wasn't for you. Just like Nathan Weisman wasn't for me." Abby's grandmother said it matter-of-factly, as if it shouldn't have come as a surprise.

Abby used to wonder if Nathan was real or merely a story her grandmother invented to make Abby feel better about her own relationships. If Nathan was real, Abby realized now, he was probably mentioned in one of Sara's journals. Perhaps Sara had written something about him that could help Abby figure out what to do about Will. What exactly did it mean if someone wasn't *for her*? How could she know? What were the signs?

Abby flipped through the pages, searching for Nathan's name, look-ing for the man that hadn't measured up. She read through dozens of names and descriptions, until, finally, she found what she had been seek-ing. The year marked in ink was 1918, the name at the top of the page: Nathan Weisman. It was underlined not only once, but twice, and the ink was blurred, as if her grandmother's fingers had traced the letters a hundred times. A ticket stub was tucked behind the page for something called "The 1918 War Show," held at the Columbia University gym.

Had Nathan gone to Columbia then? Abby had no memory of that detail, but when she read the journal entry more closely, that was what her grandmother had written. The last time Abby had heard Nathan's name, she'd been in her second year of law school. She'd recently ended things with a man she'd been seeing before heading home for her win-ter break. Over coffee and cake at her grandmother's apartment, Abby confessed the whole sordid story.

"I thought he was perfect," Abby moaned. "Handsome and funny. Great in bed, too."

Grandma Sara raised an eyebrow. "So?" she said. "What was the problem?"

"The problem was that I wasn't the only one who thought so."

"He had another girlfriend?"

"Bingo," Abby said. "Some undergraduate—a psychology major. I only found out because he called her my name by mistake, and some-how, she forced the truth out of him. Then, she looked me up in the university directory and called me up to rat him out." Abby laid her head on her grandmother's kitchen table. "I can't believe I was so trust-ing," she said. "I'm completely done with relationships now. Honestly, it doesn't seem worth the trouble."

"It will be worth the trouble when you find the right one."

"Yeah, well, I find that hard to believe. How is anyone supposed to know if they've found *the right one* anyway?"

Her grandmother smirked and put down her fork. "I could tell you, *mameleh,* but you wouldn't believe it."

"Try me."

"Fine." She pushed her plate away. "But if the brilliant skeptic doesn't like my answer, I don't want to hear any complaints." Grandma Sara closed her eyes for a moment, and when she opened them again, the smirk was gone. Her voice grew serious and low. The answer she gave was so nonsensical and odd that Abby immediately dismissed it—though she never forgot it.

"When you weep," her grandmother said, "the one you are meant for tastes the salt of your tears."

NINE

SARA

1917–1918

He Bakes Lies Like They Are Bagels

THE 1918 WAR SHOW
"TEN FOR FIVE"

FRIDAY MAY 3, 1918 8:15 pm	Columbia University Gymnasium
	GENERAL ADMISSION

No one in the neighborhood was surprised when Ida's wedding was written up in the Yiddish dailies, but when *The New York Times* wrote about it, everyone on the Lower East Side paid attention. Because the article specifically denied that the couple used a matchmaker, the *shadchanim* lost their standing to complain about Sara in public. Of course, the article did not prevent them from paying a visit to the Glikmans' landlord. The building owner hadn't forgotten the commotion the group of men had caused, and he refused to discuss the family's benefactor. "What do you care who pays the rent?" the landlord said. "Moishe Raskin is a *mensch*! The man gives charity to everyone!"

Again, the *shadchanim* could not argue. Raskin was, in fact, a charitable man. Not only did he invite five hundred of his poorest neighbors for a dinner at the synagogue before his daughter's wedding, but he and Ida personally distributed half-dollar coins to all in attendance. The entire Lower East Side buzzed with the news, and with stories of the lavish feast. *Not only pickles and herring,* people said. *There was meat and fish, kasha and kugels. His wife, God bless her, made the kugels herself.*

The wedding spectacle was a welcome distraction from the country's entrance into the war. Neighbors flooded the nearby streets to watch dozens of carriages make their way to the *shul.* At the front of the procession was the family of the groom—the men dressed in handsome black silk suits and hats, and Mrs. Lipovsky in a blue satin gown. The final carriage, draped with one hundred white roses, held Ida and her beaming parents.

Amid the more progressive population of the Lower East Side, Ida's pearly white gown was further evidence that the *shadchanim's* assertion about a brokered match was unfounded. The Raskin wedding was a modern affair, not some old-country, out-of-doors, undignified mess. There were traditional elements, to be sure—the wedding canopy and the breaking of the glass—but it was impossible for anyone to believe that Ida was marrying for anything but love. Hers was no negotiated or mercenary marriage. From her dress to the flowers to the red-white-and-blue bunting that festooned the entrance of the synagogue, Ida Raskin was a shining example of an all-American bride.

Sara's high school graduation came a week after the wedding. The night before the ceremony, Hindel washed Sara's hair and tied the damp locks into spirals. In the morning, Sara looked like a different person—an older, more confident version of herself. She wore a pale blue cotton dress, hemmed and cut down from one of Hindel's. Against the white lace of the collar, Sara's curls were dark and striking.

Her two younger brothers hollered and clapped as she marched into the courtyard with her classmates. Sara thought she could see her mother crying when she approached the podium to receive her diploma. Afterward, when some girls invited her for ice cream, her oldest brother, Joe, pressed a quarter into her palm. He squinted his cloudy gray eyes and smiled. "Go," he said. "You deserve some fun." Sara wondered whether Joe's sudden appreciation for "fun" stemmed from the fact that he'd recently registered for the draft.

A few hours later, when Sara returned to the apartment, Moishe Raskin and Rabbi Sheinkopf were sitting in the front room with her mother and Joe. Ever since Ida's engagement last winter, Mr. Raskin had taken a keen interest in Sara's family. He'd hired Joe to drive one of his delivery trucks, and he had spoken with her mother about bringing her youngest boys to live on his Long Island farm for the summer.

He was in the middle of describing the farm and the fields when Sara walked in. "Hoho!" he cheered. "The graduate is here! My congratulations to you!" Above his beard, his cheeks and forehead were glossy with perspiration.

Rabbi Sheinkopf spoke up next. "*Mazel tov,* Sara," he said. "Tell me, have you heard any more from the *shadchanim?*"

"They haven't spoken to me since Ida's wedding, but one of Grossman's sons is always lurking around the corner whenever I leave the apartment in the morning. And Shternberg is still spreading rumors. He told the ice man that I tricked my neighbor into calling off her engagement."

Raskin frowned and stroked his beard. "Shternberg has always been the worst of them. He bakes lies like they are bagels."

Sara's mother's eyes again filled with tears, but Sara tried to be reassuring. "Don't worry, Mama. Now that high school is over, I've been thinking of a plan for what to do next. With Hindel pregnant, I need to work, but I don't think I can make any matches for a while. I was hoping," she said to Mr. Raskin, "that I could have my old job at your store."

Moishe Raskin shook his head. "I'm afraid I can't do that," he said.

His rebuff was a blow she had not been expecting. As foolish as it may have been, she had been counting on that job. What other position could she hope to get? She had no skill or patience for sewing. Watching the neighbors' children didn't pay enough. She supposed she could try for a cleaning job, but the thought of it made her stomach turn. "I understand," she said to Mr. Raskin. "You've already been so generous."

He loosened the tie around his neck. "Please, indulge me with a question. Why do you want to work at the store? Your mother told me that your father's wish was for you to continue your education."

Sara didn't want to be rude, but wasn't the answer obvious? "My father hoped I would go to Hunter College, but it isn't possible."

"Ah," said Raskin. "An excellent school, and there is no cost to attend."

"But just because the classes are free doesn't mean I can afford to go."

From beneath his bushy eyebrows, Moishe Raskin's bright eyes gleamed. "I do not disagree," he said. "You can't afford to go to Hunter, not when you should be studying at Barnard College instead."

Sara's mouth fell open in shock as Moishe Raskin made his argument. "Ida has told me many times what an excellent student you are— even better than she was, she says. Rabbi Sheinkopf and I spoke to your teachers, and they said you earned high marks on your Regents exams. Barnard has agreed to accept you in the fall. You may live in the dormitory, as Ida chose to, though of course, you can go home whenever you wish. I will pay for your tuition and also for your room and board." He stopped for a moment to pat his stomach. "Ida tells me the food is not so bad, though not as good as her mother's."

"I'm sorry, but I still don't understand. I can't go to college. I need to earn money."

Sara's mother interrupted. "The four of us have already discussed it. If Eli and George do a good job this summer, Mr. Raskin promised them after-school jobs in the fall."

"But Mama," Sara said. "That won't be enough."

"It *will* be enough," Mr. Raskin insisted.

"Even if I do go to school, why can't I go on living at home? That's what plenty of the Barnard girls do—Ida told me so herself."

It was then that her brother Joe chose to speak, in a voice that sounded almost like their father's. In the eight months since he'd been working for Raskin, Joe's puny arms had grown muscled and strong. When Sara looked at his burly frame, she saw the man he had become. "Don't you see, Sara?" Joe pleaded with her. "It's better for you to go. Shternberg and Grossman won't leave you alone. They've already spoken about calling for a *beis din* and bringing you in front of the rabbinical court. If it weren't for Rabbi Sheinkopf's intervention, those pigs would have done it already."

"Rabbi Sheinkopf, is this true?"

"I'm afraid so," the rabbi said. "If they even suspect you of making a match, they will make sure there is nothing but aggravation for you and your family. They will try to take away Aaron's job. They will sabotage Joe's chances of finding a wife."

"I don't care about a wife," Joe growled. "But I don't want them making my family miserable. Listen to me, Sara. No one wants you to leave, but if you're not living in the neighborhood, the *shadchanim* can't make any accusations. Besides, think of what Papa would say about you going to a school like that. Think of how proud he would be. Please, Sara. Say you'll go."

Sara couldn't remember ever hearing Joe say so much in one sitting.

"But what if you get sent overseas? Isn't it better for me to live at home?"

"Just because I registered doesn't mean that I'll be drafted. And if I am, I'll feel better knowing that you're safe on the other side of the city, far away from those men."

Sara's mother bit her lip, but she managed to hold back her tears. She took Sara's hand and squeezed it, hard. "Papa would have wanted this for you."

❧

Barnard College was only twelve miles away, but truly, it was a different world. Compared to Sara's home on the Lower East Side, the Morningside Heights campus was spacious and serene. There were no crowded tenements, no laundry lines. The air did not smell of onions or borscht.

Sara had never spent a night away from her family. She had never once had a bed to herself. Her room in Brooks Hall should have been a luxury, but instead, it felt disorienting and empty. There were 150 women in Sara's class, but loneliness filled her long, narrow room, coating every surface like the breath of old ghosts.

Everyone who knew Sara was convinced she would love college. But the truth was, the classes did not particularly interest her, and the socializing tempted her even less. She did not want to study botany or become fluent in French. She did not want to sing in the Glee Club or join the Social Science League. There were far too many teas and readings and performances, too many concerts and plays and competitions. The Greek Games—an annual spring tradition—was, in her opinion, a waste of time. From the elaborate costumes to the choreographed dances and recitations, the exaggerated pageantry of the festival struck her as absurd. She wrote as much in a letter to her brother Joe, after he was sent to France.

I want to be doing something to help with the war, not smearing gold paint on a fake wooden chariot so a bunch of girls in white robes can pretend to be Goddesses.

It was difficult for Sara to reconcile such events with the academic rigor of the school and its students. Her peers, no matter their backgrounds, were the most ambitious young women she had ever met. They were smart and organized, well-read and curious. They were motivated in a way she felt she understood. But she could not relate to their affinity for distraction or appreciate the activities that many of them flocked to for "fun."

Delores, who lived in the room next door, told Sara that she should try to enjoy herself. "College is supposed to be an *adventure*," Delores said.

Delores, Sara knew, was from a wealthy family, with a mother who'd gone to Radcliffe and a father who made his money "in steel." Sara didn't know exactly what that meant, but she knew enough to understand that Delores never worried about things like getting evicted or paying doctor bills. It wasn't that Delores was not committed to her studies. It was that, for girls like her, college was more than coursework. It was four years of socializing, making connections, going to dances, and, of course, looking for a suitable husband.

There were other girls, of course—girls for whom college was a means to a predetermined end; these were the girls who planned to teach, who had mapped out careers as scientists, or writers. They had chosen their future professions, and they were at Barnard to begin learning their trade.

But Sara wasn't a wealthy dilettante, and she wasn't at college to find a husband. And though it was true that she wanted to pursue a career, it was certainly not a conventional one. There was no course of study the college offered that could guide her on the path she had chosen. She had known her calling since she was ten years old. But the route was circuitous and the destination unpredictable. Barnard could not help to prepare her for the role.

Of course, Sara could never admit this to her professors or even to any of her classmates. She had made a vow not to reveal her gift or to discuss it with anyone at the school. She was tired of being whispered about, tired of being the subject of scrutiny. She was certain that the other girls would despise her if she told them what she saw and what she knew. She wouldn't dare tell Delores, for example, that the handsome young man who had picked her up downstairs was a better match for someone else—the sweet brunette who lived at the end of their hall.

There were a few students at the school with a background like Sara's—Lower East Side Jewish girls, whose parents still remembered the *shtetls* they came from. Sara hadn't known any of them from home, and she hoped they hadn't heard the rumors about her. They were the students most likely to know about the tradition of the *shadchanim*, but Sara was certain that even they could not imagine the mysterious method she used.

There were other kinds of Jewish girls at Barnard, of course—the kind of Jews the administration preferred. They were the girls from more established families, whose parents spoke English without an accent. Many of them commuted, and those who boarded did not feel guilty when bacon was served with pancakes at breakfast. The majority of girls were from different faiths entirely—Episcopal, Presbyterian, Catholic. They weren't all moneyed, society girls like Delores, but Sara didn't feel as if she fit in with any of them.

The first time Sara thought about quitting was in December when Joe was drafted. In April, when Joe was somewhere in France, Sara talked about leaving a second time. "I can be of more help at home," she told her sister, but their mother insisted that Sara stay and finish out the academic year. "Don't worry so much," Hindel had said. "Rabbi Sheinkopf's niece, Esther, lives with him now. She doesn't have enough work at his house to keep her busy, so she's been helping me with the babies in the afternoons."

Sara went home every Sunday to visit, but she was careful not to leave her family's apartment or to risk being spotted by the *shadchanim*. They had finally stopped looking for her around every corner, finally stopped making fresh accusations. Her extended absence had diffused the situation, and Sara did not want to risk provoking them again.

One Friday evening in early May, the girls at Sara's dinner table offered her an extra ticket to a "War Show" at the Columbia University gymnasium. When Sara accepted the invitation, she'd been under the impression that the "show" was a lecture or some kind of fundraiser for the troops. She hadn't realized it was a substitute for the annual under-graduate Varsity Show. The typically extravagant production, usually held in the Hotel Astor ballroom, had been economized on account of the war. The songs were written by a member of the class of 1916—a young man by the name of Oscar Hammerstein.

Sara was unprepared for the crowd—almost eight hundred students filled the gym—but she was even more surprised by the show itself. The characters were played by Columbia students—even the romantic female roles. Sara had never seen anything so ridiculous—nor could she remember ever laughing so hard. The girls who invited her looked on approvingly as she howled along with the rest of the audience.

When the show was over, the orchestra kept playing. Young men cleared away the seats, and the theatergoers began to dance. Sara found herself uncharacteristically swept along with the others until, one by one, the girls she had come with were cut in on by groups of young men they knew. Sara took a seat in a corner of the room to watch the couples on the floor. Though the gym was too warm and the music too loud, she was utterly mesmerized by the sight. After months of spending her evenings alone, cramming her head with impractical knowledge, she found the burst of vitality infectious. She should have felt awkward, sitting by herself, but she was too enthralled by the dancers to care. Once or twice, she noticed a stray beam of light connecting this or that woman to this or that man, but she put the visions out of her head, determined to appreciate the moment.

As one song ended and another began, a young man she did not recognize made his way toward her. It was too loud to hear what he was saying, but it was clear that he was asking for a dance. She tried to tell him she didn't know how, but either he couldn't hear or he pretended not to.

He was good-natured enough to smile when she faltered and to laugh when she stepped on both of his feet. He was handsome enough to make her stand straighter and to wish she had worn a different dress. He was enough of a *mensch* to put her at ease on an evening when everything she thought she knew about what she wanted from college had shifted on its axis. When the music stopped, he put her out of her misery and led her outside so they could hear each other speak. When she told him her name, he wrapped his hand around hers.

"It's nice to meet you, Sara. I'm Nathan Weisman."

TEN

ABBY

1994

D r. Cooper called back on Saturday morning. *What kind of doc-tor returns calls on a weekend?* "I was surprised to hear from you so soon," she said. "I know how difficult the funeral must have been, but I'm thrilled that you're ready to talk."

The comment was puzzling. She was *thrilled*? Why did she think Abby had called? What did the two of them have to talk about? After a lengthy, awkward pause, the doctor continued. "I'm sorry," she said. "Have I misunderstood? You *did* leave me a message yesterday, didn't you?"

"Yes," Abby said. "I was calling to ask for some medical advice."

"Oh," Dr. Cooper mumbled. "*Oh.* Did you . . . want to come in for an eye exam?" The ophthalmologist sounded disappointed.

"Not exactly," Abby said. "I was actually calling about one of my clients—a woman in her sixties, with some vision issues. But . . . I guess I could use a checkup, too. I haven't gotten a new prescription for years. So. Why not? We can kill two birds with one stone."

Dr. Cooper sounded relieved. "How does Monday morning sound? I'm booked all day, but I can squeeze you in early. Would eight o'clock be all right?"

"Perfect," Abby said. "See you then."

Jessica Cooper's office was on Sixty-Third and Madison, a nice walk from where Abby worked on Sixth Avenue. The patient waiting room was spotless and sleek, with black leather furniture and bright white walls. A series of framed black-and-white photographs were hung in groups above the chairs.

The doctor was waiting for her. "My receptionist and nurse don't come in until nine," she said. She led Abby down a carpeted hallway into a small interior room. On one end sat a complicated ergonomic chair alongside the standard ophthalmology equipment. On the other end, a screen hung down from the ceiling, with an eye chart projected onto its surface.

"Thanks for coming in so early," Abby said.

"No problem at all. Anything for Sara Glikman's granddaughter."

Abby took a seat in the chair. "Sara *Auerbach*," she corrected. "How do you know my grandmother's maiden name?"

The ophthalmologist flashed her a sheepish smile. "Believe it or not, our grandparents knew each other. Your grandmother was the one who figured it out—she recognized my grandfather from a photograph in the waiting room. That's how she and I became so close. Your grandmother was more than just a patient to me. If it weren't for her, I wouldn't even exist."

"Oh my God," Abby said. "Did she . . . was she your grandfather's *matchmaker*?"

Dr. Cooper beamed. "Yes! Isn't that amazing? I can't tell you how many times I heard the story when I was growing up. Your grandmother was only a girl when they met, and my grandfather was studying to be an optometrist."

"There was something in my grandmother's journal . . . your grandmother didn't make hats, did she?"

"She was a hat trimmer! Yes! Before she got married. My mother always said she had a great sense of style." Dr. Cooper gestured to her sneakers and the rumpled white doctor's coat she wore over mismatched clothes. "Unfortunately, I did *not* inherit it."

Abby fidgeted in the chair. She was beginning to feel lightheaded now. "Do you remember anything else your grandfather said? About my grandmother, I mean?"

"I was only sixteen when he died, but I know she made quite an impression on him. He told us the same story every year, always on his anniversary. *If it weren't for that stubborn little nudge, Sara Glikman, I never would have met your grandmother.*"

"He called her a *nudge*, huh? He was right about that." Abby thought about all the times Grandma Sara had pushed her to learn or try something new. If it weren't for her grandmother, she wouldn't know how to roller skate, how to sew on a button, or how to tweeze her own eyebrows. She never would have known that eggs, lox, and onions was the most delicious combination ever concocted. She wouldn't have applied to Columbia Law School, and she probably wouldn't have gotten such a good deal on her apartment. A fresh surge of sorrow wound its way through her. What would her grandmother say to her now? Abby stared up at the ceiling for a moment before her eyes wandered down to the clock on the wall. It was already twenty minutes after eight. She swallowed the lump in the back of her throat. "Would you mind if we got started with my exam? I don't want to be too late for work."

"Of course. I got carried away—sorry. If you lean your head forward, you can rest your chin right there." Abby looked through the phoropter and read from the eye chart while Dr. Cooper adjusted the dials. "Is it better like this . . . or this?" she asked. "*A* or *B*? Better or worse?"

Next, they moved on to a smaller device that measured the inner pressure of her eye. "This helps us to check for glaucoma," the doctor said.

"That can cause blindness, right?" Abby asked.

"It can, but we have a lot of treatments these days."

"I wonder if that's what my client has," Abby said. "The one I mentioned on the phone. I brought her some papers a few days ago, but she didn't want to—or couldn't—read them herself. I had to read them to her out loud. At first, I thought she was just tired, but then she couldn't even see the signature line."

"Did you ask her about it?"

"I didn't, no. We got interrupted, and it didn't seem appropriate. Can I ask—I know you've never met this woman and I have hardly any information, but do you have any idea why that could happen?"

Dr. Cooper shook her head and frowned. "It's impossible to know without examining her. There are way too many possibilities— glaucoma, like you said, macular degeneration, cataracts. I'd be happy to see her if she wants to make an appointment."

"Thanks. I shouldn't even be asking. My boss would have a fit if she knew I was discussing a client. And I'm not sure the client would appreciate it either. Giving unsolicited medical advice isn't part of my job description."

"I don't know about that," Dr. Cooper said. "Your grandmother gave me unsolicited advice all the time. Maybe it runs in the family."

Abby almost laughed. "Are you saying I'm a *nudge,* too?"

"I don't know you well enough to decide, but I don't think it's necessarily a bad thing. It sounds like you really care about this woman."

"I do. I mean, I only just met her, but I want to help her if I can. This will sound strange, but her husband walked in when we were reviewing the papers, and I got this . . . overwhelming feeling that they shouldn't split up."

The corners of Dr. Cooper's lips quivered slightly, but she didn't say a word.

Abby continued. "I know her husband doesn't want the divorce—she's been extremely clear about that. She doesn't seem happy about it either, but she's determined to end the marriage anyway. Still . . . when I saw the two of them together, it was so *obvious*. You couldn't look at them and not see how madly in love they were with each other." Abby considered describing the sun through the window and the halo of light. But she had already said too much, and she didn't want the ophthalmologist to think she was crazy.

After a moment of quiet, Abby apologized. "I'm sorry, Dr. Cooper. You must have other patients waiting. I've taken up way too much of your time."

"Call me Jessica," Dr. Cooper whispered. "And please, please, don't apologize. I can't tell you how touched I am by what you've told me. You sound so much like your grandmother, Abby. It's . . . uncanny." Jessica's eyes clouded over with tears.

Her display of emotion caught Abby off guard. "Dr. Cooper—Jessica. When you called me, you said something about me being *ready to talk*. Was it about the fact that our grandparents knew each other, or is there something else you thought I wanted to talk about?"

Jessica hesitated. "That unsolicited advice your grandmother gave me? It was . . . marriage related." She held up her left hand and wiggled her fingers. "No engagement ring, no wedding band. No fiancé, no husband. Your grandmother noticed right away. She wanted to know if I had anyone special. When I told her no, she said she wanted to help. To do for me what she'd done for my grandfather."

"But she stopped making matches forty years ago!"

"She said she had recently come out of retirement."

Abby couldn't believe what she was hearing. She was lightheaded again, and her pulse was racing. "How long did she—?"

"Close to two years, I guess. She tried, but she couldn't find the right person for me. She said she was positive that my soulmate was out there, but she wasn't sure how to find him yet. She used to joke that it might take more time than she had left, but I kept telling her I was patient. Most of the time, she'd laugh it off, but a month or so before she died, she said something strange."

Abby was dizzy now. Her mouth had gone dry. She was afraid to ask, but she couldn't stop herself. "What did she say?"

"She told me that if anything happened to her, you would be able to help me."

When the time comes, try to remember what I taught you. Who knows? Maybe you'll make a few love matches of your own.

On her way out of the office, Abby stopped to look at the photographs in the waiting room. Closest to the reception desk was a faded picture of two men standing behind a pushcart. The older man wore a black felt hat and a dark wool coat with a lambswool collar. Although he looked uncomfortable being photographed, the young man beside him smiled heartily for the camera. It was difficult to make out what was on top of the cart, but if Abby looked closely, she could see dozens of pairs of wire-rimmed spectacles.

A second photograph showed the same two men in the doorway of a storefront. The painted signs in the wide glass windows read EYES EXAMINED and GLASSES FITTED. Over the doorway in bright white letters were the words TUNCHEL & SON.

As strange and unnerving as the morning had been, the black-and-white photographs filled Abby with comfort. Her grandmother had known both of these men. She had, most likely, been inside their store. Abby felt a connection, an invisible pull, that kept her staring at the pictures for far too long.

She couldn't remember the older man's name, but the son—Jessica's grandfather—was called Jacob. Abby stared at Jacob's smile and tried to imagine how her grandmother had ever become friendly with this man. What had made such a young and inexperienced girl think she was qualified to find him a wife? What had she seen or felt or known that had given her the courage—the *chutzpah*—to try? What had she said to make Jacob listen?

By the time Abby left the doctor's office, her head was full of more questions than answers. She was no closer to helping Evelyn Morgan, and no nearer to understanding her client's condition. She was unsure of what the ophthalmologist wanted from her, and completely confused about what to do next.

At Abby's office, things were equally complicated. By the time she made it to her desk, Diane had already left one of her Post-its stuck to the screen of Abby's computer: *Where are you? Come see me.*

The note made Abby's stomach flip. She hated this feeling—like she'd done something wrong, like she had a strike against her before the day even started.

As usual, Diane made Abby wait in the doorway before looking up and offering her a seat. "Sorry I got in late," Abby said. "My doctor had a last-minute opening."

Diane pretended she hadn't heard. "Evelyn Morgan was trying to reach you this morning. When she couldn't get you, she asked for me."

"I didn't realize—I haven't checked my messages yet. I'll go call her right now."

"That won't be necessary. I took care of it."

"Was there some kind of problem?" Abby asked. She racked her brain to think of why Evelyn might have called. Maybe she had decided to stay with Michael after all?

"Evelyn said you were interrupted on Friday, that her husband walked in while you were going over the summons."

Abby tried to sound unconcerned. "It wasn't an issue. By the time he arrived, we were already finished. I got her signature, and then I left."

"You didn't tell me Michael was there."

"He wasn't *there*, not really. He walked in when I was walking out. Honestly, I barely met him. Our paths crossed for maybe ten seconds—he shook my hand, then he saw Evelyn and went over to her. I can't say what happened after I left."

"Well, whatever happened, Evelyn is distraught." Diane was up and pacing again, back and forth between her desk and the window. "How could you have allowed him to come into the room? You're Evelyn's lawyer. You represent her *against* him. You should have demanded that he leave!" There was a nasty crackle to Diane's voice, like an electric wire that had been left exposed.

Abby knew she had to stand up for herself. "I'm not a bodyguard, Diane, and with all due respect, you weren't there. Our business was done, and I was on my way out the door. Besides, you didn't see how she embraced him, how the two of them held each other, like . . . like they couldn't bear to be apart. It wasn't only Michael, it was Evelyn, too."

Diane frowned. "We've already had this discussion, Abby. Divorce is an emotional business. People can have strong feelings for each other and still want to get out of their marriage. *Your* job is to make sure that happens while protecting the client."

"I'm doing my best, but you said it yourself—you've never seen Evelyn behave this way. Her vision loss is an added complication—maybe that's part of why she's been so upset. I'll give her a call when I get back to my office and make sure she still wants us to serve Michael with the papers."

"There's no need for that. I've already spoken with Evelyn, and she assured me that she wants to move forward."

"Shouldn't I talk to her first, especially since she called me?"

"I told you, that *isn't* necessary." Diane took a thick stack of files from her credenza and slammed it down on her desk. She pushed the teetering pile toward Abby. "These are for the Henshaw case. I want an itemized list of every penny he's spent in the seven years since he's been married."

"That won't be a problem," Abby said, "but with respect to Michael—"

Diane's glare was enough to silence her. "Michael will be served *to-day*," she insisted. "As for the Henshaw matter, I need that list as soon as possible—no later than tomorrow morning."

Abby eyed the heap of folders. It would take her all day to get through them, and she'd probably be working well into the evening. "Of course. I'll get started on it now." She balanced the pile in both of her arms and made her way slowly out of Diane's office, trying not to drop any papers on the way.

"One more thing," Diane called out from behind her. "The next time you plan on coming in late, I'd appreciate you letting me know in advance."

Abby's fingers dug into the folders, but she kept her head down and kept moving forward. Diane always liked to have the last word.

Back at her desk, Abby listened to her phone messages.

Abby, this is Evelyn Morgan. Thank you for meeting me on Friday. Getting around the city has become more difficult lately, so I appreciate your willingness to come to my hotel. I wanted to apologize for the . . . interruption we had. I'm afraid it was a bit of a scene, but I wanted to confirm that you were moving ahead with the papers and the divorce.

So, Diane was right then, Evelyn had made up her mind.

I'm afraid Michael still refuses to accept the inevitable. I don't . . . I don't know what I've done to deserve such devotion from him, but . . . oh dear. I'm sorry, but I'll leave it at that.

Or had she? The ragged edges of Evelyn's voice betrayed an obvious uncertainty.

Abby arranged for her favorite paralegal to serve Michael with the summons. Still, the echo of Evelyn's message nagged at Abby for the rest of the afternoon. As she worked through the mound of documents Diane had given her, all she could think of was the awful day when her mother had received divorce papers from her father.

Beverly and her daughters had been leaving their building when a nervous-looking man approached them from the street. Abby thought she had seen him the day before, but she hadn't been with her mother then. "Are you Beverly Silverman?" the man demanded, and when Abby's mother said yes, he shoved a slim manila envelope into her hands. "You've been served, ma'am," he said, before scurrying away.

Abby's mother had stood frozen in place on the sidewalk, stunned by the strange and unexpected encounter. Her silence sent Hannah into a fit of tears, while Abby tried to hush her sister so people wouldn't stare. Abby wondered why the man had been so rude. She wondered why he'd run away so abruptly. More than anything else, Abby had wondered what was inside the manila envelope.

Abby finished the Henshaw project by eight, but she didn't dare leave work before Diane. It felt like a petty battle of wills—whoever stayed longer would be the victor. Diane strode past Abby's open door a little after 8:15. She didn't look up or say goodbye, but Abby was certain Diane had seen her. Abby raised both of her arms over her head and stretched her torso from side to side. One by one, the muscles running down her spine unclenched. She was rubbing the back of her neck with both hands when the phone on her desk rang.

"Abby Silverman."

"Ms. Silverman, this is Michael Gilbert." *Evelyn's husband? Crap.*

"Mr. Gilbert, hello. Is there . . . something I can help you with?"

Abby tried to sound as professional as possible. Never mind what she had seen at the hotel the other day. Never mind that she shouldn't be speaking with him at all.

"I know it's late. I wasn't sure if anyone would answer." Michael Gilbert sounded jittery, like someone who'd had too many cups of coffee, or maybe like someone who'd just read about his own divorce.

"We work pretty long hours—it's part of the job."

A whooshing noise rattled the receiver, as if Michael had let out a long-held breath. "Ms. Silverman, I'm no good at small talk. I called because I received your papers. It took me all day to work up the courage to open the envelope and read them. Now that I have, I find it necessary to make clear that I *do not want* this divorce."

"Ms. Morgan has already told me that, but I'm afraid I can't do anything to change her decision. I'd be happy to speak to your lawyer . . ."

"I don't have a lawyer. That's why I called you."

"As sympathetic as I am to your situation, it isn't appropriate for us to be talking—"

"Did Evelyn tell you why she wants to divorce me?"

Abby's muscles forgot that she had stretched them. Her twenty-six-year-old body felt eighty-five. She didn't want to be speaking with Evelyn's husband. She didn't want to know any more personal information. And yet, as much as she didn't want these things, she felt powerless to end the conversation. When she didn't answer, Michael Gilbert continued.

"Evelyn is going blind. Or, at least, she thinks she is. She refuses to consult with a doctor. She's convinced she has the same eye disease as her father, and she says she won't put me through what her family endured. She doesn't want to be dependent on me. She doesn't want me to see her helpless."

Abby remembered the look on Evelyn's face when she asked her to read the summons. Evelyn was embarrassed to be asking for help. It

didn't matter that Abby pretended not to notice——Evelyn's humiliation had filled the room.

But then again, so had her feelings for her husband. Their mutual
ardor was a palpable thing, and because Abby had felt it, she could not
forget it. It was in the thickness of Michael's voice when he pleaded
with Evelyn to come home; it was in the way Evelyn bent toward her
husband, like a flower bending toward the sun; it was in the radiance
emanating from them both when the light from the window enveloped
them.

"Ms. Silverman? Are you still there?"

Abby cleared her throat. "Yes, I'm here. As much as I appreciate
your honesty, Mr. Gilbert, I don't see how this changes anything."

"Couldn't you try speaking to Evelyn? Convince her to slow things
down a bit? Suggest she see a doctor at least, to make sure she isn't
making a terrible mistake?"

Abby tried to imagine how Diane would have responded if Michael
Gilbert had called her instead. Diane would have said, *I cannot help
you* or *You're out of line* or *Evelyn is my client, Mr. Gilbert, not you.* She
would have said, *I'm a lawyer, not a therapist* or *How dare you ask me to
do something like that.* She would have been indignant; she would have
been furious. Diane would have already hung up the phone.

But Abby was still holding the receiver to her ear, thinking of the
way her mother's fingers had trembled when she pulled the legal papers
from the process server's envelope. Almost fourteen years had passed
since that day, but Abby hadn't forgotten her mother's nail polish
color—Toasted Almond, it was called, and her mother had never worn
it again.

Abby wondered what Michael Gilbert would remember from
today—the day he learned that love could be papered over like a wall
with a few short paragraphs of boilerplate language and one signature
line on a clean white page. To a man who wrote poetry, the realization

that such lifeless words could wreak such havoc must have been all the more painful to bear.

Abby's mother had known divorce papers were coming, and Michael Gilbert had known it, too. Both of them had been shaken to the core despite not being the least bit surprised. Abby rubbed her neck again, but her muscles were stiff and full of knots.

"I'll try," Abby whispered. "But I won't make any promises."

ELEVEN

SARA

1918

A Drop of Love Sometimes Brings an Ocean of Tears

Sara's last month of her freshman year was nothing like the eight months that preceded it. After the other girls saw her at the show—collapsing into laughter and dancing with Nathan—they decided she wasn't such a stick-in-the-mud after all. Sara Glikman, they said to themselves, was finally coming out of her shell.

The truth, Sara knew, was more complicated. From the day she had first arrived at Barnard, she felt guilty about leaving her family behind. While she had a room all to herself, they slept crowded together on tables and cots. While she ate three meals a day that someone else cooked, they haggled every morning for soup greens and eggs. While she studied Shakespeare and scientific equations, their minds were filled from morning to night with the business and burdens of making ends meet.

Sara had gone to college because it was her father's wish. She had gone because her family had begged her to accept the gift of a grateful,

generous man. But her acquiescence did not mean that a tide of re-
morse had not almost drowned her along the way.

It was one thing for Sara to go away to school. It was another thing,
entirely, for her to enjoy it.

The day after the War Show, Nathan Weisman invited her to the Cop-
per Kettle Tearoom on Amsterdam Avenue. In the light of day, he was
as much of a gentleman—an *edel mensch*—as the night before. When
Sara couldn't decide between cake or pie, he asked the waitress to bring
her both.

He wanted to hear Sara's "life story," so she told him about the
steamship to New York, her sister and brothers, and her father. She told
him about Mr. Tunchel's pushcart, the lemon-ice man, and New Year's
prayers on the bridge. She did not spare him the unsavory details of her
crowded apartment, her noisy neighbors, and the one shared bathroom
down the hall. The only part of her life that Sara left out was the gift
she'd been given for making matches. She did not want to lie about
who she was, but that was the one thing she could not say.

When Nathan asked if she was enjoying her first year at Barnard,
she said "enjoy" wasn't necessarily the word she would choose.

"How would you describe it then?" Nathan asked.

Sara felt her eyes well up, but she composed herself quickly, dabbing
her eyes with the soft white napkin from her lap. A single tear fell on
the chocolate cake and one or two more on the cherry pie. "Mostly,"
she confessed, "it's been lonely."

"What about the friends you were with at the show?"

"They invited me because they had an extra ticket, but I wouldn't
say any of them are my friends. It's my fault, not theirs. Most of the
time, I stay in my room."

"Why is that?" Nathan's voice was curious and free of judgment.

"It feels wrong to be laughing and having fun when everyone in my family is working so hard. My sister is up all night with her little ones. My brother is who knows where in France. I am the only one who gets to go to college. I have to work as hard as I can."

Nathan took a bite of pie. "Do you want to know what I think?" he said. "You're not making the most of the opportunity you've been given if you don't allow yourself to participate. Yes, you should study and work hard, but it isn't necessary to make yourself miserable. Some of my classmates are in France, too. Sometimes I feel guilty that I'm safe here at school while they risk their lives out on the battlefield. But it doesn't help their chance of survival if I sit alone in my room pulling my hair out."

"I'm not pulling my hair out," Sara insisted.

"Good. Though you'd be just as beautiful if you did." Nathan set his fork down beside his plate and reached across the table for Sara's hand. She felt her cheeks flush and her fingertips tingle.

Sara wished she could know what the feeling meant, but her thoughts were muddled, and her vision unclear. In all the years that she had been looking for matches, she had never thought about finding one for herself. She had never considered how she might recognize her own soulmate if he were to appear. She turned her head slightly, this way and that, searching for a flicker or filament of light. But nothing in the tearoom seemed out of sorts.

"There's only one month left before the school year ends," Nathan said. "What if you tried a different approach?"

After that, Sara made more of an effort. She went to Field Day and cheered on her classmates as they ran the relays and jumped the hurdles. She volunteered at Barnard's Boathouse canteen for soldiers who were traveling through New York City on their way home from the war. She joined Delores's study group and found she didn't mind conjugating French verbs as long as Delores played her radio in the background.

In between, Sara spent time with Nathan. He took her for ice cream and brought her flowers. He told her about growing up in the Bronx. He described the antics of his younger twin sisters and promised Sara she'd meet them over the summer. He kissed her, for the first time, on a rainy spring evening, and the heat from his lips traveled through her whole body. The raindrops caught the light of a streetlamp overhead, and, for a moment, Sara thought: *There it is.* But then Nathan said something about the light, too, and she knew that it was no preternatural force.

Sometimes, she found herself searching the edges of her sight for flashes and signs that he would be hers forever, but whenever Nathan stood beside her, her periphery was blank. She grew increasingly skittish when they were together, but, thankfully, he did not seem to notice. When he offered to borrow his father's car to drive her home the day after exams, she told him yes.

On her last day of living at Brooks Hall, Sara packed her suitcase and said her goodbyes. It came as a bit of a shock when she realized how much she would miss her hallmates. Nathan loaded her suitcase into the Model T Ford and they headed south, toward Cannon Street. While Nathan concentrated on the driving, Sara thought about how much had changed since she'd contemplated leaving school that winter.

She had learned that although her gift was considerable, she had much more to learn about people and love. A good *shadchanteh* would have to deal with every kind of personality—romantics, skeptics, snobs, and fools. Some people would naturally dismiss her input. Others would have impossible expectations. By broadening her experience in the world, by studying subjects she once presumed were irrelevant, she might be better able to serve them all. Sara had looked forward to spending the summer with her family, but now she was also enthusiastic about resuming her classes in the fall. All she had to do was maintain a low profile and avoid crossing paths with the *shadchanim*. If she could get through the summer without drawing their attention, she could get back to her education.

As soon as Nathan crossed the Bowery, Sara realized the mistake she had made in accepting the ride. People from Cannon Street did not own their own cars; they did not go driving with the top rolled down on warm June days with handsome young men. If she had wanted to return home without anyone noticing, she'd chosen the wrong way to go about it.

As Nathan turned left onto East Houston, a group of gray-haired *yentas* turned their heads. Street vendors stared while they counted out change. Sara tried to ignore the increasing attention, but when they turned on Cannon Street, it became impossible. Children ran after Nathan's shiny black Ford, struggling to keep up as it rolled down the street. When Nathan came to a stop in front of Sara's building, a handful of tenants threw open their windows. Familiar faces stared down from above, but there were no friendly waves or welcoming smiles. For reasons she could not quite discern, no one seemed particularly happy to see her.

Sara had the beginnings of a headache—the car ride and hot sun had seen to that—but her vague sense of discomfort turned to something more menacing as she considered the blank expressions of her neighbors. She wanted to tell Nathan to restart the engine, to pull away from the curb and drive somewhere else, but all the words she knew were caught in her throat. And then, just as Nathan was helping her out of the car, her sister appeared on the stoop of their building. Hindel's face was a shocking, sickly white, as if all the color had been drained from her cheeks. On her hip, she held Florence, her oldest daughter. Behind her was Esther, Rabbi Sheinkopf's niece, who'd been helping with the children while Sara was at school. Esther rested one hand on Hindel's shoulder, as if she were there to keep Hindel from toppling backward.

For Sara, there was no mistaking the wretched meaning of the piteous tableau. She ran to the steps and stumbled up them, flinging both arms around her sister and niece. Florence smelled faintly of soap and milk, but Hindel smelled of paper, ink, and sorrow. She was still clutching the telegram in her hand.

`Deeply regret to inform you that Private Joseph Glikman Infantry is officially reported as killed in action May Fifth.`

Her oldest brother had been dead for over a month and still, the world had kept on spinning. Up at Barnard, professors had continued with their lectures; the grass in the Quadrangle had continued to grow. Down on Cannon Street, the ice man still whistled on the corner, and the children still played marbles in the alleyways.

Yet Sara—who prided herself on her intuition—had somehow not noticed that anything was amiss. Incredulity and grief circled her slowly, like a two-headed snake, poised to strike. She stood frozen on the steps, afraid to move or even blink.

Nathan was oblivious to the exchange. He was still on the street, with Sara's suitcase beside him, waiting politely to be introduced. He must have been watching with increasing apprehension as Sara failed to call him over. Eventually, he approached the hollowed-out steps, climbing them quietly so as not to spook her. She passed the telegram to him, grateful that she did not have to say the words. *My brother is dead. Joe is gone.*

Ignoring the stares of the neighbors overhead, Sara allowed herself to lean against him. "I'm sorry," Nathan said both to her and to Hindel. "So very sorry for you both."

Sara forced herself to move. She turned to Nathan. "I have to go," she said. "I need to go upstairs to my mother."

His face went blank for a moment before he understood her meaning. He had expected a different kind of day—he'd hoped to meet Sara's mother, to shake hands with her brothers, to pet the soft heads of Hindel's young children. Sara knew he had expected to be invited upstairs, to see the home she had told him so much about. But no matter how kind and comforting he might be, Sara knew that this was not the time for introductions. She whispered her apology, and he promised her that he would return the following afternoon.

"Can I carry your suitcase up the steps, at least?" he asked, his brow creased heavily with concern. "It's heavy. Will you be able to manage?" But Esther stepped forward and offered to help. "I'll take it," she said. "It won't be a problem." A lock of black hair fell in front of her eyes.

Sara had met Esther many times. Her parents had sent her from Hartford, Connecticut, to keep house for the rabbi, who had no family of his own. She was a few years older than Sara and half a foot taller, with a ready smile, especially for children. She was, if what Hindel had said was true, a wonderful cook and housekeeper as well. In the nine months that she had been in New York, she and Hindel had become close friends.

Esther swung her arm out to reach for the suitcase just as Nathan was edging it toward her. For an instant, it hung suspended between them—flanked by Nathan on one side and the rabbi's niece on the other. It revealed itself then—the maddening flash that cut through the haze of Sara's torpor and grief. It was as if the suitcase were lit from within—filled with candles or fireflies instead of nightclothes and socks. The more Sara attempted to ignore it, the brighter and more brilliantly it shined. Was the loss of her brother not enough? Did she have to lose Nathan today as well?

If the glow had surrounded any other man, Sara would have been happy for him. But in that moment, the beam was a butcher's knife, cutting the hope from Sara's future, deftly shaving the golden trimmings away from something that had already died.

~⟨⟩

Nathan came the next day, exactly as he'd promised, with a basket of fruit and a note from his parents. Rabbi Sheinkopf had decided that *shiva* should begin immediately, so the apartment was full of neighbors and friends. Nathan fit into the crowded space without fuss and offered Sara's mother his condolences.

Malka Glikman patted Nathan's hand. She wore a simple black scarf over her braided hair and an even simpler long black dress. In the past twelve hours, she seemed to have shrunk, and the dress hung loosely on her tiny frame. It was hard to believe that such a petite woman had given birth to five healthy children.

"You know Yiddish?" she asked, and Nathan nodded. Her face was creased and sunken with grief, but the strength of her voice did not waver.

"Sit here," she said, motioning to the hard chair beside her. "You go to the university, too?"

"Columbia University, yes."

"Good, good. A smart boy then. Smart enough to know that my Sara is not like the other girls."

Nathan nodded thoughtfully. "I agree, Mrs. Glikman. Sara is special. The smartest, most beautiful girl I know."

"Intelligent, yes. Beautiful, absolutely." Sara's mother raised an eyebrow. "But I'm talking about something else." She pointed to where Hindel stood near the window, on the opposite side of the room. "You see my other daughter there? Also beautiful. Also smart. But not so complicated. You understand?" She gestured around the crowded apartment. "For Hindel, this world is the right size. But for Sara, this world is . . . too small. She does not think I know this, but I do."

"You're worried that she won't keep your traditions?" Nathan asked.

She patted his hand again and sighed. "When we came to this country, I knew what would be. We cannot keep everything as it was. Sara will be a good wife and a good mother. She has a good heart, and in this new world, that is worth as much as a pious one."

"I understand," Nathan said. "I think my mother would say the same about me. So, perhaps, Sara and I are well suited."

Sara's mother tilted her head. She had not yet let go of Nathan's hand. "You are a good boy, *tateleh*. I'm sure you make your mother proud."

Sara stood apart from the conversation, but she had heard every word. Even in the midst of maternal grief, it was clear that Malka Glikman hoped for a wedding. In her mind, the only antidote to death was the unbroken forward march of life.

By the time the mourning period ended, everyone in the neighborhood was talking about Sara's new beau. Caught up in the optimism and the tumult, Sara allowed herself to doubt what she had seen. But when she witnessed the light a second time, during a dinner at her home where both Nathan and Esther were present, she could no longer ignore the truth.

How could she possibly explain it to Nathan? At best, she would sound as if she did not love him, and at worst, she would sound like some kind of a witch. Even among her own family members, Sara could not disclose what she had seen. There was only one person she could tell.

Sara knocked on the door of Rabbi Sheinkopf's home when she knew he was already at the synagogue. Esther was scrubbing a spotless floor, and Sara could smell the vegetable soup simmering on the rabbi's stove. Esther's hair was in her eyes again, but her cheeks were smooth and her smile was welcoming. She was pretty, Sara thought, but it was difficult to notice because she was constantly in motion. If only she would stand still long enough, her beauty would be easier to see.

"I have something to talk to you about," Sara said. "Did Hindel ever tell you how she met Aaron?"

Esther nodded. "She told me that they met on the steamship. I always thought it was a wonderful story."

"It is," Sara agreed. "Did she mention that I was the one to introduce them?"

A whisper of pink crept into Esther's cheeks as if she was embarrassed to have known this fact. "Yes," she said. "Hindel told me." Esther lowered her head and looked away. "She said that one day, perhaps, you might find someone for me as well."

"That's exactly why I wanted to see you."

Sara could not think of where to begin, how much to say, or what to hold back. Esther was horrified at first. Nathan and Sara loved each other! Esther could never do such a thing! How could she ever come between them? What would Sara's family think?

In the end, the only way to convince Esther was to tell her everything. Sara described what she had seen on the steamship; she described what she had seen between Jacob Tunchel and Miryam. She recounted the story of the grocer's son and her teacher, of Ida Raskin and the dentist, of countless others. She told Esther there were dozens of men and women who had never once suspected her intervention.

"But what if, this time, you are wrong?" Esther asked.

Sara didn't know whether to laugh or to weep. "I'm not wrong," she said. "If I thought there was a chance that I could be, believe me, I wouldn't have come to you."

"I don't understand what you want me to do. I couldn't bring myself to look at Nathan now, let alone encourage him."

"There is nothing to do yet," Sara said. "After a suitable time has passed, we will have to come up with a plan. There will be no reason for him to return to this neighborhood, so we will have to think of something, some way for you to cross paths. We will need to be patient."

Esther frowned. "I know that I haven't been blessed with your gift, but even with my eyes, I can see that you love him. I'm sorry, Sara, but I don't understand. How can you bear to give him up?"

There was no way for Sara to properly answer. Yes, she loved Nathan. Perhaps he loved her, too. But whatever brightness burned between them, it was not brilliant enough to last. She wondered if she would ever find someone whose love she would not have to doubt. Would her gift ever reveal the man she was meant for with enough certainty to stop her searching in corners for connections between him and someone else? She had always been grateful for her calling, but now she understood the havoc it could wreak. Was this the price she would have to pay—to never be secure in a love of her own?

She would not say all of that to Esther. She would not say it to anyone, ever. And so, in order to satisfy the question, Sara shrugged her shoulders and pretended not to care. "I care for him," she admitted, but with a show of nonchalance. "But not like that. It's only a little bit of affection—barely a drop."

Esther reached for Sara's hand. "*A tropn libe brengt a mol a yam trern,*" she said.

A drop of love sometimes brings an ocean of tears.

TWELVE

‹-›═◉═‹-›

ABBY

1994

The next morning, the markup of the Henshaw document was already waiting on Abby's chair. She checked her watch, but it was only seven thirty. Most of her friends who worked at big law firms said the partners didn't arrive until ten. Diane Berenson put them all to shame—she must have gotten in at dawn.

Abby looked through the changes, but she couldn't concentrate. Why had she told Michael Gilbert she'd help him? What could she possibly say to Evelyn that would make the slightest bit of difference? What would happen if Diane found out?

In addition to the work stresses swirling in her head, Abby was still reeling from her conversation with Dr. Cooper. What had Abby's grandmother expected her to do? Give up law and become a matchmaker? Continue to practice but make matches on the side? Any possibility sounded absurd. But when she thought about the excitement in the doctor's voice, a part of Abby *wanted* to help, wanted to believe, somehow, that she could.

And what about Victor Étoile and Nicole? At their initial meeting, Abby had questioned the sincerity of the model's feelings for her fiancé. But after sitting through dinner with the couple last week, Abby was more confused than ever. Nicole was intelligent and fiercely ambitious, but that didn't negate her love for Victor. Abby had noticed a kind of coziness between them, an easy affection that she hadn't expected. But was that a good enough reason for them to be married? And did it mean the union would last?

Diane tapped on Abby's open door. "I can't make it to the fashion show tonight," she said. Diane fiddled with her giant bezel-set pearl earring and swept her eyes over Abby's desk. "I have too much other work, but I wanted to make sure that you're still going."

"Of course, Diane. I wouldn't miss it."

"Good. Just do me a favor and keep your eyes open. We both know how distracted Victor has been lately. He's so wrapped up in his feelings for Nicole that he hasn't been as forthcoming as he should be. Now that I'm in touch with his corporate lawyers, I'm sure everything will go more smoothly, but I don't want any more surprises. If he makes some other announcement, or you hear anything interesting, I want you to call me at home."

"Sure. I'll report whatever I hear."

"Good. You're welcome to my ticket, by the way. In case you'd like to bring a friend."

Abby's first thought was that she would go alone, but on the other hand, she owed Will a phone call. Inviting him to the show might make up for the fact that she'd let the whole weekend pass without phoning him back.

The problem was that Abby couldn't make up her mind about him. He'd made it obvious that he'd like to see more of her, but she couldn't quite muster his level of enthusiasm. Still, every time she considered having "the talk"—telling him that the two of them were better off as friends—she found herself unable to say the words. Abby didn't think she and Will had a romantic future together, but there was something about him that made her want to keep him around, some sense she had that they weren't done with each other yet.

"Thanks," she told Diane. "I think I will."

⁓⊚⁕

Will was delighted with the invitation. "I mean, obviously, I'm not a fashion guy, but it sounds like fun. It'll be different!"

"Absolutely," Abby said.

Outside the entrance to Victor's store, a wide silver banner hung on the stone façade. NICOLE BY ÉTOILE was printed in black, but the dot over the *i* in "Nicole" was a crescent moon, and the *i* in "Étoile" was in the shape of a star. Half a dozen spotlights were aimed at the sign, and the letters shimmered over Madison Avenue. An army of tall, black-suited men stood in front of the double doors, holding clipboards and checking invitations.

"Whoa," Will said, gesturing to the crowd that was forming. Although Abby knew none of them personally, she spotted several familiar faces—actresses, photographers, club kids, and journalists mixed with New York City's society ladies. "This is quite a scene."

Abby smiled. "Not how I usually spend my Tuesday nights."

Inside the store, all of the mannequins and clothing displays had been removed. A midnight-blue runway crossed the center of the space, bordered on both sides by rows of Lucite chairs. At the far end of the runway, another silver banner hung suspended from the ceiling. Waiters passed out glasses of expensive champagne, tiny cheese tarts, and beef brochettes, but the vibe in the room was more informal than the food. Abby had worn her Étoile scarf, but she didn't see anyone else wearing Victor's clothes. They were all too conservative for this crowd, who were mostly in jeans or black leather pants. Abby's Ann Taylor suit, which had felt like the most stylish option in her work wardrobe that morning, suddenly seemed dowdy and out of place.

At the bar, they ran into a beaming Victor, who kissed Abby gallantly on both cheeks. Abby introduced Will and extended Diane's regrets. "She's sorry she couldn't be here tonight. I'm afraid she had too much work to leave the office."

"Someone must teach her how to relax!" Victor said. He shook Will's hand and clapped him on the shoulder. "Please," he said, "promise me you won't let this beautiful young woman meet the same terrible fate. Don't let her follow in Diane's footsteps. Life cannot be only for work."

It was impossible to resist Victor's charm. "I'll try," Will laughed. "But Abby is determined. And unfortunately, lawyers work very long hours."

"That settles it then!" Victor turned to Abby. "We must find you another career." He raised an eyebrow and studied her face. "You have lovely cheekbones, *ma chère*. If you were taller, you might have modeled for Nicole's new collection."

Abby almost choked on her champagne. "I don't think so," she coughed. "Besides, without us lawyers, who would watch out for you?"

"Ah," Victor said, with a sheepish grin. "You are not only beautiful but wise as well. Will, you and I are lucky men. Abby and Nicole have such ambition! Such energy! I'm ready to start spending more time away from work, but Nicole is ready to build an empire." He tapped his watch and winked at them both. "Time for my announcement now, yes? Please, find some chairs by the runway. The show will begin very soon."

After the crowd settled in their seats, Victor stepped up to the microphone. "*Merci* and thank you!" he called out, over a rowdy burst of applause. "I feel very fortunate to welcome you all, our closest friends and colleagues, this evening." He stretched his arms out and pointed around the room. "As many of you know, this magnificent building is both my place of business and my personal residence. For the past twelve years, it has been my sanctuary. But it was only after

I met Nicole that this house truly became my *home*." Victor was forced to pause again as another round of applause erupted.

"So you see, I cannot separate my work from my home. And a home must not only be beautiful. A home must be *comfortable* as well." He gestured to his own loose-fitting jacket, linen shirt, and jeans. "When we are home, we dress for comfort, yes? We will *never* sacrifice luxury, of course, but we must have elegance *and* comfort. Nicole has always understood this concept. When we are not working, we must unwind. We must enjoy, we must *live*! And so, with all of that in mind, Nicole created this unbelievable collection for the fall. It is relaxed. It is intimate. It is *personal*. The clothes you will see are from Nicole's heart and mind, but they have the soul of Étoile!"

A moment later, the overhead lights went dark. Abby felt the heavy thump of techno music shake the floor beneath her feet. From the back of the room, pink and blue lights followed the models as they emerged. Young women stomped down the length of the runway in heavy boots, loose ripped jeans, and simple, round-necked, white silk T-shirts. A second group, wearing long suede coats over embellished miniskirts, passed by next. Following them was a line of models draped in whisper-thin silk slip dresses. Abby watched as Will's eyes snapped open. Between the teensy straps and the transparent fabric, it was as if they were wearing nothing at all.

When he caught her smiling at him, Will looked away. "Sorry, but they're practically *naked*," he whispered.

"I think that's the idea," Abby said.

"Maybe you should get one of those dresses," he ventured. "I mean, they look really . . . *comfortable*."

Abby laughed. "I guess that means the collection is a success."

At the end of the show, Nicole walked onto the runway in loose, black jeans and a black silk tank. Her hair was tousled just the right amount, and silver bangles covered both of her wrists, almost as far up as her elbows. Victor presented her with a bouquet of white roses, kissed both of her cheeks, and then scurried off the runway so she could have her moment.

Brava Nicole! Brava! Brava!

Nicole waved and blew kisses to the crowd as they rose to their feet and cheered for her. The spotlights lingered on her perfect features: her heart-shaped face, her almond eyes, her impeccably glossed, pillowy lips.

Abby snuck another look at Will and then forced herself to blink. At first, she thought that what she was seeing was the reflection of the spotlights off Nicole's bracelets. But the infinitesimal bow of light was not just beaming broadly into the crowd; it was, in fact, a deliberate strand that began with Nicole and ended with Will. It was as if a single glossy thread of spider webbing linked one of them to the other. Like most of the people in the room, Will's eyes were directed toward Nicole, but he seemed wholly unaware of the connection.

The physical phenomenon was very different from what Abby had seen between Evelyn and Michael. And yet, she felt certain—as certain as she could be—that its meaning was exactly the same.

When it was over, Abby pulled Will to the back of the room, where guests were lining up to congratulate the designer. Abby wanted to tell Nicole how much she loved the clothes, but what she wanted even more was to see Nicole and Will together. What would happen if the two of them spoke? Would there be a literal shower of sparks?

As it turned out, the meeting was unremarkable, but there was still a significance to the moment. Abby introduced Will as a "brilliant corporate attorney," which immediately caught Nicole's attention. Even with journalists and celebrities clamoring for her attention, Nicole deliberately stretched out their conversation and made a point of asking Will for his business card. "I have so many legal questions," she said. "Since you're a corporate lawyer, maybe you can help."

When they left, Will smiled as if he'd won the lottery. "Can you imagine if Nicole actually *hired* me?" he said. "Imagine how impressed the partners would be if I brought in a client like her. It would put me on the fast track to partnership!"

Abby couldn't believe that after meeting a woman like Nicole, Will was still thinking about work. "Nicole's really charming, don't you think?" she asked.

"I guess. How much do you think the new company will earn?"

"And she's beautiful, too, right? I mean, really stunning."

"I guess so, but isn't that her job? Models are supposed to look like that."

"Remember, though, she's not *just* a model. She's a designer, too, a businesswoman. Did you know she also studies at NYU? It takes an incredibly impressive person to do all of those things simultaneously."

Will looked confused. "Abby, what's going on?"

"What do you mean? I was only telling you more about her. . . ."

"You sound like you want to set me up with her or something. Nicole is engaged to be married. To your client. The woman is a *model* engaged to a *millionaire*."

"I know that, Will." Abby tried to keep herself from blushing.

"So, why do you sound like my great-aunt Helen trying to fix me up with her canasta partner's granddaughter?" He changed his voice to mimic his aunt. "*Let me tell you, Willie, this one's a real catch. So smart, and such a personality!*"

Abby snorted. "Sorry," she said. "I really admire Nicole, that's all. I can't help it if I think she's great."

Will cupped Abby's chin gently with one hand and kissed her cheek. "You know who else is great? You."

~⌒☙

Abby made a preemptive call to Diane as soon as she walked into her apartment.

"Well?" Diane said. "Did anything interesting happen?"

"Not from a legal perspective," Abby said. "The show was terrific, and the clothes were beautiful. Very different from Victor's classic line."

"And what did Victor say? Did you talk to him?"

"Yes, he was charming as ever, of course. He introduced the collection and spoke about the inspiration—a lot of stuff about combining elegance and comfort. Kind of interesting actually, but not exactly relevant to his prenuptial agreement."

"Okay, good. No mention of another company or collaboration?"

"Nope, nothing. No surprises." *Except for the possibility that Nicole's soulmate may be the guy I'm kind of dating.*

When she got off the phone, Abby went to the kitchen and poured herself a heaping bowl of sugary cereal. Her mother had always banned the stuff, insisting they eat oatmeal or whole wheat toast instead. But when Grandma Sara moved in, the ban was lifted. "Beverly, sweetheart," Abby's grandmother had said, "I can live without the beach and without my mahjong game, but I'll be damned if I'm giving up my Lucky Charms." Fourteen years later, it was still Abby's favorite.

As she spooned the green clovers and pink marshmallow hearts into her mouth, Abby thought back on the events of the evening. Had her grandmother experienced similar visions? *I see what I see, and I know what I know.* How many times had Abby heard her utter those words? But Grandma Sara had never actually described the specifics of what she saw or the details of what she knew. And as far as Abby could tell from reading her journals, she hadn't written about it either.

In spite of the surprise the night had delivered, Abby did not feel disappointed. She was not sorry to know that Will was not meant to be hers. Instead, she was filled with a sense of relief as sweet as the milk at the bottom of her bowl. There was something more, too—a snap of excitement, the electric crackle of possibility. Were Nicole and Will truly a match? She wondered whether she had done enough to set things between the two of them in motion.

Then again, what if she had done too much? A sudden wave of dread coursed through her; the cereal in her stomach turned to lead. It was one thing to ensure that Evelyn Morgan was certain that she wanted to end her marriage. But to encourage a client's fiancée to cheat on him in the middle of negotiations for a multimillion-dollar prenuptial agreement?

There was no question that if anyone found out, Abby's legal career would be over.

THIRTEEN

SARA

1918

A Stab in the Heart

For the first time since her sister got married, Sara Glikman questioned her calling. It wasn't that she doubted her abilities—she was as certain as ever of her gift—it was that the heartbreak of having to give up Nathan had taken the joy out of her occupation.

She wondered if this was part of the reason her father wanted her to marry before making matches. Had he predicted the melancholy that might come? Had he foreseen that her abilities might force her to lie to someone she loved? After a week of sleepless nights, Sara decided to pay a visit to Rabbi Sheinkopf.

She found him in his study at the synagogue, poring over a newspaper. "The War Department has met with the Jewish Welfare Board," he said. He cleared his throat and read out loud. "A double triangle will be placed above the graves of the Jewish soldiers who fall in France, instead of the cross."

"Will they do this for my brother, do you think?" Sara asked.

"I believe so, yes. At least the War Department is finally listening to the Board."

"That is good news."

"Yes, yes." He lowered his glasses and studied Sara's face. "But something else is bothering you. Is it your mother?"

Sara lowered her chin and twisted the fabric of her skirt in her hands. "She doesn't eat enough, and she has bad dreams. She calls out for Joe sometimes in the night."

Rabbi Sheinkopf sighed. "Ach, it is a terrible thing to lose a child. War has made mourners of too many mothers. Your brother-in-law, Aaron, was here this morning. He mentioned that your mother seems to perk up whenever Nathan Weisman comes to visit." The rabbi offered Sara an encouraging smile. "Soon she may have a wedding to look forward to—"

"She won't," Sara interrupted. "Nathan is only a friend."

The rabbi paused to consider her words. "Forgive me then. I misunderstood. When I met him, he seemed quite taken with you."

"He was, but he won't be for much longer. That's why I've come to speak with you. I saw something, Rabbi."

"Ah. Your gift again?"

Sara could no longer hold back her frustration. "Some days, it is no gift at all. Sometimes, it feels more like a curse."

From behind his spectacles, the rabbi's eyes softened. "My dear, you bear a heavy burden, one only you can know the weight of. The only way for you to ease it is to share your suffering with someone else. Perhaps this is why you have come to me." He rearranged himself in his chair and clasped his hands on his lap, waiting patiently for her to speak.

Sara hesitated; her shoulders tensed. She had always been honest with the rabbi. But now, for the first time, she felt embarrassed. She was afraid her story was a foolish one, one that made her sound petty and jealous. Esther was a kindhearted girl who deserved to find love as much as anyone else. Sara should be pleased to be the one to help her find it.

She should be, but she was not, because she wanted Nathan for herself.

Ever since Sara confessed the truth to Esther, she wished that she could take it back. She dreamed of telling Esther that she had been wrong, that she had, in fact, misread the signs. Love was mysterious, after all. It was difficult—if not impossible—to predict. Sara knew that Esther would not object, that she would go along with the new story. Sara could suggest a different young man. She could pick someone handsome and nice enough and convince him that Esther was the girl he should marry. Sara was certain that in the end, none of it would be difficult to do.

Was *this* the real curse of a matchmaker then: to know that most people were so confounded by love that they were likely to listen to almost anyone who professed to have superior knowledge?

Was this why the *shadchanim* insisted that anyone making matches must be married? Did they believe that the temptation to use their influence for personal romantic gain was too great? Sara knew that being married was not a guarantee of good or honest behavior. Even without lying outright to their clients, many of the *shadchanim* she knew were prone to exaggeration, half-truths, and artful manipulation.

But Sara was not like those men. At best, their pairings were based on a mix of good intentions, careful research, and a little bit of luck. At worst, they were based on money alone. Regardless, the goal was always marriage. And marriage was not the same as love.

What the *shadchanim* could never understand was that for Sara, a match was not something to be *made*. Either love existed or it did not. What Sara saw, she saw. What she knew, she knew. Her method was as pure and as unpredictable as the first purple crocus to emerge in the spring.

The rabbi was right—her gift could be a burden. But she could not shirk her obligation. She could not keep Nathan for herself. He was meant to be with Esther, even if he didn't know it yet.

And so, Sara told Rabbi Sheinkopf the entire story. She told him about the shimmering suitcase, her visit to Esther, and her plan. Sara grew teary-eyed when she confessed her fear that she would always be alone. "How will I ever be able to love a man if I'm always worried about what I'll see in his future? I did not see the truth about Nathan until it was already too late."

Rabbi Sheinkopf blinked his eyes. "Too late for what?" he asked, half-teasing. "I would argue the contrary. You discovered the truth at the perfect time. And you learned something valuable in the process."

"I did?"

The rabbi nodded. "Of course. When I met you, Sara, you were ten years old. You were a young girl blessed with the rarest of talents—a gift most of the world could never imagine. Despite your youth, you understood its significance." The rabbi stopped and lowered his voice. "And yet," he mumbled.

"And yet *what*?"

"And yet, my dear, you were still a *child*. A brilliant child, but a child, nonetheless. Of course, a child is no stranger to love. She loves her parents, she loves her family. She might love her teachers or her friends. But a child cannot know what romantic love is. And so, your talent gave you a false impression. Your gift led you to believe that love was always free of pain, always joyful and uncomplicated. It taught you that love comes in a flash of light, that it is always remarkable and instantaneous. But in all of this, I'm afraid, you were very much mistaken.

"You know that my wife died long ago, years before I came to this country. But I never told you how we met, or how she came to be my bride. We had barely spoken before we were married, and our first few months together were far from happy. Of course, it was a different time, but it was almost two years after our wedding that Rivka told me she loved me for the first time."

"What happened?" Sara asked.

"Her brother was forced to put down a cow, and he brought us a piece of meat for our dinner. Rivka did not know how to cook it—we were so poor, and such luxuries were rare." He stopped to smile at the memory. "Our hut was filled with so much smoke that we were forced to eat our meal outside. She left the charred meat on her plate, but I ate my portion and told her it was delicious. In our bed that night, she kissed my cheek and told me how much she had grown to love me." He brushed away the tear that had fallen to his cheek. "On the day my Rivka died, I knew, for certain, that I would never love another woman again."

Sara considered the rabbi's words. "I wish I had been at your wedding," she mused. "I wonder what I would have seen."

The rabbi shrugged. "Who can say? Love is not always a straight, shining line. Sometimes, love is a shady path, full of unpredictable turns."

Nathan was hurt and disappointed but, ultimately, he accepted her decision. She could not reveal the whole of the truth, but she did her best to tell him what she could.

"Joe's death was a terrible blow," she began. "It forced me to examine my priorities."

"I understand, and I want to help. I want to be there for you, and for your family."

"I can't ask that of you," Sara said. "You deserve someone who can love you freely, someone who isn't held back by grief."

"But your grief will fade. Over time, it will get easier." Nathan was pleading with her now.

"You shouldn't wait for that, Nathan. In my heart, I know that you belong with someone else. You'll meet her soon enough, I promise. Don't ask me how, but I know you will. And when you do, you'll understand that I was right."

She hadn't expected it to be so hard. She hadn't expected the words to burn as they escaped her throat. Before he left, Nathan whispered that he would always remember her, that she would always be his first love. Sara felt her heart shiver inside her chest. *What a foolish child I was*, she thought, *to believe that love was a simple thing.*

Her mother was not half as understanding.

"Fool!" Malka Glikman shouted, loud enough for all the neighbors to hear. "That man wanted to marry you!"

"Mama, calm down. You don't know that for sure."

"You think because I'm not the *expert* like you that I don't see?" She wagged her finger in Sara's face. "If it hadn't been for Joseph's death, Nathan would have already asked. He delayed his proposal out of respect!"

"Well, none of that matters now," Sara said. "What's done is done. It's over."

"Why do you have to be so stubborn? When you get back to Barnard, you might change your mind."

"I won't change my mind, Mama. And I'm not going back to Barnard."

Whatever combination of disappointment and anger Sara's mother expressed after the news about Nathan, it was nothing compared to what she unleashed after Sara said she wasn't returning to Barnard.

"*Oy! Oy!* Such a stab in the heart! Will you throw Moishe Raskin's gift in his face? Will you throw away your father's dream? How can you be so ungrateful? What kind of a selfish child did I raise?" Malka Glikman flung her arms in the air and ran from the apartment into the hallway. There, she cried up and down the corridor, tearing at her hair as if it were on fire.

It took three of them—Hindel, Aaron, and Sara—to calm her down enough to pull her back inside. Hindel went to the stove to make tea, while Aaron tugged absently at his beard. All three of Hindel's children began to wail, which only added to the chaos. Aaron led two of them outside to play, while Sara lifted the youngest onto her lap.

"Mama, please. *Please,* sit down. I'm not going to give up college entirely. I'm going to go to Hunter, that's all. Now that Joe is gone, I want to be closer to home."

"So, go to Barnard and live at home! You said that's what a lot of girls do!"

Sara shook her head and sighed. "No, Mama. No. That's not what I want. Besides, if I'm home, I can help Hindel with the children."

"What kind of nonsense are you thinking? We already have Esther to help Hindel."

"Esther won't be around forever, Mama. She'll get married and have a family of her own soon enough. Besides, I never should have gone to Barnard in the first place."

"Says who?"

Sara shrugged. "It's just a feeling I have."

After one or two minutes of quiet, Hindel came out of the kitchen with a glass of tea. "Here you go, Mama," she said, soothingly. "A nice glass of tea, made the way you like." But their mother pursed her lips and pushed it away. "I don't want any tea," she snapped. She turned her attention back to Sara and glared. "Just a *feeling,*" she muttered. "You and your feelings. How are you going to *feel,* I wonder, when that nice young man marries someone else?"

Sara didn't want to think about that. She bounced her tiny niece up and down on her knee. "I'm sorry you're upset, Mama. I truly am. But Nathan Weisman is not my *bashert.* He and I were never meant to be."

FOURTEEN

ABBY

1994

W ill called Abby at work the next morning. "I have a meeting with Nicole tomorrow!" he said. "Can you believe it? I asked one of the senior partners to join us for the meeting—you should have seen his face when I told him about Étoile. He's taking me to lunch this afternoon."

"That's great," Abby said. "Congratulations!"

"She never would have called me if you hadn't brought me to the show."

"It was nothing, I had an extra ticket, that's all."

"It wasn't nothing. It was amazing! If you hadn't talked me up to Nicole like that . . . I mean, without you, I never would have gotten this chance. Alan—he's the partner who's helping me—said business generation is all about synergy. He said I have to keep making connections with people, keep trying to figure out how each person I know might work best with the others. Sorry, I'm rambling . . . I don't need to tell *you,* you already get it. Look at the way you introduced me to everyone last night. I mean—connecting people is like your superpower."

Abby felt a knot in the center of her stomach. "My superpower, huh? Well . . . thanks."

Her morning only got more uncomfortable from there. When her phone rang again, an hour later, it was Evelyn Morgan.

"Why is it that Michael has asked me three times whether you and I have spoken yet?"

"Good morning, Ms. Morgan. Um . . . I'm not . . ."

"Abby, please, spit it out. It's obvious that Michael wants you to talk to me about something. He's never been good at keeping secrets. I'm not angry about it, but I need to know."

"Mr. Gilbert called me on Monday night," Abby admitted. "I tried to tell him it wasn't appropriate for us to speak, but since he doesn't have a lawyer . . ."

"What did he say?"

Abby knew it was no use trying to lie to Evelyn. "He told me you may be going blind—that you think you're going blind, at least. And he asked me to speak to you about reconsidering the divorce. He thinks it's a mistake. He wants to take care of you."

Evelyn released an exhausted sigh. "I know he does. He's a wonderful man. But I can't put him through that, not after everything I've witnessed."

"What do you mean?"

"My father had retinitis pigmentosa. Do you know what that is?"

"No, I'm sorry, I don't."

"It's a genetic condition that causes blindness. My father was a brilliant man, but his vision problems prevented him from fully enjoying his life. By the time he was sixty-five, he was almost completely blind. Despite his health, he agreed to work with me on building my first hotel. He introduced me to all his contacts and helped me line up the investors. But once the Morgan was built, my father gave up. He stopped seeing his friends, and he became deeply depressed. Caring for him became my mother's whole world. Michael reminds me so much of my mother—he has the same sweetness, the same sense of loyalty. He's just as devoted to my happiness as my mother always was to my father's. She had been a very social, vivacious woman, but when my father lost his vision, she stopped living, too. There were no more dinner parties, no more bridge games, no more matinees or trips to the Met. She had no more time for any of the things that used to bring her so much joy. If he couldn't experience it with her, she no longer wanted any part of the outside world. I would never forgive myself if I did that to Michael."

"But don't you think you should see a doctor? What if you have a different diagnosis?"

"The odds seem unlikely, don't you think?"

"Not necessarily, and your father died twenty years ago. Who knows what new treatments might be available now? There's probably been a ton of research."

"Perhaps. But then I'd have to go through all the appointments and tests. My parents cycled through false optimism and then disappoint-ment, over and over. I don't want to go through that roller-coaster ride, and I don't want to put Michael through it either. My mother would get so excited for every new appointment—she was always sure the next doctor would have all the answers. I won't build up Michael's hopes that way, only to break his heart all over again."

"Ms. Morgan, I don't mean to overstep, but . . . when I visited your hotel last week, I saw the way your husband looked at you. The way you looked at him. It's obvious that the two of you still love each other. I don't think you should throw that away without being absolutely sure."

Abby took the silence on the other end of the line as an encouraging sign. Evelyn must have been mulling it over. After a minute or so, her voice returned. "Fine," she relented. "I'll see a doctor. But I don't want Michael to know."

Abby took a swig from the cold cup of coffee on her desk. "Actually," she said. "I know a wonderful ophthalmologist—she's very thorough and very discreet. And if it turns out that you need further tests, I'm sure she can give you the names of some specialists."

"Can she examine me after hours? I don't want anyone to recognize me."

"I'm sure she'll try her best to be accommodating. She's a . . . family friend."

"Fine. I'll wait to hear back from you. But this doesn't mean I'm putting the divorce on hold. I want you to proceed with it as planned."

"Absolutely," Abby promised. "I'll call you back after I speak with Dr. Cooper."

After Evelyn hung up, Abby put her head down on her desk and groaned. How had she gotten herself into such a mess? Somehow, she'd gone from being Evelyn's divorce attorney to some kind of medical concierge. Not to mention what she'd set in motion with Will. Maybe something was wrong with *her* vision, too. Maybe *that* was the explanation for what she'd seen at the fashion show.

As she sat at her desk with her head in her hands, Abby felt a familiar panic surge through her. Whether it was the phone calls with Will and Evelyn Morgan, or the three cups of coffee she'd already downed, she felt a sudden need to be outside, to stretch her legs and get some fresh air. She told Diane's assistant she'd be back in an hour. "If Diane comes looking for me, please tell her I'm on an errand for Evelyn."

Her assistant stared at Abby as if she'd grown another head. "Did you forget? Diane's in Miami, speaking at that conference. She's staying through the weekend—she won't be back until Monday."

"Oh my God, Lisa, I could *kiss* you." A break from Diane's prying questions! A respite from the angry stares! Relief buoyed Abby all the way to the elevator, down seventeen stories, and into the lobby. She whistled as she walked north on Sixth Avenue, breathing in the early lunchtime scents of the city. She waved at the couple selling gyros on the corner and smiled at the falafel man stationed beside them. On the next street up, she passed the baked-potato cart and then the cheerful woman selling honey-roasted nuts. Her feet took her east, toward Fifth Avenue and Madison, then ten more blocks north, to Dr. Cooper's office.

She did not have an appointment, she told the frowning receptionist, but she was happy to wait as long as she had to. "I won't take more than a few minutes of her time," Abby promised. "Please tell her it's Sara Auerbach's granddaughter."

The receptionist's frown softened into a grin. "Sara Auerbach? Oh goodness, what a gem she was! We all loved your grandmother, you know. She was everyone's favorite patient. I'm so sorry for your loss."

"That's very nice of you to say," Abby told her.

"Don't move, okay? Let me tell Dr. Cooper that you're here."

A few minutes later, the receptionist returned. "Dr. Cooper asked if you wouldn't mind waiting. She should be finished with her patient by noon."

"Of course. That's great. Thanks so much." Abby plopped down on the sleek leather sofa and picked up *The New York Times* from that morning. An ad for the new Nicole by Étoile collection took up half of an entire page. Abby threw the paper back on the coffee table and tried to ignore her budding headache.

"Abby! What a nice surprise!" Though Dr. Cooper wore the same sneakers and rumpled white smock, her thick brown hair had been freshly highlighted with streaks of caramel and blond.

Abby stood from her seat. "Hi, Dr. Coop—Jessica. I like your hair!"

The doctor ran her fingers through her newly lightened locks. "Is it too much?" she asked. "I felt like I needed a change, you know?"

"Absolutely. It looks fantastic. I'm sorry to show up unannounced like this. I didn't mean to mess up your schedule. . . ."

"Please don't apologize! I don't see my next patient for another hour. Do you want to grab a quick lunch with me? There's a place with great coffee and sandwiches a few blocks up."

"That sounds perfect."

On Sixty-Seventh Street, they slipped into a small French bakery where women in blue aprons took their orders from behind a lengthy marble counter. Stacks of freshly made sandwiches were displayed behind glass, along with croissants, pastries, and assorted macarons. As they stood in line, Jessica confessed that she came to the bakery a few times a week. "I have a thing for their macarons," she said. "The sandwiches are great, too—the *pan bagnat* is my favorite. It's like a Niçoise salad on a baguette. If you don't like tuna, the one with goat cheese and tomato is delicious."

They carried their sandwiches and drinks to a round bistro table in the back of the room. "I feel like I'm in Paris," Abby said. "This whole place smells like butter and chocolate."

Jessica took a whiff of the air. "It's amazing, right? I love it here." She grinned sheepishly at Abby. "So . . . this is embarrassing, but I have to ask. You haven't found a match for me, have you? I mean, it's totally fine if you haven't. It's just, you know . . ."

Abby struggled to swallow the bite of sandwich she'd taken. She shook her head. "I'm so sorry, Jessica. I didn't mean to get your hopes up like that. I know my grandmother told you I could help you, but the truth is, I don't think I inherited her gift."

"I wouldn't be so sure," Jessica said confidently. Her initial embarrassment was gone. "Remember what you told me about your client and her husband—the one you thought shouldn't end her marriage? The way you sounded when you described them reminded me an awful lot of your grandmother."

"That client is actually the reason I came to see you." Abby looked around the bakery and lowered her voice. "Have you heard of Evelyn Morgan?"

"Of course I have! Wait. Is that your client? *She's* the one with the vision issues?"

"Shh, please," Abby whispered. "It's confidential, but yes. I spoke to Evelyn this morning and she told me her father had some sort of condition—retina . . . retino . . . pigmenta . . ."

"Retinitis pigmentosa?"

"Yes! That's it. Apparently, her father had it, and Evelyn is convinced that she has it, too."

Jessica put down her sandwich. "I'm not sure about that, actually. Retinitis pigmentosa usually presents in early childhood. There are some late-onset cases, but even then . . . Evelyn must be in her sixties now, right?"

"She's sixty-three."

"The disease almost always presents by the patient's mid-forties. Also, women are usually only carriers. It's very rare for them to have it."

"Would you mind telling her all of this? She's agreed to let you examine her."

"Of course. When can she come to the office?"

"She doesn't want anyone to find out she's seeing you. Would you mind staying late one day for her?"

"For Evelyn Morgan? Of course! My nurse and receptionist leave by five, so if she comes at five thirty, I'll be the only one there. I'm free tomorrow, if that fits with her schedule. Just call the office and let me know."

"I can't tell you how much I appreciate this." Now that the awkwardness of discussing Evelyn was behind her, Abby realized how hungry she was. She bit enthusiastically into her sandwich, savoring the salty black olives. "This is *so* good."

She and Jessica were finally beginning to enjoy their lunch when a disruption near the counter caught their attention. A man was in the middle of placing an order when his daughter—about four or five years old—began to cry. As the young girl's sobs echoed off the tile floor, she wrapped her arms around her father's knees and buried her face in the side of his leg. From where Abby sat, the girl was visible, but it was harder to get a good look at the man. Though Abby could only see him from behind, something about him seemed familiar.

"I'm so sorry, *monsieur*," said a woman from behind the counter. "We have no more raspberry macarons." She tried to get the little girl's attention. "The lemon are delicious," the woman said enticingly. "Or, maybe you like pistachio?"

But the little girl only pushed her face deeper into the folds of her father's trousers. He patted her gently on the top of her head and rubbed her back in soothing circles.

When Abby glanced up from her sandwich, the ophthalmologist looked as if she might cry, too. Jessica nodded to the small white bag on the table. "I bought the last raspberry macarons," she whispered. "I'm going to give them to her."

Before Abby could open her mouth to respond, Jessica was already at the counter. She tapped the girl's father on the shoulder. "Excuse me," she said. "I think I can help." Jessica bent down to the little girl and held the white bag out to her. "I have four raspberry macarons," she said. "I think maybe you need them more than I do."

The little girl pulled away from her father, wiped her tears, and widened her eyes.

"You are very kind," Abby heard the stranger say. "But I couldn't let you give up your dessert." Abby turned her head to look, but she still couldn't see the man's face.

Jessica patted her hips and laughed. "I'm sure you would be doing me a favor." She bent down again to speak with the girl. "Want to know why the raspberry macarons are my favorite?" she asked. "Don't tell anyone, but it's because they're *pink*."

The little girl smiled. "Pink is my favorite color!" she said. "Right, Papa?"

The man pointed to his daughter's pink dress and pink hair ribbons before saying something Abby couldn't quite hear. He held out his right arm to shake Jessica's hand, and when their fingers touched . . . there it was.

Not again, Abby thought. It was as if a miniature lightbulb had been tucked between their palms and someone had suddenly flipped the switch. An iridescent glow lit their hands from within and flashed, for a moment, before the handshake ended.

The ophthalmologist and the stranger chatted a minute longer before he caught the attention of one of the women behind the counter. Soon, she handed him a paper bag and he, in turn, passed it to Jessica. When the stranger turned around to lead his daughter out of the store, Abby was finally able to get a glimpse of his face.

She almost choked on her baguette.

Jessica returned to the table then, with a thoroughly satisfied grin on her face. "What an adorable little girl!" she said. "She was so excited for those macarons!" Jessica held up a fresh new paper bag and shook it triumphantly. "Her father was so sweet—he insisted I take these in exchange. He says this bakery makes the best chocolate croissants in the city."

Abby remembered her first meeting with Victor Étoile and the box of croissants he'd brought to the conference room. Frantically, she rubbed her temples. "They do," she said miserably. "Their croissants are delicious."

FIFTEEN

SARA

1921

If You Stay at Home, You Won't Wear Out Your Boots

The crowd at the wedding of the Pickle King's daughter was nothing compared to the crowd at his funeral. On the day Moishe Raskin was laid to rest, nearly five thousand Lower East Siders paid their respects. They waited outside his house and his store. They kept vigil on the steps of his synagogue. A melancholy chorus filled the sidewalks of Rivington Street all the way from the Bowery to the East River, chanting the words of the mourner's *kaddish* into the muggy July air.

When the humorist Sholem Aleichem had died, a hundred thousand people lined the streets to watch the funeral procession pass down Second Avenue. Moishe Raskin, of course, was no Sholem Aleichem, but the people who knew him would always remember the whole-hearted laugh that came with his half-sours. A sentence from a story was easy to forget, but it took only one whiff of Raskin's pickled herring for the memory to live on in a customer's nostrils forever.

When Sara had told him she was transferring to Hunter, she'd worried that he would be insulted. "You're not upset that I'm making a different choice?" she asked.

Moishe Raskin smiled and patted his stomach. "Ho!" he chuckled. "Where would a man like me be without choices?" He counted off flavors on his fingers. "Sweet, spicy, dill, hot, extra sour. Cucumbers, tomatoes, carrots, radishes, onions, cabbage, peppers—the list goes on and on, my dear. Without variety, I'd be out of business."

He never mentioned it after that, but Raskin continued to pay her family's bills. When she told him it was no longer necessary, he pretended he hadn't heard. Sara knew his generosity could not last forever.

And, as usual, she wasn't wrong.

When Moishe Raskin died, his sons inherited the business. Max preferred working at the farm on Long Island, while Herschel took over the day-to-day operations. When he examined the books with his personal accountant, Herschel identified several payments that seemed to have nothing to do with the business. Ida, who had encouraged her father's generosity, begged him to speak with Rabbi Sheinkopf before making any decisions.

"My sister says you have answers for me," Herschel said. He'd appeared early that morning at the rabbi's apartment without an appointment or any notice. The rabbi led Herschel to his study but left the office door purposefully ajar. Inside, the young man continued to press. "What exactly is my father's connection to the Glikman family?"

A few minutes into their conversation, the men heard the scrape of a metal key turning in the rabbi's front door. "It's nothing," Rabbi Sheinkopf assured the young man. "A congregant who helps me with the housekeeping, that's all."

Herschel Raskin settled back into his seat, waiting for the rabbi to continue.

"As I'm sure you will remember," Rabbi Sheinkopf said, "it was Sara Glikman who introduced your sister to her husband. Your father was extraordinarily grateful, especially after what Ida went through with her first engagement. He considered Sara to be the *shadchanteh* for the pair."

"But Ida has been married for over five years! This is no *shadchanus gelt*—it sounds more like some kind of . . . extortion!"

The rabbi's mouth fell open. "Extortion? What would make you say such a thing?"

"Because what you describe makes no sense, Rabbi. Why would my father continue these payments? A single fee is all that would have been required. The Glikman girl must have been playing some game."

"I can assure you that there were no games of any kind. You've seen where the family lives—it's certainly no luxury building. Six adults and three children living in three small rooms. If there was anything improper going on, your father would have paid for a more elegant apartment."

"Maybe . . ."

"Sara's eldest brother was killed in the war. Before that, her father passed away. Moishe was trying to help the girl—to supplement the family's income so she could go to college."

"From what I hear, she graduated in June."

"She did."

"Well then, she achieved her goal. Since you know the family so well, I leave it to you to let them know that my father's arrangement will be terminated."

"And what about the two boys? Eli took over the delivery job and George is on Max's farm for the summer."

"Tell them to look for other work. I don't know if I can trust them."

Rabbi Sheinkopf steadied his voice, but it was difficult to suppress his disappointment and rage. "Herschel, I urge you to reconsider. Think of the effect this will have on the family. Can't you let the boys keep their jobs, at least? They're hard workers, both of them. Ask anyone."

Herschel sighed. "Max can keep George on the farm this summer, but when autumn comes, I don't want them in my employ."

The rabbi tugged at his beard in frustration. He saw Herschel out, said his goodbyes, and then walked quietly into his kitchen. Sara stood frozen in the center of the room, having abandoned preparations for the rabbi's breakfast. An egg was on the counter, waiting to be boiled, and the teakettle sat neglected on the stove.

"You heard?" the rabbi asked, his face etched in a frown.

Sara nodded. "Every word."

Shortly before Sara graduated from Hunter, Esther had married Nathan Weisman. The couple moved to the Bronx to be near Nathan's family and were expecting their first child that winter. Once Esther left, Sara filled in, cooking and tidying the rabbi's apartment.

In the afternoons, she looked for a job. After earning her degree with high honors in math, she tried to find a position where she could utilize her skills. Math, she had learned, was the best antidote to matchmaking. There was no wondering or guesswork, only tangible figures. Whenever she was tempted by a flash of light, she turned her thoughts instead to the numbers on her page. Her matchmaking instincts were still there, of course, but she wanted to avoid the *shadchanim*. She was still trying desperately to keep her promise, the one she had made to her father long ago.

She visited her friend Jacob at his new eyeglass store to ask whether, perhaps, he needed a bookkeeper. Tunchel & Son had been open for a year, but Jacob was still building his reputation in the neighborhood. He offered to hire her one day a week. "I wish I could give you more work," he said. "But, for now, at least, that's all we need."

Still, one day of work was better than none, and Sara was grateful for the job. She loved walking into the tidy store, with its modern glass cases and meticulous displays. Baruch Tunchel and Miryam worked behind the counter, while Jacob performed eye exams upstairs. There was no business office, per se, but Sara worked at a table in the rear of the store, going through the receipts, tallying expenses, and updating the ledgers once a week. Most of the time, she ignored the customers, but every once in a while, someone caught her attention.

There was the morning, for instance, when the sudden stench of onions and potatoes overwhelmed her senses to such an extent that she was forced to look up from her ledger for the cause. A gangly young man in a dark green apron had burst frantically through the wide shop doors and was standing in the center of the room with a pitiful expression on his face. Miryam began to offer her assistance, but before she could finish, he dropped a pair of spectacles on the counter between them. "The left lens is smashed," he groaned. "And the frame is all twisted. Please, can you help me? Can they be repaired?" Baruch Tunchel stepped forward to inspect the damage and tutted as he held the eyeglasses in his hand. "There's not much left here to work with," he said. "Your best bet is to get a new pair."

"My husband performs thorough eye examinations," Miryam told him. "It's important that you get an accurate prescription."

"But I have no time for an examination!" the man shouted, and Miryam Tunchel took a few steps back.

"I'm sorry," he stammered. "I apologize. Please . . . I work at the knishery over on Delancey, and I'm needed back soon for the lunchtime rush. My father will kill me if I'm gone for too long, but I told him I couldn't work without my glasses. I dropped them and stepped on them—can you believe it? Please, is there anything you can do?"

Miryam's eyes softened. "Papa," she said to her father-in-law, "can you show this customer some of your old ready-made spectacles? See if any of them will do for now?"

The young man clapped his hands together. "Thank you! The knish store closes at five o'clock. Could I—do you think I could come back then for an exam? My eyes—they've been bothering me quite a bit as of late."

Miryam nodded politely. "Of course. We stay open tonight until six o'clock. You can borrow a temporary pair for now, and then Jacob, my husband, will fit you properly."

Baruch Tunchel brought over a box of wire spectacles left over from his pushcart days. The young man tried each one on in a frenzy. When he shoved the fifth pair onto his face, he smiled and laughed. "These will do nicely! Thank God!" He laid a few coins on top of the counter, but Miryam pushed the pile away. "Come back before six and we'll work it out then."

The man nodded his head and hurried out of the shop. "Thank you!" he called again from outside. "I will be back before six o'clock! I will see you soon!"

Miryam smiled and waved through the glass, but her father-in-law was far less pleased. "How can you be so sure he'll return?" he grunted.

Miryam shrugged. "If he doesn't, we know exactly where to find him," she said. "The knishery on Delancey Street."

"Humph," Baruch Tunchel grunted again. "I'm going to open the door to let in some air. That *meshuggeneh* brought the whole kitchen with him."

Curiosity kept Sara late at the store until the pungent man returned. This time, along with the greasy green apron, he wore a vaguely sheepish grin. "I didn't even introduce myself earlier." He held out his hand to Miryam. "Morty Finkel. Thank you again for your help this morning." He tapped the spectacles resting on his nose. "These little beauties saved me today."

Miryam smiled at him and pointed toward the stairs. "My husband is waiting for you," she said. "I'm glad the spectacles were helpful, Mr. Finkel. But you should have a real examination. Otherwise, you might end up with terrible headaches. Or your vision could worsen from the strain."

Morty nodded obediently and made his way up the narrow stairway. In the meantime, Baruch Tunchel reached into his pocket and placed Morty's damaged spectacles on the counter. Baruch had removed the broken glass and molded the frame back into shape. "They're missing a lens," the old man said. "But I thought he might want to have them back."

At half past five the front door opened again, and a woman approximately Sara's age bounded energetically into the store. She tilted her head as she moved farther inside and sniffed the air with obvious interest. Miryam noted the woman's gesture and apologized for the unusual aroma. "We've just had a customer from the knish shop," she said. "I hope the smell doesn't bother you."

The young woman smiled and twirled one reddish curl around the tip of her pointer finger. "The knish shop?" she asked. "Do you know which one?"

"I wasn't aware there were two," Miryam said.

"Oh yes," the young woman said earnestly. "They're directly across the street from each other—a few blocks west, on Delancey Street. I prefer the knishes from Klein's myself."

"I can't say I've visited either," Miryam admitted.

Baruch Tunchel chimed in from the corner. "*Ach,* all this talk is making me hungry."

"It's no wonder," the young woman said, grinning. "It's getting late and I don't want to keep you—I'm here to pick up a pair of spectacles for my father." She cleared her throat. "His name is Abe Klein." She winked.

Miryam laughed. "That explains your personal preference then! Let me go fetch them for you, Ms. Klein. I won't be more than a minute."

While she waited, the young woman walked the length of the shop, scanning the eye charts and examining the displays. When she saw Morty Finkel's broken glasses on the counter, she wrinkled her nose. "I hope these aren't for sale," she said.

"No, no," Baruch told her amiably. "A customer stepped on them—a real *klutz*."

"That explains it." She reached for the glasses, arched a single eyebrow, and placed them jokingly on her own face. "How do I look?" she asked, striking a pose.

The flash of light that burst forth from the frames caused Sara to look up from her ledger book. She sucked in a breath and put her head back down.

Baruch chuckled and tapped the counter. "On such a pretty face, I wouldn't even notice they were broken."

"What a sweet thing to say!" Miss Klein answered. "I hope you're still hungry tomorrow, Mr. Tunchel, because I'm going to bring you the best knish you ever tasted."

That night Sara lay awake in the dark, debating what to do about what she had seen. The bills were coming faster than ever now, and she knew only one way to make them stop. Having made good on the first of her promises to her father, she was no longer sure she could keep the second. "I finished school, Papa," she whispered to herself. "But I do not think I will ever marry, and I can't postpone my calling forever."

When Esther and Nathan Weisman had wed, Sara refused to accept payment of any kind. Other than the rabbi and Esther herself, she had spoken to no one about the match. Her mother and siblings suspected, of course, but she never revealed the specifics to them. Still, the wedding of Sara Glikman's former beau to Rabbi Sheinkopf's beloved niece was too much of a coincidence for the *shadchanim* to ignore. The wedding had resurrected their suspicions about her, and they had revived their campaign of silent harassment.

Shternberg's nephew and Grossman's sons seemed to be lurking everywhere now—skulking on her corner when she left in the mornings; hanging about the market on her shopping days; following her home from the rabbi's apartment and glaring at her from across the street. She told herself it was best to ignore them, to stay inside as much as possible rather than to risk their intimidating stares. When she was little and would run to a library twenty blocks away instead of visiting the branch closer to home, her father would say: *Why push so hard, Sara? Why look so far away? Better to stay close and be satisfied with what is here. Better to stay home and help your mother and sister.* When Sara had asked why, her father had looked sad, and when she pressed him further, he had murmured something quietly under his breath.

If you stay at home, you won't wear out your boots.

But as the days wore on, and the stack of bills grew higher on her mother's bedside table, Sara felt a restlessness stirring from deep within. It woke her one night with a vicious start, like a splintering in the center of her chest. It was a break so sharp and blatant and real that it made her sit up and gasp for air. At first, she thought it was her vow—the promise to her father she could no longer keep.

But then, as her heart quieted itself, she realized what had finally shattered was her fear.

Since she was thirteen years old, Sara had followed the *shadchanim*'s rules. For eight years, she had molded herself according to the whims of a covetous group of unfeeling old men. She had let them bully and intimidate her—not only into abandoning her gift, but into forfeiting a lucrative livelihood as well. Everyone she knew—even those who loved her most—had taught her that this was the only way to survive, that conformity and submission to ancient traditions was, in the end, for her own good.

And so, for eight years she had hidden her talents, squirreled them away like so many nuts in an endless, sunless, frozen winter. She had made herself small. She had cowered in corners. She had allowed the *shadchanim* to erase who she was. And what was the result of all that obedience? Her family was hungry. Her sister, exhausted. Her brothers humiliated and unemployed. They lived together in a place that could barely contain them—without privacy, pleasure, or modern plumbing. She was lonely and unfulfilled. What did she have left to lose?

In one swift motion, she flung off her blanket, sprung up from the bed, and threw back her shoulders. She would wait no longer to accept her vocation; she had already waited long enough. She was twenty-one years old, a woman fully grown. She'd been blessed with a gift the *shadchanim* could not fathom, and she knew that if she used it, she would succeed. Those men could not see what Sara saw. They could not know what Sara knew. They chased matches like children chasing pennies in the street, but her matches bound one soul perfectly to another. Her matches were made of light and love, and *that* was why they were so afraid.

She was done pretending to be less than those men. Done burying her talents to appease their egos. Done waiting until she found a husband before she allowed herself to live. She would advertise in the papers. She would hang out a sign. She would be paid a fair fee so that she could provide for her family. Her mind drifted back to her sister's wedding, when Rabbi Sheinkopf had explained to her what she was. *You are a matchmaker, Sara Glikman. A* shadchanteh *for this strange, new world.*

The time had come for her to embrace her calling and to free herself from old-world constraints. It did not matter that she was a young woman, that she was unwed, or that her methods were strange. She would no longer hide from the flashing sparks that danced around the edges of her sight.

From now on, she would pursue the light with her eyes wide open, braced for the sun.

SIXTEEN

ABBY

1994

After what she'd seen at the bakery, Abby was grateful for the walk back to her office. She needed time to clear her head and to convince herself that she wasn't losing her mind. First Will and Nicole. Now Jessica and Victor. Was the universe playing some sick joke? Or was the continued stress of Abby's job causing her to see things that weren't there?

In the afternoon, she spoke with Evelyn Morgan to confirm the eye appointment. "I'll meet you there tomorrow," Evelyn said, which Abby found more than a little presumptuous. Still, Abby didn't have the heart to make her client go to the ophthalmologist alone.

Victor called a short while later. "I understand Diane is away," he said, "but I have some real estate documents she wanted—valuations for the Madison Avenue building, the New York atelier, and my apartment in Paris. Are you free tomorrow morning to pick those up? Nine o'clock at my apartment?"

Abby had so many questions she wanted to ask, all of them regarding what she'd seen at the bakery. But she forced herself to stick to the matter at hand. "Of course, Mr. Étoile. I'll see you then."

For the rest of the day, Abby was useless. No matter how much she tried to focus on work, she couldn't stop thinking about the designer and the ophthalmologist together. As a couple, Nicole and Will made sense. They were both young and ambitious, both business-oriented, driven. Instead of going to clubs with the other models, Nicole preferred staying home to watch *Star Trek* reruns. "Can you believe she thinks Jean-Luc Picard was better than Captain Kirk?" Will joked. Nicole may have been a fashion model, but behind her beautiful, semi-famous face, she was as much of a nerd as Abby's soon-to-be ex-boyfriend.

But Victor Étoile and Dr. Cooper? Abby was no fashion plate, but she was sure that even she cared more about fashion than Jessica. What would Victor Étoile talk about with a woman who was happiest wearing frumpy lab coats and who couldn't be bothered to know the difference between satin and suede? What would a woman of science like Jessica discuss with a man whose entire existence was focused on something as unscientific as fashion?

Abby left work early and walked home, eager to escape her spiraling thoughts. She could feel the sweat dripping down her back, causing her silk blouse to stick to her skin. When she got home, she changed into shorts and a T-shirt, flopped on the couch, and called her sister.

Hannah had chosen college in California because she'd wanted to get as far as possible from the never-ending tensions between their parents. After school, she had taken a tech job in San Francisco, and, as far as Abby could tell, she was never coming back.

Though both sisters were close with their mother, it was Hannah who spoke more regularly with their father. As she had explained on more than one occasion, "I'm happy to have a relationship with him. I just prefer to do it from three thousand miles away." Abby wondered whether she would speak to her father more often if she, too, lived across the country. It would be easier to forgive his canceled dinner plans and forgotten coffee dates if there was no opportunity to make them in the first place. Somehow, after all these years, Abby's father still managed to disappoint her. What was more, she suspected that he had never forgiven her accusation of being stingy with Beverly during the divorce.

Abby dialed Hannah's work number and waited for it to ring. "Hey, Han, it's me," she said.

"Abby! Are you okay? You never call me this early."

"That's not true!"

"Yes, it is. You never call until you get home from the office."

Abby checked her watch. It was five thirty in New York, which meant it was only two thirty for Hannah. "Yeah, well, I *am* home actually. I left work early today, that's all."

"You left work early? Is something wrong? Are you sick?"

"I'm fine." Abby paused. "You know how Grandma left me those journals?"

"Oh my God. Did you find something scandalous? Did Grandma have another husband? Does Mom have some sibling she doesn't know about?" Hannah's voice grew giddier with every question.

"Hannah, stop! What's wrong with you? Grandma did not have another husband!"

"Bummer. We could use a few more cousins. So, was there anything interesting? How could you even read them? Isn't Yiddish written in Hebrew letters?"

"The first journal started out in Yiddish, but it switched to English pretty quickly. There isn't much personal writing, though. They aren't diaries. They're actually lists, some of matches that Grandma made and others of people she wanted to set up. I found a few newspaper articles, too. Remember how she used to tell us about the Pickle King?"

Hannah started to laugh. "Of course I do! Wait, did Grandma write about him?"

"Yes! I found an article about his daughter's wedding. And get this—it's from *The New York Times*!"

"Wow. I guess she was telling us the truth—I could have sworn she was making up half of what she told us."

"I know, me too," Abby agreed. "But it turns out, those stories were based on real people. Speaking of which . . . remember that doctor I was talking to at the funeral? The ophthalmologist who came up to me before we left the cemetery?"

"I think so. Why?"

Abby told her sister the story of Jessica's grandparents. "I read about them in one of the journals. Her grandfather sold eyeglasses from a pushcart before he went to optometry school. Grandma introduced him to his wife."

"For real?"

"Yup. And when Grandma found out Dr. Cooper wasn't married, she tried to make a match for *her,* too."

Hannah whistled. "That's insane. I mean, Grandma was ninety-four years old. I thought her matchmaking days were long behind her."

"I haven't even told you the weirdest part."

Hannah sucked in a breath. "Is the ophthalmologist related to us? Did Grandma have a guy on the side after all?"

"Hannah! Grandma did *not* have a guy on the side." Abby laughed in spite of herself. "But Dr. Cooper did tell me something else. It freaked me out, actually. And ever since then, things have been weird. Like, I'm having these *flashes* about people I meet. About my clients and Will. I can't even describe it."

"What did Dr. Cooper tell you?"

Abby walked into her kitchen and opened her refrigerator. She pulled out a half-empty bottle of Chardonnay, pulled out the stopper, and took a long swallow.

"Abby? Are you there? What did she say?"

Abby took a second swallow straight from the bottle and let the wine trickle down the back of her throat. "Dr. Cooper thinks I could be a matchmaker, too."

The next morning, Abby arrived at Victor's apartment a few minutes before nine o'clock. She assumed he would hand her the appraisals and dismiss her, but when the designer opened the door, he invited her inside. He was dressed as impeccably as always, but a pair of dark circles bloomed beneath his eyes.

"I don't want to keep you from your work," she said. But Victor wanted her to stay.

"I have a few questions," he began. "Please, may I offer you a cup of coffee?" His voice was soft and melancholy, lacking its usual confidence and flair.

Abby panicked—she knew absolutely nothing about real estate valuations, and she didn't want to embarrass herself, or the firm, in the process. But as Victor waited for her answer, she got the feeling that his questions had nothing to do with the appraisals. It wasn't as if she could refuse. "Of course," she said. "I'd love some coffee."

She followed him into the dining room, where two china place settings had been laid out. Victor poured piping-hot coffee from a silver carafe and gestured to a plate of chocolate croissants. "Please," he said. "Help yourself." He plucked a croissant from the pile. "The last time you were here, you mentioned to Nicole that many of your friends are getting married."

Abby nodded. "Yes, that's right."

"And these friends of yours . . . do they tell you much about what they are planning for their weddings?"

"Oh God, absolutely. They never shut up about it."

"What exactly do they talk about?"

"Which dress to pick, how they want to do their hair, what the song for their first dance should be. The food, the band, how many bridesmaids they want. Where they're registering, what their bouquet should look like. It goes on and on. They're all obsessed."

"I see." Victor stared into his coffee cup.

Had she said something wrong? "I'm sorry, I must be boring you. You probably hear about all of this from Nicole."

He looked up from his coffee and shook his head. "No," he said softly. "I do not. Nicole does not talk about the wedding. Everything you describe—the excitement, the *obsession*? Nicole speaks that way about her new clothing line, she speaks that way about her classes and the business. When she talks about her new designs, her eyes light up. She smiles, she laughs . . . she is radiant. But when I ask about the wedding—or any of those details, she tells me she would rather have me decide. She says she doesn't have time to discuss it."

"I'm sure it's only because she's been so busy."

"And your friends—are they not busy as well?"

Abby thought about her friends who had gotten engaged most recently. One was in the first year of her surgery residency at Columbia, one worked ridiculous hours at a law firm downtown, and the third traveled constantly as a consultant for McKinsey. She tried to look Victor straight in the eye. "They're very busy women," she admitted.

"And yet, they still find time to 'obsess.'"

"Yes," she answered honestly. "I guess they do."

Victor smiled sadly. "Thank you for indulging my questions, Abby."

She wasn't sure what else to say. A world-famous designer—a man she barely knew—had just revealed a painful and personal truth. She thought back to the way Diane had first described him. Diane had painted Victor as a difficult man, someone with an enormous ego. But from everything Abby had observed, Diane's description was far from the truth. "May I ask *you* a question?" Abby said. "I know you have children, but I don't know anything about them. How old are they? What are their names?"

Victor smiled. "I have two little girls. Isobel is eight and Chloé is four. I picked Chloé up early from preschool yesterday so we could go to the bakery together."

"That must have been a treat for you both," Abby said.

"It almost ended with a tantrum," he confessed. "But a very kind woman came to our rescue. She gave Chloé the last raspberry macarons." Victor's expression turned suddenly wistful. "She had a remarkable way with my daughter," he said. "She was lovely, actually." His voice trailed off for a moment before he caught himself. "Goodness," he said, glancing at his watch. "It's getting late, and I'm afraid I must go. Thank you, Abby, for your honesty."

"You're welcome," she said. "I'm sorry I couldn't be more helpful."

He put his hand on top of his heart. "Honesty is always helpful," he said.

For the second day in a row, Abby found herself in Dr. Cooper's reception area. While she waited for Jessica to examine Evelyn Morgan, she studied the collection of black-and-white photographs on display. She returned to the picture of the eyeglass store and then moved on to the one of Jacob's father staring at the camera from behind his pushcart. In addition to the two familiar photographs, there were plenty of others she hadn't seen yet. Some were formal family portraits, while others were more candid shots. A few were street scenes from the Lower East Side—tenement buildings and laundry lines. Closest to the reception desk was a cluster of small photographs that had been taken of store awnings: a men's clothier and a cigar shop. A barbershop and a bakery. The last photograph showed a tailor's sign, with a small, striped awning tucked behind it. When Abby examined it more closely, she could just make out the words "Klein's Knishes." She stepped back from the photograph and laughed. She wished her sister were there to see it.

Back in high school, *Romeo and Juliet* had been required reading for every freshman. Hannah inherited Abby's copy, but she struggled with the language and the story. "Shakespeare is the worst," she said to Abby and her grandmother over dinner one night. "Honestly, why do people still read this stuff?"

"*Ach*, that story," their grandmother said. "What a heartache! The problem was the families—terrible people. There wasn't enough fighting in the world? They had to fight over a wedding, too? Believe me, I've dealt with family feuds before. If Romeo and Juliet had a good matchmaker, I'm telling you, both of them would have survived."

Abby and Hannah burst out laughing.

Grandma Sara was offended. She silenced them both with a furious stare. "You think I don't know what I'm talking about? Believe me, I do. I made a match between two families who hated each other like they were at war. And still, I succeeded."

"Why did they hate each other?" Hannah asked.

"Business, *mameleh*. Always business. Finkel's Knishes opened first, with a line of people out the door. For five cents you got a piece of heaven, a delicious knish, the best you ever had. Then, Klein's Knishes opened next—a few months later, across the street. Klein's knishes were also delicious, and he sold them for only *four* cents apiece. Like I said, it was war."

Hannah was even more intrigued. "So, how were you able to make the match?"

Grandma Sara lifted her chin and made a gentle scoffing sound. "*Pfft*. The same way I made all the others. I paid attention, I took a risk. I saw what I saw, and I knew what I knew."

After forty-five minutes, Jessica led Ms. Morgan back into the waiting room. The hotelier wore a loose silk shift, a Mobe pearl necklace, and a pair of oversized dark glasses. With the glasses on, it was impossible for anyone to properly read her expression.

"How did it go?" Abby asked. For the last fifteen minutes, she'd been pacing the waiting room, fidgeting with her hands, and trying to stay calm.

"Very well," Jessica said. "I dilated Ms. Morgan's pupils so that I could better examine her retina. There are, in fact, pigment deposits, which are the cause of her vision loss."

Abby turned toward Ms. Morgan. "Does that mean you have your father's disease?"

"I don't think so," Jessica interrupted. "The onset of the symptoms is very late for that, and retinitis pigmentosa rarely affects women. Luckily, we had a long discussion about Ms. Morgan's medical history."

"I don't like to talk about my rheumatoid arthritis," Evelyn admitted. "I've always kept my medical conditions private. When you're a woman in a man's business like I am, your competitors will seize on any kind of issue to gain an advantage or to paint you as weak. I broke my leg once in the early eighties, and I almost lost out on a new hotel because of it. My rival at the time told all the investors that I suffered from a debilitating orthopedic condition."

"It's a good thing I dragged the information out of her," Jessica said. "Ms. Morgan takes Plaquenil for her arthritis—a drug which has been known to cause pigment deposits."

Abby glanced at Evelyn again, searching her face. "But that's fantastic news, isn't it? If you stop taking the Plaquenil, will your vision go back to normal?"

"It may not be quite that simple," Evelyn said. "But Dr. Cooper has given me a great deal of hope. She's recommended a retinologist, and I will consult with my rheumatologist tomorrow." Evelyn reached for Abby's hand. "I know I've been stubborn," she admitted. "But I want to thank you for convincing me to come today."

Abby felt herself blush. "It was nothing," she murmured.

"I disagree. I've had countless lawyers over the years. Some were brilliant, some were abysmal, but none of them possessed your power of persuasion. You, my dear, are the only one who ever made me do something I did not want to do."

"She's a loveable *nudge!*" Jessica chimed in, and Abby's cheeks grew even redder.

"It's a personality flaw," Abby said.

"Not at all," Evelyn Morgan said. She lowered her sunglasses just enough so that her eyes peered at Abby over the top of the frame. "What you have, Abby, is a gift."

Though it was almost seven o'clock, Abby returned to the office. She needed to get in a few more billable hours, especially since she'd left so early the day before. She was in the middle of writing a memo for Diane when Will called to cancel their Friday night plans.

"I'm so sorry," he repeated, as if he'd never broken a date before. "Nicole won't be done with her shoot until six, and she asked if I could go over some new licensing agreements. Believe me, I wish I could tell her no."

Abby couldn't help wondering whether Will and Nicole would get around to something more than business, but she kept that to herself. "It's not a problem," she said. She'd been planning to have "the talk" with Will tomorrow—the one where she intended to explain that the two of them would be better off as friends. It was a conversation she dreaded having, and she was happy enough to put it off.

"Are you mad?" he asked.

"Not at all! I completely understand. Bringing in a client like Nicole is a really big deal. You can't turn down a meeting with her."

The firm's receptionist, Tom, tapped on Abby's door. "Hey," he said, waving an envelope in his hand. "This just came for you by messenger."

The envelope was made of thick ivory paper, with Victor Étoile's name embossed on the back. When she pulled out the flat, ivory card, two tickets fell onto her desk.

Abby,

Thank you again for your visit this morning. I enclose two tickets for tomorrow evening's New York Shakespeare Festival production. My sincere apologies for the late notice, but I do hope to see you there.

Kind regards,
Victor Étoile

Tom nearly passed out when he saw the tickets. "Lucky!" he said to her. "I'm dying to go, but I never have time to wait on those lines."

The Shakespeare Festival had always been one of Abby's favorite New York traditions. The program staged two plays every summer at the Delacorte Theater, an open-air theater in the middle of Central Park. Tickets were technically free, distributed on the day of the performance. But because people lined up hours beforehand, getting tickets was a nearly impossible task. Some people bought resold tickets at exorbitant prices; some paid others to stand in line for them. Abby knew there had to be other ways, especially if one was a generous donor to the Public Theater, the nonprofit company that produced the shows. Abby couldn't say how Victor came by his tickets, but she was certain he hadn't stood on line for them.

Abby had been to the festival twice before—once when she was a teenager and a second time in law school—but she hadn't been back for several years.

On the bus ride home, she thought about the extra ticket and who she wanted to invite. Will would be busy with Nicole at their meeting (perhaps that was why Victor had offered Abby the seats?), and her mother was still out of town for work. Abby was trying to decide which girlfriend to ask when the bus reached her stop, and it was time to get off.

She remained undecided as she swapped her work clothes for a pair of shorts, as she searched her grandmother's journals for an entry about a young woman named Klein, and as she ran her fingers over the yellowed newspaper clippings that she discovered between two of the faded pages—advertisements for Finkel's and Klein's Knishes.

Not until she hung up with the deli on the corner after ordering a pastrami on rye and a potato knish did Abby finally make up her mind.

Everything about the decision was reckless. Her choice of companion was foolish, at best. The evening would surely be messy and awkward and odd, and she was probably going to regret it for a long time to come. She was certain her grandmother would approve.

For the first time ever in her life, Abby was going to try making a match.

SEVENTEEN

SARA

1921

Some of the Best Shoemakers Go Barefoot

> Finkel's Knishes
> The Best Knish in New York
> 5 cents each
> 146 Delancey Street

> **KLEIN'S KNISHES**
> BETTER THAN THE BEST
> Quality Ingredients, Inside & Out
> ONLY 4 CENTS EACH
> 151 Delancey Street

From now on, Sara Glikman decided, she would go about her work in a professional manner. No more hiding what she was doing. No more pretending she wasn't a *shadchanteh*. And, most importantly of all, no more working for free.

She'd been keeping secret records of her matches for years—scribbling down details in two mismatched journals, starting from when Hindel first married Aaron. Sara told no one about her writing; she had tucked the journals deep in the bottom of the chest that her family had brought from their home in Kalarash. Now, with the last of her spare coins, Sara purchased a third notebook. She had made up her mind to chronicle her endeavors, to keep careful records of her future successes. When the story of Ida's wedding was printed, Sara began saving newspaper clippings as well, tucking them between her handwritten pages as further proof of her efforts. With any luck, she would need a fourth notebook soon, and then—God willing—a fifth after that. Her journals, she decided, would be her personal archive—one of hope and of love.

She would begin by visiting Miss Klein, the spirited young woman from Tunchel's eyeglass store. In an attempt to avoid the "lunchtime rush," she made her way early to Klein's Knishes. Delancey Street was already crowded—packed with shoppers and peddlers of all kinds. As Sara passed by the open door of the cigar shop, the tang of smoke and tobacco hit her nose like a slap. Coughing, she made her way across the street, toward the tailor's shop whose windows were filled with signs handwritten in both English and Hebrew.

Past the tailor's shop, the morning sun fell across a bright yellow-and-white-striped awning. Even from twenty feet away, the smell of warm dough, butter, and potatoes beckoned Sara inside. The bell on the door rang as she entered, and the familiar young woman from the eyeglass store greeted her from behind the counter. "Welcome to Klein's," the girl said with a smile. "One knish, or do you want two?"

"One please," said Sara, caught off guard. She'd meant to begin her career by collecting money—not by being the one to pay. But she wasn't quite sure how to start, so she pushed four pennies toward Miss Klein, accepting a steaming hot knish in return. "My name is Sara Glikman," she offered. "Do you mind me asking—what is your name?"

"Beryl Klein," Miss Klein told her. "Did you want something else, Sara Glikman? If you don't mind my saying so, you look nervous."

Sara tried to brush off the young woman's words. She had never had to sell her services before. "I'm not nervous," she corrected. "I'm excited."

"Excited, you say? And why is that?"

Sara cleared her throat to buy some time. She was going about the matter all wrong—she should have asked to speak to Beryl's parents first. "Are your parents here?" she asked politely. "I'd like to meet with all of you together."

"My father is drunk and sleeping it off. My mother is busy in the back. What's this about? Are you looking for a job? Are you selling something?"

"Neither," said Sara. "Well, not exactly."

"Look," said Beryl. "You seem nice enough. But I have a mountain of potatoes to peel, and my mother will be yelling for me any minute. Why don't you just say what you want, and then I'll see if I can help."

"I'm a matchmaker," Sara blurted out. "And I have a proposition for you."

Beryl's eyes widened. "You're very young. And I've yet to meet a *shadchan* without a beard."

"Yes." Sara nodded. "But I know what I'm doing. I've made dozens of matches—fifty, at least."

"And yet, I've never heard of you," Beryl said.

"The neighborhood *shadchanim* don't approve of me. They don't want me taking away their business. For years, I tried to pacify them—I worked in secret and I took no payment. But now, with my family's debts piling up, I can't go on that way any longer. I don't have the luxury to worry now about what the *shadchanim* think or say."

Beryl looked at Sara with newfound admiration. "No one wanted my mother to open this shop," she admitted. "The landlords kept asking where her husband was, and he was never sober enough to meet them. But my mother is smart and she works hard—harder than any man I've known." Beryl rested her hands on both hips. "As far as I'm concerned," she said, "we women can do any job we want. Why shouldn't you be a matchmaker if you want to? Especially if you're good at it."

"Thank you," Sara said.

"Don't thank me, yet. I support your choice of occupation, Sara, but I'm afraid I have no personal use for it."

"I understand," Sara said. "But I would not have sought you out without good cause. I make love matches, Beryl. I swear. And I came to tell you that I have found your *bashert*."

Beryl threw her head back and laughed until the tears poured down her cheeks. "I'm sorry," she said, wiping her eyes with her apron. "But how could you know who my soulmate is?"

"I can't explain it," Sara admitted. "But I've been doing this since I was ten years old, and I haven't been wrong yet. I see what I see. I know what I know. Please, all I ask is that you give me a chance. If you don't like the man, you'll tell me so. What could be the harm in that?"

Beryl bit down on her lower lip, considering the strange proposal. "You say you've already found him then?"

"I have. Though your match is not without complications."

"What do you mean, complications? Is he married? Divorced? Is he an old man?"

"No, no, nothing like that at all. He's young and handsome. He's never been married. His family has a successful business."

"Well, what is it then? What's the problem? Why do you speak to me in riddles?"

"Because the man is Morty Finkel, from the store across the street."

This time, Beryl did not laugh. Her lips curled into an angry frown. When she spoke again, her voice was low, as if she did not want to be overheard. "What kind of trick is this?" she whispered. "Who have you spoken with? What do you know?" She reached across the counter and grabbed Sara's wrist. "Tell me now, or you'll regret it."

With great effort, Sara yanked her hand away. "I did not mean to upset you," she said. "I'm only telling you the truth."

"But how, *how*? I've told *no one*. Not even Morty himself."

Sara felt a buzzing of joy in her chest. "So, you already feel it? You already know?" It was her turn to admire Beryl now.

"Of course I do. But how do *you* know?"

Sara tried to explain herself then, to tell Beryl a bit of what she had seen. "The feelings come to me unannounced. I can't predict them. I can't control it."

Beryl's eyes were full of sympathy. "It is for you as it was for me. I can't control my emotions either. If I could, I wouldn't fall in love with a man I could never hope to marry."

"Why would you say such a thing?"

"You said it yourself—there are complications. Our families are practically at war. The Finkels have hated us from the very first day we opened this shop. My mother wanted a store closer to the Bowery, so as to avoid a rivalry. But none of the other landlords would rent to her. This was the only place she could find."

Sara nodded. "I understand."

"And it isn't only that the Finkels hate us. My parents have no fondness for their family either."

This time it was Sara who reached for Beryl's hand. "If you will trust me, I promise you, I will bring about the match."

Beryl looked down at Sara's bare fingers. "I don't understand. You're not even married. If you're so gifted at finding love for other people, why have you found no one for yourself?"

Sara shrugged. "Some of the best shoemakers go barefoot, they say. Now then, will you trust me, Beryl? Will you allow me to do this for you?"

Beryl's green eyes filled with tears. "Please," she said. "Do whatever you can."

Beryl and Morty were married four months later. By the end of the year, if she included the knish makers, Sara had made a total of five successful matches. One by one, the stack of bills on her mother's nightstand disappeared.

At first, the *shadchanim* were confused. They were not prepared for Sara's boldness, so when she began making matches in the open, they did not know how to respond. They began by increasing their intimidation tactics—sending more men to follow her, spreading false rumors, and stealing her signs from the local shop windows. But as her reputation grew and flourished, the group of old men became increasingly desperate.

Sara knew it was only a matter of time before they tried something more daring. She was not at all surprised when she received a summons to appear before the *beis din*—the rabbinical court.

Rabbi Sheinkopf had already given her the news of what the *shadchanim* had planned. The *beis din* was not a centralized court. There was no formal courthouse, and no jury to convene. All that was required was to bring together a panel of three rabbis to hear the case. Rabbi Sheinkopf would be one, but the other two were men Sara did not know. As a woman appearing all alone, Sara would be at a disadvantage. Had her father or her brother Joe been alive, they would have accompanied her to the hearing as her advocate. Aaron offered, but Sara knew that he was too passive of a man to be effective.

Before the *beis din* was scheduled, Sara made up her mind to seek professional help. The Educational Alliance was a settlement house that served the whole of the Lower East Side. In addition to classes, a children's theater, and an art school, the Alliance also offered legal assistance. When one of Aaron's friends had a problem with his employer, an attorney from the Alliance's Legal Aid Bureau helped to collect the salary he was owed. "You should go see them," her brother-in-law suggested. "The lawyers there are very smart. The *beis din* isn't a typical court, but even so, it couldn't hurt."

The Alliance building stood on the corner of Jefferson Street and East Broadway. Sara wore her new wool coat for the meeting, and a hat trimmed with green velvet ribbon to match. It was the first new coat she'd ever had; knowing she had purchased it for herself gave her a boost of confidence as she entered the lobby.

She was directed upstairs to the Legal Aid Bureau, where a long line of people had already formed. After giving the clerk her name and address, she took a seat. More than an hour later, her name was called, and she was brought to the office of a pleasant-looking young man who sat waiting behind a wide wooden desk. Stacks of papers covered every surface, including the side table and the windowsill.

"Come, have a seat," the man said to Sara. "How can I help you today?" His smile was cheerful and sincere. His cheeks, clean-shaven and smooth as glass. Amid the mess on top of his desk was a nameplate that read GABRIEL AUERBACH.

"Well, Mr. Auerbach," Sara said. "I'm afraid my story is not a short one." She did not reveal how she went about making her matches, but she gave Gabriel a sense of the number of marriages she had brought about and the lengths to which she had gone to avoid confrontation with the neighborhood *shadchanim*. "I eschewed my calling for many years," she explained.

"And now?" Gabriel asked. "What has changed?"

"I won't let them scare me any longer. The *shadchanim* are convinced that only a man can do what they do. They think that because I am young and unmarried, I don't have the right to earn the same living. And now, because I won't obey them, they're bringing me in front of a *beis din*, exactly two weeks from today."

"Ah," Gabriel said. "Now I see." He tapped his foot against his desk and chewed on the end of his pencil. "It's complicated," he admitted, taking the pencil from his mouth. "A *beis din* is a religious court. It has no state or federal authority. Its power is limited only to those who agree to be bound by its jurisdiction. Legally, you don't have to appear before them, and they can't enforce any judgment they pass. If they impose a fine, you can refuse to pay. If they say you can't work, you don't have to listen. Neither the police nor the court system can hold you accountable for whatever it is that they decide." He paused and leaned back in his chair. "In other words, it is a court of public opinion."

Sara pursed her lips together. "In my line of work, public opinion is important."

"I understand. But I want to make clear that this is not something you *have* to do. You are not beholden to those men."

"That doesn't mean that there won't be consequences if the panel decides against me. My business could dry up, my family could be shunned. Even worse—the local rabbis could refuse to marry any of the couples I match. In trying to bring two people together, I could be the cause of keeping them apart."

"Ah," Gabriel said. "That could be problematic."

"Yes. That is why I must appear before them." She opened the sturdy woven bag she had carried to the appointment and pulled out three books of various sizes. "These are my journals," Sara said, passing the notebooks across the desk. "I've kept records of all the matches I've made, beginning with my sister Hindel's. Most of the parties mentioned in these books had no idea of the role I played in helping them to find their spouses. Until recently, I never received a traditional payment. When I was very young, a man gave my father a bracelet. Another man—a cherished family friend—paid my family's rent and other bills for many years after I introduced his daughter to her husband."

Gabriel skimmed through the books, stopping periodically to read a few entries more closely. He called out the names he recognized, either in amusement or disbelief. "Jacob Tunchel?" he said. "From the eyeglass store? And Sam, the Grand Street grocer's son?" He whistled when he came to Ida Raskin and the clipping from *The New York Times*. "The wedding to the dentist was *your* doing?" he asked. "But the article specifically says—"

Sara interrupted. "Moishe Raskin, may he rest in peace, was a very well-connected man."

Gabriel put down the notebook and stared. "In all my years as a lawyer, Miss Glikman, I have never heard a story quite like yours."

Sara studied Gabriel's face—the smooth, soft skin and bright brown eyes. "*All* your years? You can't be more than twenty-five."

"I'm twenty-seven. In any event, your story is unique. In fact, you are the first professional matchmaker I have ever met."

"I'm surprised," Sara said. "You never sought out a matchmaker's services then?"

Gabriel chuckled and shook his head. "I don't believe in such outdated practices. When it comes to finding love, I prefer a more modern method."

Sara stiffened. "What do you know of my methods, Mr. Auerbach? I haven't told you how I make my matches."

"I assume you follow all of the usual criteria."

"Oh?"

He ticked them off one by one on his fingers. "Appearance, age, occupation, family status, dowry size . . ."

"You think I'm just like the others then? Those terrible men who care nothing for love?" Suddenly, Sara had had enough of this man, with his condescending speculation and his cynical tone. She gathered her journals from his desk and stuffed them back into her bag. "I should go. I'm sorry to have wasted so much of your time."

Gabriel stopped chewing on his pencil and frowned. He stammered in protest. "But . . . how can you leave now when we haven't come up with a strategy yet? I thought you needed an advocate to assist you?"

Sara silenced him with a glare. "On second thought, Mr. Auerbach, I've decided to advocate for myself. That would be the *modern* method, wouldn't it?" Before he could answer, she swept out of the room, rushed down the hallway, and ran out of the building. Sara cursed Gabriel Auerbach under her breath all the way home to Cannon Street.

It wasn't until she was back in her apartment that she allowed herself to wonder why it was that a man she had only just met managed to exasperate her so completely.

For the next week, Sara thought about what she would say when she was called in front of the *beis din*. She considered returning to the

Educational Alliance and asking Gabriel Auerbach for his advice, but every time she thought about seeing him again, her face grew hot. *How dare he question her matchmaking methods! How dare he imply that she was old-fashioned!*

Sara complained vociferously to her mother. But every time she mentioned Gabriel's name, Malka Glikman seemed preoccupied with other matters. For the past few days, Sara's mother had been on a kind of cleaning rampage—wiping and mopping, dusting every surface, and clearing out every nook and cranny of their home. Sara had just begun a fresh litany of Auerbach's faults when her mother started rummaging through the cannisters near the stove.

"Honestly, Mama, are you even listening? He was the most infuriating man I've ever met."

"I know, I know. You told me already."

"Well, I'm sorry to repeat myself," Sara huffed.

Malka Glikman finished with the cannisters. "Forget him," she said, clapping her hands. "Poof! Put him out of your head."

"That's just it. I can't stop thinking about how rude he was."

Sara's mother rolled her eyes. "When a woman can't stop thinking about a man, it's usually for one particular reason."

"Mama! How can you even *think* such a thing? That's it! I'll never mention him again!"

"Very good. A wise decision. Don't waste your breath on a person you hate."

"I never said I *hated* him," Sara said, sulking.

"No? Well then. My mistake." Sara's mother went back to her cleaning—this time to look through the drawers of the sideboard.

"What are you looking for?" Sara asked.

"What makes you think I'm looking for something?"

"Mama, please. I'm not blind. You've been tearing this whole place apart. Why don't you tell me what you're looking for, and I'll try to help you?"

But Sara's mother would not be swayed. "I'll tell you what it is when I find it," she said.

~⌒⌒

A few days before Sara's hearing, Gabriel Auerbach knocked on their door. He stood in the hallway with his hat in his hands, his brown curls combed neatly to one side. His smile was intact, as sincere as before, but the sight of it made Sara almost want to scream.

"What do you want, Mr. Auerbach?" she asked. She did not invite him to come inside.

"Hello, Miss Glikman. I hope you don't mind, but I obtained your address from our intake clerk. He keeps the addresses of all our visitors—"

"I'm well aware of what a clerk does, Mr. Auerbach."

"Of course you are. I didn't mean to imply—"

"What do you want?" Sara repeated.

He pulled a handkerchief from his pocket and mopped the sweat from the back of his neck. "I've been thinking about your case," he said. "Quite a bit, actually. I would like . . . if you'd allow . . . I would like to be of help to you. I would be happy to accompany you to the proceeding."

"You think you can do a better job of representing me than I can myself?"

Gabriel Auerbach shook his head. "No! Of course not! It isn't that. I only thought you might like some support."

"I appreciate your offer, but I prefer to handle it alone."

"I understand, but if you change your mind—"

"I won't."

He hesitated, as if he wanted to say more. "Well then, I hope you will accept my very best wishes for your success."

"Thank you, Mr. Auerbach. Goodbye." Sara shut the door in one swift motion, but she regretted her rudeness immediately. Her heart thumped furiously in her chest; it was so loud that she thought for sure he could hear it even from the other side of the door. After a few moments passed, she looked through the peephole to see that Mr. Auerbach had not moved. His pervasive smile had disappeared, and his shoulders drooped like a scolded child's. Sara watched as he pressed his hand to the door, as if he might consider knocking again. She held her breath and continued to watch as he pulled his hand slowly from the door and shoved it into the pocket of his coat. A moment later, he took a step backward and let out a long, heart-heavy sigh.

Sara had a lump in her throat for the remainder of the day.

EIGHTEEN

ABBY

1994

Judging from the way she was gasping for air, Jessica must have run to the telephone. "Did something happen to Evelyn?" she panted. "Is she okay? What's wrong?"

Abby felt a twinge of guilt. "No, no, everything's fine, I promise. Really. Evelyn is fine."

"My receptionist said it was an *emergency*."

"I'm sorry. I didn't mean to scare you. But I really needed to ask you something." She tried to sound casual. "Do you have any plans for tonight? Because I have tickets for the Shakespeare Festival in the park."

There was a long pause before Jessica spoke again. Her voice was heavy with frustration. "Abby, I was with a *patient*. Couldn't you have waited for me to call you back? And yes, I do have plans tonight. I'm supposed to have dinner with some friends after work."

"Cancel."

"Excuse me?"

"Sorry, that was rude. Cancel, *please*? Come with me to the play instead. The weather tonight is going to be perfect. The show got wonderful reviews . . ."

"Abby, listen. I appreciate the invitation, but I'm not going to cancel on my friends—"

"There's a man!" Abby blurted out. "I mean, there will probably be a *lot* of men at the theater. But there is one particular man I want you to meet."

Jessica's voice grew soft. "Are you serious? I thought you said you didn't know how to—"

"I don't. I mean, I *really* don't. For the record, I didn't go looking for him. He just, sort of, you know, *appeared* . . . I can't explain it. Don't ask me to try. I just think it would be good for you to meet him."

"Abby, this is amazing news, but can't I meet him another night?"

"No. It has to be tonight."

"Okay . . . I suppose I can change my plans. Can you tell me a little bit about him? His name? His age? What he does for a living?"

"No."

"*No?*"

"I don't mean to be difficult, but you know I've never done this before. I don't know what will happen, but I think it's best if you don't go into the evening with any preconceived ideas of who this guy is."

"But he's not a serial killer. Right? And he's age appropriate? I'm thirty-seven. Have I told you that? Because I don't think we ever discussed my age."

Abby sighed. "He is definitely not a serial killer. He is absolutely age appropriate. He has a very successful career. Other than that, I don't want to say more."

"Fine. I'll go. He already sounds a million times better than every date I've had this year. What time does the play start anyway?"

"Eight o'clock at the Delacorte Theater. Go into the park on the Fifth Avenue side at Seventy-Ninth Street, by the Met. Follow the signs to the theater, and I'll meet you by the entrance at seven thirty."

"Sounds good."

"And Jessica—leave the white coat and sneakers at the office, okay?"

Jessica chuckled. "So now you're telling me what to wear? You're really embracing this *yenta* thing, huh?"

Abby groaned. "Never call me that again."

It was a perfect New York summer night. All of the humidity had disappeared. Central Park felt lush and alive—filled with breezes, birdsong, and the silvery laughter of thousands of fascinating strangers. It was the kind of night that made Abby feel like there was no better place in the world to be.

If only she weren't about to do something so stupid.

She spotted Victor first, waiting on a pathway, watching his two daughters chase each other in the grass. Abby recognized the younger girl from the bakery. She was surprised that Victor had chosen to bring them—it seemed like a sophisticated outing for children so young. Then again, for all Abby knew, maybe the children of millionaires studied Shakespeare in preschool.

"Abby! Come, meet my daughters!" He called the girls over as Abby walked toward them. Both of them had Victor's golden-brown eyes, the color of just-warmed maple syrup. "Isobel, Chloé," Victor said, "this is Abby."

Abby lifted her hand in an awkward wave, which the girls immediately returned. They wore simple sundresses in plain white cotton, flecked here and there with fresh grass stains.

"Is your friend Will joining us?" Victor asked.

Didn't Victor know that Will was with Nicole? Why hadn't Nicole mentioned the meeting? It took a moment for Abby to regain her composure. "No," she said. "Not tonight. Unfortunately, he had to stay late for work. But I invited a different friend—she should be here any minute."

Victor nodded. "I understand. Nicole had to work late as well."

"Is that why you brought the girls tonight? *The Two Gentlemen of Verona* is an . . . interesting choice for children."

Victor looked amused. "You think my daughters are too young for such a performance?"

The last thing Abby wanted to do was offend him. "Please, don't go by me. I don't know the first thing about kids."

"For better or worse, Isobel and Chloé have been forced to spend many evenings in the company of adults. I can assure you, they know how to behave. I had planned on bringing only Isobel, but Chloé insisted on coming as well. She has agreed to sit on my lap, where I'm sure she'll fall asleep."

Abby was reminded of some of the evenings she and Hannah had spent with their father on "his" weekends. There was the time they had begged him to see *E.T.*, but he had dragged them to *An Officer and a Gentleman* instead. "You can see *E.T.* anytime," he'd told them. "Richard Gere is Tanja's favorite."

Victor's voice pulled Abby back to the present. "The girls adore any kind of theater. Isobel has already announced that she is going to become an actress when she grows up."

"Well in that case," Abby said, smiling, "I suppose it's best to learn about Shakespeare early."

The girls ran over to their father, squealing. "Papa! Do you see the truck? Can we have some ice cream before the show?"

"Ice cream?" Victor said, patting his stomach. "Of course, we need ice cream! Wait one minute!" He turned back to Abby. "Would you like some, too?"

"No, thank you," Abby said. "You go ahead, and I'll wait here for my friend. We'll meet you and the girls inside the theater." Abby hadn't had ice cream since she was twelve, since that awful day at Rumpelmayer's. She watched Victor joking with his girls and thought about her own father again. Victor's choice of outing for his daughters may have been unusual, but at least he seemed genuinely happy to spend time with them.

A moment later, Abby spotted Jessica approaching from the opposite direction. Abby's shoulders relaxed when she saw that Jessica had left her ratty sneakers behind. Instead, she wore a floral print dress with a long, flowy skirt and leather sandals. Her newly highlighted hair swung just past her shoulders, and her lips were tinted with a pale mauve gloss. She lifted a foot and wiggled her toes. "See?" she said. "I'm wearing real shoes."

"You look great," Abby said approvingly.

Jessica smiled and flicked a stray hair off her forehead. "Thanks," she said. "So, is he here? He's coming, right? He didn't cancel?"

"Of course he's coming," Abby said. "In fact, he already arrived. He took his daughters to get some ice cream. We're going to meet him at the seats."

"His daughters?" Jessica said, her mouth falling open. "You didn't tell me he had kids!"

"I thought you like children," Abby said, remembering the way Jessica had behaved at the bakery.

"I do. I *do*. I'm just . . . surprised."

"All I ask is that you keep an open mind. I told you, I didn't go looking for this match. I think it can work. I really do. But that doesn't mean it's going to be straightforward. Love isn't always a walk in the park."

Jessica snorted. "We are literally walking in a park right now, Abby."

"Fine, make jokes," Abby huffed. "But don't pretend you don't know what I mean."

When they entered the theater, Jessica nudged Abby's arm. "Look at what they've done with the set," she whispered. An elaborate "river,"

complete with real water, had been built to wrap around the semicircu-
lar stage. There was also an enormous billboard featuring a half-naked
supermodel. "I have no idea what that has to do with the play," Jessica
admitted, "but it certainly is provocative."

As the audience members took their seats, there was a palpable excitement in the air—a combination of the crowd, the fantastical set,
and the stunning fuchsia sky darkening softly overhead. "You were
right," Jessica said, her voice practically giddy. "Even if the guy doesn't
show, I'm already glad I came."

"He'll be here any minute," Abby assured her. Out of the corner
of her eye, she could see Victor and his girls make their way toward
the seats. Isobel climbed the steps on her own, but Victor held an exhausted Chloé in his arms. As the three of them approached Abby's
row, Chloé lifted her head and spotted Jessica. "Papa," she said. "It's
the bakery lady."

"Don't be silly," Victor said. At the end of the row, people stood
from their seats to allow Victor and the girls to pass. "Excuse me," he
murmured. "So sorry, excuse me." It wasn't until he was directly beside
Jessica that he realized Chloé was correct. He froze in place. "It's you,"
he said.

Abby was sure that if Jessica hadn't been seated, her legs would have
given out from beneath her. The look on her face was shock and be-
wilderment, slowly giving way to wonder and delight. She reached for
Abby's hand to steady herself. "Hello" was all she could manage to say.

Luckily, Chloé broke the silence. "I ate all the macarons you gave
me. Isobel was mad because I didn't save her any."

"She's right. I was," Isobel chimed in. "Do you have any macarons
with you now?"

"I'm sorry, but no. I wasn't expecting . . ."

"That's okay," Isobel said. "We just had ice-cream cones anyway."
She climbed onto the seat next to Jessica while Victor took the next
chair over. "I didn't introduce myself at the bakery," he said, reaching

out a slightly trembling hand. "Victor Étoile. It's wonderful to meet you." He patted Isobel's shoulder. "This is Isobel, my eldest. Of course, you and Chloé have already met."

"It's so nice to see you again," Jessica said, still recovering from the surprise.

"This is my friend Jessica," Abby offered. "Dr. Cooper, I mean. She's an ophthalmologist."

"I know what that is," Isobel announced. "That's a doctor for people's eyes. Papa is a fashion designer. He makes very expensive clothes."

"Really?" said Jessica, trying not to laugh. "That's impressive!"

Isobel nodded as if she already knew. "He's famous, actually. Have you heard of him?"

"I'm afraid I haven't. I don't know very much about fashion."

Isobel pointed to the billboard above the stage. "We've met *her* loads of times," she said. "She wears the clothes at Papa's shows."

Victor put a finger to his lips. "Shh now, Isobel," he said. "Pay attention to the stage. The show is about to start."

By intermission, Chloé was fast asleep on Victor's lap, so Jessica offered to bring Isobel to the ladies' room with her. "Are you sure you don't mind?" Victor asked, but Jessica assured him she did not.

As soon as Jessica and Isobel were out of earshot, Victor spoke up. "How did you find her?" he demanded. "How on earth did you know?"

"Excuse me?"

"Your friend is the woman I mentioned yesterday. The one from the bakery who was so kind to Chloé."

Abby decided the safest course of action would be to say as little as possible. She shrugged. "It must be one of those crazy New York City coincidences."

But Victor Étoile did not agree. "I don't believe in coincidences," he said.

When the show was over, they waited in their seats for the bulk of the crowd to dissipate. "What did you think of the play?" Abby asked Isobel.

"I liked the river, but the story wasn't my favorite. I prefer *Romeo and Juliet*. The ending is depressing, but the play is much more interesting."

Abby laughed. "My grandmother never liked that ending either."

"If I was Juliet," Isobel said, "there's no way I would have died in the end. I would have loved whoever I wanted, and I wouldn't have felt bad or run away."

"Sounds like you've got the right idea," Abby said.

They said their goodbyes outside the theater, in the grassy spot where the girls had played tag. Victor was headed east with his daughters, but Abby and Jessica were headed to the west side. "Thank you so much for the tickets," Jessica said. "It was a wonderful surprise to see you again."

"It was my pleasure," Victor murmured. He shook Abby's hand, but when he reached for Jessica's, he pressed his lips to it instead. There was a quiet tenderness to the moment that made Abby want to look away.

Jessica and Abby walked in silence until they reached the edge of the park. They emerged from the greenery to see the avenue teeming with Friday-night traffic. Central Park West was a mass of taxis and cars—headlights beaming and bouncing off the pavement like a hundred mismatched constellations. When they had crossed the street, Jessica stopped on the sidewalk. "How did you find him, Abby?" she asked. The question hung heavily between them, and Abby could not avoid giving an answer.

"Victor is my client," she admitted. "He didn't notice me at the bakery—it was way too crowded in there that day. I spotted him though—just for a minute, but that was enough."

"I never thought I'd see him again."

Abby nodded. "That's why I wanted you to come with me tonight."

"I still don't understand what made you think . . ." Jessica's voice trailed off for a bit before she erupted in a fit of laughter. "He's a *fashion designer,* of all things! And from what his daughter said, a famous one, too. The man hangs out with *Kate Moss.* Meanwhile, I can barely put an outfit together!"

"Yeah, I know," Abby said. "But at the end of the day, none of that actually matters."

They made it only two blocks farther before Jessica came to a stop again. "You said Victor is your client. Does that mean he's in the middle of a divorce?"

"No—he was divorced a few years ago, actually."

"Phew," Jessica exhaled. "That's a relief. I'd hate to get caught up in someone else's mess."

Abby wrinkled her nose.

"Uh oh. What is it?" Jessica said. "What's with that face? What aren't you telling me?"

"The truth is that Victor is . . . don't be upset, but he's engaged. We're in the middle of negotiating his prenup."

Jessica looked as if she might be sick. "Engaged? Abby, what the *hell*? Why did you tell me to come tonight? Why did you go and get my hopes up if he's already in love with someone else?"

"Because he isn't in love!" Abby said. "Infatuated, maybe, but not in love. And she *definitely* isn't in love with him. From what I can tell, she's not a bad person. She's just young and ambitious and honestly, Jessica, I think she's in love with the business, not him. From everything I've seen so far, he's more of a mentor than a fiancé."

Despite the explanation, Jessica was distraught. "Honestly, Abby, this is too much. It was nice of you to invite me tonight, but I don't think this arrangement is a good idea after all. I shouldn't have bugged you about it in the first place." Jessica darted down the street, leaving Abby no choice but to run after her.

"Jessica, wait!"

By the time Abby caught up to her, Jessica's eyes were filled with tears. "I don't know anything anymore, Abby. For years I kept telling myself to be patient. I watched so many of my friends fall in love, and I kept thinking, eventually, it would happen for me, too. But maybe it's time I let it go. Maybe it's time that I faced the fact that some things aren't meant to be."

"Let me ask you something," Abby said. "What did you feel when you were with Victor?"

"Energized, I think. A little breathless. He's not like anyone I've ever met. He's completely charming. Sweet with his daughters. If you want to know the truth, I haven't been able to stop thinking about him since that day at the bakery."

"He was thinking about you, too. Not only that, he said you were *lovely.*"

Jessica stared at her. "But none of this makes any sense."

"Of course it doesn't! Come on, Jessica. Why did you believe my grandmother could help you? Why did you believe what she said about me? It certainly wasn't for any rational reason. None of this is rational. None of it makes sense."

Jessica sighed. "I know," she said, wiping a tear from her cheek. The side street they had turned onto was darker than the avenue, but a flash of light caught Abby's eye.

Abby gasped. "Don't move," she whispered, reaching slowly for Jessica's hand. There, between Jessica's knuckles and wrist, exactly where Victor Étoile had kissed her, a perfect lip-shaped circle glowed.

"Do you see it?" Abby asked. But even as she traced the mark with her fingers, the shimmering circle disappeared.

"I don't see anything," Jessica said.

Abby shook her head and closed her eyes. How had she gotten into this mess? Spending her Friday night with her grandmother's ophthalmologist? Taking advice on love from Victor's eight-year-old? Five weeks ago, Abby was a kick-ass lawyer on the path to early partnership. Five weeks ago, she'd been in complete control. She knew exactly what she wanted and how to achieve it. Now she spent more time med-dling in her clients' marriages than she did working on their cases. Now she analyzed her grandmother's journals more closely than the latest court decisions. She was chasing invisible premonitions and looking for imaginary lights in the dark.

And yet, she could not stop herself. Her unexpected connections to these people—to Evelyn and Michael, to Jessica and Victor—had given her a newfound sense of purpose. As much of a mess as she might be creating, she felt as if she was fulfilling a promise to her past. Her grandmother's voice was strong and certain in her head. *Maybe you'll make a few love matches of your own.*

Slowly, Abby opened her eyes. "Jessica, don't give up now," she begged. "Please, trust me for just a little bit longer."

NINETEEN

SARA

1921

When a Thief Kisses You, Count Your Teeth

Under normal circumstances, the *beis din* would have met in one of the participating rabbis' studies. The proceedings were generally not open to the public, and there was rarely a need for a bigger space. In Sara's case, however, the number of interested parties necessitated a larger venue. The hearing was scheduled to be held in the sanctuary of a synagogue led by Rabbi Pearl of Orchard Street. It was not nearly as grand as Rabbi Sheinkopf's synagogue, but the room could accommodate one hundred congregants.

Not wanting to burden anyone in her family, Sara went to the proceeding alone. Three rabbis sat behind a narrow wooden table that had been placed in the center of a stagelike platform. The wrinkled man in the center was the ancient Rabbi Pearl, well into his eighties and known to all as a prodigious scholar and a compassionate leader. To his left was the sour-faced Rabbi Kaufman, a longtime supporter of the *shadchanim*. To his right, thank goodness, sat Rabbi Sheinkopf, loyal friend to the Glikman family.

The *shadchanim* were seated in the first three rows, to the right of the center aisle. The synagogue did not have a women's balcony—only a small space in the back of the room separated from the front rows by a wooden screen. Sara refused to sit behind the partition. If she was going to be accused, she would make them do it to her face. Instead, she took a seat in the front row, across the aisle and to the left of the men. She wondered whether any of them would object, but none of them even acknowledged her presence. She was the only woman in the sanctuary.

As the most senior of the three rabbis on the panel, Rabbi Pearl was to call the proceeding to order. He would be the head of their small court, and each of the rabbis would act as a judge. When Rabbi Pearl banged his cane on the pocked stone floor, Sara felt the vibrations through her boots, all the way up to the lump in her throat.

"Identify yourselves, gentlemen," he said. "Each of you in turn. Name, age, and what has brought you here today." One by one, the men came forward, twenty-eight of them in all, ranging in age from thirty-six to eighty-three. As the self-proclaimed representatives of the group, Shternberg and Grossman spoke up first. For the next several hours, the *shadchanim* spouted one accusation after another.

"She is too young."

"She is not qualified."

"She has lied to all of us for years."

"She takes the bread from our children's mouths."

"She steals the matches from behind our backs."

"She is an unmarried woman who has no shame."

"She defiles our customs and spits on our ways."

"She is a witch!"

In an attempt to make their condemnation appear more thoughtful, some of the men asked questions instead.

"Does the law not say she must be wed before she can practice our profession?"

"Who is she to hold herself out as a better matchmaker than any of us?"

"With no proper teacher or mentor for the trade, how can she be trusted with her task?"

Others preferred to use their time to petition for the consequences they felt should be imposed upon her.

"She should be banned from making any further matches."

"She must submit her records and be made to reimburse us for the money we have lost."

"Our rabbis should refuse to marry any of her future matches."

There was more, of course. So much more. Voices were raised in a furious chorus of insults and curses, exaggerations and lies. Hour after hour, she was forced to endure the storm of vitriol.

And yet, this time Sara was not frightened. She was no longer a child hiding in the balcony. She was a woman facing her accusers head-on. She had not yet decided how much she would say about the nature of her gift, but she would not allow these men to demean her. When she was finally called upon to speak, her cheeks did not flush and her knees did not quake. She was barely over five feet tall, but she stood straight and firm and unafraid.

"There have been many things said about me today, but I would like to begin with what is true. Of everyone here, I am the youngest. I am also the only woman. These are facts I cannot change. It is also true that as a *shadchanteh*, I have certain talents that the men in this room do not have."

Her assertions were met with a series of grumblings from the other side of the room.

"As for the claim that I am unqualified, I have been making matches since I was ten years old."

"There—you see?" Shternberg spat. "Now she admits it! For years, she claimed she made no matches. Do you see how she lies?"

Sara waited until Shternberg finished his outburst. When he was done, she began again. "You and your colleagues spoke for five hours, Mr. Shternberg, and I did not interrupt any of you. Now that it is my time to speak, I expect you to extend the same courtesy to me."

A few of the men raised their voices again. "What impertinence!" "What gall!"

The prune-faced elder, Rabbi Pearl, brought down his cane on the floor again. "Silence!" he shouted. "She is right. The *beis din* is a sacred institution, bound by *halacha*, by Jewish law. The law demands integrity and civility. There will be no more outbursts. Is that understood?"

The men quieted down, but they did not look pleased.

"Thank you," Sara said calmly. She pulled three journals from her bag and carried them to the judges' table. "These are my private records," she said. "Records I have kept for the past eleven years. In them, I have detailed all of my matches, including any amounts I was paid. Before the wedding of Beryl Klein, I received no personal payment for any match I made."

Grossman snorted. "'No *personal* payment,' she says," he mumbled under his breath.

Sara ignored his whisperings. "My first match was for my sister, Hindel. By now, many of you have heard the story. I did not make another match until I turned thirteen years old. That was when I met Jacob Tunchel and his wife, Miryam Nachman. There was no contract for that match. Indeed, I have never used a contract."

"You don't use contracts, even now?" Rabbi Kaufman interrupted.

"I do not pair people in the usual way, so I do not find it necessary. I only advocate for a match when I am certain it will be a success."

Rabbi Kaufman looked skeptical. "How can a *shadchan* ever be certain? Surely, you must have made many introductions that failed to result in marriage proposals."

Sara shook her head. "With all due respect, I have not."

The *shadchanim* grumbled on their side of the aisle, and Rabbi Pearl banged his cane a third time.

Because Sara had no idea how long she would be allowed to speak, she thought it best to forge ahead. "In any event, it was the Tunchel match that first brought the *shadchanim* to my father. The Lewis Street matchmaker came to our home and demanded to know what I had been paid. I was brought into the room to be questioned, and I swore that I had received no money." She hesitated. "I later learned that the father of the bride gave my father a gold bracelet as a token of his appreciation."

The bearded men were on their feet as the sanctuary erupted. Shternberg screamed louder than all the others. "This *proves* she is a liar!" he said. "This proves that we have always been right!" He turned to his grim-faced colleagues. "What do I always say? When a thief kisses you, count your teeth!"

Rabbi Sheinkopf stood from his chair. "The next man who speaks out of turn will be ejected from these proceedings! All of you—take a seat or leave!" He stopped for a moment to catch his breath. "Miss Glikman has revealed this new information regardless of how harmful it is to her case. I would argue that this admission proves her intentions to be honest and fair. Furthermore, the gift was made over eight years ago. This panel will draw no conclusions until the proceeding is complete." He turned to Sara. "You may continue."

"Thank you." Sara nodded. "After the Tunchel wedding, I hid my efforts. If I sensed that a man and a woman should meet, I put them in each other's path, but I did so without anyone's knowledge. In order to avoid the issue of payment, I made sure no one knew of my endeavors."

Rabbi Kaufman strummed his fingers on the table in front of him. "Although you reaped no financial benefit from those matches, there is, nonetheless, an argument to be made that you deprived the *shadchanim* of the money they would have earned if they had matched the parties themselves."

"Perhaps," Sara said. "But I would assert that had I not intervened, most of those people—especially the women—would have remained unmarried to this day. When I matched my teacher, Miss Perelman, for example, she was twenty-seven years old. The neighborhood had declared her a spinster, and the *shadchanim* had given up on her."

Rabbi Sheinkopf interjected. "An excellent point."

"It was the same with Ida Raskin," Sara said. "After she broke off her first engagement, the *shadchanim* proclaimed her too difficult to match."

"A very high-profile wedding," Rabbi Pearl mused, stroking the long gray strands of his beard.

"For which you were paid handsomely," said Rabbi Kaufman.

"The benefit my family received was not as simple as that," Sara corrected him. "Moishe Raskin gave my family food. He gave my brothers jobs. He paid our rent. But he never discussed a fee with me. In fact, we never discussed money at all. He continued to pay my family's bills— not out of any contractual obligation, but out of human decency and friendship. At the time, my family was about to be evicted. We did not have enough food to put on the table. Moishe Raskin was a generous man."

"So generous that he paid for you to go to Barnard College." Rabbi Kaufman did not hide his smirk.

"That is correct," said Sara plainly. "Mr. Raskin knew that a college education was my father's dying wish for me. I left Barnard after one year, however, and continued my education at Hunter College."

Grossman and Shternberg rose from their seats. "If I may speak now?" Shternberg asked. Before Sara could object, Rabbi Kaufman bowed his head in agreement.

"I believe we have heard enough from Miss Glikman. She admits that she was paid for the Tunchel match. She admits that Moishe Raskin paid her family's bills. She has lied—both outright and by omission. She has manipulated the truth for her own gain." Shternberg paused for dramatic effect. "Can this young woman do what we do? Perhaps. But when Abraham wanted a wife for Isaac, he sent his servant Eliezer to find a match. He sent a man, not a woman, to carry out the sacred task. Miss Glikman wants us all to believe that she is singularly blessed with the gift of finding people love." Shternberg gestured to the rows of men behind him. "But why should any of us believe her?"

The sudden sound of footsteps on stone echoed from the back of the sanctuary.

"Because all of what she says is true!"

Sara recognized the voice; she turned to see five familiar women marching up the center aisle. Together, they were an undaunted band—holding their graceful heads high and swishing their skirts shamelessly across the cold, hard floor. They came to a stop at the front of the room, taking their places beside Sara, whose heart swelled at the sight of them—Beryl Klein, Ida Raskin, Miryam Tunchel, Sophie Perelman, and Hindel Ambromovich, Sara's sister.

Rabbi Kaufman stood to object. "This *beis din* is not open to the public. This is a private proceeding."

Beryl Klein, who had already spoken, stepped forward and pointed to the rows of *shadchanim*. "Then what are all of those men doing here?"

"They are parties to the case. What happens here today is of personal interest to them."

But Beryl would not be deterred. "Seeing as Sara was the matchmaker for all of us, what happens here is of personal interest to us as well."

Rabbi Kaufman grimaced, but Rabbi Sheinkopf stood firm. "Let them speak," he insisted. "We have listened to testimony from twenty-eight men. Surely, we can find the patience to listen to these five women."

Rabbi Pearl pulled at his beard. "I agree. I would like to hear what they have to say." He blinked his eyes. "Who will speak first?"

Beryl Klein crossed her arms over her chest. "I will begin. When I entered the sanctuary, you were debating Sara's talent and character. I am here to vouch for both. When Sara first came into my knish shop to tell me she had found my *bashert*, I did not believe it was possible. I was certain there was no hope for me to marry the man I loved. When Sara spoke his name out loud, I thought she had lost her mind. She swore to me that no matter the complications, she would bring about a wedding. She made a match between two families at war—a match none of the men in this room would have attempted. She did not let the difficulty of the job dissuade her. I will owe her my happiness for the rest of my life."

It was Ida Raskin who spoke next. Marriage had agreed with her— she carried herself with even greater confidence than Sara remembered. Well into the middle of her second pregnancy, Ida rested her hands on her rounded belly. "I am Ida Lipovsky," she said. "Formerly Ida Raskin. I am sure my father has been the subject of much of your discussion today."

"He has," Rabbi Pearl admitted. "What can you tell us about the compensation he paid to Miss Glikman and her family? Was there a contract for her services?"

"There was never a contract," Ida confirmed. "My father considered Sara a close family friend. He never referred to her as a matchmaker. It wasn't until long after I was married that I ever knew of her chosen profession."

"But she introduced you to your husband, yes?"

"She did," Ida said. "Outside the synagogue on Yom Kippur. In truth, my father never got over the fact that my husband and I met that day. He could not see how anyone could fall in love on a day of fasting and repentance."

"And yet, your father covered the Glikmans' debts for many years?"

Ida nodded. "He did, but you must understand: my father loved

Sara as if she were his own family. She gave him the gift of his daughter's happiness. Whatever money he donated on behalf of the Glikman family, he gave out of love, not business obligation."

"That money could have gone to one of us!" the Lewis Street *shadchan* shouted.

Ida's eyes blazed with fury. "Never!" she said. "After what happened with my first fiancé, my father was disgusted with all of you! Besides, after I ended my first engagement, none of you introduced me to anyone suitable."

"They considered me unworthy of their attention as well." It was Miss Perelman now who stood to speak. It had been half a dozen years since Sara had last seen her favorite teacher, but it was as if she had not aged a day. Her eyes were as bright and as thoughtful as they had been in the classroom. "I am Sophie Potashman, formerly Perelman. Until a few days ago, I had no idea that Sara played any part in bringing about my marriage."

"I find that hard to believe," Rabbi Kaufman said, sneering.

"Believe what you like, but it is true. At twenty-seven, I was considered too old to marry. The men in this room declared me unlovable. One day, Sara encouraged me to visit the grocer on Grand Street for strawberries. She was adamant that I go. At the time, I did not think much of it, but she had already met my husband, Sam. I don't know how, but Sara *knew* what would happen when Sam and I met."

"And she never contacted you later for payment?"

"Never," Miss Perelman insisted.

"She asked for nothing from my family either." It was Miryam now who had decided to speak.

"And yet, we just heard that your father gave Mr. Glikman a gold bracelet."

"I did not learn about that until recently," Miryam said. "I suspect it was my mother who insisted upon it. She is very superstitious, and she would have wanted to ensure that the marriage was a happy one by offering something to the family."

"Still," Rabbi Kaufman continued. "Mr. Glikman lied about this gift, and Sara Glikman lied as well."

"The matter of the bracelet is unfortunate," Rabbi Sheinkopf admitted, "but perhaps—"

"I will resolve it!" Hindel called out, stepping up to the table where the three judges sat. She slowly pulled a small felt bag from the pocket of her coat and placed it on the table. "My family is prepared to return the bracelet in order to set the matter right."

The *shadchanim* fidgeted in their seats and craned their necks to see what Sara's sister had brought. Slowly, she slipped the bracelet from its pouch and held it up for the room to see. "Our mother hid this years ago, but in her quest to keep it safe, she forgot where she put it. Luckily, she recovered it this morning."

Sara's lips curved into a smile. *So that was what her mother had been searching for.*

Rabbi Pearl held his hands up for silence and paused for a few moments to think. Eventually, he cleared his throat. "Thank you, ladies, for your testimony. Rabbi Sheinkopf, Rabbi Kaufman, forgive me if I am wrong, but I believe the only question left to discuss is the question of Miss Glikman's marital status."

Sara tried to maintain her composure, but inside, she burned with indignation. "With all due respect," she said, "I believe it is wrong to impose marriage as a condition of this vocation. Furthermore, I do not believe that it is a requirement under our law." She pointed to the *shadchanim.* "Many of the men in this room are widowers. They are unmarried, and yet, they still work."

"That," Rabbi Kaufman scoffed, "is an entirely different matter."

"I do not believe it is," said Sara. "In any event, I do not intend to marry."

Rabbi Pearl's face went white with surprise. "Why do you say this?" he demanded. "Why have you come to such a decision?"

"The decision is . . . an unfortunate consequence of my particular matchmaking method." Sara searched for the right words to explain. "When the inspiration to make a match strikes me, it often comes without any warning. Sometimes I am moved to match strangers, but often I am struck to make a match for someone I already know. What would happen if my inspiration comes for the man I intend to marry? What if I find his true soulmate only after he and I are wed? How can I marry knowing that such heartache may be waiting in both our futures?"

"You are certain of matches for other people, but you cannot be certain for yourself?" The sneer on Rabbi Kaufman's lips took over his entire face.

Beryl wrapped a protective arm around Sara. "Some of the best shoemakers go barefoot," she said. "So, I don't see why a matchmaker must be married."

Despite the incredulity of many in the room, Rabbi Pearl nodded as if he understood. He pulled a watch from his pocket and studied it carefully. "I believe the time has come to adjourn this proceeding. I will meet now with my fellow judges, and we will reconvene tomorrow morning to announce our ruling. Does either party have any final words?"

Shternberg and Grossman shook their heads, but Sara raised her hand to speak.

"I would like to say only that it has been my greatest honor to bring these marriages into the world. No matter what the court decides, I will never regret the work I have done."

The *shadchanim* swarmed out of the room, each of them avoiding Sara's gaze. Rabbi Sheinkopf helped Rabbi Pearl descend from the platform, and the three judges retired to Rabbi Pearl's study. Meanwhile, the women who had come to Sara's aid crowded around her.

"You were so brave," Hindel said. "Papa would have been proud of you."

"You spoke beautifully," Miss Perelman assured her. "With the same intelligence I remember from my classroom."

Beryl and Miryam complimented her poise, while Ida threw her arms around Sara's waist. "Oh, how I wish my father were here. He would have praised you to the heavens and spat in the faces of those wretched men."

As thrilled as Sara was to have the women by her side, she wondered about their unexpected appearance. "I cannot thank you all enough for being here," she said. "But how on earth did it come about? The rabbis did not advertise the gathering to the public. How did you know where and when to come?"

Hindel squeezed her sister's hand. "It was Gabriel Auerbach's doing. He paid each of us a visit."

Miryam nodded in agreement. "He was adamant that we should come to your aid. He did not want you to face the *shadchanim* alone."

Sara felt her legs wobble beneath her. For hours, even as the *shadchanim* attacked, she had managed to maintain her strength. But now, in the face of this new revelation, a sudden weakness overcame her. No one had ever done for her what Gabriel Auerbach managed to do.

"He seemed a truly sincere and earnest young man," said Miss Perelman.

Beryl winked. "Handsome, too."

"Who knows?" Ida Raskin teased. "Perhaps our Sara might change her mind about a wedding after all."

The next day, the women returned to the *shul*. Hindel held tight to Sara's hand as they waited for the *shadchanim* to take their seats. Once everyone was in place, Rabbi Pearl banged his cane for order.

Gabriel was waiting for her outside the *shul*. His smile was hopeful but apprehensive—he was uncertain not only of how Sara would receive him but also of whether she had won or lost her case. It was Sara's sister who spotted him first. Hindel whispered into her ear. "He's waiting for you, Sara. Go, talk to him. I'll see you at home. Remember, be *nice*."

After saying goodbye to her companions, Sara made her way across the street. The weak March sun swept away the morning clouds, and the first hint of spring was in the air.

"Hello, Mr. Auerbach," Sara said.

"Please," he insisted. "Tell me, quickly—what did the *beis din* decide?"

Sara stepped closer until she was beside him. He smelled like coffee and buttered rye bread. "Miss Glikman," he whispered impatiently. "What did the court decide?"

"They found in my favor," Sara finally answered. "Rabbi Pearl told the *shadchanim* to stop harassing me. I was ordered to return Miryam Tunchel's gold bracelet, but no other fine was imposed. I am free to work as a *shadchanteh*, despite the fact that I am unmarried."

Gabriel's eyes were glued to hers. "I am very happy for you," he said. He blinked a few times and searched her face, rubbed his eyes, and blinked some more.

"Is something wrong?" Sara asked.

He blinked again. "I do not think so, no. No. I'm sure it's only the sun in my eye. It is only . . . there, it's gone again. A kind of light around your face . . ."

Sara felt a flutter in her chest, but she did not press Gabriel to explain further. She took a step closer. "Thank you for what you did for me. I must say, I was a bit surprised. I thought you did not see the need for matchmakers."

Gabriel leaned into the space between them. "I believe I've changed my mind," he said. "Sometimes there is beauty in the old-world way of doing things."

"Sometimes," Sara agreed. "But there is beauty in what is modern as well. Tradition should never be used as an excuse to keep people from reaching their potential."

"Perhaps we will agree on a compromise then—to take what is best from both the old world and the new?"

When Gabriel reached for Sara's hand, she took it without hesitation.

TWENTY

ABBY

1994

O n Sunday evening, Abby braced herself for the inevitable chaos of Diane's return to the office. She had just pulled a yogurt from her refrigerator when Diane called her from the Miami airport. A cluster of thunderstorms had delayed her flight, and now the airline had canceled it. "I can't get another flight to New York until early tomorrow morning," she said. "Victor is coming in at eleven, and I may be a little late. Keep him occupied until I get there, please. Lisa will print out the revised draft of the prenup."

"Of course," Abby said. "No problem at all."

But when Victor walked into the conference room on Monday, Abby barely recognized him. The dapper, stylish man she knew looked as if he hadn't bathed for days. His hair was greasy, his shirt untucked, and instead of his trademark butter-soft suede loafers, he wore a pair of muddied sneakers.

"Mr. Étoile!" she exclaimed, unable to mask her surprise. "Is everything okay?"

He lowered himself into a chair and shrugged. "I am not myself, Abby. I am . . . adrift."

"Did something happen?"

He rubbed the stubble on his chin. "Nicole was so busy with work this weekend, she barely had time to speak to me. Of course, she is far more productive than I ever was—efficient and focused—a perfect business partner. But our house feels more and more like an office—not the home I hoped to make for my girls."

"How are Isobel and Chloé?"

"Since Friday night, they have not stopped talking about your friend."

"What friend?" Diane swept into the conference room. Despite the fact that she had come straight from the airport after a harried morning of travel, Diane was as put together as ever.

Abby tried to tamp down her nerves. "Diane! You're back! How was your trip?"

"The trip was fine. What friend are you talking about?"

"Oh, Mr. Étoile was kind enough to share some extra tickets with me—for the Shakespeare Festival in the park on Friday. I brought a friend of mine, that's all."

"It was a lovely night for the performance," Victor added, in an unfamiliar, wistful voice.

Diane shook off her confusion. Abby knew she wouldn't ask too many questions, not while Victor was in the room. "How nice," Diane said. "Now then, let's get to business, shall we? Why don't we begin by going over the changes to your agreement?"

Victor rubbed his eyes and yawned. "I apologize, Diane—I haven't been sleeping well. If it's all the same to you, I will take the documents home and go over them tomorrow. May I call you then?"

Diane did not seem pleased. "Victor, your wedding is in six weeks. And your engagement party is Saturday. I thought you wanted to wrap this up before then?"

"Of course. But I'm afraid I don't have the energy today." He pointed to a thick pile of papers on the table. "I assume that is for me?"

Diane looked stunned. "Yes."

Abby tucked the document into a heavy manila folder. "Here you go, Mr. Étoile."

He rose from his chair. "I'll call you in the next few days. And I'll see you at the party, yes? Both of you should feel free to bring guests." He tucked the folder under his arm and pushed his way through the conference room doors.

Diane waited until he was out of earshot. "What on earth happened to him?" she said. "Did you see what he looked like? He's a total mess." From across the table, she glared at Abby. "What was all that about the show? Did something happen that I should know about?"

Abby felt a throbbing in her temples. "What? Of course not! He sent over two tickets and I brought my friend, that's all. Victor had his daughters with him."

"And what about Nicole? Where was she?"

"He said Nicole had to work late."

"That doesn't sound good. Did you see the look on his face when I brought up the wedding?" Diane slammed her hand on the conference room table. "Damn it!"

Abby chose her words carefully. "What would happen if they didn't get married?"

The tone of Diane's voice was bitter. "Prenups are a mind game," she said. "Putting people through a hypothetical divorce right before they promise to love each other forever? It's a miracle they ever get signed. But people want them, and more important, they want a scapegoat to go with them. *We're* the scapegoat, Abby. That's our job. Bride-to-be thinks her fiancé is a secret greedy bastard? *Oh no, darling,* he'll say. *It isn't me. It's the lawyers. If it were up to me, there'd be no prenup at all ...* Do you know how many times I've heard my clients say that?

"As you know," she continued, "Victor's engagement has been in all the papers and magazines. The wedding is a highly anticipated event coming after his *very* public divorce. Everyone knows there will be a prenup, and everyone knows we're the ones doing it. If Victor doesn't get married when he's supposed to, people will assume it's the fault of *this* firm—that we were too tough in the negotiations, or we made things too difficult, or maybe, that we're just bad luck. And that could mean that future clients might not want to work with us."

Diane tapped her manicured nails on the conference room table. "You're sure nothing else is going on? Did he say anything strange on Friday? Anything to make you think he was having problems with Nicole?"

"Nothing that jumped out," Abby lied.

"What was he saying about your friend and his daughters?"

Abby shrugged. "Just that Jessica—my friend—was sitting next to them. She's an ophthalmologist, and she's great with kids. I guess the girls really liked her."

"What about Victor? Did *he* like her?"

Abby forced herself to meet Diane's eye and to answer like the lawyer she was. "Jessica isn't Victor's type. She barely said a word all night, and when she did, it was mostly to his daughters." This, at least, was true, Abby thought.

Diane gave Abby one last look, as if she could sense the hesitation in her answer. "Fine," Diane said. "I'll wait until I hear from Victor. In the meantime, let's hope he gets himself together before the party."

"Let's hope," Abby repeated, with forced enthusiasm. She fled from the conference room and back to her office, where she cradled her pounding head in her hands. *Let's hope I don't lose my job.*

The rest of the morning was uneventful, but the peace and quiet did not last long. At around one o'clock, the receptionist knocked on her door, carrying a tall glass vase filled with pale yellow roses and the softest blue hydrangeas. "What's this?" Abby asked.

The receptionist shrugged. "It was delivered just now," he said. "Diane got one, too."

Abby opened the card that was tucked between the blossoms.

Dear Abby,
Michael and I are forever in your debt. The divorce is off! We can't
thank you enough.

With every good wish,
Evelyn Morgan

The sentiment was lovely, but Abby knew what was coming. Diane was going to have a fit.

It took less than a minute for the phone to ring.

"Abby, I need you in my office. *Now.*"

There, in the center of Diane's desk, was a second arrangement of roses and hydrangeas. Diane waved the tiny card in the air. She tossed it at Abby. "What is *this*?" she spat. "What the hell did you do?"

Abby scanned Diane's card.

Dear Diane,
What an amazing young attorney you have in Abby. Thanks to her
persistence, the divorce is off! We can't thank you both enough.

With every good wish,
Evelyn Morgan

"She seems happy," Abby said, in her cheeriest voice, but Diane was not smiling.

"What did you do?" Diane repeated. "What were you so *persistent* about?"

"Well . . . ," Abby stammered. "Right before you left for Miami, Michael Gilbert gave me a call."

Diane crossed both arms over her chest while Abby struggled to continue.

"Remember how I told you about Evelyn's vision problems? Michael told me that Evelyn was convinced she was going blind. Apparently, her father had a rare eye disease, and Evelyn thought she had the same condition. She believed that it would make life very hard on Michael, but she refused to see a doctor about it. Michael had just been served with our papers, and he called because he was hoping that I might . . . encourage her to see someone before she made any final decisions."

"And?"

"And so, I arranged for her to see an ophthalmologist . . ."

Diane looked as if she might explode. "Let me guess," she said, with a sneer. "The same ophthalmologist you invited to the show—the one Victor's kids can't stop talking about?"

Abby gulped. When Diane put it that way, it did sound suspicious. Abby tried to sound confident. "Yes," she said.

"And what was the result of the doctor's visit?"

"It was terrific news, actually. Turns out Evelyn is on some medication for her arthritis that is causing the problems with her vision. Last I heard, she was making appointments with some specialists. I guess they decided the damage is reversible." Abby paused. "It's a happy ending, isn't it?" she asked. "I mean, if she sent us flowers, she must be really pleased."

Diane considered this for a moment before taking a seat behind her desk and flipping through her Rolodex. "Sit," she ordered. "We're going to call her."

Evelyn answered after two rings. "Evelyn?" Diane cooed over the speakerphone. "It's Diane Berenson. Abby and I couldn't wait another minute before we called to congratulate you."

"Diane! Did you get the flowers?"

"We did, we did! What an incredibly thoughtful gesture. Abby and I are thrilled for you and Michael."

"You know," Evelyn said, "I owe it all to Abby. I realize now how stubborn I was. I almost made the biggest mistake of my life. I will never be able to thank you both properly."

"Don't be silly," Diane assured her. "Your happiness is thanks enough."

"How sweet you are. I suppose it's a bit of a novelty in your business—having a client with a happy ending."

"Oh, I wouldn't say that." Diane was laughing through tightly clenched teeth. "I assure you, we have many happy clients. At least that's what their accountants tell us!"

Evelyn chuckled politely.

"In all seriousness, Evelyn, please remember that we are always here for you."

"Thank you, my dear. Michael and I are so grateful to you both. I will be in touch. Both of you, be well."

"You too, Ms. Morgan!" Abby chimed in.

After the call, Diane didn't speak. Abby was used to Diane's frenetic movement, her barking of orders, her pacing back and forth. This still and silent version of Diane made Abby feel uneasy and spooked. After five full minutes of quiet torture, Diane looked at Abby and told her to leave. "You need to go now," she said.

"Of course," Abby answered. "Absolutely. I'll finish the Henshaw papers and drop them off later."

"No," Diane told her. "You don't understand. You betrayed my trust, Abby. You interfered in a longtime client's personal relationship without even bothering to tell me about it."

"Are you firing me?" Abby whispered.

"I haven't decided yet. You're talented, Abby. There's no doubt about that. But you keep getting sidetracked. Suddenly, you think you know better than our clients about what it is they need or want for their lives. Maybe Evelyn Morgan likes it, but I cannot tolerate that kind of behavior."

"Please, Diane. I should have told you about Evelyn. I'm sorry about that. It was—inexcusable. But you heard yourself how happy she is. She only has good things to say about our work."

Diane nodded. "Yes, that's true. Evelyn is happy. But Victor Étoile is miserable, and the more I sit here and contemplate why, the more I think *you* had something to do with it."

"Please, Diane, if you could—"

Diane held up one hand to silence her. "I don't want to hear any more today, Abby. Go home. I need time to think. I'll decide what to do after the engagement party—assuming the party still happens, of course."

"Is there anything I can say that will change your mind?"

"No. It's settled. I'll see you on Saturday."

It would have been less frightening if Diane had lashed out. If she had cursed or slammed her office door. Abby was used to that side of her boss; it was a side she knew how to manage more easily. But Diane hadn't so much as raised her voice, and Abby didn't know what to say next.

"I'm sorry, Diane. I truly am."

Diane turned her chair and stared out the window. "I never set out to become a divorce lawyer, you know. I had much more lofty dreams about what I would do: civil rights law, immigration policy. But it was made very clear to me early on that if I ever wanted to become a partner, it would have to be in a field that the men I worked for considered suitable for women. 'Family law' was the only specialty they thought a woman was capable of handling. It was the only chance they were willing to give me, so I took it, and I got very good at it. I've worked my entire life to earn the reputation I have today. When I joined forces with Richard to form this firm, I thought I'd found a real partner—a colleague I could trust. But Richard Gold only looks out for himself, which means I need my associates to look out for *me*. I can't risk having someone at this firm who doesn't respect me enough to be completely honest."

"But I do respect you! And your work! Please, Diane, please hear me out."

Diane kept her eyes on the window. "You should go, Abby. I'll see you on Saturday. In the meantime, enjoy your time off."

Enjoy my time off? How the hell am I supposed to do that?

Abby got into the elevator with her head still spinning. When she pushed her way through the glass doors of the lobby, the late July heat was like a slap in the face. It was too oppressive to walk more than a few blocks, so she hailed a taxi and got inside. Without thinking, she gave the driver the address of her grandmother's apartment.

When the taxi pulled up, Abby's heart felt heavy. The last time she had been inside the building was the last time she had seen her grandmother alive. She fished into her purse for money to pay the driver and forced herself to get out of the car.

The doorman greeted her with a hug. Paul had to be in his sixties, at least, but to Abby, he never seemed to age. His white mustache was as thick as ever, and the jacket of his uniform still fit to perfection.

"Abby," Paul said, his voice heavy with emotion. "I'm so glad you came by. We've missed seeing your face around here."

"I've missed you, too," Abby said. "It's been . . . hard with her gone."

Paul nodded sympathetically. "She was one of a kind. Everyone in the building loved her."

"That's so sweet of you to say. Do you think you could let me into the apartment? My mom has the extra key, but she's out of town."

"Of course! Let me get it—I'll only be a minute. I'll take you up myself."

Ten minutes later, Paul was turning the key into the door of 11G.

Whenever they had visited the apartment as children, Hannah liked to say, "The *G* is for grandma!"

"Thank you, Paul," Abby told him. "I'm not sure how long—"

He interrupted with a reassuring smile. "Take however long you need," he said.

The spacious one bedroom was as spotless as ever, but the silence felt unfamiliar and strange. The scent of lemon Lysol hung in the air, erasing the memories of other, cherished smells—roasted chickens, cheese blintzes, and oatmeal cookies, heavy with chocolate and walnuts. Before her trip, Abby's mother had been by to clean and to begin what would surely be the lengthy process of packing up all of Grandma Sara's possessions. The evidence of those efforts was all around—the bare bookcases, the empty coat closet, and the neat rows of half-filled cardboard boxes pressed against the living room wall. Abby dug her nails into her palms. She did not have the courage to walk into the bedroom, the place where her grandmother had breathed her last breath.

She scanned the boxes on the floor, looking for the one her mother had mentioned, the one with Abby's name written on the top. Abby found it, eventually, on the coffee table, next to the crystal dish of candies that had been wrapped to look like tiny strawberries. Abby took a candy, twisted off the wrapping, and popped the rock-hard sweet in her mouth. She bit through the shell to the viscous center—a dollop of cloying strawberry syrup. It was as if her grandmother were sitting beside her, holding her hand, whispering in her ear. *We begin in dust and end in dust. In the middle, it's good to have something sweet.*

When the last bit of candy was finally gone, Abby opened the flaps of the cardboard box. It was largely empty—only two speckled composition notebooks were inside—the kind her teachers used to give her in high school. One was new, but the older, yellowed book seemed remarkably familiar. As Abby lifted it onto her lap, she suddenly remembered the last time she had seen it. It had been a cold and rainy day when she was fifteen or so. Grandma Sara had asked her to fetch

an umbrella, and Abby had scoured the bottom of Sara's front hall
closet. Behind the winter boots and the pile of shopping bags, Abby
had found the timeworn notebook. She had brought it to her grandmother, along with the umbrella, and asked what it was.

"It's a book of memories," her grandmother had replied, a smile
playing on the edge of her lips. "You're welcome to look through it if
you want." But Abby had been busy with her schoolwork, and the book
seemed too old and shabby to be of any interest. She remembered that
it had been filled with newspaper articles, but she'd had neither the
patience nor the desire to read even one.

Now, of course, all that had changed. Carefully, she flipped back
the cover of the notebook to see a myriad of wedding announcements
from *The New York Times*, cut out and glued onto the pages. The first
clipping, dated August of 1946, consisted of only a single paragraph.

YOUNG REFUGEE COUPLE WED YESTERDAY

Emma Buchbinder, 20 years old, and Benjamin Teplitz, 22,
who survived two Nazi death camps, were married yesterday
at the Hebrew Sheltering and Immigrant Aid Society, 425 La-
fayette Street. A wedding reception followed the ceremony.

The second article was printed in November of 1947.

SURVIVORS OF NAZI DEATH CAMPS MARRIED

Two recently arrived displaced persons who lost their families in Nazi death camps were married yesterday at the Mar-
seilles Hotel, the national reception center maintained by the
United Service for New Americans.

The bride, Anna Weiss, 28, spent two years in the Buchenwald camp. She lost her mother and father, three sisters, two married brothers, and nine nephews and nieces.

The groom, Harry Kranz, 29, escaped with his brother from a sealed train taking them to Oswecim (Auschwitz). The brothers lost their mother, father, and two sisters.

Anna and Harry met in a camp for displaced persons shortly after liberation. Distant cousins of Anna's father arranged for her to move to New York, but Harry and his brother were still overseas. When Rabbi Samuel Cohen of the Bronx relayed Anna's story to Sara Auerbach of Manhattan, Mrs. Auerbach coordinated with United Jewish Appeal to relocate both Kranz brothers to the United States.

The third article was from 1948, about a wedding that took place on Coney Island. The outdoor wedding, it was printed, "is an old Jewish religious custom, the open sky symbolizing the roof of the traditional canopy." According to the article, the bride and groom both fled Poland after the German invasion. The families of both had been "wiped out." Over five hundred people, including fifty rabbis, were in attendance at the ceremony.

Abby's hands shook as she turned the pages—more and more wedding stories from the late 1940s, all of them, presumably, her grandmother's doing. When a fresh wave of European Jews began arriving in New York, Sara had been approached by a group of community leaders who encouraged her to use her prodigious gifts once more. The matches she made—and the children that resulted from them—would help to rebuild some of what her people had lost. While Abby knew a bit of what Sara had accomplished in those early post-war years, those were the stories her grandmother glossed over. Those were the names Abby didn't know.

Abby wondered whether this was why Sara still read the wedding announcements with such devotion. Her grandmother had insisted that even if she didn't know the couples, reading the love stories lifted her spirits. "Love is a light in the dark," she would say, waving her newspaper in the air. "These stories are proof of love. And proof of love is proof of life."

In the last few pages of the notebook, a different type of entry caught Abby's eye. The first was dated 1955, with a woman's name written and underlined on top: <u>Marlene Fishman</u>. Below the name came standard information:

Husband: Artie Fishman
Children: Annie, 7, Steven, 4
Address: 165 West 82nd Street
Phone number: Traflgr 4–0495

None of that, of course, was particularly unusual. What *was* strange, however, was what came after. Notes had been added on different days, some in pencil and some in ink. When read together, the tale they told was a far cry from Sara's typical stories. It was clear that Marlene and Artie Fishman were *not* one of Sara's love matches.

3/6/55: Met Marlene and Artie at Purim carnival
3/20/55: Saw Marlene at park
3/25/55: Marlene limping
4/8/55: Marlene's arm in cast, bruises on face
4/11/55: Coffee with Marlene at my apartment
4/12/55: Called, no answer
4/14/55: Called, no answer
4/16/55: Visited Marlene's apartment
4/19/55: Calls with Marlene
4/20/55: Purchased suitcase for Marlene
4/24/55: Purchased train tickets for Marlene
4/29/55: Marlene called from Connecticut. Will be staying with her sister

Abby read the list half a dozen times—more certain with each reading that her grandmother had, undoubtedly, saved Marlene Fishman's life. At first Abby wondered why her grandmother hadn't mentioned these kinds of stories to her and her sister. But the longer Abby sat there pondering, the more she realized that, perhaps, Sara had tried.

There had been that day when Abby learned about her father's engagement, and Sara had brought her to the park for pretzels. *There are worse fathers, sweetheart. Believe me. Some of what I've seen . . . well, I'll tell you one day when you're older.*

And then, there had been the conversation they'd had when Abby announced she would be a lawyer, like her grandfather. Sara had been so proud when Abby got into law school, bragging to everyone who would listen. *She's going to Columbia Law School, you know. This one's got a mind like you wouldn't believe!*

But Abby had been nervous to tell her grandmother when she decided on the job with Diane's firm. "Divorce law then?" her grandmother had asked. "Your grandfather did a few of those. It wasn't his specialty, of course. He was a jack-of-all-trades—real estate, business. You're sure that's what you want to do full time?"

"I'm sure," Abby said. "When Mom got divorced, nobody fought for her. I want to fight for people now."

Grandma Sara raised an eyebrow. "Fight *for* people or fight *against* them?"

"Look, Grandma, I've heard all your stories. All the love matches, all the perfect couples. But look at my parents. We both know the world isn't all happy endings. Honestly, I wish you'd stop pretending it was."

Her grandmother's face crumpled like a broken cookie. "*Pretending?*"

"You know what I mean."

Sara's eyes flashed with fury. "You think *I* don't know from heartache? You think I don't know from miserable endings? Just because I didn't tell you *those* stories, Abby, doesn't mean I don't have plenty to tell."

Abby's voice rose in indignation. "Well, maybe you *should* have told me them then! Maybe you should have been more honest with me!"

"You and your sister had enough *tsuris* with your parents—you think I should have given you nightmares, too? Look what happened when I was honest with Hannah about that *fakakta* royal wedding!"

"I only mean—"

"Abby, sweetheart, I'm not a fool. I know how your parents' divorce affected you. I know that you have something to prove. When I was younger than you, I had to prove myself, too. I represented *myself* in court—a rabbinical court, but a court just the same. There were twenty-eight men arguing against me. *Twenty-eight* men! Can you believe it? They said I shouldn't be allowed to make matches. They called me a liar. They thought I wasn't worthy. At the end of the day, I won my case. I understand your need to fight. Whatever job you take, I'll be proud of you. But you need to remember to fight *for* something."

"I'll be fighting for my clients. Isn't that enough?"

Abby's grandmother shook her head. "Clients are only people, sweetheart. Some will be worth fighting for, and some will not."

"Don't you think you're being melodramatic?"

Sara placed both hands on Abby's shoulders and kissed her granddaughter softly on the forehead. "There is too much cruelty in this world. I've seen it, and I know you've seen some, too. It isn't enough to fight against cruelty. For my whole life, I fought *for* love. Not just romantic love, you understand. The love of a parent for a child. The love of one friend for another. Fight *for* something, sweetheart. Not just against. That's the best advice I can give you. And if you can't decide what you want to fight for, love is as good a cause as any."

TWENTY-ONE

SARA

1955

Trust One Eye More Than Two Ears

Sunday 3 P.M.: A Carnival Day, to celebrate Purim, will be open at Congregation Shaare Zedek, 212 West 93rd Street. Games, prizes, and refreshments for children ages 6-13.

S ara looked forward to volunteering at the carnival. She was certain that seeing the little ones in their costumes would bring back precious memories of six-year-old Beverly, dripping in scarves and fake gold bangles, pretending to be brave Queen Esther.

Beverly and Eddie were both grown-up now, both in college, but at schools close enough to make it home for dinner most Sunday evenings. Since Gabe had passed away last year, the three of them had become even closer. Sara knew Gabe would be proud of their children and the way they had handled his untimely loss. Every morning she woke with the same thought in her head: *How foolish I was to put off marrying him for so long. What I wouldn't give now for just one more day.*

Gabe began courting her immediately after the *beis din* made its final decision. But for two years, Sara refused to marry him. "What if I find out you're meant for someone else?" she said. "What if I see something I don't want to see?"

Gabe's patience with her was seemingly limitless. "The only woman I see is you," he promised. "There will never be anyone else for me."

The wedding itself was an absolute blur—Rabbi Sheinkopf performed the service, and Rabbi Pearl offered a special blessing of his own. Sara's mother danced with the women, clapping and shouting as she spun on her heels. The banquet table was heaped with platters of roasted chicken, five kinds of pickles, and, of course, knishes from Klein's.

After years of miscarriages, Sara gave birth to Eddie when she was thirty-five years old. Beverly came along two years later—a second miracle for the couple. They moved to an apartment on the Upper West Side, and Sara devoted herself to caring for her young children. Though she stopped making matches, she retained her reputation; when the war finally ended, rabbis from all over the city visited her home to beg for assistance. Six million Jewish souls had been taken. Would she help to ensure that their people survived?

She agreed, of course, and began searching again—scouring the shadows for glimmers of light. Every match she made was a candle in the darkness, a beam of hope after an endless eclipse. For eight years, she was tireless in her efforts, but when Gabriel died, her intuition grew cloudy, and the edges of her vision blurred like wet paint. With Gabe gone, she was a dancer without music, a writer devoid of paper and ink. Her passion became an inaccessible thing; her senses dulled from technicolor to gray.

She began volunteering at her *shul*, filling her days with committees and meetings. When she was asked to staff a booth at the Purim carnival, she accepted the task without hesitation.

Because the holiday had come so early that year, it was decided that the carnival would be held indoors, inside the *shul*'s vast social hall. The teenagers were in charge of selecting the games—pin the tail on the donkey, tossing balls at tin cans, and popping balloons were among

the most popular. Parents and other adult volunteers collected dona-
tions, handed out tickets, and generally curbed the overall chaos. The
high-ceilinged room echoed with laughter and the squeals of overex-
cited young children. The floor was littered with popcorn kernels, candy
wrappers, and *hamantaschen* crumbs.

When Sara arrived, she was assigned to the prize booth, where
children traded in their winning tickets for flimsy toys, coloring books,
shiny trinkets, and paper dolls. At first, she was charmed by the adorable
faces and the way their brows furrowed as they made their selections.
But after almost two hours, she grew tired, and her back turned stiff
from standing in place.

Sara was coming to the end of her shift when an attractive young
mother in a green floral dress approached with a boy around four or
five years old. Perched atop his curls was a silver foil crown, and at his
waist hung a homemade cardboard sword. After reaching the booth,
he held out his chubby fist and deposited a small pile of tickets on
the table.

"Hello!" said Sara. "What would you like for your prize?"

The boy pointed shyly to a small tin car, and Sara placed it gently in
his open palm. His mother lifted him onto her hip. "What do you say,
Steven?" she asked.

"Thank you," he whispered, and Sara smiled.

Steven's mother introduced herself. "I'm Marlene Fishman. And
this is Steven. Thank you so much for helping with the carnival. It's
been such a lovely day for the children."

"It's a fun event," Sara agreed. "It's nice to see all of the little ones
so happy."

Just then, a handsome man in a sports jacket approached the table
with his daughter. Like all the other girls, she was dressed as Queen
Esther, adorned with a pile of shiny beaded necklaces. "Mommy!" she
said. "I got so many tickets! Daddy showed me the best way to knock
down all the cans!"

"Wonderful, Annie! Now, what will you choose?" Annie's father complimented Steven's car. "It looks like you picked out a fast one," he said. "We'll test it out when we get home." He turned to Sara and flashed a smile. "Artie Fishman," he said, extending his hand. "Great carnival, isn't it? Terrific, really."

"Sara Auerbach," Sara said. "I'm so glad to meet all of you. It's wonderful to see so many young families."

With Sara's help, Annie chose a butterfly coloring book. Afterward, Sara watched as the young family stopped for popcorn at the busy refreshment table. Steven fed his father a handful of kernels while his mother and sister looked on, giggling.

When the flash came, it was a total surprise.

It had been more than a year since the last time she'd felt it—the streak across her periphery, the tickle just outside her sight. It had always filled Sara with a sudden burst of warmth, a giddy rise in temperature and in spirit.

Only this time, the feeling was completely different. This time, the flash was sharp and searing, as ominous and jagged as a strike of lightning. Sara reached for the table to steady herself. She studied the couple from across the room, but their smiles revealed nothing out of the ordinary. On the outside, they seemed to be happy and loving. But Sara was certain something was wrong.

In bed that night, Sara reflected on what she had seen in the social hall. She pondered whether she had a duty to investigate the meaning of whatever it was she had felt. Both Gabe and Rabbi Sheinkopf were gone—she had run out of people to call upon for advice. She passed sleepless night after sleepless night for the next two weeks.

And then came the second hair-raising jolt, as she was walking through Central Park. The playground was crowded with parents and children, but Sara spotted Steven out of the corner of her eye. A further scan revealed his father behind him and Marlene to his left, pushing Annie on a swing. The same feeling of dread swept its way through her, so Sara found a seat on an empty bench nearby. What was the problem between Marlene and her husband? What was causing this sensation that rushed so ominously into Sara's head?

When Sara saw Marlene next, at Friday-night services, the young mother limped into the sanctuary. "What happened, dear?" Sara asked, but Marlene waved the question away. "Just a little accident," she said. "So nice to see you again, Mrs. Auerbach." A few weeks later, after Passover, Marlene Fishman's arm was in a cast, and it was obvious that she had used a good deal of pancake makeup to cover the bruise on the right side of her face. "Klutzy me," she said, when Sara inquired. This time, Sara was insistent. "I'd like you to come over for coffee," she said. "On Monday, after your husband goes to work. Bring the children, I don't mind. Come at ten—my address is in the membership directory."

At 10:15 on Monday morning, Marlene Fishman knocked on Sara's door. Steven was with her, but Annie was in school. "She's in first grade now," Marlene explained. "She loves her teacher and her friends."

"How wonderful," Sara said. "Please, both of you, come in. I just brewed a fresh pot of coffee." She set out a plate of oatmeal cookies, along with paper and colored pencils for Steven.

"Tell me," Sara said. "How are you, my dear?"

It was over an hour before Marlene admitted it, and even then, she couldn't say the words. "Artie begs me for forgiveness every time," she said. "And he promises it won't ever happen again. He always knows the right thing to say."

Sara sighed and pointed to the bruise that was still in bloom on Marlene's cheek. "When a man does this with his hands, you cannot believe what comes out of his mouth. Believe what you see, not what you hear. *Eyn oyg hot mer globin vi tsvey oyern,*" she said.

"I'm sorry, but I don't understand Yiddish," Marlene whispered.

"Trust one eye more than two ears."

That Friday, the Fishman family did not come to services, so on Saturday, Sara looked up Marlene's address. They lived in an elegant prewar building only a few blocks from Sara's. Sara avoided the doorman by entering the lobby with a large group of women on their way back from shopping. In the rush, Sara passed by undetected and rode the elevator up to the Fishmans' floor. She was about to knock on the door of apartment 9A when she heard the shouting.

"Who the hell are you to throw my whiskey away? I paid good money for that bottle!"

"Artie, please, I thought we agreed. When you drink too much, your moods—it's not good for the children. It frightens them."

"Now I'm not a good enough father either? What kind of ungrateful bitch—"

Sara knocked loudly on the door. She hoped to diffuse the situation, but Artie sounded too far gone to care. "We're busy!" he shouted, as she knocked again. "Whoever it is, come back later!"

Across the carpeted hallway, the door to 9D opened, and a gray-haired man in his seventies poked his head through the opening. "He won't let you in," the old man said sadly. "He's a drinker, that one. Not bad when he's sober. But lately he's been on quite a tear. If you have something for them, you can leave it with me. I'll drop it off when things calm down."

Sara told him she had stopped by for a visit. "Would you tell Marlene that Sara Auerbach was here? I want to help her if I can." The man nodded before retreating back into his apartment.

The next few weeks were filled with whispered phone calls and the cautious but continuous making of plans. A suitcase was purchased. Train tickets were obtained. Marlene's sister in New Haven pledged her support. On the twenty-ninth of April, while Artie was at work, Marlene picked Annie up early from school. She stopped by Sara's apartment for her suitcase, as planned, before taking a taxi to Grand Central

Station. A few hours later, Marlene and the children were on the train to Connecticut.

Sara told no one about the part she played or what she had seen at the Purim carnival. At first, she wondered whether her gift had been irreparably altered. She questioned her purpose going forward—what was it that she was meant to do now? She was a *shadchanteh,* after all—a maker of matches, not an enforcer of vows. She did not want to trade her occupation for the work of a bodyguard or a policeman.

And yet, Sara knew that if the sensation struck again—if she were ever moved by another menacing flash—she would fight to protect any woman whose secret pain was revealed to her.

TWENTY-TWO

ABBY

1994

When she finished reading through the first journal, Abby wandered into her grandmother's kitchen. Sara's presence was everywhere, from the bag of Zabar's coffee on the counter to the recipe box on the windowsill. According to the clock on the stove, it was almost three thirty. Abby hadn't eaten a thing since breakfast, and despite the stress of being "almost" fired, she found that she was actually starving.

She was rummaging through her grandmother's pantry when she remembered their last conversation. *Mrs. Levitz is coming tomorrow at ten. I promised her I'd make the cinnamon babka, but I don't like to rush around in the morning, so I made two of them this afternoon. I put one in the freezer for you.*

Abby held her breath while she opened the freezer door. Her mother had probably thrown the babka away, along with the rest of the refrigerator's contents. It was silly to get her hopes up like this, to imagine tasting Sara's handiwork one last time.

As soon as she spotted the foil-covered loaf, Abby felt a lump in the back of her throat. She carried the bag of coffee and the frozen babka to the living room and put them into the box, beside the two journals. She would come back later with her mother and go through her grandmother's other belongings. For now, what she had would be enough. On her way out of the building, she asked Paul to make sure the door to her grandmother's place was locked.

By the time Abby got back to her own apartment, the frozen babka had almost thawed. She turned on her oven to warm it a bit and filled her coffeemaker with her grandmother's ground beans. Just as the water began to hiss, Abby's phone rang.

"Abby! It's Jessica. Your secretary said you'd gone home already. Is everything all right? Are you sick?"

"Hi, Jessica. No, I'm fine—"

"Good," Jessica interrupted. "Do you have a minute to speak?" She lowered her voice. "I have a patient waiting, but I just saw Victor. I ran out for a coffee at the bakery, and he was sitting at one of the tables in the back. He said he'd been waiting there since before noon, hoping I might come in again. Can you believe that?"

"Wow," Abby said. "That's . . . wow. What else did he say?"

"He wanted me to stay and have coffee with him, but I had to get back for my patients. He looked terrible, Abby—like he hadn't slept or showered. Then he asked me to have dinner with him tonight. I couldn't say no. He looked so desperate. You don't think it's wrong of me to meet him, do you?"

"Wrong? Of course not! I already told you, there's something between the two of you."

"I know, but you also told me he's engaged."

"Engaged isn't married. He's obviously having doubts."

"But how do you *know* that?"

Abby sighed. "Victor was at our office this morning. He was supposed to meet my boss to discuss his prenup. She rushed back from

Miami for the meeting. But like you said, Victor was a mess today. He told us he couldn't focus, and he left the office without even looking at the documents. If he didn't have doubts about the wedding, he would have stayed to go over the agreement."

"Maybe."

"Jessica, last week you told me you couldn't stop thinking about him. You told me he was charming. You said he made you *breathless*."

"I did, didn't I? Okay, I'll go to dinner. Oh my god, it's four thirty already—I have to run. I'll call you tomorrow to let you know how it goes."

When she got off the phone, Abby pulled the babka from the oven. Her apartment smelled like someplace else—the coffee, the cinnamon, and the yeast transported her back to her grandmother's kitchen. If she closed her eyes, she could see her grandmother's hands, patting the babka dough, sprinkling the filling, and tucking it all into the narrow loaf pan. Abby cut through the golden outer layer to the gooey center of the cake. As the cinnamon crumbs dissolved on her tongue, the lump in her throat gave way to tears.

She carried her plate and mug to the couch and opened the second journal from her grandmother's apartment. Abby figured she would read a bit and then watch something on TV. There couldn't be more than a few entries, at most. The first journal went up to the late 1950s, and Sara had given up matchmaking after that.

Or had she? The book looked newer than it should have, and as Abby scanned the dates jotted down inside it, she grew increasingly confused—the entries spanned from 1990 until the last month of Sara's life. The realization was shocking at first, then inspiring, and, finally, hilarious. Her grandmother hadn't come out of retirement just for Jessica. In Sara Auerbach's tenth decade on earth, she had begun actively matchmaking again! And, from everything Abby could glean from the pages, Sara hadn't lost her touch.

This last journal was different from all the others. The names of the clients were from varied ethnic backgrounds; they were twenty-somethings, octogenarians, and every age in between. Was it possible for an eighty-year-old man to find love? Abby's grandmother certainly seemed to think so. Not only that, but there were other surprises, too. These new pages showed that Sara had matched women with women, men with men, people from all religions and races. It seemed that in her final years, Sara saw no barriers to love.

Abby smiled when she saw the name of her grandmother's door-man, Paul, among the pages.

Paul McCormick, age 62
Occupation: Doorman
What a mensch *Paul is! Such a caring and wonderful man. I have known him for almost twelve years.*
In all that time, I don't believe he's dated anyone. But there is a lid for every pot. I won't let such a treasure of a man be alone!

The notes in this journal felt more personal than the others. Perhaps it was because the pages were written not by the twenty- or fifty-year-old version of Sara, but by the version of the woman Abby knew and loved so well. These words *sounded* like Abby's grandmother— heartfelt, determined, and filled with purpose.

"Did you like being a matchmaker?" Abby had asked once, when her grandmother had first come to live with them in New York.

"Darling, it was the greatest honor of my life. To make a true match, to see two souls united—I wish everyone could experience it."

"Did you like it better than being a mom and a grandma?"

"Oh, sweetheart. Nothing could be better than that. I love being a mother and I love being your grandma. But I'm grateful that I was a matchmaker first. It taught me that I could support myself, and that I have something valuable to offer. One day, no matter what your career is, I hope it makes you feel that way, too."

Abby thought about her grandmother's hopes. She certainly knew she could support herself, but did working for Diane make her feel valued? Evelyn Morgan appreciated her, but that was because Abby had gone above and beyond the normal parameters of her job. Although Abby hadn't made a match, she'd prevented Evelyn from throwing her marriage away. In her heart, Abby knew that what she'd done for Evelyn was more meaningful than much of her other work. She thought, perhaps, she was closer to understanding some of what her grandmother wanted for her.

The phone rang again, but Abby let the machine pick up. It was Will, sounding slightly confused. Like Jessica, he had tried reaching her at the office and had been told that she'd gone home for the day. Abby resolved to call him tomorrow—for now, she wanted to be alone. She scraped the remaining crumbs off her plate.

This was the last of her grandmother's babkas, and she would not waste a single bite.

The next morning, Abby slept later than usual. She might have gone on dozing into the afternoon if Jessica hadn't called at nine.

Although it was Jessica who'd woken Abby, the ophthalmologist was the one who sounded half asleep. "Abby?" she whispered dreamily. "It's me."

"Jessica? Hey—how was dinner?"

"Abby . . . I . . . I don't even know what to say. It was the most amazing night of my life."

"Victor must have taken you to one hell of a restaurant," Abby said.

"Let me guess. Le Bernardin? Bouley? That new one—Daniel?" Abby sighed. "I'd love to go to Daniel."

"No, nothing as fancy as all that. We went to a tiny bistro over on First Avenue. I've never had anyone ask me so many questions. Victor made me tell him my entire life story, starting with the hospital where I was born. He wanted to know why I became a doctor, why I'd never been married, why I loved sneakers so much."

Abby groaned. "Please don't tell me you wore your sneakers to dinner. . . ."

"I had no choice! I met him right from work. There was no time for me to go home first."

"Did he shower before he met you, at least? He was kind of rank yesterday morning."

"Yes, he showered, but he still looked tired. He hasn't been sleeping well lately. Abby, he told me all about Nicole. How they met, their work together. She sounds incredibly smart and creative. That's what drew him to her. They have a wonderful working relationship."

Abby hesitated. "Did he say whether he's still planning on marrying her?"

"He's having doubts, like you said. He feels connected to Nicole in terms of their work, but not in other important ways. Victor is finally settling into a good routine with Chloé and Isobel, but Nicole isn't interested in spending time with them. It's been a painful realization for him. He told me he wants to find someone who loves his daughters as much as he does." Jessica paused. "I told him how I've always wanted children and how I used to think it was too late for me. Anyway, Nicole only wants to talk business these days. She's been distant with him lately, and he thinks she may have found someone else. He isn't sure what either of them wants."

"What about *you*? What do you want?"

"I don't know, Abby. It's so . . . confusing. The way Victor looks at me—I've never felt so beautiful. We stayed at the restaurant until one in the morning. We never ran out of things to say."

"Did he kiss you? Did you guys—sorry, is that too personal?"

Jessica laughed. "We kissed, yes. But that was it. He's still engaged." For a few moments, there was silence on the other end of the line, and Abby wondered whether Jessica had hung up the phone.

"Jessica?" Abby asked. "Are you still there?"

Eventually, Jessica spoke again. "I'm here," she said. "Sorry about that."

"Are you going to tell me how the kiss was?"

Jessica's answer was barely above a whisper. "I didn't want it to end."

Abby had another piece of babka for breakfast. She made more coffee and called Will at work. "Do you have time for lunch today?" she asked. "I can meet near your office—I have the day off."

"A day off?" Will asked. "That doesn't sound like you."

"Long story," Abby told him. "How's twelve thirty?"

Abby arrived at the diner first and scored one of the leather banquettes in the back. She scanned the twelve-page laminated menu and tried to decide what she felt like eating. She was still pondering when Will walked in wearing new glasses——a pair of speckled tortoiseshell frames. She waited until they got their food before she complimented him on them.

He flashed her a slightly sheepish grin. "They're a lot snazzier than my old ones, I guess. More fashionable, maybe?"

"They look good!" Abby told him. "Did Nicole help pick them out?"

Will almost choked on his poppy seed bagel, but Abby had made up her mind to be honest. While he was still coughing, she tried to explain. "Whatever is going on with the two of you is a good thing. But I'd love it if you and I could still be friends."

Will wiped his mouth with a paper napkin and cleared a few poppy seeds from his throat. "I don't . . . how did you know about Nicole? Not that anything's happened—it hasn't, I swear. But—"

"But you spent the entire weekend together and you're starting to have feelings for each other."

Will stared at her, wide-eyed. "Are you some kind of fortune-teller or something?"

"Let's just say I'm a particularly observant person."

"Abby, I hope I haven't hurt your feelings. I really do think you're amazing. But I never really felt like you were that into me."

"You're right," she agreed. "The two of us aren't a match, that's all."

"Yeah, well, Nicole's getting married in a month, so it's not like she and I are a perfect match either."

Abby shook her head. "You don't know that, Will. A lot of couples have to overcome obstacles. Have you told Nicole how you feel?"

Will frowned. "Not in so many words. We speak on the phone about her business a million times a day, but I'm pretty sure most of it is just an excuse for us to keep talking to each other. Neither of us ever wants to hang up. We make each other laugh . . . I can't stop thinking about her."

"Then why not tell her that?"

"You *know* why, Abby—she's *engaged*."

Abby took a bite of her sandwich while she contemplated what to say to Will next. She thought about her conversation with Jessica that morning. How much was Abby willing to give up in order to help Will and Jessica find love? Was she really willing to sacrifice her career?

What if Abby decided to choose her job instead? She could tell Will that Nicole would never break off the engagement. She could persuade Jessica that her matchmaking intuition had been wrong, and that Victor was meant to marry his fiancée. All Abby had to do was tell a few lies, rebuild Diane's trust, and bide her time. Then, everything could go back to the way it used to be.

But as Abby stared down at her plate, she realized "the way it used to be" was no longer what she wanted. Her grandmother had known what Abby was capable of. Sara knew Abby would never become a full-time matchmaker, but she also knew that Abby needed to open her eyes to the possibility that there was still more for her to discover: more fulfillment to be gained from her career, more confidence to be found within herself, more love in the world than she could have imagined.

Abby swallowed her food and turned to Will. "Just because Nicole is engaged doesn't mean she's going to get married. If you truly think the two of you share something special, you owe it to yourself—and to her—to tell her how you feel."

After lunch, Abby went back to her grandmother's building, where Paul was waiting behind the front desk. "Back so soon?" he asked her, smiling. "Wait one minute and I'll get the key."

"That's okay," Abby said. "I don't need to go up. Actually, I came by to talk to you."

"Me?" Paul asked. "Well, that's a nice surprise. Is there something I can help you with?"

She wasn't quite sure how to begin; she bit her lower lip and paced in front of his desk. "Paul, did you know that my grandmother used to be a matchmaker?"

Her reticence seemed to amuse him. "Don't look so worried—of course I did! Mrs. Auerbach wasn't shy about it. *I've come out of retirement,* she used to say. She had a special name for it. A shadko . . . shadcho . . ."

"*Shadchanteh,*" Abby told him.

Paul snapped his fingers. "That's it!" he said. "Like I told you, everybody in the building loved your grandmother. She practiced her hobby on a lot of us, actually." He frowned. "Only I'm not supposed to call it a hobby—your grandmother didn't like me saying that. Anyway, whatever you want to call it, Mrs. Auerbach was responsible for quite a few couples in the neighborhood." He began to list them on his fingers. "Mr. Singh in 11B, Dr. Salcedo in 5A. The pharmacist at the drug store on the corner, Mr. and Mrs. Lee's granddaughter, Vicki . . ." He began to blush. "Me too, of course."

"Paul! That's wonderful!" Abby told him.

Paul nodded. "Albert is a special man," he said softly. "And we owe our happiness to your grandmother. Marriage isn't legal in New York for us yet. But we're going to fight until it is." He pointed to a chair in the corner of the lobby. "She used to sit there with a book every morning and watch the tenants come and go."

Abby stopped pacing and smiled at Paul. "My grandmother loved you, you know. She called you a *mensch*—the highest compliment she ever gave." Abby took a few steps toward the upholstered chair and pictured her grandmother sitting on it, offering greetings and advice to passersby as unreservedly as always.

If you can't decide what you want to fight for, love is as good a cause as any.

TWENTY-THREE

SARA

1990

There's a Lid for Every Pot

Sara Auerbach returned to matchmaking on the eve of her ninetieth birthday.

Beverly and Abby took her to dinner at her favorite Italian
place near Lincoln Center. When they got to the restaurant, Eddie
and Judy were already there, along with their sons, Jason and Bobby.
The biggest surprise of the evening was Hannah, who had flown in
from California that day. Eddie asked the waiter for two bottles of
champagne, and as soon as everyone was holding a glass, the family
went around the table, making toasts.

"To ninety more birthdays."
"To the most wonderful grandma."
"The most supportive mother."
"Who makes the best kugel."

"And the most delicious babka."

"Who tells the funniest stories."

"Thank you for always being there for us."

Sara ordered her favorite—eggplant parmesan—but she made sure to save room for dessert. Not only did the waiter bring her a giant dish of tiramisu, but a few minutes after the coffee was served, a group of waitstaff headed toward them with an extravagantly decorated pink-and-white cake. It was three tiers high, like a mini wedding cake, swathed in buttercream flowers and ten sparkling candles. "We thought ten candles was probably enough," Abby explained.

Both the servers and the people at the tables surrounding them lifted their voices to serenade Sara. When it was time to lean forward and blow out her candles, she felt as if the entire restaurant was watching. At first, the tiny flames on the cake resisted, but, eventually, Sara's breath won out.

She hadn't seen a flash at the edge of her vision for at least thirty years. After Gabe passed away, Sara had stopped matchmaking, and although she'd seen flickers of a different sort for Marlene Fishman and a handful of others, even those darker bits of intuition had petered out by the time she reached sixty. She was entirely caught off guard, therefore, when one of the cake candles bounced back to life, leaving a whisper-thin trail of light for her to follow. It pinged back and forth between two of the waiters before the candle sputtered out again. An electric thrum traveled from Sara's lips down the tunnel of her throat and to her chest. She imagined it felt something akin to the sensation of switching on a pacemaker. A renewed sense of purpose pumped its way through her as she called the two waiters over with a flick of her fingers.

"Darlings," she said softly, so the others wouldn't hear. "Thank you so much for the beautiful singing. If you don't mind my saying, you make a lovely couple." She pulled a crisp twenty-dollar bill from her purse and pressed it into the hand closest to hers. "Do an old woman a favor, will you? When you're done here tonight, get a drink together. I think the two of you will have a lot to talk about."

After her birthday, more matches revealed themselves—not as regularly or as brightly as they had in her youth, but just frequently enough to make Sara feel useful. She began sitting in the lobby of her building with a book—sometimes reading, but more often chatting with her neighbors and taking mental notes. There was Dr. Salcedo, the cardiologist from the fifth floor, who liked to ask Sara about her novels. There was Mr. Singh, from 11B down the hall, who was always carrying canvases and boxes of art supplies through the lobby and to the elevator. Sara sensed a latent loneliness in both of them and made up her mind to do something about it.

Was it wrong of her to schedule an appointment with Dr. Salcedo despite the fact that she had no coronary complaints? Perhaps, but she did not think anyone would question a ninety-year-old asking for a checkup. Was it nosy of her to knock on Mr. Singh's door to ask if she might take a look at his work? Perhaps, but who would refuse an art lover's request, especially if the art lover was as old as she was and holding a homemade cinnamon babka?

In this not-so-subtle but charming way, Sara became closely acquainted with the two neighbors. And, after putting in several months of effort, she was able to find love matches for both of them.

After Mr. Singh announced his engagement to a lovely poet Sara had met in line at the grocery store, Paul—her favorite of the building's three doormen—scolded her. "You're going to get yourself a reputation," he said.

"I don't know what you're talking about," she answered. She pulled a shiny compact mirror from her purse and checked to make sure her lipstick hadn't smudged. Paul raised his eyebrows and wagged his finger. "You might fool some of the other tenants," he said. "But I see you down here every day. Sitting in your chair, pretending to read, watching the others come and go."

"I am not *pretending* to read!"

"Snooping, stalking, meddling in people's business . . ."

"Is it wrong to be interested in my neighbors? Is it a crime to help other people find love?"

"I suppose that depends on whether you believe in it."

"Paul!" Sara put a hand to her chest as if his words had mortally wounded her. "Don't tell me *you* don't believe in love? You're one of the most loveable men I know."

The doorman laughed. "Mrs. Auerbach," he said. "That sweet talk isn't going to work on me."

After that, Sara focused her attention on Paul. He was sixty-two years old and he had never been married. He had eight nieces and nephews, but no children of his own. He'd been working as a doorman for over twenty-five years, long before Sara ever moved to the building. Before that, he had worked as a security guard, at an office building all the way down by Wall Street.

"Don't look at me that way," he told Sara one morning, as she peered at him over the pages of her book. She had begun carrying her coffee to the lobby in the mornings, sipping from a mug while she flipped her pages. Sometimes, she brought Paul a cherry danish or a piece of her homemade apple strudel. She always dressed nicely for her lobby mornings—a jewel-toned cardigan and a crisp white shirt. Sometimes, she regretted her plain black slacks, but her legs just weren't what they used to be.

"Like what?" she said innocently. "How am I looking at you?"

"The same way you used to look at Dr. Salcedo."

Sara sighed heavily and snapped her book shut. "Fine," she admitted. "I'm *looking* at you. But that's only because I want to help. As my people say, there's a lid for every pot."

"No disrespect, but I've been lidless for a very long time."

Sara rose from her chair and made her way to the reception desk, behind which the doorman was currently sitting. She lowered her voice just enough to sound mysterious. "I'm going to tell you a little secret. I was a professional matchmaker, once. I've been making matches since I was ten years old."

"Ten years old?" Paul said. "Well now, that's really something." His feigned admiration came off too sweetly, and Sara could tell he was trying to humor her.

"Don't you patronize me, young man," she snapped. "I made *hundreds* of matches in my day. I might be a little out of practice, but I assure you I haven't lost my touch."

Paul hid his laughter with a few well-timed coughs. "Whatever you say, Mrs. Auerbach."

A few weeks later, Sara was sitting in the lobby, reading *The Remains of the Day* for the second time, when a middle-aged man she did not recognize led a wide-eyed young couple into the building. The man wore a soft tweed jacket, a blue bow tie, and an old-fashioned fedora on top of his head. He was obviously a Realtor, there for a showing, and told Paul as much when he stopped at the desk. "Albert Campbell to show 12F," he said, passing Paul a card from his jacket pocket. After he checked the schedule book on his desk, Paul handed Mr. Campbell the key.

When the key was passed between the two men, the flash of light was unmistakable. Sara hid her smile behind her book and waited for Albert to return to the lobby. Half an hour later, when he passed the key back to Paul, the light shone as brightly as before.

Sara told Paul the next day, without mincing words. He blinked a few times and scratched his head, uncertain of how much he should say. "Things are different for young people nowadays," he said. "But when I was growing up, I had no one to talk to. I had three older brothers, and everyone assumed I'd grow up to be exactly like them. I knew I was different, but I didn't have the words to explain how. Even if I had, I don't think my parents would have understood."

Sara laid her wrinkled hand over his. "I'm sorry, Paul. It must have been difficult."

Paul shrugged his shoulders. "It wasn't easy, but it got better. These days, I'm happy with my life. I have some wonderful friends I can be myself with—friends who accept me as I am. But I never had much luck in the romance department. I'm sixty-two years old, Mrs. Auerbach. I'm pretty sure that ship has sailed."

"Oh, sweetheart," Sara said, straightening her shoulders. "I've been on my fair share of cruises, and those ships always turn around. You're going to have to trust me, *tateleh*. In eighty years, I've never been wrong."

TWENTY-FOUR

ABBY

1994

For the rest of the week, Abby worried what Victor's engagement party would bring. She went to Bloomingdale's for something to wear, but on her way to look for dresses, she found herself drawn to the lingerie department.

"You need a new bra," Grandma Sara told her, on one of their last afternoons together.

"What's wrong with my bra?"

Sara pointed to the fraying shoulder strap peeking out from the side of Abby's tank top. "Never underestimate the power of a quality undergarment. A well-fitted brassiere is a wise woman's armor."

When Abby thought about seeing Diane at the party, she decided that a little armor couldn't hurt. So, she followed the overeager saleswoman to the dressing room and let herself be measured from every embarrassing angle. She left with three bras—two beige and one black. The prices were high for a few scraps of fabric, but Abby bought them anyway. Finding a dress was far less complicated. She chose a simple

black sheath that was just chic enough so that she wouldn't feel embarrassed in a room full of couture.

On the way out of the store, she bought a fresh lipstick—one more
layer of protection to help her face her boss. Though Abby usually favored
soft pinks and mauves, this time she chose a bolder hue. The saleswoman
nodded in approval while Abby rubbed her lips together. She turned the
tube over to check the name of the shade. Bulletproof Burgundy.

"I'll take it," Abby said.

Back at her apartment, half a dozen messages waited for her on the
machine.

Hi, Abby, it's Jessica. I have something to ask you.

It's Jessica again. It's about Victor's party. He wants
me to go, but it's obviously complicated. Am I missing
something? It is his engagement party, isn't it? Anyway,
please call me back.

Hey, Abby, it's Will. So . . . Nicole invited me to her party
tomorrow night. It's kind of weird, I guess, but I'm thinking I should go. It's a good chance to network, and I figure
I'll bring a lot of business cards and make the rounds.
Are you going to be there? Let me know.

Hi, honey, it's Mom. I just got back from my trip. Do you
want to meet for lunch tomorrow? Can't wait to see
you. Love you. Bye!

Abby. Where are you? Victor just sent over a gazillion
roses and two giant towers of raspberry macarons. My

office is starting to look like Versailles—without the
mirrors, but *still*. He wrote a note begging me to come
to the party. Abby, what should I do? *Call me back!*

Abby, it's Diane. I haven't heard a peep from Victor, and
he isn't returning my calls. If you have any idea what the
hell is going on, now would be a good time to tell me.

Abby called her mother first and made a plan to meet for lunch.
Next, she left a message for Will, confirming that she would see him at
the party. The third call she made was to her boss, but Diane's assistant
picked up instead.

"Diane is in a meeting, but she's *losing it*," Lisa whispered. "Victor
Étoile is MIA, and the Henshaw negotiations are falling apart."

"At least she can't blame me for that—I've never even met Mr.
Henshaw. Anyway," Abby continued, "I'm returning Diane's call.
Please tell her that I haven't spoken with Victor since the meeting
Monday morning."

"I'll let her know," Lisa said. She lowered her voice to a whisper
again. "Get back here as soon as you can, okay? This place does *not* run
well without you."

After Abby hung up with Lisa, there was only one phone call left to
make.

She had never heard Jessica sound so frantic. "Abby! Thank God!
I've been avoiding Victor's calls all afternoon. I had my nurse tell him
I'm with patients. What do you think is going on?"

"Honestly, I have no idea. I'm sure he's having doubts about the
wedding. But this whole plan of going ahead with the party and inviting you to come makes no sense to me."

"You don't think he wants me to be his *mistress*, do you? Mistresses
are much more accepted in France, I've heard."

"Jessica! You're not going to be anyone's mistress."

"I know, I know. I'm just looking for some kind of explanation."

Abby sighed. "Let's think this through logically. Victor clearly wants you at the party. For now, neither of us can figure out why. The only way we're going to find out is if you accept the invitation. If you stay home and Victor goes through with the wedding, you're always going to regret not going."

After a long pause, Jessica concurred. "You're right," she said. "I have to be there. Would you mind if we went together? I don't want to show up by myself."

"Of course," Abby promised. "Try not to worry—everything is going to work out." She sounded more confident than she felt. By the time she got Jessica off the phone, her head was buzzing with all the different ways the engagement party could go wrong.

Tomorrow night was going to be chaos. Just *thinking* about it was enough to give her a headache. Why had Nicole invited Will? Why had Victor invited Jessica? How long would it take before Diane lost her temper and Abby lost her job?

On Saturday, Abby met her mother for lunch at their favorite coffee shop on Broadway. Beverly smelled like lemons and oranges. Her hair was longer than usual, her cheeks more freckled, and her nose was slightly sunburned. After visiting with Hannah in San Francisco, she'd continued on to Hawaii to coordinate conferences for two of her travel agency's corporate clients. Abby hadn't seen her for almost a month, and their hug lasted for a very long time.

They found a booth, ordered omelets, and sipped at their coffee while Beverly described the highlights from her trip. Abby wasn't sure how much to say about her grandmother's journals and Jessica Cooper, but it turned out that her mother already knew.

"So, have you found a match for the ophthalmologist yet?" Beverly asked.

Abby tried not to choke on her coffee. "I should have guessed Hannah would tell you. Aren't you even a little bit surprised?"

"Surprised that your grandmother was still making matches or surprised that she thought you could make one, too?"

"Either, both, I don't know! Seriously, Mom, don't you find any of this *strange?*"

Beverly chuckled. "I grew up on your grandmother's stories. The Pickle King, the knish war, the stalking *shadchanim.* What could be stranger than any of that?"

"I thought she stopped matchmaking after Grandpa Gabe died."

"She did, but she could never give it up entirely." Beverly shrugged. "It was in her blood."

"But why would she tell Jessica Cooper I could help her? I help people get *divorced,* for God's sake. What made her think I could help anyone find love?"

Abby's mother reached for her daughter's hand. "You've never understood how perceptive you are. You've always had a sixth sense about people, sweetheart. Remember our old upstairs neighbor, Mrs. Adelson? Her husband died before you were born. When you were seven years old, we saw her here, having a cup of coffee at the counter. She waved at you and you waved back. Then you turned to me and said, clear as day, "Frank loves Mrs. Adelson.""

"Who was Frank?"

"The waiter who worked behind the counter. A year later, they moved in together."

"I have no memory of that."

"Well, it happened. And when I told your grandmother, she wasn't surprised."

"You make it sound like I was some kind of freak."

"Not at all! It was just that every once in a while, you seemed to . . . *know* things about people. You knew your piano teacher was pregnant before she was even showing. And remember when your father and I took you to Rumpelmayer's? He wanted to make it a big, fun outing, but you *knew* something bad was coming. You *knew* we were going to get divorced."

Abby grimaced. "Well, yeah, that certainly rings a bell."

"After the divorce, you stopped having those . . ." Beverly paused for a moment to find the right word. "*Insights.* Or maybe you just stopped talking about them. It was like you turned off a switch to protect yourself. Maybe your grandmother wanted you to flip the switch on. Maybe she thought you might be able to help a few people the same way that she did." Beverly paused again. "I guess what I'm trying to say is: none of this is as strange as you think it is."

That night, on the way to the party, Abby asked her taxi driver to stop by Jessica's apartment. When Jessica opened the door to the cab, Abby's mouth fell open. The ophthalmologist's hair hung in soft, smooth waves. She wore a silk chiffon, off-the-shoulder black cocktail dress, with a triple-strand pearl choker around her neck. Her black silk heels were definitely *not* sneakers.

"Please don't look so shocked," Jessica said. "It's not as if I don't know how to get dressed."

"You look stunning," Abby told her.

"Stunning for a thirty-seven-year-old ophthalmologist—not for a twentysomething fashion model. Of which there will be *many* at this party, I'm afraid."

"You look stunning, period."

The party was on Greenwich Street in Tribeca, at a former factory turned celebrity restaurant. Vaulted ceilings and uneven walls were covered with the factory's original bricks. It was one of the hottest reservations in town, but there would be no customers there tonight. Instead, two hundred invited guests filled the exquisitely cavernous space.

The room smelled like an overwhelming mixture of designer perfume and expensive alcohol. No matter where Abby looked, she saw important and vaguely familiar-looking people—people she had seen in *The Wall Street Journal, The New York Times,* or the pages of *Vogue.* When she looked more closely, her head began to pound. There was Diane, chatting with Victor, in front of the ornate mahogany bar. Jessica didn't know who Diane was, but when she spotted Victor, she grabbed a glass of champagne off the tray of a passing waiter and downed it in a single gulp. "Come on," Jessica said, looping her bare arm through Abby's. Before Abby could extract herself, Diane caught her eye and waved her over. There was no escaping now.

At least Victor looked like himself again. The puffy eyes and greasy hair were gone. He wore another perfectly tailored jacket, made to fit easily over his broad shoulders. When Jessica approached, he reached for her hand and gave it a single, tender kiss. "You have no idea how happy I am to see you," he said, his voice heavy with emotion. "Please, allow me to introduce you. Diane Berenson, Dr. Jessica Cooper. Jessica, this is my attorney, Diane." After an awkward pause, his eyes drifted toward Abby. "Abby!" he said, as if she'd suddenly appeared. "Thank you for coming." He leaned forward. "And thank you for encouraging Jessica to attend." The last part was intended for Abby's ears alone, but Abby knew from the look on Diane's face that her boss had heard every word.

Victor did not let go of Jessica's hand. "If you will excuse us," he murmured, "I have something to discuss with Dr. Cooper in private." He led Jessica to the other side of the room and ushered her through an unmarked doorway. Diane frowned. "Let me guess—*that* was the ophthalmologist. You didn't tell me she was so glamorous."

"Jessica isn't glamorous," Abby said. "She normally wears a doctor's coat and sneakers. And for the record, I didn't invite her to the party. That was all Victor's doing." Abby decided it was best to keep quiet about the macaron towers and the roses.

"Well, why does he want her here? What did he tell you?"

"Honestly, Diane, I have no idea. I haven't spoken to Victor since Monday."

Diane considered Abby's answer. "Before you ask, I haven't decided whether you still have a job. Victor has ignored my calls all week—he's no closer to signing his prenuptial agreement than he was on Monday morning."

Abby tried her best to sound confident. "I'm sure he'll sign it soon," she said. "He wouldn't throw this lavish engagement party if he didn't intend to get married."

Diane picked up her glass of wine and sauntered off in search of some food. She called out to Abby over her left shoulder. "For your sake, I certainly hope you're right."

Abby needed something stronger than the champagne the waiters were offering. With Diane gone, she settled in at the bar and asked for a vodka martini. She was rifling through a crystal dish of mixed nuts when Will took the empty seat beside her. "So that was Diane Berenson, huh?"

"How did you know?"

"I've seen her picture in the paper a couple of times." He asked the bartender for a beer, glanced around the room, and whistled. "This is some party," he said. "Have you seen Nicole? I can't find her anywhere."

"Nope," Abby mumbled, through a mouthful of cashews. "Did you take my advice? Were you honest with her?"

Will looked sheepish. "Yeah," he said. "I felt like an idiot, though.

Can you imagine how many times she's heard that speech? Guys fall in love with girls like her every day."

Abby felt a dangerous combination of self-doubt and vodka coursing through her veins. What if she was wrong about what she had seen? What if this attempt at her grandmother's calling was nothing more than a means to cling to old memories? What if the lights and signs she perceived were only flashes of lingering grief?

"What did Nicole say when you told her?"

"Well, she didn't seem surprised. She told me she had some things to sort out and that she didn't want to promise me anything yet."

"*Yet*, huh? That has potential."

"Maybe, but it was impossible to tell. Later, she left a message on my machine asking me to come tonight and saying we would talk." Will put down his beer and gestured to the crowd. "But what is there left to talk about? We're at her engagement party, for God's sake. She's never going to turn down Victor Étoile for some nerdy guy like me."

Abby ordered a second martini. "Don't count yourself out yet," she said. "This evening isn't exactly going according to plan."

As if on cue, Victor and Jessica emerged from the door on the other side of the room—this time, accompanied by Nicole. "Excuse me," Abby asked the bartender. "That door over there. Where does it lead?"

"That's the stairway to the rooftop terrace."

"Is there another party there tonight?"

The bartender shook his head. "Mr. Étoile reserved the whole venue. He's planning a surprise for the guests later this evening."

"Is there going to be dancing?" Will asked.

The bartender put one finger to his lips. "Sorry, sir, but I've been sworn to secrecy."

"Don't look now," Abby said to Will. "But it looks like Nicole is on her way over."

Nicole's long blond hair hung sleek and straight. Her slip dress was similar to the ones from her fashion show, but not quite as sheer or as long. Abby couldn't help but be impressed by the speed with which she crossed the room in her strappy four-inch heels.

"Will!" Nicole gushed. "You have no idea how happy I am to see you." When she leaned forward to kiss Will's cheek, Abby quickly averted her eyes. She was too tipsy to look for light flashes now. She busied herself with the bowl of nuts, picking through the almonds in search of cashews, before she felt Nicole tap her shoulder.

"Abby! Can I speak with you for a minute? Will—would you mind excusing us?"

Will was surprised but perfectly agreeable. "Sure," he said, grabbing his beer. "I'll be over by the cheese table if anyone needs me."

"First of all, Abby, thank you so much for coming." Nicole tugged nervously at the hem of her dress and tucked a stray hair behind her ear. "I hate to ask this," she continued, "and I'm afraid you're going to think I'm awful. But . . . what is the situation with you and Will?"

Nicole looked so serious, so painfully concerned, that Abby almost wanted to give her a hug.

"Me and Will? We're friends, that's all. Truly—nothing more than friends."

Relief blanketed Nicole's delicate features. "I hope you don't think—"

"You don't have to say any more," Abby assured her. "Will is a wonderful guy."

Nicole beamed. "He's the only person I know who doesn't tell me to *slow down* or to *relax* and *stop working so hard* all the time. Not that the people in my industry don't work hard—but there's this expectation to never actually *show* that you're working, you know? It seems like we're always supposed to be having fun and living these glamorous, fabulous lives. Will is just so completely real."

Abby nodded. "Absolutely." Out of the corner of her eye, Abby noticed Victor making his way toward Diane. In the meantime, she spotted Jessica heading for the ladies' lounge. "It looks like he's waiting for you," Abby said, pointing across the room to where Will was pacing in front of a table piled high with Brie and Camembert. "You should go rescue him. I'm going to say hello to a friend."

Abby left her drink at the bar and followed Jessica to the bathroom. Inside, three willowy twentysomethings stood in front of the oversized wall mirrors, quietly chatting and touching up their perfectly symmetrical faces. Jessica had disappeared into a stall, so Abby waited on the tufted bench near the door. She stared at the black-and-white-checked marble floor and tried to calm her fraying nerves.

She'd been sitting for only a minute or two when Diane pushed her way through the doorway. "There you are!" Diane hissed, her eyes flashing with anger. The women by the sinks turned their heads in unison—their lipsticks and mascara wands paused in midair. When Diane saw them staring, she reconsidered her outburst and lowered her voice.

"He isn't going to sign," she said cryptically, careful not to mention any names. "He hasn't given me any real explanation, but in the meantime, I've made up my mind. You can pick up your things on Monday, Abby. As of this moment, you are fired."

Diane left as quickly as she had arrived, leaving both Abby and the trio reeling. For a moment, the bathroom was painfully quiet. Abby's eyes began to tear, and a moment later, the three tall strangers gathered around her in a show of support.

The first handed Abby a tissue, while the second offered a mint from her purse. The third woman—Abby swore she knew her from somewhere—asked if Abby wanted a glass of water. "I can run to the bar and get you one," she volunteered.

"Thanks," said Abby, dabbing her eyes. "But I'm okay."

"No offense," said the woman who gave her the tissue, "but your boss seems like a terrible person."

The woman with the mints nodded emphatically. "We have good instincts about these things." She lowered her expertly shadowed eyelids and stared at Abby. "You seem really nice though. I bet you weren't happy working for her anyway."

There was something about this circle of strangers that Abby found oddly comforting. They were right. The worst was behind her. Abby had been so worried about losing her job that she had stopped asking herself whether she still wanted to keep it.

The familiar-looking woman who'd offered her water flashed a cover-worthy smile. "It's all going to work out," she said kindly. "Now, get back to the party and try to have fun. And may I just say, for the record, that your boobs look *really* good in that dress."

It was the first thing to make Abby laugh in weeks. "I just bought this bra yesterday!" she said. "My grandmother told me I needed a new one."

The young woman nodded. "Smart lady," she said.

Never underestimate the power of a quality undergarment.

No sooner had the three women left than Jessica emerged from the stall. "I could only hear half of what was going on," she said. "What on earth was happening out here?"

"Victor won't sign the prenuptial agreement, Diane fired me from my job, and I'm pretty sure Christy Turlington just complimented me on my boobs?"

Jessica took a seat on the bench. "Wow," she sighed. "That's a lot for one trip to the ladies' room."

"It is," Abby agreed. "Diane thinks I meddled in her clients' personal lives, and I can't honestly say she was wrong."

"Are you losing your job because of *me*?" Jessica looked as if she was about to cry.

"Jessica, no. It's not because of you—I promise. Ever since my grandmother died, my life has been . . . complicated. I've been having flashes, like when Victor kissed your hand. Little things only I seem to see. And I get these feelings about people . . . things no one else seems to know. It's been a mess, but it's not only you. It happened with

Evelyn Morgan and her husband." She took a breath. "It happened a few weeks ago with Nicole, too."

A blush crept into Jessica's cheeks. "Victor told me they're calling off the wedding," she whispered.

"I figured," said Abby, hugging her friend. "The only thing left to figure out now is why they still went ahead with this party."

"Victor said they're making some sort of announcement. I think it's going to happen soon."

Abby spent the next half hour trailing the waiters who carried the tastiest hors d'oeuvres. If it hadn't been for Victor's surprise announcement, she would have already gone home. The events of the evening had already depleted her, and there wasn't much left for her to do. But curiosity won out over exhaustion, and she vowed to stay for as long as the miniature hamburgers held out. She was in the middle of consuming her fourth when the servers requested that everyone make their way to the stairs. "Mr. Étoile and Ms. Blanchard invite you to join them on the rooftop."

From up on the terrace, the city sky was a swath of blue ink and crystalline stars. The moon had shrunk to a crescent shape, but it shone with a soft and pearly luster that lit up the terrace in such a way as to make the guests gasp out loud. The rooftop floor was covered with a white velvet runway lined with rows of chairs along both sides. Near the edge of the roof, behind a podium and microphone, an enormous white silk sign was suspended. It bore the silver Étoile logo with the words "et Soleil" added in gold.

After the guests had taken their seats, Victor and Nicole approached the platform. Under the lights—both electric and celestial—both of them looked especially radiant. "Welcome, everyone," Nicole said. "You know, when Victor and I first thought about this party, we intended to celebrate our engagement. Now that the evening is upon us, however, we have decided to celebrate a different kind of union." Nicole ignored the murmurs of the crowd and continued with her speech. "When I first met Victor Étoile, I fell in love with his creative vision. He was the only designer who spoke to me as an equal. He encouraged my questions and my ideas. We embarked on a relationship of mutual admiration and respect. Eventually, as all of you know, we began a romantic relationship as well." Here, she paused and took Victor's hand. "Over the past several weeks, however, Victor and I have come to realize that although we are a perfect match creatively, our hearts are meant for other people." The murmurs of the crowd grew exponentially louder, and Victor stepped up to the microphone.

"Some of you know that Nicole and I collaborated on a line of clothing this summer. Tonight, we are thrilled to announce that we will be making that collaboration permanent." He turned slightly and gestured to the sign behind him. "The Étoile brand will now be known as 'Étoile et Soleil.'" He winked at the crowd and pointed to Nicole. "If I am the stars, this woman is certainly the sun."

It was Abby who began clapping first until, eventually, the entire crowd joined in.

Nicole held her hands up to quiet them. "Thank you. Without the support of many special people, Victor and I would not be standing in front of all of you tonight. We want to thank our families, especially my mother, who has been so encouraging. We also want to thank everyone at Étoile et Soleil for their hard work and their discretion as we mapped out this new business venture."

Victor ran a hand through his hair. "As some of you may know from personal experience, a good matrimonial lawyer is hard to find. It takes a good lawyer to negotiate on your behalf. But it takes a *great* lawyer to look beyond all the posturing and to put the happiness of her clients first.

"I first met Diane Berenson years ago, when she represented me in my divorce. A month ago, I hired her again—this time, of course, for the opposite reason. And this time, my friends, she had the wisdom to assign a secret weapon to my case." Victor scanned the rooftop for Abby's face and pointed her out to the crowd. "Abby, it is because of your resourcefulness, your empathy, and your insight that Nicole and I are so truly happy this evening." As all of the guests began to clap, Jessica took Abby's hand and squeezed.

"Did you tell him to say all that?" Abby whispered.

"Of course not! All I said was that you deserved a thank-you."

As the event photographers snapped her picture, Abby felt Diane staring. A few minutes later, the music began, and dozens of models wearing the latest designs from the new Étoile et Soleil collection filled every inch of the runway. When the crowd rose to their feet for a standing ovation, Abby gave Jessica a peck on the cheek. "I'm going to get out of here while I can," she whispered. "Please, give Victor and Nicole my best."

Before Jessica had time to respond, Abby bolted down the narrow stairway into the now empty restaurant. Five minutes later, she was in a taxi on the way home to the Upper West Side. Her stomach was churning from the mini hamburgers, her head was spinning from the vodka martinis, and her heart felt as if it was beating at twice its usual speed.

She'd been fired from her job. She'd stopped a wedding. She'd made a match between a world-famous fashion designer and her grandmother's ophthalmologist. She'd made a second match between a supermodel and her own sort of ex-boyfriend. Victor Étoile had publicly acknowledged her and thanked her for his happiness. Christy Turlington had complimented her boobs.

What should she make of these occurrences? What did any of it mean? A wave of nausea overcame her, but she got back to her apartment just in time. After emptying her stomach into the toilet, Abby kicked off her heels, crawled under the covers, and fell into a dreamless sleep.

The next morning, Abby took two Tylenol and brewed some of her grandmother's Zabar's coffee. She put the last piece of babka on a plate and carried it over to her sofa. Most of Sara's journals were in a stack on the floor, but she pulled the most recent one from the pile. She took a sip of her coffee and flipped to the final entry in the book.

Dr. Jessica Cooper, ophthalmologist
Granddaughter of Jacob and Miryam Tunchel
   Jessica is a lovely woman—brilliant and sensitive, like her grandparents. I am doing all I can to find a match for her, but I cannot seem to find success. I have been wondering why this is so. Jessica has taken up her grandfather's occupation. She has inherited his talent and his passion. I know my Abby does not wish to be a matchmaker, but I believe she has some of my gifts within her. Aside from my sister, Jacob Tunchel was the first real match I ever made. Perhaps it makes sense that his granddaughter should be my granddaughter's first match as well. Abby is too skeptical to believe in such things, but perhaps, in time, I can convince her.

There was nothing for Abby to do but laugh. In the end, it hadn't mattered how skeptical she was or that she hadn't believed what she was capable of. She had stopped a divorce, thwarted a wedding, and made not just one match, but _two_.

She hoped her grandmother would have been proud.

TWENTY-FIVE

SARA

1994

It's Never Too Late to Die or Get Married

Sara wasn't wrong about Paul and Albert. She wasn't wrong about the pharmacist or the florist either. She wasn't wrong about the man who sat beside her at the movies or the people she met waiting in line at the soft-pretzel cart. But when Sara tried to find a match for Jessica Cooper, she could not seem to find Mr. Right.

After eighty-four years of making matches, Sara was feeling more tired than usual. She still went on her walks and baked her babkas, but she fell asleep earlier and slept more deeply. She began having vivid dreams of Gabe, dreams where they danced together like they used to. When she woke in the mornings, her heart ached for her husband. It took longer to get out of bed and get dressed.

Sara made the decision to tell Dr. Cooper about Abby at her next eye appointment. "My granddaughter is not going to like the idea," Sara explained. "I can't be the one to tell her. It's going to have to come from you."

"Me? But I've never even met her. I can't chase your granddaughter down and beg her to be my matchmaker." Jessica helped Sara up from the exam chair and walked her to the reception area. "Mrs. Auerbach, I'm so grateful for all you've done to try and help me. But it's been almost two years—if *you* can't find anyone, I don't see how anyone can. It's probably too late for me."

"Nonsense," Sara said emphatically. "In my day, the girls got married at eighteen. When I met Gabe, I was well into my twenties, and a lot of people already called me a spinster. But my mother, may she rest in peace, never gave up. *I refuse to die before you find a husband,* she said. So, I told her she was going to live forever. You should have seen how angry she was! She balled up her fists and shouted at me loud enough for the whole block to hear."

Jessica smiled. "What did she say?"

"*It's never too late to die or get married.*"

TWENTY-SIX

ABBY

1994

When Abby went to clean out her desk on Monday, one of Diane's Post-its was waiting for her: *Please come see me.* So many of Abby's days had begun with those notes—with a pit in her stomach, a mad dash to Diane's office, and a humiliating wait in Diane's doorway. But today, Abby decided, she would not run. If Diane wanted to talk, she knew where to find her.

Abby was already sorting through files when the receptionist, Tom, poked his head in her doorway. "Holy crap, Abby! That party was crazy!"

"I guess Diane told you?"

Tom rolled his eyes and waved a hand through the air as if he were swatting an invisible fly. "Diane? That woman never talks to me."

Abby tilted her head. "How did you hear about it?"

"Seriously, Abby? You don't know? Oh my God. Wait right there."

Tom was back in a flash with his copies of *New York Newsday* and the *New York Post*. Both had covered Victor's party. Aside from the gossip about who had been invited, the canceled wedding, and the new collaboration, the fourth biggest story turned out to be Abby. Who was the "mystery attorney" Victor Étoile had praised so highly? Was Diane Berenson grooming her "secret weapon" to become the next partner of the firm?

"This is crazy," Abby said. "Diane fired me Saturday night."

"She *what?*"

"She fired me," Abby repeated, pointing to the thick manila folders covering her desk. "I'm only here today to clean out my office."

Tom pulled the Post-it off Abby's computer and studied the words on the small yellow square. "At least this time, she said 'please.'"

Not long after, Diane passed by on her way to get some coffee. "Abby!" she said, when she saw the open door. "You're here. Didn't you see my note?"

"I did," Abby answered, but she made no excuses. Diane Berenson was no longer her boss.

"About Saturday night," Diane began. "I looked for you when the fashion show was over, but your ophthalmologist friend said you'd already left."

"There wasn't any reason for me to stay."

"A lot of people were asking for you. They wanted to meet my 'secret weapon.'"

"Did you tell them you already fired me?"

Abby thought she had rendered her boss speechless, but it didn't take long for Diane to recover. "I'd like to talk to you about that," Diane said, taking a seat across from her. "It seems that I underestimated the appeal of your approach. I've already gotten some calls this morning from a few potential new clients—people who'd like to meet with us."

"Well, as you know, today is my last day."

Diane frowned. "Look, Abby, I'm not big on apologies. Was I wrong to fire you? Maybe, maybe not. As I already made clear, you betrayed my trust. You ignored my instructions on two separate cases and took matters completely into your own hands. What I'm proposing now is a business arrangement that involves you staying on at the firm. I'm offering you the opportunity to build your legal career—to benefit from my experience, my contacts, and my reputation. We both made some regrettable decisions, Abby. But you've tapped into something that people are interested in—a different style of representation. As long as you don't keep fighting against me, I think we can work together."

Abby didn't answer immediately. She picked up the photograph on her desk—the one of her with her sister and her grandmother. In the picture, Sara's eyes were bright, her smile was wide, her face was full of joy. *Fight for something, sweetheart,* her grandmother had told her. *Not just against. That's the best advice I can give you.*

Abby put down the frame. "The thing is, Diane, I *don't* regret my decisions. I don't regret listening to Michael Gilbert or encouraging Evelyn to see a doctor. It might not be the way you would have done things, but because of me, they're still together, and that is something I'm proud of. I don't regret following my instincts about Victor and Nicole getting married either. I don't regret introducing Victor to my friend, and I certainly don't regret that the wedding was canceled.

"I wasn't fighting against you, Diane. I was fighting *for* all of them."

The only thing Abby took home from her office was the photo of her grandmother. When she got home, there were three long messages from legal headhunters on her machine.

She thought the story would die down in a few days, but then *New York Magazine* ran a piece on Evelyn Morgan. Both the hotelier and her husband credited Abby as the person who had saved their marriage. The magazine published a picture of the couple standing in front of the window in Evelyn's office. It was the same place where Abby had seen them embrace, where she had known for sure that they should be together.

In a moment of inspiration, Abby tore the article from the magazine and pasted it into her grandmother's most recent notebook. The journal was half empty, after all, and Abby saw no harm in filling its pages. She thought, perhaps, she might continue the tradition her grandmother had begun so long ago.

After the *New York Magazine* article was published, job proposals came in from unlikely places. Abby's sister, Hannah, called from San Francisco, with the phone number of the friend of a friend. "His name is Gary," Hannah said, "and he wants to talk to you about some website he's starting. It's for dating, I guess, but it sounds pretty strange. Match dot com. What do you think?" Abby told Hannah she knew nothing about computers and could she please tell Gary thanks but no thanks.

Diane's two biggest competitors called to offer her positions. Like Diane, they specialized in high-net-worth clients and celebrity divorces. Abby told them she'd get back to them, but in her heart, she already knew her answer would be no.

For a week she stayed home, poring through her grandmother's journals, reading about all the matches Sara had made. She went back to the pages about Marlene Fishman and the other entries from the late 1950s. Her grandmother had never told her these stories, but she had left the journals for Abby to find. The stories proved that there was more than one way to use the gift that she'd been given.

When Abby had first decided to become a divorce attorney, she was only twelve years old. She had wanted to fight for women like her mother—ordinary people who needed an advocate to guide them through a difficult time. She wondered, sometimes, what would have happened if her mother had been able to hire a better attorney— someone savvy enough to defend Beverly and her daughters from the hostile battle Abby's father had waged, someone compassionate enough to reassure Beverly that she was not alone in her plight, someone strong enough to convince her that no matter how tired and depleted she was, she owed it to herself to stand up for what she deserved. But somehow, instead of representing women like her mother, Abby had ended up going to work for Diane. What if she went back to her initial inspiration for becoming a lawyer in the first place? What if she looked to her grandfather's career and his devotion to Legal Aid? What if she used her skills and her training to fight for the women who needed her the most? She called back a few headhunters and reached out to law school friends who'd chosen public interest law instead of big firms. By the end of the week, she had lined up a few meetings and was ready to think about her next steps.

Two weeks after the party, Jessica met Abby for a walk. August in New York was notoriously oppressive, and the heat that day was no exception. They entered Central Park on Sixty-Seventh Street and decided to walk north toward the lake, hoping for a breeze off the water. It was too hot to go very far, however, so they found an empty bench in the shade and fanned themselves with some newspaper pages someone had left on the bench next to theirs.

Abby filled Jessica in on her job search, and Jessica told her about Victor and his girls. After a few minutes, Jessica pulled a black velvet pouch from her purse.

"I have a gift for you," she said. "For everything you've done for me."

"Jessica, that's sweet, but it really isn't necessary."

"Please. It's important. It belonged to my grandmother. It was supposed to be the fee for her match."

"Jessica, I'm not a *real* matchmaker. You don't need to give me anything."

"But I do," Jessica insisted. "It's tradition. You don't want me to have bad luck, do you?"

Abby chuckled. "Come on, you don't really believe that stuff."

"Maybe. Maybe not. The only thing I'm certain of is that your grand-mother was my grandparents' matchmaker and now, decades later, you are mine." Jessica pulled a polished gold bracelet from the pouch and held it out for Abby to see. "Here," she said. "This was my grandma Miryam's bracelet. Her father gave it to your great-grandfather, and then your grandmother was made to give it back. I don't know all the details of the story. All I know is that it should have been hers, and now, it belongs to you."

Jessica slid the bangle over Abby's hand and helped to fasten the clasp around her wrist. The outside surface was etched with leaves in an intricate hand-carved design. "It's beautiful," Abby said, holding it up to the light. "Thank you."

They walked back on the path in the afternoon heat, their hair-lines damp and their faces shiny. When they emerged from the park at Sixty-Seventh Street, a soft-serve ice-cream truck waited near the en-trance. "I'm dying for some ice cream," Jessica said, reaching for Abby's hand. "What do you say? Do you want a cone?"

Images of a melted Rumpelmayer's sundae flashed through Abby's brain—she saw her father's ice-cream soda and the cheap, silver, heart-shaped lockets he had once offered his daughters as his first bribe.

She was about to say no when her eyes settled on the flash of solid gold at her wrist. Inside her chest, something loosened, wiping child-hood hurts away. Suddenly, after fourteen years, an ice-cream cone sounded like a good idea.

EPILOGUE

1995

The next spring, Evelyn Morgan and Michael Gilbert invited Abby to their vow-renewal ceremony. It was a small affair—only thirty guests—and Abby was touched to be included. Michael read a poem he had written for his wife, and Evelyn read some words of her own. The couple faced each other, teary-eyed, under a wedding canopy made of roses.

After the ceremony, guests were invited into the courtyard of the Morgan Hotel, where shimmering lights, sweet-smelling flowers, and elegant food awaited them. In one corner, a small jazz band was playing, adding to the intimacy of the atmosphere. Abby had just made her way to the bar when Evelyn approached her with a young man. He was wearing a simple black tuxedo, and he looked, Abby thought, to be around her own age.

"Abby!" Evelyn said, with real warmth in her voice. "I'm so thrilled you could join us, dear. Thank you for coming."

"I wouldn't have missed it for anything," Abby said.

"I want to introduce you to my nephew, Noah." Evelyn put her arm around the slim young man, whose self-conscious smile revealed dimpled cheeks. "The rest of my guests are all hideously old, but the two of you might have some things to talk about. Noah just moved to New York," Evelyn explained. "He's been working at the Morgan Hotel in LA."

Noah shook Abby's hand. "My aunt says wonderful things about you," he said.

"Evelyn thinks much too highly of me."

"Nonsense," said Evelyn. "If it weren't for you, we wouldn't be here celebrating today, would we? Noah, make sure Abby has a drink. I'm going to ask my husband to dance."

They ordered margaritas from the bar and found a cocktail table away from the music. Noah was almost a foot taller than Abby, and it was less awkward for them to chat once they were seated. He wanted to know more about how Abby had managed to keep his aunt and uncle together.

At first, she was nervous about revealing too many details of what she knew was an unconventional story. But after they finished their first round of drinks, Abby's tongue loosened, and she began to talk about her grandmother.

The waiter brought over two more margaritas just as Abby was telling Noah about Sara's journals. She told him about Jessica, about Paul and Albert, and about the other tenants in her grandmother's building.

"It's coming up on a year since she died," Abby said. "Honestly, I can't believe it."

"My grandparents have all been gone for over a decade," Noah told her. "It's wonderful that your grandmother was able to see you grow up."

There was something about the way Noah said it that made Abby's eyes fill with tears. She hadn't realized before what a gift it had been—all the time she'd been lucky enough to share with her grandmother. Grandma Sara's love and old-world wisdom had helped to shape Abby's adolescence. Her unwavering presence had helped Abby to navigate a world that might have been a much darker place without her grandmother's steady hand. Before Abby knew it, she was full-on crying—and then scrambling to wipe the tears away with the cocktail napkins from the bar. "I'm sorry," she apologized. "This is supposed to be a happy day."

"Everyone cries at weddings," Noah said good-naturedly. "There's nothing to be sorry about." Abby held up her fresh drink, tapping it against his, and they both took a sip. Abby's drink tasted fine, but Noah frowned at his and crinkled his nose.

"What is it?" Abby said.

"No worries," he replied. "It's just, I thought we told them no salt on the margaritas. I can't see any on the rim, but I swear I can taste it."

"Let me try," Abby said, taking a sip from his glass. She swirled the alcohol back and forth on her tongue. "I don't taste it," she said. "But here, take mine instead."

They swapped their glasses and clinked them again while Evelyn and Michael glided by, smiling. The jazz band broke into another number, and Noah asked Abby if she wanted to dance.

It wasn't until she got home that evening that Abby remembered her grandmother's words.

When you weep, the one you are meant for tastes the salt of your tears.

AUTHOR'S NOTE

In March of 2020, when the pandemic began, my daughter, Ellie, and her roommate, Adelle, were given five days to pack and move out of their dorm. We brought them home from college and spent the spring together, navigating our strange, new normal. My husband learned to take depositions over Zoom. My son had a virtual high school graduation. We baked and took the dog for long walks. At the time, I was working on a novel, but it wasn't coming together the way I had hoped.

That summer, Adelle told me about her grandmother, who had once been an Orthodox Jewish matchmaker. Her grandmother had been such a success, in fact, that in 1977, *The New York Times* ran an article about her. The article stuck with me and, eventually, inspired me to think about a matchmaker story of my own. I discussed the idea with my agent, Marly Rusoff, who, in turn, spoke to my editor, Sarah Cantin. It was because of their enthusiasm and encouragement that I decided to put aside the novel I had been writing and focus on this new idea.

After reading about "Love on the Lower East Side" on the Museum at Eldridge Street's website, I decided to anchor my fictitious matchmaker in that same neighborhood during the 1910s and 1920s. Although the pandemic made it impossible to travel to the Lower East

Side streets I wanted to write about, I was aided in my research by the online collections of the Tenement Museum, the Center for Jewish History, the New York Public Library, and, of course, the Museum at Eldridge Street. It was from these sources, as well as others, that I learned about the wedding of "The Pickle Millionaire," the real knish war of 1916, and the formation of matchmaker unions. In my novel, I reimagined these events and altered them in order to best suit my story.

Before I began my research in earnest, I assumed that the typical matchmaker at the time was an older and somewhat meddlesome woman. In my mind, she was Yenta from *Fiddler on the Roof* or Dolly Levi from Thornton Wilder's play. I assumed that there were just a handful of such women, but my assumptions couldn't have been more wrong. Not only were there thousands of Jewish matchmakers in New York, but the majority of them were men. According to a 1910 *New York Times* article, there were, by "a conservative estimate, about 5,000 professional *schatchens* in the city. . . . The traditional picture is the man of the tenements with a three-pound watch chain and a polka-dotted vest, whose work in life is to see his neighbors happily married."

In order to explore the portrayal of matchmakers in early 1900s New York, I turned to the Gimpel Beynish cartoons, a popular comic strip by Samuel Zagat, which ran in at least two daily Yiddish newspapers (including *The Warheit* and *The Forward*) beginning in 1912. Gimpel was a matchmaker who constantly found himself in problematic and amusing situations. I drew inspiration from fiction as well, including Bernard Malamud's short story "The Magic Barrel," Tashrak's novel *Shulem the Shadchen*, and Abraham Cahan's *Yekl and the Imported Bridegroom and Other Stories of the New York Ghetto*.

While I rethought my vision of the typical early-1900s matchmaker, I realized that my character would be facing challenges I had not previously considered. She would be a young, unmarried woman in a business dominated by established, older men. As the character of Sara Glikman took shape, I began to understand that her struggles were no different from those working women still face today.

Of course, I also researched modern-day matchmakers. I spoke with Aleeza Bracha Ben Shalom, also known as "The Marriage Minded Mentor," to understand what drew her to matchmaking as a calling. From Aleeza, I learned that a matchmaker must be married in order to satisfy religious modesty rules. Aleeza taught me about *segulas*— lucky charms and customs thought to encourage positive outcomes such as a successful marriage. Dr. Laura Shaw Frank, a law school classmate, reached out to offer me the opportunity to read her recent dissertation on "Jewish Marriage and Divorce in America from 1830–1924." My law school roommate, Michele Pahmer, helped me to understand the various religious customs surrounding traditional rabbinical courts.

In my quest for accuracy in portraying a rabbinical court scene, I reached out to Rabbi Shlomo Weissmann, the director of Beth Din of America. Through Rabbi Weissmann's contacts, I was eventually directed to Dr. Zev Eleff, president of Gratz College in Philadelphia. Dr. Eleff was generous with both his time and his knowledge and ex-plained the unstructured nature of a *beth din* (*beis din*) at that time in America. Although I found no specific precedent for the court scene in my story, it seems very likely that a woman such as Sara—a woman whose gift compelled her to defy long-held customs and traditions— would have attracted the ire of the many men with whom she com-peted for work and payment.

Dr. Eleff also shared with me an article from *The Jewish Observer* by Chaim Shapiro about *shadchanim*, which helped me to develop a clearer picture of what the world of the early-1900s matchmaker may have been like, the kinds of concerns they would have had, and the methods they might have used. The article drove home the esteem with which a *shadchan* was held in his community, as well as the idea that a *shadchan* was considered an "agent of heaven," fulfilling a divine mission.

For assistance in understanding the experience of immigrants on the Lower East Side in the 1910s and 1920s, I read a variety of memoirs, including: *Out of the Shadow: A Russian Jewish Girlhood on the Lower East Side*, by Rose Cohen; *Streets: A Memoir of the Lower East Side*, by Bella Spewack; *The House on Henry Street*, by Lillian Wald; and *The Button Thief of East 14th Street: Scenes from a Life on the Lower East Side 1927–1957*, by Fay Webern. I also consulted the following works of nonfiction: *World of Our Fathers: The Journey of the East European Jews to America and the Life They Found and Made*, by Irving Howe; *America's Jewish Women: A History from Colonial Times to Today*, by Pamela S. Nadell; and *The Wonders of America: Reinventing Jewish Culture, 1880–1950*, by Jenna Weissman Joselit.

Although writing a dual-timeline novel can mean twice as much research, Abby's story was made easier by the fact that in 1994, I, too, was a young lawyer living and working in New York. As a trusts and estates lawyer, I worked on a few prenuptial agreements, but in order to better understand the intricacies of divorce law, I turned to my former colleague Laurie Ruckel, matrimonial attorney Sherry Weindorf, and family friend Mark Koestler. All of them were kind enough to share their knowledge. In addition, my optometrist, Dr. Alec Perlson, was generous enough to brainstorm with me in order to come up with an ailment for my character Evelyn Morgan in the story.

Over the course of the novel, as my character Sara ages, the nature of her matchmaking changes. In order to portray the kinds of matches I thought she would have made in the post–World War II era, I turned, once again, to *The New York Times*. In reading over the wedding stories of European refugees, I was better able to appreciate and portray the obligation Sara would have felt to help connect Holocaust survivors.

Readers of *The Matchmaker's Gift* will find a good deal of Yiddish sprinkled throughout its pages. In the course of my research, I found several different spellings or transliterations of the Yiddish word for matchmaker. I chose to use the spelling *shadchan* in my story, but there are several other possibilities, including *schatchen*. A female matchmaker is most often referred to as a *shadchanteh*, and the plural of the word is *shadchanim*. Both Susan Kleinman and Adelle Goldenberg were instrumental in helping me to find the proper Yiddish words and phrases.

For those interested in reading the *New York Times* articles that helped to inspire *The Matchmaker's Gift*, I offer the following:

- "Finding a Find, Catching a Catch, For Brooklyn's Orthodox Jews," January 31, 1977
- "Karp Wedding Glory Dazzles East Side," June 24, 1909
- "Rates for Husbands on the Increase: Prices for Desirables Now Run as High as $25,000, so the East Side's Schatchens Say," January 16, 1910
- "Rivington Street Sees War. Rival Restaurant Men Cut Prices on the Succulent Knish," January 27, 1916
- "Jewish Match-Makers Form Protective Union in Warsaw," March 3, 1929
- "600 at Outdoor Wedding: Rabbi and Bride Met in U.S. After Fleeing from Poland," April 12, 1948
- "2 Young Survivors of Nazidom are Wed," October 28, 1949
- "Couple Who Lived in 4 Nazi Death Camps to Culminate Romance at Wedding Here," August 10, 1946
- "Refugee Couple Wed Here," August 12, 1946

ACKNOWLEDGMENTS

Some of you may know the Yiddish word *bashert*, which is often translated to mean "soulmate." But *bashert* has a broader meaning as well: that of "destiny" or "fate." For many reasons, the writing of this story was *bashert* for me.

First, I want to thank all of my readers. I am so grateful for your continued support.

Love and thanks to Adelle Goldenberg, who told me the story that lit the spark for this book.

Thanks to my agent, Marly Rusoff, and her partner, Mihai Radulescu, for pushing me to put this novel on paper. Thanks to my editor, Sarah Cantin, for reading this story with such care and for providing me with such sincere and constant encouragement. Thanks to Kathleen Carter for her diligence, humor, and friendship. A thousand thanks to the entire team at St. Martin's Press: Jennifer Enderlin, Lisa Senz, Anne Marie Tallberg, Sallie Lotz, Drue VanDuker, Katie Bassel, Beatrice Jason, Rivka Holler, Brant Janeway, Michelle McMillian, Michael Storrings, Ginny Perrin, Gail Friedman, Hannah Karena Jones, Susannah Noel, and Deborah Friedman.

I am grateful to the following people for helping me to navigate the medical, legal, historical, and religious details of this story: Dr. Alec Perlson, Laurie Ruckel, Sherry Weindorf, Mark Koestler, Dr. Laura Shaw Frank, Michele Pahmer, Aleeza Bracha Ben Shalom, Rabbi Shlomo Weissmann, Dr. Zev Eleff, and Rabbi Stacey Bergman.

I would never have survived the past two years without my Thursday Zoom crew of Jamie Brenner, Fiona Davis, Nicola Harrison, Suzy Leopold, Amy Poeppel, and Susie Orman Schnall.

Thanks to all of my author, book influencer, and bookselling friends for their love, humor, and patience. To Lisa Barr, Elisabeth Bassin, Jenna Blum, Kimberly Brock, Jenny Brown, Jillian Cantor, Christina Clancy, Jackie Friedland, Ashley Hasty, Jane Healey, Robin Kall Homonoff, Elise Hooper, Brenda Janowitz, Pam Jenoff, Andrea Peskind Katz, Susan Kleinman, Pamela Klinger-Horn, Sally Koslow, Mary Kubica, Greer Macallister, Lauren Blank Margolin, Rachel McMillan, Kristina McMorris, Annabel Monaghan, Zibby Owens, Kate Quinn, Allison Pataki, Alyson Richman, Jamie Rosenblitt, Heather Terrell, Heather Webb, Rochelle Weinstein, and Lauren Willig: your presence in my life—whether in person or virtual, frequent or intermittent—has only served to make it better. Please know how much your kindness means to me.

Thanks to the Jewish Book Council for all it does to ensure that Jewish stories survive.

Thanks to Leslie Powell, Grey Salcedo, my mahjong crew, and all of my wonderful Chappaqua friends for humoring me.

Finally, a million thanks, love, and hugs to my family—both immediate and extended. And to my greatest gifts: Bob, Ellie, and Charlie—without you, there would be no stories worth telling.

1. *The Matchmaker's Gift* alternates between Sara's narrative and Abby's narrative. Was there one perspective that you connected with more than the other?

2. Sara is a matchmaker and Abby is a divorce attorney. How does the juxtaposition of these two careers work to move both the narrative and the two character arcs forward?

3. Discuss Abby's father. How do you think he influenced Abby's life decisions and her opinions on love?

4. Consider the weight of the statement, "Love is not always a straight, shining line. Sometimes, love is a shady path, full of unpredictable turns," on page 161. How does the truth of this come to light throughout the novel? In what specific instances does love feel the most complicated?

5. In *The Matchmaker's Gift* there are several unique and strong female characters. Each of these women tells us something important about the two time periods explored in the novel. What qualities and strengths do these women express, and where are they illuminated in the novel? What do these women reveal about the times and places in which the novel occurs?

6. On page 246, Sara says, "If you can't decide what you want to fight for, love is as good a cause as any." Which character in the novel do you believe fought the most for love?

7. Consider the statement on page 231: "Tradition should never be used as an excuse to keep people from reaching their potential." In what ways does tradition work to hold back the characters in the novel? In what ways does it work to benefit them?

8. In your opinion, what is the biggest gift / lesson that Sara leaves Abby with, both from the time she was alive and from Abby's reading of her journals?

9. *The Matchmaker's Gift* asks the question of whether being able to find true love is a blessing or a curse. When you initially learned of Sara and Abby's ability to sense a true match, what was your opinion on this? Did it evolve over the course of the novel? In what moments does matchmaking seem like a gift? In what moments does it seem like a curse?

10. Overall, how did the end of the novel make you feel? What do you think comes next for Abby? Do you think she will continue to make matches? Do you think she will find love for herself?